ALGONQUIN BOOKS
OF CHAPEL HILL

LARGE PRINT

MEN LIKE US

A NOVEL

Carson Markland

ALGONQUIN BOOKS OF CHAPEL HILL

LARGE PRINT EDITION

for my parents, Kelly and Kevin

CONTENTS

PART I

1952–1956

PART I

1952–1956

CHAPTER 1

Backstage

"YOU DON'T MISS A THING, do you?"

It's Jack saying this: Jack with his back to Bobby; Jack with hands like a running tap, twisting a button on his jacket, tugging at his socks; Jack with a razor on the edge of his voice.

So you are nervous, Bobby thinks. His brother studies his notes; Bobby studies their opponent.

Here's the senator from Massachusetts, gliding in at the last possible minute before the debate's set to start, while they, the Kennedys, have been here for an hour already, sitting, standing, fidgeting. Senator Lodge walking in like a winner, like he's got somewhere else to be. His smile gleams like emergency lighting, fluorescent bright. His arrival has stirred up a breeze in the stifling backstage air, and on that breeze: the scent of oranges.

Bobby tightens his tie. Loosens it. Side-eyes his brother. Senses the annoyance rolling off of Jack a moment before his brother says, "Crowd check," and then Bobby takes off through an ill-lit corridor cluttered with music stands and the set pieces of theater productions.

This isn't his high school, but it reminds him of the ones he went to. This dim, semi-abandoned wing off the auditorium stage—this would have been the spot boys used to trade cigarettes and chewing gum and stories about what their older brothers were doing in the war. And Bobby always with an ace up his sleeve: Two brothers. One fighting the Germans. One fighting the Japanese.

"One minute," someone says, and Bobby wipes the sweat from his palms on the thighs of his pants. Thinks something eloquent, something like *Shit, shit, shit.* Presses one eye to a slit in the curtains.

Every seat is filled, and then some. Men offer up their chairs to women, and the women smile and take them. Others crouch in the aisles or stand together, smoking, at the back. But who are they all here for? His brother, or Senator Lodge?

"Full house," Bobby says, returning to where Jack sits, folded into a corner, his mouth moving with silent words; reciting talking points, or prayers. He seems not to notice Bobby. Bobby doesn't know whether to stay or go; he feels, right now, every inch of the eight years between them. For most of his life, Jack's been a voice on the phone, a laugh in the other room; someone talked about but rarely seen, like God or the Pope. His brother an ace up the sleeve, but also a stranger.

A stagehand appears, motioning that they're ready for Jack; across from them, someone is giving the same signal to Lodge. Jack stands, a silent negotiation between himself and his body as he pushes himself upright through his wrists, trying not to aggravate his back, his face starched with pain.

"Kick his balls off," Bobby says, but Jack isn't listening, already moving away.

They meet in the middle, his brother and the senator. Lodge sinks his palm into Jack's without looking at him, instead waving to the crowd. The ease of a veteran politician in his element. For Lodge, this was the plan all along: the first son of a political family, born to hold office.

Lodge is here, Bobby said as the senator arrived backstage. And Jack's response: *You don't miss a thing, do you?* Bobby supposes that it's always obvious when men like that enter a room. Men who're supposed to be there. Not like his brother, who barely looks old enough to run for class president, much less the United States Senate. Who's only here because their brother Joe is not, killed in a plane crash during the war. No remains recovered, nothing of him to bury.

Seated now, the senator sips from a water glass,

unbothered. *Lodge might have incumbency*, his sisters had joked earlier, what feels like years earlier, *but Jack has Catholic mothers.* Catholic mothers sending up prayers across the state. Catholic mothers chanting *Aves* for the Congressman from the Eleventh District.

He thinks of his father, ten miles away listening to the radio in his hotel room, wearing a track through the carpet in his smoking slippers. He'd have known the right thing to say to Jack before he went out there. Some final piece of advice that would have spurred him to victory. But their father didn't want to give the press something to talk about besides his son. Even a decade after being exiled from politics, he's still a divisive enough figure that any public appearance would mean blowback for Jack.

Bobby looks at Lodge, with one leg crossed over the other, and then at Jack, with both feet planted firmly on the floor. He looks at Lodge, and he hates him beyond reason.

All of the advisors have agreed: as long as Jack holds his own, it'll prove they're equals. A draw is good enough. But Bobby doesn't want good enough. He wants to gut Lodge. He wants to hoist up his brother's noodle of an arm at the end like a victorious prize fighter's. He wants, and wants, and keeps on wanting.

So here they are: one brother on stage, one waiting in the wings. The moderator asks the first question, and they both take a breath.

CHAPTER 2

Kennedy for Senate

BUT FIRST THERE'S THIS:

Early spring in the year of our Lord 1952, six months before the debate with Lodge, and Bobby's listening to his father on the phone, trademark Joe Kennedy: "I don't give a damn how much it costs—if we're not reaching markets outside of Boston, we're not going to win!"

First—before the lights, the audience, the stagehands, the senator, before Bobby will stand in the wings with skin too tight for his body, a snake of nerves constricting his throat—first he has to become the campaign manager. And this is how it happens, six months before debate night: with him summoned to his father's room at the Ritz to be given the keys to the castle. At least in title. It's not that they actually need him as campaign manager, just that he's a convenient buffer between Jack and his father.

This is the plan; his father's plan. The castle or the outhouse. The world, or nothing. Why? Because they're Kennedys. Because when his brother was born, their grandfather crowed that he'd be president of the United States.

Except Jack's the wrong brother; that story was about Joe. A three-headed grief twists inside him; not only Joe, but also Kick, killed in a plane crash four years ago, and Rosie—not dead, but gone, hidden away in a facility somewhere that he and his siblings know better than to ask about. Even when it comes to tragedy, his family beats everyone. No matter the metric, Kennedys don't lose.

Although he's seated, his father seems to be towering—this has to be a trick he learned on Wall Street. Some people have fathers who swing them up on their shoulders, or read to them before bed. He has a father who was once ambassador to England and is still referred to by the title, even by his own children, a father who plays the stock market the way his mother plays the piano, adeptly and without error, who looks at his children the way Saturn might have: certain of their potential, ready to devour them whole.

But his third son; his third son he's never known quite what to do with. He hangs up the telephone and gazes at Bobby now with that familiar unfamiliarity.

They say the only similarity between the Ambassador and Bobby is the color of their eyes. The Ambassador wrote a friend once that he was afraid Bobby was growing up a sissy because he's surrounded in age order by girls, with sisters above and below him. Bobby's sure that, given the choice, his father would have put Eunice in charge. Eunice who's tough as nails and will give you a piece of her mind whether you asked for it or not. But he must have thought they had enough working against them as it was; better a sissy in charge than a woman.

"Now look," his father says. "Dalton was a fine campaign manager. Ask anyone and they'll tell you: a completely competent operative. Do you know why I got rid of him?"

He was there; he watched Dalton get ripped a new one about campaign spending. His father's exact quote, he believes, was, "You've spent ten thousand dollars of my money and you haven't accomplished a damn thing."

But no conversation with his father is just a conversation. It's also an aphorism, a fable, a lesson delivered to a lecture hall of one.

"Why?" he asks.

"Because we're Kennedys," his father says. "We don't settle for competence." He spreads a map of their state on the table in front of Bobby. "What do you see?" his father asks.

"Massachusetts" isn't the answer, but it's the one he gives.

"A springboard," his father says, tapping the map with an impatient hand. "We need people who'll think bigger." He looks Bobby over with a gaze that settles as heavily as a suit of mail. "What are you going to contribute to your family?" his father asks. "We could build something here if your brother would just listen to me."

"You know Jack," Bobby says. "He likes to go things alone."

His father rounds on him. "You can't go a campaign alone. And if he loses—" His father winces, as if physically pained. "Everything out the window."

"Everything?" he asks without thinking, one of those throwaway comments you have to be careful of making in front of his father. Surely their entire future cannot rest on Jack's winning this election. Surely the sun will still rise, the earth will still turn—his father's eyes narrow to slits the size of coins.

"I would hope, Robert, that someone with your intelligence wouldn't fail to grasp the magnitude of the situation. Or have I overestimated your intellect?"

There's a story his family tells about him: when he was very young, maybe three or four, he jumped off the boat and into the bay. He didn't know how to swim yet. When Joe hauled him back onboard, Jack said, "That either took a lot of guts or no brains at all."

"The latter I think," his father muttered.

This is who he is to the Ambassador: a brainless boy merrily trying to drown himself. You can't fire family, but maybe he'll be shunted off into the corner and Eunice will be called up after all, woman or not.

"If he loses, that makes all of us losers," his father says, each word crisp and black, as if punched out on a typewriter. "What future do you see for a family of losers?"

He's silent.

"That wasn't a rhetorical question," his father says. "Name a family that got somewhere by losing."

He returns his father's gaze. "I can't," he says.

"You can't." His father nods, satisfied, turning back to the window. His glasses pick up the reflection of the clouds, obscuring his eyes. As a young man, their father looked like Joe, or Joe looked like him. Strong chin, sharp nose, pleasant smile. Handsome. Men who look ready to conquer their fates.

And he and Jack? Jack looks like he's just gotten over a bad fever, or is on the verge of catching a new one. Bobby sometimes doesn't recognize his own face in photographs. He looks at pictures of himself and has no idea who that man is.

"There aren't many people who have what you all have," his father says.

"We know," he says.

"Then don't waste it, damn it," his father says.

CORNERED. ANOTHER THING he's been lately.

Cornered by his sisters in the same restaurant their father used to take them to when they were children. They were already seated when he arrived, three screws preparing to be turned in him. There was no small talk in this family. He'd barely poured himself a glass of water when Eunice said, "The old man wants you in Boston." Her jaw set, digging in for a fight. Her eyes, like all of their eyes, changeable with her mood, and aggressively blue that day.

"I have a job here," he said.

"You're a Kennedy first," Eunice said. First, now, always.

He turned to Pat, usually an ally. The smoke haze of her cigarette like a spell cast around her head. The sharp smell of mint.

"Are you on menthols again?"

"Do you want one?" The lazy flick of her wrist offering him the pack. She was only there because she had nothing better to do, and she enjoyed the small dramas of life: being caught gossiping by the person you're talking about, flirting with your best friend's husband, fights between her siblings.

And Jean nervously shredding a straw wrapper, there to referee in case things got ugly.

He looked between his sisters: variations of the same pattern. Russet-haired. Light-eyed. Bright white teeth waiting to tear into you.

And then Jean said something unthinkable in the blunt, quick way of younger sisters who aren't used to getting very many words in: "He might lose."

Silence.

"It's that bad?"

"You know how Jack is."

"You know how *Dad* is."

They told him about the feud that had been bubbling up between Jack and the Ambassador. King Henry and the wayward prince Hal. Jack, who hadn't been taking their father's calls, or advice. Jack, who seemed to forget that their father had once tread the highest halls of power. Their father, who seemed to forget that Jack wasn't Joe, not happy to go along, not someone who had believed his whole life he was destined for politics.

"What does Dad think I'm going to be able to do?" he asked.

Eunice: "We're as confused as you are." In his family's eyes, he ranked somewhere north of "inadequate" and just shy of "completely useless." And Eunice could do a better job; she knew it and he knew it, too. "You could always tell Dad you don't want it," she added. "It'll be a lot of work. One big headache."

She should've been in ancient Rome, he thought, although if she'd been in Brutus's shoes, she wouldn't have needed forty other senators to fell Caesar. She'd have done it in one stroke.

"Did Jack—I mean, does he want me out there?" He tried to say this casually, like he was asking the time.

Pat shot him a pitying glance. "Of course he does," Pat said, which meant *No, not at all*.

BUT NOW HE'S HERE, in Boston, whether his brother likes it or not.

And it's *not*, if he had to guess. Jack doesn't look at him with the cold distance of their father, but with a closer, more intimate annoyance. This is worse.

Jack keeps a campaign the way he used to keep his room: messy, books thrown everywhere. The campaign itself is a bigger mess. No statewide infrastructure to speak of. No network. Just a bunch of aides who don't know whether to listen to his brother or the Ambassador. The politician, or the purse.

"How have things been going on like this?" he asks his brother. "What have you been doing this whole time? How was nobody on top of this?"

It's March; his brother's plan was to start months before anyone else would even dream of it. Give him time to connect with the voters. To have a chance at competing with the immediate name recognition of "Lodge." The man they're running against, whose seat they hope to steal—Henry Cabot Lodge, say it out loud to yourself—when he bleeds, it's blue; his ancestors were in the Senate. Bobby's were starving. The Kennedys are—rich? Yes. The good kind of Irish? Yes. But still Irish. Still immigrants. It counts in this country; counts against you.

And sure, Jack's been speaking everywhere that'll have him, but what good does that do without donors, volunteers, organization?

"Please Bob—one question at a time." Jack massages his jaw, all good humor gone in an instant. This is the effect Bobby has on his brother.

"To land a statewide position, you need statewide support," Bobby explains slowly, to which Jack rolls his eyes. "And from the sound of things, you're pissing off your biggest donor," he says lightly, toeing out onto the ice. "What kind of strategy is that?"

Jack's face pinches, then slips back into carefully crafted amusement. "Wait until it's you, Bobby," he says. "See how you like it when Dad sits you down and tells you who you're going to be and what you're going to do—heads he wins, tails you lose."

I'm never running for office, he almost says. Would say, if it were Ted. But not to this brother.

"You sound like a teenager," he says instead, expecting the sudden heat of Jack's retort.

But Jack only laughs, unbothered. "I made a good teenager. The drinking, the sneaking around. The girls."

His eyes fall away, down some cellar of memory, some corridor that Bobby can't follow. Bobby was always too young, wasn't he? Wandering the fields around Hyannisport catching baby rabbits, smuggling them into the house to live in the bottom drawer of his and Ted's dresser until his mother got wise to his act and started making him turn out his coat pockets before he came inside. When he was a boy, his brothers were men. When he was a man, one brother was dead, and the other one had taken his place.

He looks at his brother, surrounded by the clutter of the campaign. Jack seems small in his suit, or maybe it's the room that dwarfs him. He notices, for the first time, the bags under his brother's eyes.

"I can't be the candidate and the manager," Jack says. "And I can't let Dad have free rein—don't look at me like that. You know his politics are the kiss of death."

This he can't argue. Their father has a tendency to end up on the wrong side of history; just look at how his own career ended. One day the ambassador to England, with a door opening up for his own presidential run, the next a resignation in disgrace because he thought the Nazis should be appeased and made the mistake of letting people put his opinions in print.

They're silent for a minute.

"Why did you agree to it?" Jack asks at last.

He offers part of the truth: "I heard it was a shit show," he says.

Jack gives his best imitation of a smile. "Dalton was a doormat," he says, looking at Bobby. "Are you going to be a doormat?"

Bobby's lived in this family long enough to know a challenge when he hears one.

"You worry about shaking hands," he says. "I'll worry about the rest."

"I THOUGHT THE POINT of New York was to have your own life," Pat says, watching him from a seat in his new office. The badger's stripe of blonde dyed in her hair gleams as she cocks her head to the side, studying him. "Are you sure this is what you want?"

"I want Jack to win," he says.

"That's what Dad wants," she says. "What do *you* want?"

He stares at her hard, getting frustrated. "Am I supposed to run off to California?" he asks. "Will that solve all my problems?"

It's a cheap shot, and Pat stiffens. He shouldn't hold it against her, her disappearance across the country, but he does anyway. It feels like not just a repudiation of him, but of their entire family, an attempt to distance herself from the uncertain claim of being a Kennedy.

He remembers how, when they were children, they'd put on Christmas plays: the nativity, the wise men's journey, the birth of the Christ child. He never got a say in his role: Kick had always cast him as the camel, or once "Backup Angel (Silent)." So maybe this is why he took the job: he wants to be written into the script.

"You don't owe them anything," Pat says at last, and it seems like she's speaking as much to herself as to him. "You can say 'no.'"

"It's just until November," he says.

She hooks her hair behind her ears and stubs her cigarette out in the nearest ashtray with three angry taps. "I'll see you tomorrow," she says. He can't help but feel he's disappointed her somehow, but then he's always disappointing one member of his family or another.

She pauses at the door, and looks at him with something that could almost be pity.

"It's all well and good to give up your life for him," she says, "but you might want to ask yourself if Jack would do the same for you."

CHAPTER 3

Campaign Manager

NO TOWN IS TOO SMALL or too Republican.

That spring Bobby drives from Lawrence to Pittsfield, tapping the most well-connected men he can find to run Kennedy for Senate clubs. Their campaign can't count on support from the Democratic machine or the party leaders—none of them give a shit about Jack. To their mind, it'd be wasted effort on a hopeless campaign. So the Kennedys will do it themselves, build their own machine, some combination of grassroots and guerilla campaigning.

Jack flies in from DC every Thursday; he leaves every Sunday. In the interim, he crisscrosses the state, speaking to any group that'll have him. Veteran's leagues. Church picnics. Women's clubs. Their sisters march from door to door to talk to voters, hosting "Coffee with the Kennedys" events around the state. They return home at the end of the day, feet lined with blisters from a full day in heels. Even Teddy, stationed in Paris with the army for a year, is doing his part. He's convinced the other boys from Massachusetts in his unit to vote for his brother come fall. Six Kennedys are running; only one is on the ballot.

When he's not organizing, Bobby has the dreaded task of speaking, which often means standing on a chair in the middle of a bar. Fifty eyes on him, and none of them friendly. A flurry of questions that barely let him get a word in.

"Well why should we vote for him? Lodge is a veteran, too."

"And he's proved he can do the job—why switch horses mid-race?"

"Hasn't your brother voted against unions?"

It's not a matter of natural enmity—he's deep in Democratic territory—it's just that Boston Irish aren't friendly to anyone.

"No," he says. "That's untrue, he voted against the Taft-Hartley Act because he felt it would weaken unions, whereas Lodge—"

Some newcomers muscle toward the front.

"You look a little young to run for office," one man says.

"*I'm* not running," he protests. "It's my brother—"

His wife Ethel enters the bar with a lit cake.

Chocolate and ablaze with a regiment of small white candles striped pink, blue, and yellow.

"I heard someone turned another year prettier," she says. Addressing this room full of strangers in South Boston as if they're her sorority sisters.

"Come on," she coaxes. "Don't be shy."

Sheepishly, one man steps forward with a raised hand. "This Saturday," he says.

"Happy birthday," Ethel crows. "How old will you be?"

And that's all it takes for a previously indifferent crowd to become theirs. Ethel cuts the cake, she asks the men their names, what they do, what issues they're concerned with.

"What are we doing for veterans?" one says, and she nods and rattles off Jack's record. Cost of housing, another says, and she tells him about the forthcoming legislation Jack's sponsoring in that area. As natural with a crowd as any of his siblings. As natural with a crowd as a Kennedy should be. Although she grew up Republican, you'd think she'd been studying Irish pols her whole life. He remembers their early acquaintance; Jean would bring home her college friends to campaign for Jack's early races for the House. Most of them were only good for licking stamps. But not Ethel.

Somehow when he and his siblings were sent out canvassing, he was always stuck with her, the girl who wouldn't shut up. The two of them walking door to door handing out fliers and trying to convince people to vote Kennedy. Climbing walk-ups around Boston in the summer heat and knocking on stranger's doors. And the whole time, Ethel talked. Asking them about their sons and daughters; the babies they were expecting; where they were from; what they wanted, all while he sat there mute, picking at the tablecloth like her idiot cousin. By the time they left, she'd usually secured not just a vote, but also an invitation to dinner, knitting circles, christenings, vacations.

"You're good at this," he told her once as they left, and she said, "One of us has to be."

And before they went into the next house, when they were still standing at a stranger's door, strangers themselves, she'd look at him sideways in the dim of the hallway and say, "Knock, knock," like it was the start of a joke just between them. It's the kind of thing that makes you fall in love, after a while.

She gets them singing now, a bar full of men belting out "Happy Birthday." Then she slips over to where he stands alone, at the edge of the room. It works the same way it used to: she talks, he watches.

She cuts a bite of cake off with the edge of her fork and offers it to him. "Here comes the airplane," she says.

"How did you know it was his birthday?" Bobby asks.

"If you get a hundred people together, it's always close to someone's birthday," she shrugs. "And if not, you still have cake."

"Good trick," he says.

She winks at him. "Wait'll you see my next act."

AFTER A FEW MONTHS of this, the Kennedy organizers report: "high level of enthusiasm among young voters; voters responding well to most recent attack on Lodge's attendance record; a visit from the congressman would be well received." Bobby reads everything that comes across his desk. He writes back and tells them how to adjust course, sending Larry O'Brien and Ken O'Donnell out across the state to see that his orders are followed. O'Brien is Jack's man, knows state politics better than the rest of them combined, and O'Donnell is his, a stoic, dark-eyed Irishman who played football with Bobby at Harvard.

But most important, Bobby meets with their father so Jack doesn't have to, his father who uses the telephone like it's an instrument of war, drawing up battle plans, issuing commands, demanding information about enemy troops.

"The Democrats are finished in November. Mark my words: it's a red wave."

His father is fond of making apocalyptic declarations with a *Mark my words* or a *Just you wait*, like some Shakespearean villain plotting his revenge.

"People want peace and prosperity, not proxy wars," his father continues. "They want to own houses. They want dishwashers—I don't know how the party doesn't see it."

"Dishwashers have never been a significant plank of the party platform."

His father, forgetting himself, laughs. "I suppose that's true," he says. "As true as anything." He claps his hands together as if to bring the meeting back to order, one of those gestures seared into Bobby's brain from childhood, loud rooms filled with chattering siblings who suddenly fell silent on command. He supposes you develop these cues over time when your children outnumber you nine to one.

"Jack can win," Bobby says, "red wave or not."

"As long as we get the Irish, the Catholics, the women," his father says. "And as long as we keep Joe McCarthy out of the state."

McCARTHY: VOTED THE WORST senator in office by the Washington press corps his first year on the job. No one believed he'd be reelected.

A lesser man might have accepted his fate. Taken his one term in Congress and returned home to the bank or law office or university he left. But this is Washington, land of sudden reversals of fortune and violent political tides. It favors strong swimmers, and on Lincoln Day, 1950, McCarthy invented a new stroke. Standing before the Republican Women's Club of Wheeling in the ballroom of the McClure Hotel, stocky, already balding but concealing it with a combover, giving the women there what might, on another face, be termed a smolder, but on his was brooding and violent.

People, McCarthy knew, wanted something to be afraid of. They wanted their fears named and given form as simply as possible. They would rather be told that it's the Soviets who are threatening their way of life than their own complacency. They would rather fear the bomb than the fact that technology has produced power beyond man's control. They want an enemy, not an enigma. And McCarthy gave it to them. He told them that the State Department was thoroughly infested with Communists—*infested*, he said, and the women thought of lice, bedbugs, rats. Things that needed to be eradicated.

And that was all it took. "McCarthyism," his detractors branded it, but he took the term for himself, deemed it "Americanism with its sleeves rolled." Every campaign he touched in 1950 turned to gold. A Republican sweep. Finally, people said, someone who's going to do something about Communism.

Now, two years later, his popularity has only increased. The Irish in Massachusetts are crazy for McCarthy—one of their own, is how they see it. They've got his picture nailed up right next to the Pope. If Lodge gets an endorsement from McCarthy, they can kiss their one advantage over him goodbye. The Irish, the Catholics, the women, in that order.

LATE AT NIGHT, it's just Bobby in campaign headquarters, just him and poll after poll he's trying to bend to his will. He works by lamplight and old coffee, making notes to himself on the curled yellow pages of a legal pad.

"What are you still doing here?" Jack asks, unfolding himself from the shadows voice first, like the Cheshire cat's smile dancing out on a tree limb.

He's surprised to see his brother. Mostly they communicate via clipped phone calls that Jack always hangs up on first.

"You look tired," Bobby says. The Candidate can't look tired.

"That's the funny thing. I'm not tired. Not at all," Jack says. And maybe it's true, but not in this light. His brother's eyes are two wounds in a thin face. He limps when no one's looking, his back troubling him again, always.

Jack studies a poster of himself tacked to the wall and turns away. "What are you working on?" he asks.

"How to reach the women of Hampden County."

Jack nods like he suspected as much. For a moment, it sounds like a torrent of rain has unleashed outside, but it's only the wind. "I'm going for a drive," he says. "Want to come?"

They park below one of the LODGE FOR SENATE billboards that have started to taunt the roads of Boston in recent weeks. Someone on the Lodge campaign has realized he has an opponent after all, although the senator himself is still out of state, organizing the Eisenhower presidential campaign. It never stops once you enter politics; this is why Bobby never will.

Is this what you used to do with Kick and Joe? he doesn't ask, sitting on the hood of the car as his brother cracks open two beer cans. The Golden Trio, the British press dubbed his siblings when their father was the ambassador to England. Joe, the eldest; Jack, the wittiest; Kick, the prettiest. A nickname that cored Bobby because he wasn't a part of it. And Jack, now, the sole survivor.

"You could make a career out of this," Jack says, reclining against the windshield, wincing as he does.

"Don't tell Eunice that."

Their sister's been stiff with him since he came to Boston, still resenting him for signing on as campaign manager. Jack gives him a knowing glance; he's noticed it, too. They were raised as a tribe unto themselves; even now, grown up and separated by geographical distance, they're attuned to each other's moods.

"Don't take it personally," Jack says. "She hates me a little, too. She thinks she should have been the politician." Takes a swig of beer. "And she's right."

Elizabeth I at Tilbury, that's Eunice. Body of a weak and feeble woman, heart and stomach of a king. The muddy field, the Spanish threat, the princely queen in white gown and plumed helmet, wearing an iron corset and wielding a truncheon of steel.

"In any case," Jack says, "You're better than the last guy."

"Only because I know how to deal with Dad," he says, flicking the metal rim of his can. "I practically have a degree in it by now."

"Can you imagine the coursework," Jack asks, "for a master's in Joseph Kennedy studies?"

"The Castle or the Outhouse: A Seminar on Achievement," he suggests.

"Kennedys Don't Lose," Jack starts, and then cuts himself off, not in the mood. So it's just Jack sitting here with him, not the Candidate. No charm. No jokes.

"Sometimes," Jack says carefully, "I can't tell if I do what I do because of him or because of me."

"You mean running for office?" he asks.

"I mean everything."

There are days he wonders if his brother's heart is in this thing at all. You can tell when it's Jack who's shown up to an event and not the Candidate. Jack blurts out a speech; he hovers next to their mother in receiving lines to let her do the talking. He sits there and looks not a bit bothered when setbacks are discussed.

But he's also seen the Candidate, who'll climb a ladder to shake a window cleaner's hand, his back be damned. Who'll stop, even when he's being rushed to the next event, to ask a girl with an Irish accent which county she's from and tell her about their own relatives in Wexford.

Jack the now-eldest. He can feel their brother's ghost behind him and doesn't dare look. *We're just filling in for the dead, aren't we?* he wants to ask Jack. But he doesn't. They're not those brothers. Maybe they never will be.

The orange haze of the streetlight casts a pall like

memory, like something you lost a long time ago. A shadow passes just out of sight: a feral cat, or maybe something else.

"We should get back," he says reluctantly. "No time to lose."

"There's still plenty of time to lose," Jack says. To Bobby, it almost sounds like a wish.

He clambers down off the hood of the car and hurls his can at the Lodge billboard. It doesn't come close, falling in an arc and skittering across the gravel and into the weeds. "You'll get us arrested," Jack laughs, and Bobby says, "Prison would be a vacation compared to getting you elected," but in his head he's chanting *us, us, us*.

WHILE THE REPUBLICANS have their national convention, the Kennedys play football. They collide and tumble on the lawn of the summer house in Hyannisport. It's white and benevolent and perched on the coast, although it represents another slight; they weren't welcome in Cohasset where the WASPs vacation, so his father had to buy here instead. Jack sends a delicate spiral toward Pat, who lays out to catch it. They dart in and out of the house between downs for updates, the whole thing broadcast live for the first time ever.

"Someone is listening to your prayers, children," their mother informs them from the porch, inciting a mad scramble inside. They're hoping for an Eisenhower nomination in order to keep Lodge busy in the fall.

And they get what they want: Eisenhower showered in confetti, bald and grinning so widely his head gives the impression of an egg about to crack open. It's hard to square this kindly old man with the engineer of D-Day. He looks more like someone you'd find behind a gas station counter in a flat Midwestern state.

Pat sighs heavily. "Eisenhower's just *so* unsexy, isn't he?"

After the RNC, Lodge takes off for the Virgin Islands to recharge for Eisenhower's general campaign. The Kennedys have agreed that they'll rest in November.

Every week, his brother is kissed by hundreds of women he doesn't know at their tea parties. Old, young, none are immune. They wait in receiving lines that wind through ballrooms or rented hotel halls, straining around each other, standing on tiptoes to get a peek. They peck Jack on the cheek as they file past. The mothers wish he was their son, the bachelorettes wish he was their husband, or so the papers say.

"I bet most of them couldn't even tell you what office he's running for," Eunice says through her teeth, standing in the receiving line at one of their Kennedy Teas. "They just want to look into his eyes."

"They're here for Mother," Jean says as one woman pauses for an extended colloquy, holding up the entire line. Their mother, the daughter of a former Boston mayor, the dark-haired beauty who's been campaigning since she was seventeen, filling in for her own mother, who had no taste for politics. Like a true expert, she pulls an Irish Switch: still smiling at the first woman while shaking the next woman's hand and reaching for a third.

Their tea parties have been a success, their system devised and perfected on Jack's previous campaigns. In each town scheduled for a tea, the campaign organizes a committee of fifty prominent women. Those fifty women each reach out to invite ten friends to the tea. Those ten friends invite ten friends themselves and so on and so forth until they have an audience of thousands built by the women themselves. It's a novelty for most women, the opportunity to see up close a family they've only read about. The women's vote, Jack has said from the start. That'll be what puts him in office. The women's vote, and the women's work. When they canvass, Eunice knocks on twice the number of doors she's assigned. If Jack can't make an event, she's his go-to surrogate on the campaign trail. And now, at the tea parties that she resents having to attend, she shakes hands with a vigorous pump that seems to startle most of the women on the receiving end. *But that's how a man shakes hands*, their faces say.

Bobby scans name tags as the women file by: O'Leary. Kelly. O'Sullivan. Too many Irish. He makes a mental note to reach beyond their base, to Italians, French, Poles. No vote they won't chase down with Earl Grey and petit fours. He'll make sure that each woman today receives a thank you letter encouraging them to help out at Kennedy for Senate offices near them. These letters will be written by the previous round of tea party attendees, who've since been converted into volunteers themselves. Some of the women today—excited to get something in the mail besides a bill—will march in to volunteer. So who cares if they moon over Jack? They'll mail out invitations for the next tea. The cycle will continue. The columns of votes will shift. Maybe it'll be enough.

"I'm told they're quite pleasant little affairs, and I'm sure they're nonfattening," Lodge is reported to say of their teas.

Laugh while you can, Bobby thinks.

THE INVITATION COMES in late August: Lodge wants a public debate with Jack.

"Absolutely," his father pronounces. The Ambassador's hotel suite has been turned into a temporary war room. Even Jack has come, willing to call a truce with their father in the face of Lodge's challenge.

"Go show them an Irish boy has just as much smarts as the upper crust." The disdain in his father's voice is palpable. This, coming from a man who is himself a millionaire several times over.

O'Brien nods in agreement. "It either means he's scared or overconfident," he says. "Both are good for us."

"Scared," his father decides. "He's finally realized he has some real competition and not a whipped dog."

"We won't have time to recover from a mistake," Ken says. "Do you want your campaign decided in one night?"

"Eunice?" Jack asks, and Bobby knows this will be the deciding vote. She's the one Jack turns to now that Kick, who he was even closer with than he was with Joe, is gone.

"You're the underdog," she says. "You need to play offense."

So it's decided. Bobby starts to stand, but then Jack knits his fingers together and turns to him. "Bobby?"

Resentment shadows Eunice's face, there and gone before anyone else can spot it. The miracle at Tilbury came down to chance, he reminds himself. A change in weather that day, and Elizabeth's army would have fallen to the Armada. Sometimes the wind's in your favor; sometimes it's not. When it is, you'd better be ready with the sails.

His brother is waiting for an answer. A mistake head-to-head is all that some voters would need to swing to Lodge. But he's seen his brother turn it on when he wants to. Jack can win as long as he shows up as the Candidate and not himself.

"Do it," Bobby says.

"Good," Jack says. "I've already told them yes."

CHAPTER 4

Debate

SO HERE THEY ARE. Jack and Senator Lodge onstage. Bobby in the wings.

Across the stage, Lodge's people stand with clipboards and expressions ranging from unconcerned to bored. He thinks, *We should have brought clipboards.*

Jack pauses before he starts speaking, letting the last of the applause die down. "I've been traveling this state since January," he says, his voice a flat nasal pitch like an insect, entirely unpleasant, meant to be swatted away—

"Getting to know her people, her industries, her problems. I have been campaigning in this state because I'd like to serve this state."

Yes, good, hit hard, hit early—

"My opponent has only recently entered Massachusetts at all—perhaps after he saw one of my television ads."

Laughter, and something unknots in Bobby's spine. "Are they laughing as hard as they did for Lodge?" he asks Ken. O'Donnell's only answer is to purse his lips, which means, in his friend's laconic way, *Shut up and watch the game.*

"Massachusetts needs someone who is equipped to deal with her particular problems," Jack continues, "not someone who is going to let our industry flee to the South and our jobs disappear."

He hands the microphone back; the crowd sounds their approval. Lodge looks at Jack for the first time all night. Bobby wishes he had a camera to capture it, the brows knitted in confusion: *This was supposed to be easy.* But his mind is camera enough.

Lodge's answers are concise, crisp. His brother's answers are concise, crisp. If you were hoping for a dog fight, you've come to the wrong place. Other than the occasional jab at someone's record, they're entirely civil. The only one to draw blood is Bobby, chewing a hole in the wall of his cheek, the taste of iron warm across his tongue.

Lodge seems to take up more than his side of the stage, more than his chair, sitting there with a profile the papers call "regal" when what they mean is that a single glance from him makes you think he owns the place. Lodge studies the crowd; Jack studies the stack of papers arrayed in front of him, suit jacket hanging off of him like he's just a coatrack. You could fit a whole other arm in his sleeve. Would Bobby vote for that man? That scarecrow in a suit? He falls back on that old rosary: *War hero. Best-selling author. A voice for the next generation of Americans.* Everything his brother has going for him. A platform that's not a platform, so much as a confederacy of parts.

Splitting hairs, you might call the ballot this year. A well-educated war hero. A liberal Republican to Jack's conservative Democrat. Except for one distinction: beating Kennedys is in Lodge's blood. All the way back to 1916, to the same families, the same contest. Lodge's grandfather, the Old Senator, the man Lodge was named for, against the man Jack was, their grandfather, John Fitzgerald. The Old Senator ran a bad campaign by all accounts and still trounced their grandfather by thirty thousand votes.

Bobby's seen it up close, how you are the people who came before you, or you become them over time. Look at Joe, who everyone said was a natural politician, out-going, popular, solicitous. And now look at Jack, who used to hide from them in closets on summer days so he could read his books in peace. Look at him running for office, sitting on a stage telling people "Pick me."

There's a limit to who you can be—to *what* you can be—and it's mostly decided the moment you're born. It's not just the color of your hair or the shape of your nose that you inherit. It's also your force of will, the ability to align destiny with opportunity, the size of the swath you'll cut through history. The past isn't just present, it's running the show.

"A draw," O'Brien decides as the debate winds down, and, seeing the look on Bobby's face, "That's as good a result as we could have hoped for. I bet he's changed a few minds."

Lodge is making his closing argument onstage, hammering the Democrats. "Unstaunched corruption. Flimsy efforts to halt the Communist Tide…"

Bobby looks out at the crowd, their faces lost behind a corona of spotlight. Is a few minds enough? Was it a mistake to let Jack debate Lodge? But perhaps the bigger mistake was Bobby taking this job in the first place. What does he know about electoral politics? What does he know about anything? He's twenty-six years old; he's still a boy in the fields of Hyannisport with baby rabbits sleeping in his pockets.

"A president who lost China and is losing Korea—is this the party you want to serve you?" Lodge demands, finishing with a flourish.

The microphone is handed off to Jack. There's no pause this time.

"If we are to be blamed for all the failures, surely our successes should be counted as well," Jack says. "Over the past twenty years, under the Democratic Party, this country has reached landmarks in social legislation, in civil rights legislation—the Republicans are quick to accuse us of everything that went wrong, but we are also responsible for everything that went right."

There's applause now—real applause—but Jack isn't done. He's got one more line; he's got a period to end the sentence.

"Do you want someone who represents the party of the past or the party of the future?" he demands, looking out at the crowd.

The applause is instantaneous; it shakes the room with the thunder of their approval. Bobby thinks, *God bless the people of Massachusetts*. A second wave builds from the back of the room to the front, cresting over his brother anew.

It's a better point than Lodge has made all night. The party of the future. That has a ring to it. Off the cuff? Or some little phrase his brother has been rolling around in his head for weeks now?

The moderator has given Lodge the opportunity to respond, but the senator fumbles, saying he agrees—the second rule of politics, never agree with your opponents—that the Democrats have had their share of successes, that if he's sent back to the Senate, he'll continue to work along bipartisan lines with good men on both sides of the aisle—

JACK CALLS THEIR FATHER from the hotel room. "How was I?" he asks, in a voice that sounds two feet tall.

Bobby's itching for a copy of tomorrow's paper, for

the words they'll use to describe his brother: Collected? Boyish yet self-assured? Dignified?

On the way out, Lodge had shaken Jack's hand with a cheery smile, telling his brother, "Hell of a way to make a living, isn't it?" Hardly the portrait of a defeated man. Probably thinking: *Good for the Paddy, getting a few blows in.*

Jack listens to their father's response, eyeing the floor as he does and nodding absently. Bobby slides his tie off while he waits, letting it run like water through his hands, twisting it into a noose. Tomorrow, he thinks. And every day after that until November.

Jack hangs up. Enters the bathroom. The sound of water disgorging itself from the faucet, thundering against the bottom of the tub. He reclines in the water, stripped down to his boxers, an ashtray balanced on the lip of the tub with a cigarette he seems to have lit for show, his eyes closed, his hands resting on his bony kneecaps.

Bobby sits on the countertop, leaning back against the cold fist of the mirror, letting out a breath that he's been holding in all night.

"Think he'll ask for a rematch?" Jack asks.

"Not if he's got half a brain," Bobby says with more confidence than he feels. He sees Lodge on stage in a dark blue suit, shaking his brother's hand like he's doing him a favor. That look of surprise. Someone who's never considered an Irish Catholic his competition.

"Is it enough?" Jack asks. "It feels good tonight, but is it enough?"

"I don't know, Johnny," Bobby says, and for some reason, the briefest smile twitches across Jack's sleeping face.

"There's not much time left," his brother says.

The spare change of September. October. All that's left to prove to the people of Massachusetts that John Kennedy is their man. "He might lose," Jean said. Still true, just a different month.

"Have faith," he says.

"Yes, Father," Jack mocks him. "Forgive me, Father."

"I don't know what I'll do," Jack adds after a moment.

"If you lose, Dad will find you a job. Writing. Managing a baseball team. Teaching. If you lose you can do anything."

Jack's eyes flicker open then. He looks at Bobby briefly, takes one drag from his cigarette, and closes them again. A door shuts out in the hall. The sweet odor of tobacco hangs heavy in the muggy air.

"I meant if I win," Jack says. He runs a hand through his damp hair, down his face. "What have I done, Bobby?"

Bobby prays for a qualifier, prays his brother isn't asking this in the existential sense of things—

"Six years in the House and what do I have to show for it?"

"You made it here," he says.

Jack shakes his head, his jaw going tight. "I don't want to make it," he says. "I need to do more than make it."

And for the first time, he feels completely certain that Jack does want to win this thing. Bobby uses a pinky to trace his initials in the fog on the mirror. *RFK.* Jack sinks by degrees into the water until it's just his head above the surface. This brother who's more often than not a mystery to him contained beneath a faintly pulsing temple, a twitch at the corner of his closed eye.

"Come down here," Jack says. Maybe the first time he's ever made that request. "I feel like I'm talking to God."

Bobby sits on the bath mat amidst his brother's discarded clothes. Jack offers him the cigarette, and he takes a drag and hands it back.

"You know I went flying once?" Jack asks. "After I got back from the war. Florida." *Tap* goes the cigarette into the ashtray. Steam hovers over the water. "I wanted to be like Joe," Jack says.

"Good thing you weren't," he says. The last plane their brother flew ended up in pieces.

"It'll have to be different," Jack says. "*I'll* have to be different. If I win..." He trails off, massaging his temples. "I've spent too much time in politics to do anything else."

Bobby tries to see through his brother's skull to the membrane of thought attached there, sticky, pink, and hard to explain. "You don't have to stay in politics," he says.

But Jack isn't listening, watching the end of the cigarette murmur ash into the ash tray.

"Nixon, Smathers, McCarthy," Jack rattles off the names. "They got to the Senate before me. Fine. Maybe Nixon will be the next vice president. But I'm going to do what they're not." Here his brother's eyes flash, not ice or steel or whatever the women are always saying, but pure, liquid want.

What would their father say? What would Joe say? Something hard and polished, something you could crack between your teeth. The words come to him like a reflex, tapping the right nerve and watching a knee kick out.

"Let's see it, then," he says.

CHAPTER 5

Election Night

IN THE FINAL WEEKS of the campaign, his father calls him two, three, four times a day asking for updates, demanding the most recent numbers. He directs staffers to pay fifty dollars to large families for "volunteering at the polls." Ethel reminds him to eat more often than not, though she's worse than he is, leaving the hospital the day she gives birth to make a campaign stop. He hears Lodge and his wife are throwing copycat Kennedy tea parties.

On election night, headquarters is a logjam of staff, volunteers, press, family. Everybody wants to be the first to embrace the winner or abandon the loser. His brother's fate is a coin flipping in the air. The heat of so many bodies makes the windows steam.

"What do you say, Bobby? A toast?" Pat asks, yoking an arm around his neck. He can smell the booze on her. Pat tips a flask toward him, whose contents nearly singe his eyebrows off.

"A toast to what?" he snaps. "We haven't won anything yet."

Pat flicks him in the head.

They shoulder their way through throngs of people, thanking volunteers for their hard work, knowing they won't be in the mood to do it afterward if they lose. We did everything we could. Did we do everything we could? He runs through towns, districts, counties in his head as he smiles and shakes hands—should we have done another tea in Lowell? Targeted the Italians more effectively?

Eunice and Jean have commandeered one of the tables in the middle of the office and Jean waves them over. Eunice looks pointedly in the other direction as he sits, ignoring him. "Have you seen Jack?" Jean asks.

"I was going to ask you."

His leg bounces uncontrollably beneath the table. He tries unsuccessfully to turn himself to stone.

"Isn't this exciting?" Pat asks, craning her neck to peer over heads. "You could power a city from all the nerves in here."

"You could power a city from Bobby alone," Jean says. "Do you think we'll win?" she asks, a little voice at his right elbow.

"Of course," he says. And, "I think I might puke."

"It's a little sad that it's ending," Pat says. "It feels like the end of summer, doesn't it? Packing up the house…"

Eunice blows a pillar of smoke out of the corner of her mouth. "Weren't you just complaining about your blisters?"

"That doesn't mean I'm not sad."

The radios are tuned to the national stations; people are guessing which states have gone Eisenhower, which have swung Stevenson. "What do you think, Bobby?" Pat asks. "We all think Ike."

"Anybody with half a brain thinks that." Everything out of his mouth stings.

Pat rolls her eyes. "Well excuse me."

Eunice has decided he exists again, and looks at him coldly. "You're out of a job tomorrow," she says with what he thinks is a touch of malicious delight. "What'll you do next?"

His sisters grin: merciless. "Somebody's got a fun conversation with Dad in their future."

O'Brien is calling him from across the room: the returns are coming in over the wire. He'll figure his life out tomorrow. Tonight, he's still got a job, and the phones are ringing just for him.

He reaches O'Brien at the same time Jack does. "Nice of you to show up," Bobby says.

"How does it look?" Jack asks.

Bobby grabs his slide rule, starts calculating on the fly as the votes pour in by the thousands, fielding calls from various secretaries reporting on their town's polling, trying to keep score. County by county. Town by town. Jack stands next to him, peeking over his shoulder, asking who it is on the other end.

A pattern starts to emerge. A pattern that leans Lodge.

"It's fine," Bobby says, double-checking his numbers, making sure he hasn't lost a few thousand votes for his brother somewhere. "It's coming in from the Cape. He's got strong support there anyway..."

Jack's face is taut, serious. A man being stretched on the rack. This is how he imagines his brother looked when a Japanese destroyer sliced through the hull of his cruiser during the war, when he watched his boat burn knowing they were miles from anywhere with enemies on all sides.

He waits for a lull in the counting to call his father.

"Are you seeing this?" he asks.

His father is unexpectedly calm. "It's a long night, Robert," he says. "Put your brother on."

After the initial pour of votes, it comes in spurts. Reporting from Boston. Lowell. Worcester. He keeps telling the journalists that he feels optimistic about his brother's chances, that nothing is certain yet. His sisters are chain-smoking in the corner. It's starting to feel less like a party.

He gathers his siblings in the coat closet. "It's not over yet," he says.

"It's not over yet," they agree, except Jack, who stares at the floor with arms crossed.

"Do you have a concession statement?" he asks.

Jack smiles a grim little smile. "I'll improvise."

"We should walk over to Lodge headquarters. If… to shake his hand. Be a good sport."

"Fuck that," Eunice says. "Would he do it for us?" Her face looks especially angular in this light, a bare bulb overhead casting shadows down the length of her thin face.

"All right," he snaps. "Enough of that. Go out there and put a smile on your face. All of you."

To his surprise, they listen.

He slips outside, presses the heels of his palms into his eyes until television static blooms on the back of his lids. *Everything down the drain*, his father said all those months ago, and he realizes now that it's not just Jack, Jack's future, but also his father, his father's past, that this was meant to be a kind of redemption, a kind of rectification. His father hasn't been able to go near politics since he was ambassador; his own chance for political office is far past. But the sting of that would be erased if his son could have what he couldn't.

Ethel finds him out back, praying and smoking and hopeless. She takes his cigarette from his hand and puts it out against the step, leaving a black burn mark against the concrete. It looks somehow accusatory.

Once, complaining of her thirst while they were out canvassing, Ethel led him into a church. Crossed herself at the door and then, taking a cursory look around, dipped both hands into the holy water font and drank by the palmful. He copied her; it was the first but not the last sacrilege they performed together. Their sweat drying, making them shiver, they sat in the nave, joking about the water moving through them and making them holy. He could almost feel it tingling inside him, changing his blood to soda fizz, but maybe that was just being with Ethel.

Like the good Catholic children they were, they started quizzing each other on the martyrdom of saints. Saint Denis? Beheaded. Saint Peter? Crucified upside down. Saint Eulalia? Rolled in a barrel of glass down a hill.

"Saint Longinus?" she asked.

Arrows? Burning? Head cut off and from it sprang a white dove?

"I don't know," he admitted.

She smiled. "That one's easy. They cut out his tongue."

She leaned forward over the back of the pew in front of him, head resting on her arms. "The nuns at school used to threaten me with that one because I'm a motor mouth. But I only talk to remind myself I'm here," she said. "Sometimes I don't feel real if my siblings aren't around. Does that make sense? I only know what I am because of what they are—louder than my sister, faster than my brother."

"It's the curse of a big family," he said. To be defined by what you are in relation.

Now he reaches to light another cigarette, but Ethel

stays his hand. The wind picks up, and he imagines it's votes rushing past them, brushing against his sleeve, invisible, flying through the air. A burst of laughter from inside makes him jump. What are they laughing at? he wonders.

"Why did I agree to it?" he asks.

Ethel looks at him now like he's very young. Her answer is unexpected. "Because you love your brother," she says.

Is that what love is? He looks at her doubtfully.

"It is in your family," she answers his unspoken question.

O'Donnell's on him as soon as he reenters the room, his face uncharacteristically animated. "Come see this."

It's still close, not enough to put Jack ahead, but he's pulling even. He wants to run over to the Lodge campaign to see what the mood is there, but it might be bad luck. He stays exactly where he is; he holds his breath.

The numbers are good. The numbers are bad. Then the coin lands.

His brother will be the next senator from Massachusetts.

Cheers that have been held in all night explode across the room like uncorked bottles of champagne. Confetti rains through the air like snow, settling on tired up-dos and jacket shoulders, a miniature version of the V-Day parades. He climbs onto a folding chair to read out the returns while his brother stands beneath him, grinning. Jack steers him toward the waiting press as onlookers pound them on the back and say they knew it all along.

Sitting in front of the television cameras, they study the returns. He lets Jack do the talking as he toys with the papers in front of them like they require his undivided attention.

"Well, I'm just sure glad it's over, aren't you Bobby?" Jack asks.

"I am, Jack," he reads his line.

They push their chairs back from the table with the same motion, standing as one. A call is waiting for Jack; he watches his brother's face slide from confusion to interest before settling on amusement.

"Dad?" he asks when Jack hangs up.

"Lyndon Johnson," Jack says, "wishing me congratulations. That guy must never sleep."

The Senate majority whip calling to be one of the first to talk to Jack: he's not trying to curry favor. You don't curry favor with your inferiors. And he's not just being friendly, either. There's no such thing in politics. So what does the senator from Texas want? A hand closes on his throat; he brushes it aside.

"Lodge is coming to concede," O'Brien says, his shoulders epauletted with confetti.

"You heard that from his people?" Jack asks.

"Somebody saw him leaving his headquarters. He's on his way over."

They hustle Jack to the door to save Lodge from having to walk through their celebration. Tactful, as his mother would say. His sisters are waiting, ready to form the Kennedy receiving line. "That's his car," Eunice says, nodding at the approaching vehicle.

"How do you know?"

"We thought about egging it."

They wait for the car to roll to a stop at the curb, for Lodge to disembark, maybe with his wife, maybe alone, to shake Jack's hand. *Hell of a way to make a living, isn't it?* He can see the unmistakable profile of Lodge through the car window, even in the dark, even from here. It's the same view Bobby had of him when Lodge sat across from Jack on a stage and didn't think he could win.

The car slides past.

If he's not mistaken, he hears the engine pick up.

Doesn't need to see Eunice's eyes saying *I told you so.* Doesn't need to see Jack's face when his brother says, "High class."

"He's a bastard," Bobby says calmly. "And he's a loser. Let's be done with it." He pushes his siblings back inside toward the party. Tonight, they'll celebrate. But he has a memory like a steel trap. Forgive nothing. Forget nothing.

The main room is swollen with people, more than they started the night with. A crowd is forming on the street; people know a party when they see one. It'll be hours yet before he gets another word alone with his brother, hours before Jack turns to him in the car with the headlights of passing cars screaming across his face and says, "You did this." An accusation. An acknowledgment.

Jack's being passed around the room by eager well-wishers. Bobby can catch only glimpses of him at a time. The back of his head. The slope of his shoulder. Hard to say if his feet touch the ground.

Their father will want to know the details, so he looks; he listens; he pays close attention.

Dad, he'll say, *they were singing "Sweet Adeline" and raising toasts to him, Irish whiskey in paper cups. There were people coming in off the street asking what we were celebrating and the girls were telling them it's a birthday, it's a baptism, it's Christmas come early. Euny's necklace popped, and we found every pearl on the floor but one. I think I heard somebody say that Jack would be president.*

He finds Pat. He says: "I'll take that drink now."

CHAPTER 6

Jackie

THE DEBUTANTE, HIS SISTERS call her. *Her Royal Highness of Rhode Island.*

So. This is the girl Jack's been calling at every campaign stop, finally come to their Palm Beach house for a week to see if she can survive the Kennedys. His sisters watch her with the pointed smiles of ocean carnivores. They've grown bored in the lazy weeks after the election. They've grown bored, and in their boredom: brutal. They're convinced she'll go the way of Jack's other conquests soon enough, and Bobby's inclined to take their side.

And yet what is it about this one that so provokes his sisters' ire? The reporter. The step-daughter of a

Standard Oil scion. The former Newport debutante, such a standout in her season she was dubbed "Queen Debutante of 1947." All they really know about her is a loose collection of nouns. Jack met her through mutual friends; leaned over the asparagus at a dinner party, according to him, and asked her out.

She sits across the dinner table from Bobby now, what should be a prime vantage point, but he's finding it difficult to stare. Her eyes fly to his the moment he so much as glances in her direction, catching him out.

So, this is Jackie.

She looks on as his family's conversation ricochets around the table, never offering an opinion of her own, but—he's certain—carefully cataloging each of theirs. If she were a man, you'd only think she was quiet, but as she's a woman, silence is never neutral, it has shape and shades.

Every night since the election has been a postmortem; Jack's victory aside, it was a bad year for Democrats. For the first time in twenty years, there's going to be a Republican in the White House.

"Throwing in the towel after one term—" their father says about Truman, shaking his head, about to go on—

"He couldn't have been elected again even if he'd tried," Jack says.

"Of course he could have—it's all about nerve. It's about having the stomach for power." His father's eyes flash.

Pat asks sweetly: "What do you think about the new president, Jackie?"

The question isn't meant as a way of including her. It's meant to expose, to embarrass, to call attention to her silence that's lasted through the meal. Because they're used to good sports. People who show up and sparkle, telling clever stories and funny jokes. They want to be impressed, not ignored.

Jackie glances up from her plate and he feels like it's the first time he's gotten a good look at her all night.

"I haven't really been keeping up with it," she says. "Reading about Eisenhower I feel like I'm having my eyeballs painted beige."

This should be points off. Don't bother coming to dinner if you haven't read the *Times*, *U.S. News & World Report*, *Foreign Affairs*, and the *Economist*, their friends have joked before. But his father does a startling thing: he laughs. So does Jack.

"She speaks," Ethel mutters under her breath.

And what a voice it is. Looped and feathery, like an airplane spelling out letters in the sky. As soon as she stops, you want to hand her a quarter, make it go again.

"What *does* interest you?" Eunice asks.

Jackie pauses, deciding what she's willing to share with them. "I enjoy riding," she says. "And I'm interested in history."

"Very good," his father says. "I always say you have to know about your country's history if you want a hope of changing its future—"

"Oh, no, I'm afraid I'm not as well versed in American history as I ought to be," she interrupts, and his sisters exchange looks. "I much prefer Europe." She looks up from beneath her eyelashes slyly. "More gossip."

His father laughs *again*. Ethel starts combining food on her plate, heaping mashed potatoes onto her peas, the motion of her wrist a small act of violence again, again, again.

"Europe," his father says. "You're French, correct?"

"On my father's side. My mother claims she's related to the Robert E. Lees, but she's been known to exaggerate," Jackie says with just a touch of weariness. "On my father's side, we're just cattle farmers. *Bouvier* comes from *boeuf*, beef." She shrugs as if it's all the same to her.

"What does your father do?" the Ambassador asks, though Bobby's certain Jack has already explained these things to him in private. It's like confession, he thinks. It doesn't matter if God already knows what you've done; he wants to hear you say it.

"He lost most of his money in the Crash," Jackie says carefully. "He hasn't had much luck since."

"Your stepfather's in stocks?" the Ambassador asks, tossing her a lifeline. "The Auchinclosses got their start in oil, is that right?"

Stepfather, Pat mouths to Eunice. Bobby feels a short, hot flare of hatred for his sisters.

Jackie's hand drops to her lap. Two bright spots of pink flame in her cheeks.

"My father never met a vice he didn't like," she says, throwing her head back. "Gambling, smoking, drinking. He does it all."

He understands the look on her face—the pride, of all things. Understands what it's like to love a man few others do. To have as a father a man few others would want to claim.

"But you've never met someone who's such fun," she finishes.

The table is silent. Then the Ambassador raises his glass to her. "Your father," he toasts Jackie. When she drinks, she drains her glass.

THE NEW THING becomes imitating Jackie's voice, trying on her strange inflections, the misplaced pauses.

Ethel has particular venom for her: "It sounds like there's a little girl in the bottom of her throat calling for help," his wife says, making his sisters laugh. "Or like she's been buried alive and is running out of air."

Normally, Bobby would be laughing with the rest of them. But something about hearing them mimic Jackie's voice turns his stomach. In their mouths, the softness of her voice becomes babyish; the cadence, cloying; the hesitations, artificial.

They take issue with her clothes—too put together, trying too hard. The fact that her parents are divorced—she's a gold digger just like her mother.

What bothers them most, he's decided, isn't her, but Jack. The way he treats her, the way he watches her.

The way he follows her from room to room as if he doesn't want to miss a single thing.

"FOR THE RECORD, I don't want to be doing this," Bobby says.

Ethel just shushes him and motions for him to follow her. They've been sent out on reconnaissance by his sisters.

"What if they're . . . intimate?"

"Cover your eyes if you need to," Ethel says.

They creep along the hedges, just out of view from the pool, where Jack and Jackie were last spotted sitting on deck chairs. He's following his wife on some half-baked intelligence plot; his sisters want to know what Jack and Jackie talk about when they're alone, and now the two of them are hunched over and moving silently through the yard.

"Hey, wait a minute." He stops suddenly, struck by an idea. "Did you do this kind of thing when I was dating your sister?"

Her look tells him everything he needs to know.

They're in earshot now. Ethel motions him down. He kneels in the dirt next to her.

Jackie's telling Jack about a time she was angry with her mother, and left a dead snake in a hatbox outside of her door.

"Where did you get the snake?" Jack asks.

"Roadkill," Jackie says, and Jack laughs.

And then there's a silence. A long silence.

He and Ethel pop their heads up, over the wall of shrubbery. It's worse than kissing; they're holding hands, staring at each other quietly. He thinks of Howard Carter holding forth a flickering candle as he pried open King Tut's tomb. The whispered question behind him. *What can you see, Carter?* The answer: *Wonderful things.* That's the way Jack and Jackie look at each other. Like treasure in the desert, a room of gold buried under the sand.

They duck back behind the bushes. Ethel mimes retching. Bobby feels strange. Sarcasm, jokes told at each other's expense, beating the hell out of each other in games of football: that's how his family shows affection. Holding hands is something foreign, something you see in movies.

He starts to stand again, wanting another look, but Ethel grabs him by the shoulder, forcing him back down.

"Are we as bad as you expected?" Jack asks on the other side of the bushes.

A pause. "You're a strange family, from the outside."

"Eunice is a bear with everyone, don't mind her. Pat doesn't have a filter. Jean's probably the only one you can trust, but she takes a little while to warm up. As for my brothers—"

"I thought you had another sister."

A slight pause. "Kathleen. She's dead."

"Besides her."

"Oh. You mean Rosemary." A pregnant pause. "She teaches schoolchildren in Wisconsin."

It's a lie Bobby's repeated enough times himself that he knows how it sticks in the throat, how it almost refuses to come out.

"Will I ever meet her?"

"She's very private," Jack says vaguely.

"Even with her own family?"

"Especially with us," Jack says. "You have to be careful in my family. The snakes we leave for each other are live."

Bobby would like, more than anything, to see the expression on Jackie's face right now.

"And your brothers?" Jackie asks.

But before he can hear what Jack has to say about him, a shadow falls over him and Ethel. Jack looms over them in dark sunglasses. His expression is one of measured annoyance.

"Don't you have anything better to do than lurk around?" Jack asks.

"We're not lurking—" Bobby starts.

"We're creeping," Ethel says.

Jack turns over his shoulder. "Do you see what I have to deal with?" he asks.

They stand, and Bobby's eyes meet Jackie's for just a moment. She seems faintly amused, or maybe this is only how she wants to appear. The moment passes too quickly for him to get a fix on her. She turns away, kicking one foot idly, her sandal flapping softly against her heel.

As they turn to go, Bobby takes Ethel's hand. They

walk like that for a few steps, then stop. Look down at their hands. Give them an experimental swing. He knows they're thinking the same thing: it'd be hard to run like this, harder still to catch a pass. Holding hands was invented for stiller people.

They let go of each other at the same moment.

"DAD WANTS A MARRIAGE," Eunice says one day in low tones by the pool.

"How would you know?" Bobby asks. His sister's always acting like she's privy to secret cables the rest of them are too young to know about.

"A bachelor at thirty-five and you start to look light in the loafers," she says.

The thunder of violins drifts from the house. They all pointedly ignore this. It's been their father's ritual since the war for grieving his son. Music as loud as the opera, and solitude. *Joe time*, they call it.

"At least Shriver earned it," Pat says, kicking her feet through the water at the edge of the pool. "He's been around … what, seven years? Eight?"

Sargent Shriver: the man their father's put in charge of his business in Chicago. He's been pining after Eunice forever; he's been an inside joke for almost as long.

"He hasn't earned anything," Eunice snaps.

"She's still having a torrid affair with Stevenson, remember?" Jean says. It's a dangerous joke to make given Eunice's likelihood of retaliation, but when you're in the youngest tier of siblings, sometimes you have to prove that you know as much as everyone else.

There are rumors of a fling between Eunice and the recently defeated presidential candidate. So she was seen a few times in Chicago at the same events Stevenson was. So he neglected his donors to dance with her. So she tried to hand him back his jacket through the window of a taxi and he said, "Keep it." It doesn't mean she's in love. The rumors have gotten her in hot water with the Ambassador. Bobby doesn't know what the greater sin is in his father's book: Stevenson's status as a divorced man or his ignominious loss at the hands of Eisenhower.

Pat remains conspicuously silent as they argue, trying not to draw attention to herself. She's been seeing a man who's older than her by an inappropriate amount. Her life is a soap opera: a series of betrayals by friends; men she promises her heart to before breaking it off; secret trysts; cliff-hangers; twist endings.

"I'd pick one of them soon," Jean is telling Eunice, "before you end up an old maid."

Stretched out with her eyes shut against the sun, Jean doesn't see it coming. Eunice upends her glass in their sister's face. Jean comes up sputtering, cursing Eunice a thousand different ways, reaching for the nearest thing to retaliate with, which happens to be a sandal.

There's laughter inside: not unusual, except that it's coming from his father, loud enough Bobby can hear it over the music. He retreats from the squall of his sisters, creeping down the hallway, ready, at any moment, to bolt in the other direction.

More laughter, throaty and unfamiliar to him. Through the crack in the door: a sliver of crossed ankles. One hand that gestures with red-lacquered nails. *Who is this woman?*

"Bobby," his father's secretary, Mr. Moore, says behind him, and he whips around. "It's not polite to look through keyholes." Mr. Moore shuffles him to the side, rapping on the door. He takes advantage of Moore's entrance, following him inside. "The Luces have stopped by," Moore announces.

Jackie turns; her eyes seem to take up her whole face. She doesn't look worn down, defeated, or resigned. In other words, she doesn't look like someone who's been conversing with their father at length. She's dressed in pink; she's the brightest thing in the room.

His father stands. "To be continued," he tells Jackie with the familiarity of an old friend, and follows Moore out of the room. Bobby's shock erases what would normally be reserve, what would normally prevent him from saying a word to her.

"You were in here," he says, "when my father was playing his music."

"Is that another rule?" she asks dryly, without looking at him. "I just came to listen. I love Toscanini."

"You made him laugh," he says, and then, realizing he's speaking with what Jack calls "the bomber voice" for its high, insistent whine, softens his tone. "That's practically a state secret."

She stands. He thinks she's going to leave, but she only walks over to his father's desk and takes a cigarette from the holder. She lights it not the way some people light it, when they want you to know they've been at parties with artists on balconies in Paris with blue smoke drifting from their lips; she lights it with her back to him, only facing him when she's done as she leans against the desk.

"Not the Luces who run *Time* and *Life*?" Jackie asks.

"Friends of my father," he says.

"Of course," she says, ashing her cigarette. "Who else would it be in Kennedyland?"

She dislikes us, he thinks. He goes to the Victrola, wanting something to do with his hands. Removes the record carefully. "We used to throw these off the roof," he says, "when they got too scratched. They go for miles. Joe swears he hit the water once."

He remembers, then, the press of his brother's arm around his middle, yanking him back from the roof's edge after an overenthusiastic throw sent him hurtling toward danger. But it was always fun back then. It was always Joe laughing, saying, "Jiminy, Bob, you trying to break your neck?" He thinks of his brother; which makes him think of his sisters. Back then, if you fell off the roof, you bounced; if you flew in a plane, it landed; if you went to the hospital, you came home after.

The sound the record makes as he slides it back into its cover fills the whole room.

"Can I try?" Jackie asks.

This is how they find themselves on one of the balconies facing the water, the gulls swooping around them like hall monitors trying to put a stop to this foolishness. She tests the weight of the record they've selected in her hand, then lets it fly with a short, quick snap of the wrist, a spinning black shard that might cut the sky in two.

"You're with the *Times Herald*, right?" he asks. He's learned to ask questions so that he doesn't have to talk about himself. But this isn't the reason he asks this particular question.

"Inquiring Camera Girl," she says.

"What do you inquire about?"

" 'Are you or are you not a supporter of the institution of marriage?' " she says. " 'Do you think the President should be paid a higher salary?' " When she looks at him, her expression is lethal. "It's a demanding job," she says, "but that's the price of delivering hard-hitting journalism to the people."

Is she joking? Or isn't she? Her face gives nothing away. "So that was you that just won the Pulitzer," he says slowly.

"The one and the same," she says.

There was a day not long after she arrived in Hyannisport that he and his sisters went through her valise in search of clues as to who she was. A silk chemise (interesting), a blouse with the tag still on it (is she trying to impress us?), a pair of striped socks (childish). His sisters deducing her character from each object, though to him they'd just seemed like clothes.

He wishes now he hadn't done it. Almost blurts an apology, but bites his tongue at the last minute.

She tilts her face to the sun, bronze threading the dark brown of her hair where the light touches it. Strange to be strangers. Strange to stand in the sun with someone and know that, depending on your brother, this person will either be someone to you, or no one at all.

"YOU CAN'T JUST LET HER throw records," Eunice says.

"Why?" he asks. It is, to him, a reasonable, logical question, but the look his sisters give him dispels any such notion.

They're cross with him after this and say you can't trust men, how all men are the same. They treat it like a betrayal.

"They were never like this with Ethel," he complains on the phone to Ted.

Ethel was like having another sister around; hair going a million different directions, a laugh loud enough to break glass, a leg sticking out to send you tumbling in their games of football. She comes from a family even rowdier than theirs; for fun, she and her siblings used to shoot tin cans off each other's heads with pellet guns.

But his sisters mock Jackie. She doesn't play football, telling them in a voice arch with sarcasm, "I'd rather keep all of my limbs, thank you." When she's not with Jack, she buries her nose in a book or walks alone on the beach. Her stepfather's a Republican, and her father, as far as he can tell, is an itinerant drunk. If you mark her on the usual scorecard, it's failing marks.

Yet she's understood intuitively that it doesn't matter if he or Ted or any of the girls like her, or even if Jack does. There's only one opinion that counts. She sits with their father on the porch, their heads bent in conversation, their conversation bent with laughter. Never in the history of their house has someone new so instantly earned their father's affection. He invites her to go riding with him in the mornings, an event that's only ever been reserved for his children.

"Everything's different with Jack," Ted says. "So what's she like? Fanged? Covered in scales?"

"She's funny."

"Funny odd or funny ha-ha?"

He thinks about it. "Both."

"Is she Kennedy material?"

"You'll just have to see for yourself."

CHAPTER 7

McCarthy

THE CAMPAIGN MAY BE OVER, but politics is a year-round game, and his father can still play with the best of them. Bobby's used to the Ambassador's maneuverings. No visit is ever random; no friendship, coincidental. It's all a careful calculation by his father, and tonight, just a month after the election, Senator McCarthy's here for dinner.

He's swilling gimlets with their father, his dark brows knitted together in concentration as he listens to the Ambassador. But why is he here, among them, the most famous Republican of all? Bobby knows McCarthy as a friend of his father's, though "friend" can mean anything from acquaintance to business partner to political tool.

He thinks his father sees McCarthy as a kind of charm, a rabbit's foot he can palm—proof that an Irish American can win in Washington. Maybe his father's thinking of luck by association. In politics, there's no ritual too ridiculous.

The glass in the senator's hand appears comically small; McCarthy had told them that he used to be a boxer, and you can see it as the senator leans forward in his armchair, composing his next answer like a blow to the temple.

Their father's playing that old favorite of his: *America can never survive as global policeman.*

"There are boys dying in Korea over a war that doesn't need to be fought," his father says. "A war we never should have gotten involved in to begin with. Sons and brothers, good American boys—"

"But surely you wouldn't have us just roll over for the Red Tide," McCarthy says. "We've never lost a war, Joe, we aren't going to start now."

"Yes," Jack says, toying with a loose thread on a throw pillow, "or else it'll be our turn to ask 'Who Lost Korea?'"

McCarthy laughs a great, booming laugh that erases the brooding look on his face. "As you should," he nods to Jack. His brother crosses one foot over the other, revealing a flash of mismatched socks, one black, one white. Jackie has gone; Jack's back to dressing himself in the first thing he finds. He'll go back to Washington soon, to be sworn in as a senator. Maybe that's the Ambassador's angle with McCarthy, to get Jack in early with the figures in power.

"Jack and Bobby were in that part of the world only last year," his father says. "Tell him."

"Me too," Pat says. "I was there, too."

Last fall; he, Jack, and Pat visited seven different countries in as many weeks, one of the recurrent trips abroad their parents send them on that are more like military campaigns than vacations. Meetings with foreign dignitaries, prime ministers, generals. Jack caught a fever and fell into a coma in Japan, but the important thing was, the trip beefed up Jack's foreign policy resume ahead of the Senate race.

"So you've seen the Red Menace firsthand," McCarthy says. "Myself, I haven't been in the Pacific since—since the war I suppose. How did you find it?"

"Incredibly volatile—" Jack starts.

"We met the prime minister of Pakistan just a few days before he was assassinated," Pat interjects.

Jack nods. "You get the feeling that the course of the next century could be decided in the Middle East, in the Pacific, India," he says. "It's important, I think, to win their minds—"

"Those poor souls," McCarthy agrees. "They don't know any better, and so they blindly chain themselves to the yoke of communism."

"Perhaps we haven't presented a strong enough alternative," Jack says.

"Freedom and democracy," McCarthy says. "What could be a stronger alternative?"

"It's difficult, though, when the Americans offer you democracy and the Communists offer you bread," Pat says, her voice loud enough to silence the room.

McCarthy turns to her. "You went with your brothers, is that right?"

Pat takes a breath. Her face has gone grim and red.

"Yes," she says.

"Joe, what a modern father you are," McCarthy crows, turning to the Ambassador. "Sending your daughter out to the edges of civilization—what a thing!"

"She was popular with Nehru," Jack teases, shooting an appeasing glance at Pat. It was a joke they had at the time, the prime minister of India's obvious infatuation with their sister.

"Patty Cake can handle herself," the Ambassador says. "I could have sent her alone and she'd have done just fine, but these two—" He gestures at Jack and Bobby with his glass as if their hopelessness is physically evident. "You drop Pat in the desert, though—she'll find water."

His sister straightens up, adjusting to the weight of a compliment from their father. Such a heavy thing it is.

"Did you sense much Communist feeling among the people?" McCarthy asks.

Bobby clocks the motion of his brother's hand, twisting the thread around and around and then, with a flick of the wrist, snapping it off. "I'd say it was more anticolonial than procommunist," Jack says.

"Surely you would agree though, Senator, that regardless of what motivates Communist leanings, it presents a danger to our national interests."

Jack smiles, coy. "I'm not a senator yet," he says. Playing politics even now, in their living room.

Their mother enters, announcing dinner, and they disband to the dining room. Bobby is the last to leave, lingering by his mother's side. She's just returned from a trip alone to France, and part of her is still an ocean away.

"Did you hear the latest?" he asks her. "About Jackie?"

"He seems like a nice boy," his mother says. "He wrote me a lovely thank you note—"

"*She*, Mother. She's a woman."

"Ah. Well."

She gives a little wave of the hand. The recent years have brought a practiced absence about her. If our father's a puppet master, Pat says, our mother left at intermission for concessions and was last seen driving west.

McCARTHY SITS NEXT to their father, accepting a refreshed drink from their mother.

His father to McCarthy: "You must be pleased with the results of the election."

It's been a Republican sweep. House, Senate, and

presidency. McCarthy grins, his smile making him appear more youthful than the comb-over suggests. "And about time," he says with mock exasperation. "You only had the keys to the castle for twenty years."

"'Twenty years of corruption,'" Jack counters, parroting the Republican line. "Give us credit where credit's due."

"Believe it or not, I used to be one of you," McCarthy says, looking around the table with dramatic flair. "An FDR man through and through." The Ambassador saws through his roast with determination. "A loyal Democrat. Blue down to my—"

"What happened?" Eunice prods, impatient to move the story along.

"Truman became president."

Genuine laughter; the senator in private is a far cry from the biting headlines you see in the papers. Jovial and smiling, his face flushed red with good humor. Bobby likes him; unlike his father's other politician friends, who, even in private, have a tendency to either pontificate or speak in dull platitudes about the issues, McCarthy talks like a real person. He's unpolished, genuine. And unlike those other politicians, his main concern isn't keeping his seat for another term—it's the country, and what's actually going on in the world.

"I'll tell you this," his father says. "It's almost enough to make me change parties. I'd like to wash my hands of the whole administration."

"Some Democrat you are, Dad," Bobby says.

"You cheered Truman when he was elected," Jack reminds their father. "You said you were sick of the Hyde Park set—"

"Truman wasn't all bad," Eunice says. "Besides the influence peddling and his attorney general being a criminal and the Hiss affair..."

Hiss, a former State Department official, accused of being a Communist by a former party member: at first it seemed like nothing but hot air—no one wanted to take the word of some Commie against a government official.

His father shakes his head. "Talk about a career maker for Nixon."

"A windfall," Jack says, his voice prickly. "It could have been anyone."

"But Nixon didn't let it drop," his father continues. "That's why he's vice president now. Tenacity. Stubbornness—"

"Some might call it pigheadedness," Jack says.

"Call it what you want, he's laughing all the way to the bank."

"The Soviets don't need to beat us in Korea," Bobby says. "They're already beating us here. Can you imagine what the Hiss case did for their propaganda?"

"Wind him up and watch him go," Eunice mutters. Normally, Bobby's opinions have all the cachet of a drunk soothsayer's.

But McCarthy raises a glass to him. "I'll drink to that," the senator says. Unexpectedly, Bobby's said the right thing for once. McCarthy's approval warms him through, warding off Eunice's cold glare.

Jack turns to McCarthy, his voice a light note of curiosity that wouldn't register as false unless you'd spent your life listening to him. "Surely you know of others," Jack says. "Other communists in the government."

All eyes turn to McCarthy. The senator doesn't hesitate. "I couldn't say in the presence of ladies."

"We're not ladies," Pat says. "Ask anyone who knows us."

The senator leans in, his voice going husky like he's telling a ghost story. "I'm not at liberty to disclose specifics," he says, "but I can tell you this: something is rotten in the state of Denmark and I intend to get to the very bottom of this black and pernicious conspiracy and pull it out by its roots and salt the earth behind me."

A long beat of silence.

"Best of luck," Eunice says finally.

McCarthy sits back in his chair, satisfied. "No luck," he grins. "Only shaping destiny with your own two hands."

"Is that it?" Jack asks. "Or does destiny produce the man for the hour?"

But nobody's listening except Bobby.

AFTER DINNER, THEY GATHER in his father's study. He, Jack, McCarthy. None of the girls have managed to muscle their way in, not even Eunice. The Ambassador pours McCarthy a drink—his fourth? His fifth? McCarthy accepts it happily.

Who else with McCarthy's power would be seen talking with the disgraced Joe Kennedy? But McCarthy's no coward. And his reputation is like the *Titanic*, too big to sink. Bobby remembers how his own law school classmates booed the Ambassador once when he came to speak, and he feels an unlikely swell of gratitude toward McCarthy.

"So," the Ambassador says, sinking into his chair, "tell us about this committee of yours."

McCarthy takes a seat next to Bobby, unbuttoning his suit jacket as he does. He has the heft and build of a linebacker—the couch springs pop as he settles in. "It's thankless work," McCarthy says, smiling, "but I suppose that's the bedrock of democracy."

"Who have you got with you?" his father asks, oddly intent. "Your staff?" Bobby wonders what his father's interest is.

"I've just hired a young lawyer out of New York," McCarthy says. "Roy Cohn."

"Cohn?" Jack asks. "Wasn't he involved with the Rosenberg trial?"

"You can see why I wanted him as chief counsel." McCarthy takes a long swig of his drink. "A remarkable young man. Photographic memory—why, he graduated from law school before he was old enough to legally practice."

"Chief counsel?" the Ambassador asks, his voice cool and blue as the tide.

"Oh yes," McCarthy says. "I don't mind taking a chance on a young man when he's got a track record of hunting down Reds. He comes highly recommended from J. Edgar Hoover in fact. He's quite the catch—Roy's handled all kinds of subversion, espionage—"

"Who will you investigate next?" Jack asks. "Now that we're not in the presence of ladies."

"If I didn't know better, I'd say you were angling for a spot on my committee," McCarthy says, wagging a finger at Jack.

"I couldn't," Jack demurs. Bobby realizes then that Jack doesn't like McCarthy. It's subtle; everything is, with his brother. But Jack has a tendency to retreat, yanking up the drawbridge behind him, when he's uncomfortable with a person. That's twice now he's deflected. It makes Bobby wonder where he's gone wrong, that he and Jack could come to the opposite conclusion about the same man.

Confusion arrows through him. Why's McCarthy here, if not as a potential ally for Jack in the Senate? He tries to ask his brother with his eyes, but can't decipher Jack's answering look.

"That's all right," McCarthy says. "You'll have your turn. And you, Bob—what'll you do next?"

Bobby's caught off guard by the question, by the genuine interest with which McCarthy asks it.

"We may run him for governor," Jack says.

This is the first he's heard of it; ice grips his insides.

"My advice—stay out of elected office as long as you can," McCarthy says, the ice in his glass tinkling as he gestures.

It doesn't matter to Bobby that the senator's drunk; he's been waiting for someone to say these words.

"People get all kinds of ideas about you," McCarthy continues, "all kinds of ideas about the man you are. You don't want to be some five-inch column of newsprint. No sir."

He understands what McCarthy means, even as his father and brother exchange a glance. And McCarthy, eyes hooded with drink, understands him in a way that perhaps even his own father doesn't.

The Ambassador says, "Shall we retire for the evening?"

"A lovely evening," McCarthy says as Bobby leads him toward the guest room. His words are thick and syrupy. "It's always fun with the Kennedys."

Bobby stops at the doorway. "Here we are," he says. The senator lists to one side, slumping against the wall. "Congratulations," McCarthy says, clapping a hand on Bobby's shoulder, "on Jack's election. I heard you did good work. Any politician worth his salt needs a man like you—take it from me."

Like what? he wants to ask. But he says instead, "We were certainly helped by your staying out of the state."

"I told Lodge—I told Lodge I'd only campaign

for him if he asked for it. *Publicly.*" McCarthy grins, his eyes heavy. "And we both know that would never happen."

"Why not?" McCarthy's the most popular figure in his party; anyone would be lucky to have an assist from him.

"We're just gutter Irish to them. No matter how far we claw our way up. You understand."

He thinks of Jack, himself, their sisters lit from one side by a victory party, lit from the other by the headlights of Lodge's passing car. Anger flares in him anew.

He says, "I do."

BACK IN HIS FATHER'S STUDY, his father and brother are arguing.

"You didn't have to keep pouring him drinks," Jack says.

"Nobody's going to say that Joe Kennedy keeps his guests dry," the Ambassador says.

"Not when you have a gin runner reputation to uphold," Jack replies, voice laced with sarcasm.

"Put to bed?" his father asks, turning as Bobby enters.

"Yes."

"What do we think?"

His father leans over the desk, fists on the wood, the pose you take for closing a deal. Bobby looks to Jack, expecting to see his confusion mirrored, but Jack's already been clued in, evidently. Bobby's surprised at the annoyance he feels; and then annoyed by that surprise. *Did you think winning one campaign made you part of the club?* It's still just his father and Jack, Jack and his father.

"It might be giants and it might be windmills," Jack says.

"Look at the Lodges," his father says. "While one was in the Senate, the other was in the House."

"So let Bobby run for something," Jack says. "He could use the practice. So could Ted."

"The next election isn't for two years. He needs experience."

"He can work for me," Jack offers without offering. "I need someone to sort the mail."

"What's this about?" Bobby asks.

"Rest is for losers," his father says, pacing. "You did a good job with the campaign. It's time for you to do a better job with something else."

So the fun conversation has arrived. The Ambassador has been dogging him since the election. Since he came out of the voting booth, really.

"What about my old job?" Bobby asks hopefully.

His father whirls around. "Out of the question," the Ambassador says. "You're not going to be some coat boy at the DOJ. Your brother is a US Senator now."

Something he's taken to reminding them. To reciting like a prayer. *Your brother is a US senator now.* And why shouldn't he be proud? He's the one who paid for it.

An ambassador's son. A senator's brother. But where's he in any of this? he wonders. Where's anything he's done?

"Dad wants you to work for McCarthy," Jack says.

"Why would McCarthy want me?" Bobby asks, a sinking feeling in his stomach.

Jack and his father exchange a look.

"You're my son," his father says. Meaning, *He owes me.* Meaning, *It has nothing to do with you.* His father's not only a genius at stocks, but at debts. At placing money in the right hands long before he'll ever need it, and calling it in when the timing is right.

"The Republicans are trying to put him out to pasture," Jack says. "And now he has a president from his own party—do you think Eisenhower's going to be a whipping boy for McCarthy like Truman was?"

"I don't know what Eisenhower's going to do," his father says. "Men change in that office. They're different people to what they pretend on the campaign trail."

"It's good experience," his father adds. "Real work on a Senate subcommittee."

"It's courting controversy."

"Power is where power goes, and right now McCarthy has a full deck to play with."

"For now," Jack says. "Until he's the snake that tried to swallow an elephant. He could drag Bobby down and all of us, too."

"It won't come to that," his father dismisses Jack.

Jack throws up his hands, harassed. "I know you

think you have the ability to control the motion of the sun in the sky, Dad—"

"It won't come to that," his father repeats.

"People on the left can't stand him. People on the right can't stand him. Nobody's going to touch Bobby if he works with him."

Tailgunner Joe, they call McCarthy for his fudged wartime stories. He'll show you scars he claims were from surviving a plane crash under heavy fire, when in reality it was an overenthusiastic party on deck that had maimed him, although McCarthy sticks to his story.

"I thought you liked him," his father says. "The press seems to think so."

A casual twist of the knife. Jack's mouth pinches. Uncomfortable with the association. "We get along in social settings. I agree with *some* of his premises—"

"How do you think the Lodges became the Lodges? The Tafts? The Roosevelts?" his father asks, cocking his head to one side. "By winning one race? No, I don't think so. And none of them have anything that you don't have."

This is directed at both of them. A warning. A reminder about what he's worked to give them. He glances at Jack; his brother looks like he's holding his breath.

"Success follows success," his father says. "But it's like money. You have to chase it. You can never make enough of it." He gestures to Jack. "Look at the people who came into the House with you. Smathers spent half the time you did before jumping into the Senate. Nixon's got his bread buttered. Were they harder workers? Or simply better politicians?"

His brother's jaw is tight, coiled, a snake about to strike. His eyes: liquid glass.

"The McCarthy job," Bobby says before his brother can speak. "I'll consider it."

JACK CATCHES HIM in the hallway, the house quiet except for the far-off sound of their sisters' laughter like a jolly ghost.

"You'll consider it, or you've already made up your mind?" Jack demands.

"I trust Dad," he says. Although it's too dark to be certain, he imagines Jack rolls his eyes.

The truth is, he'll take any job that keeps him out of office. Maybe he's fighting the inevitable; his father won't be content with the Senate for long. But he doesn't have what Jack has. If he ran, he'd lose. And Kennedys don't lose.

"He's tough," Bobby says. "If I work for him nobody will be able to say we were Communist sympathizers."

He finds himself warming to the idea as he speaks. So what if McCarthy's controversial or in the opposing party; at least he's *doing* something about Communists. The Soviets have professed as their goal the end of democracy; they've stolen how to make the bomb. And while the rest of Washington wrings their hands, McCarthy's the only one willing to fight fire with fire. Bobby's twenty-seven years old and certain of nothing in his own right, so he'll bank on someone else's certainty. He wants to be tough, like McCarthy. Taken seriously. He wants to have something of his own. Something that'll show that his help with the Senate victory was more than a fluke, a stroke of luck, a windfall.

His brother rubs his jaw as if he's been punched. "It's not up to you to rehabilitate Dad's reputation."

"It's not about Dad," he says. "You got Lodge for being soft on Communism by the skin of your teeth. Next time—the next Republican—you might not get so lucky."

Jack looks at him for a long moment; he's not sure what his brother can see, the two of them no more than outlines in the black hallway.

"If you want the job, take it," Jack says, "but don't do it on my account. And don't do it on Dad's."

MAYBE JACK'S RIGHT to be wary. After all, the Ambassador's played political games before and lost. But Bobby sees it differently; their father lost, so why shouldn't Bobby, his son, give him a chance to win again?

He remembers how it was before the Ambassador's exile; he remembers how the British press cheered his father when he first arrived in 1938, family in tow. An Irishman in a WASP's post. A novelty. Nine children who made for excellent copy. He thinks of how his father told the press that in order to avoid further strains on the British housing problem, he was bringing his children over to England in waves. Laughter all around.

His father had been given smaller roles in the administration up to that point—SEC chairman, head of the Maritime Commission. Now he wanted Secretary of the Treasury. Felt he was owed it. Got Ambassador to England instead. The president gave his little gifts and what could he do but accept them? Smile. Thank him for his generosity.

Bobby was just a boy, unconcerned with Hitler and Hirohito. In his memory, England glints: a diamond tiara in the dark nest of his mother's hair; the photo flash as Kick and Rosie curtseyed in front of the Queen at their coming out; a cut-crystal glass of milk handed to him at a party for which he was allowed to stay up late, listening to a string quartet; the shine in his father's eyes when he described the weekend he and their mother spent as guests at Windsor Castle—"We're a long way from East Boston," the Ambassador said.

But then the Germans started annexing pieces of Europe. London was filled with barbed wire and blackout curtains and their debates at dinner began to turn to just one question: Do you think there'll be war? He could tell by the way Jack and Joe leaned forward and shot each other sideways glances, that they hoped the answer was *Yes*, and by his father's closed study door that they were right.

The Ambassador sent his children back home in

waves too, not as a joke this time, but to avoid German U-boats and mined harbors. Kick showed up at every meal in those final weeks with eyes raw from crying, having failed to convince their father to let her stay behind with her posh friends and help with the war effort.

His father refused to mince words even if the one job of an ambassador was to smile and support the president's foreign policy. So when he was asked about the future of Europe, with panzer divisions rolling in, he said, "Democracy is finished in England. It may be finished here." The epitaph to his own political career. They started calling him a coward. Defeatist. Un-American. And the cruelest: Nazi sympathizer. *Sympathizer*. The worst thing a person can be, implying something spineless.

He got the sack in fairly short order. Then America joined the war. Joe died. Their older brother always first. Beating the rest of them even at this. The president killed my son, his father started saying, and Bobby found the picture of his father and Roosevelt that used to haunt the bookshelf shattered in the trash, frame and all.

Sometimes when Bobby hears Brahms thundering from his father's Victrola, he remembers those London nights, his siblings—who he still needed two hands to count—all in the corner, and he remembers how, after he'd been sent to bed, he'd lay on the floor of his room to feel the vibrations through the floor, his ribcage shuddering with music. Now if he hears strings, he knows to get out of the house.

Their father lost a job, then a political future of his own, then his eldest son, in that order. To Jack, it's a fate to avoid; to Bobby, it's an undeserved slight from a political class that never meant to let them hold power for long. To Jack, a warning; to Bobby, a wrong waiting to be righted.

CHAPTER 8

Part of the Club

THE McCARTHY COMMITTEE OFFICES come to a boil every day just before noon and just before six; the feeding frenzy happens like clockwork because McCarthy gives the reporters a scoop right before their print deadlines. It's a win-win; their bylines are automatically bumped to the front page, and McCarthy can say whatever he wants because the newsmen don't have time to fact-check or source quotes from the opposition. In the competition for headlines with over five hundred other members of Congress, it's rather brilliant.

Men in suits vie for position—you can tell which ones are aides and which ones are journalists by the metal flasks flashing in and out of the latter's hip pockets. All of them waiting for McCarthy to emerge from questioning the accused in one of his closed-door executive sessions. No press inside. No witnesses. No one except Roy Cohn, McCarthy's sneering chief counsel, who clings like a shadow to McCarthy and fancies himself a co-senator. Eunice makes a joke about the Stasi after he describes it to his siblings.

Bobby himself isn't sure what to think. It's just the way things are done, others on the committee tell him. Some witnesses will only talk in private. The line he hears parroted a hundred times a day: If these people had nothing to hide, they wouldn't be called in for questioning to begin with. Bobby takes comfort in its assured logic. It's not personal, he reminds himself, just politics.

And yet it nags him anew every time he sees McCarthy swaggering out of an executive session, Cohn following behind him with the bloodless eyes of a dead fish, muttering something in McCarthy's ear with lips that barely move, the witness exiting last, gray and slumped as a pre-Renaissance Christ.

But mostly he's too busy to linger on these moments of doubt. Bobby's been assigned an investigation into trade with Red China. He reports to a man named Flanagan, one of several ex-FBI men on staff who are easy to pick out with their crew cuts and square jaws, their way of standing with feet shoulder-width apart, as if on a firing range. He follows the money, looking for suspicious trade with the Reds. It suits him, the quiet. His only company is the draft of air that sometimes toys with the strip of skin between his pant leg and his sock. By the time he emerges most days, the world has turned cool and blue.

It feels good to be doing something again, to have a purpose he's been missing since Jack's campaign ended. More and more, he finds himself using McCarthy as justification in arguments with his siblings. "That's not what the senator thinks," or "I heard from the senator" become part of his daily repertoire until Jack tells him one day, "You know the girls have developed a drinking game around this charming new verbal tic of yours. Every time you enlighten us as to what 'the senator' thinks, they drink. Last I heard, the house has become a dry county." After that, he's careful to only use this line with acquaintances.

When he tells people who his boss is, he can feel how they're both awed and intimidated. He's close to power, or closer than he's been before, and it gives him a certain sheen people recognize. Out recently with Pat, who'd been in town for the weekend, the woman they'd been talking to at a cocktail party had grabbed his sleeve when he told her he worked for McCarthy.

"Oh, wow," she said. "Do you know him personally?"

"He *does*," Pat said, mimicking her breathless tone so effortlessly the woman didn't see she was being mocked.

"What's he really like?" the woman asked. "He can't be as serious as they show him on TV."

"Well, he's certainly serious about Communists…"

Bobby said, a little distracted by Pat nodding along eagerly. To a stranger—to this woman—it would have looked like genuine interest, encouragement to go on. But in the code of siblings, it translated to Pat calling him a blowhard.

"What are you working on now?" the woman asked.

"Sorry," Pat said, grabbing Bobby's arm to extricate him. "Requires a clearance Secret or higher." She dragged Bobby away through the crowd. "Didn't realize I was out with the big man on campus," she said, and for the rest of the night, she made him tell people he worked at the Department of Agriculture.

BOBBY'S BEEN ON THE JOB nearly a month when he receives a summons from McCarthy. "Don't go on an empty stomach," Flanagan warns him.

And soon he sees why: McCarthy pushes a drink into Bobby's hand the moment he sits, knocking a stack of files to the floor, the papers fanning out over the carpet. The glass in Bobby's hand is cool like his father's warning: *We're not that kind of Irish.* He bends down to gather the papers.

"How do you like it?" McCarthy asks.

"The work? I'm enjoying—"

"No, no, the whiskey." McCarthy laughs, waving a hand. "Work, work, work," he says. "Flanagan says you work like a dog. He says he's not sure if you breathe. But I told him—I told him, 'Look here, even the boy's own father says he's a hard-driving son of a bitch—'"

Bobby takes an infinitesimal sip of his drink. It burns a hole in the back of his throat. *She could make friends with a door*, his father used to brag about Kick. *Show me something Joe can't do.* The simplest of all reserved for Jack: *That's my boy.*

And him: a hard-driving son of a bitch.

"We can't be these men, Bobby, who only talk about work. Who forget we're people outside of our causes. Another?" McCarthy asks, his own glass empty.

"That's all right," he says.

McCarthy unscrews the cap and tips a heavy finger of honey-colored liquid into his glass. "Your children," McCarthy says, watching the pour. "Tell me about your children."

"Kathleen turns two in July," he says. "She likes having her picture taken. And Joe—Ethel thinks his head is crooked. But he's a happy boy nonetheless."

"He'll be all right," McCarthy says, a merry glint in his eyes. "You can get far with a good strong name like 'Joe.'"

The senator considers his glass with heavy-lidded eyes. His face deflates, showing his age all at once. "I wanted children myself," McCarthy says. "A whole team of them. A whole choir. But who wants a father who's the most hated man in Washington?" His voice is small, hopeless.

"Children don't see it like that," Bobby says, thinking that his father claimed the same title, once.

"Ah, but she'll never have me," McCarthy says with a sad smile. Bobby doesn't have to ask who. McCarthy's red-headed secretary has been working for him longer than any of the rest of them.

"I thought the same thing about Ethel," he says. "She wanted to be a nun."

Ethel coming down to Charlottesville to break his heart. Ethel arriving the way she always arrives: tripping out of her cab, purse tangled around one wrist, one glove unbuttoned. Telling him it was over between them, that she'd decided to dedicate her life to God. "Don't bother to call," she said. "I've told my sister to answer, and I said she can be as mean as she likes to any of the Kennedys."

"How did you change her mind?" McCarthy asks.

"I didn't," he says. "I got lucky."

"The luck of the Irish," McCarthy says, looking up at the ceiling. "If ever I could use it…"

"We'll have you for dinner," he says. "Ethel likes to play matchmaker."

"I'd like that," McCarthy says. "I can't tell you the last time I had a dinner that wasn't about fundraising." He sighs and rests his head against the back of his chair. "I saved my first dinner invitation," McCarthy says. "Left it propped on the mantel for a month.… And of course now I barely look at them. But it's all very exciting in the beginning, isn't it?

"That first win. That first race. The day I was sworn

in, I remember thinking 'This is what it's all about.' Being part of the club. Not pressing your nose to the glass, but actually inside."

Bobby marvels at the change in him. The McCarthy the world sees, the communist hunter—he glowers and swaggers and insists. But this private McCarthy seems uncertain. *Why don't you show this face to the world?* Bobby wants to ask. Could this man not accomplish the same things the other McCarthy has? Or can you only win by being the worst?

"I told you I used to be a New Deal Democrat, didn't I?" McCarthy asks, head lolling toward Bobby. Bobby nods. "Four terms Roosevelt had. The longest-serving president there ever was."

Bobby expects McCarthy to comment on his admiration for FDR, his iron grip on power—but he only shakes his head. "It makes one terribly sad for him."

"Sad?" Bobby asks.

"There are more important things, aren't there?" McCarthy looks at him heavily. "Wouldn't we all be happier if we were fathers instead of politicians?"

The most feared man in Washington feels the same way he does. He takes another small sip of his drink and it runs a hot line down his throat.

"I always thought politics would be temporary," McCarthy says, holding his own glass now almost like Yorick's skull. "But once you're in, you can never get out. You're like the tiger who's tasted man. Nothing is ever as sweet again."

The janitor comes in with his cart; it's that late. Ethel will come looking for him if he doesn't get home—that's the last thing the city needs, his wife bombing through the streets at dark. She's enough of a menace in the daylight hours.

Bobby stands. "I won't keep you."

McCarthy's voice is low and mournful. "Don't be a stranger," he says.

CHAPTER 9

Balancing Act

"BUT YOU ONLY SEE HIM at work, don't you? You don't socialize with him?" Jack asks Bobby.

He wouldn't call it socializing, exactly, him stopping by McCarthy's office to talk every now and then. So it's not quite a lie when he tells his brother "No."

Luckily, Jack doesn't press him further, too preoccupied of late with learning his way around the Senate and *socializing* of his own. In amidst legislative briefs, his desk is cluttered with books of French history. He took Jackie as his date to Eisenhower's inaugural. He's reportedly been asking if twelve years is too big an age gap for marriage.

Bobby's sisters and Ethel turn it over endlessly on the telephone: the Jackie problem.

Apparently there was a previous engagement she broke off last spring. He's heard different things from different sisters. The man was unfaithful. Jackie's mother pressured her into saying yes. She didn't want to become a housewife. He didn't make *real money.* Whatever the story, it's in the past now. *If he's serious,* they agree in sideways, slanted voices, *I hope he marries her quickly, before she trades up again.*

But it's Eunice who gets engaged.

Over the phone, Pat reads Bobby the telegram Shriver sent their parents:

AM FURIOUS AT YOU KNOW WHO STOP TYPICALLY SHE DID NOT ALLOW ME TO BE PRESENT WHEN SHE TOLD YOU THE NEWS STOP DESPITE THIS AND HER OTHER PECULIAR IDEAS AND ACTIONS I LOVE HER MORE THAN ANY TELEGRAM COULD SAY STOP THANK YOU BOTH FOR MAKING HER POSSIBLE FOR ME.

"What do you think that means, 'making her possible for me?' Do you think he cut some kind of deal with Dad—"

Pat's sigh is dry. "Bobby," she says, "you've really been spending too much time with your boss."

But he has good cause for unease. "Keep your wits about you," his father told him after the election. "Everyone will want a piece of the pie now."

Look at what Shriver stands to gain from marrying

into their family: not just money, but political legitimacy. He's a proud man, full of liberal ideas, and, when Bobby's willing to admit it, decent on the stump. He doubts Shriver's going to be content as a strategist on another man's campaign forever.

"We're nobody's *springboard*," he tells Pat.

His sister is nonplussed. "Dad says I'm to make sure you call Shriver and congratulate him like a man."

On paper, it's a good match—Catholic family, Yale graduate, et cetera, et cetera—but as a person, Bobby finds him insufferably earnest, too eager to please, a boy scout. Just look at his cable: I LOVE HER MORE THAN ANY TELEGRAM COULD SAY. He imagines Eunice would rather walk barefoot across a bed of glass than ever put a sentiment like that in writing.

"I thought she wanted to take holy orders," he says, puzzling through it one night in bed with Ethel.

Ethel's response is immediate: "How would a nun in the family look to voters in West Virginia?" Sometimes she's more of a Kennedy than he is.

"What made you change your mind when we got married?" he asks. "She can't be in love."

"I don't know that it has to do with love," she says. "Not in the way you're thinking." She stretches her arms above her head, the streetlight through the blinds cutting stripes in her skin. "Your sister's not a romantic."

No, he thinks. None of us really are. Romance is for people who haven't dealt with death.

He thinks of his sister in church, white-knuckling her prayers like she's clinging for dear life to a tether from God, not the smooth serenity of the Virgin Mother, but the unyielding agony of some early martyr. He used to see her on her bedroom floor sometimes, face down in supplication, a rosary clutched so tightly in one palm that her fingers had turned purple from a lack of circulation.

"If you would focus less on God and more on getting a man, it would be a great relief to your brother," Jack wrote her once. And Eunice probably wrote back with a Bible verse and her usual signature, e.de.m, *enfant de Marie*, "child of Mary."

"Are you happy?" he'd asked his sister when he called to confirm this wasn't an elaborate hoax. "I mean, this is something you want?"

"Am I happy?" she'd asked mockingly. "God, Bobby. Grow a pair."

Ethel's hand comes up, covers his eyes. "Go to sleep," she says. "I can hear you thinking."

"You didn't answer me," he says, "on why you changed your mind."

She yawns. "I prayed on it again," she says, "and even God agreed a Kennedy was too good to pass up."

WHY SHOULD A HAPPY *bachelor get married?*

How much should a man spend on an engagement ring?

Do you think a wife should let her husband think he's smarter than she is?

These are the questions in Jackie's "Camera Girl" column in the *Times Herald*. Husband, wife, marriage, his sisters point out. She's certainly thinking about it.

They start to suspect that Jack's already proposed in secret. But Bobby knows better; he runs into Jackie at the Capitol one day, and she tells him the news. She's been assigned to London for the summer to cover the Queen's coronation.

So this is how it ends. She'll go away to Europe, and Jack will lose interest. Come fall, it'll be a new girl. He's surprised to feel disappointment.

"Maybe I'll swing by your old house while I'm there," she says.

"Check the wine cellar," he advises her. "My father had to leave behind all his nice champagne when we left. It was supposed to be for entertaining the toffs. An Irishman serving the English glasses of French wine in the American embassy."

Jackie looks at him funnily. "Jack said the same thing," she says. "About the champagne." She laughs shortly. "Sometimes I think you all share the same brain."

"SOMETIMES, THEY CAN SENSE it coming, in which case you have to act quickly," McCarthy says. "And then you simply…" Here he swings his arm in a circle, demonstrating the proper technique for killing a chicken.

They're having that dinner, the one he promised McCarthy.

"You haven't known cold until it's four in the morning in a Wisconsin winter," McCarthy says, shaking his head fondly. "It's like another world."

Ethel studies the pair across their dining room table, McCarthy and the secretary who won't have him.

"You make a handsome couple," she says. She's determined that if she can get McCarthy hitched, he'll move Bobby up in the ranks of the committee.

Jean Kerr laughs and shifts in her chair, twisting her wristwatch with one manicured hand. She reaches for her drink. "Oh, I don't know about that…"

"How long have you worked with Joe?"

"Since 'forty-six," Jean says.

"She's my right-hand man," McCarthy interjects. "I don't know what I'd do without her."

"He exaggerates," Jean says, but Bobby can tell she's flattered.

"It's important to find someone who understands your work," Ethel says.

"She understands it," McCarthy says. "She practically runs the place."

Jean pats his arm as if to settle him down, as if to shut him up.

"How did you two end up together?" Jean asks.

"He was dating my older sister," Ethel says. "But he traded her in for a newer model." She winks at Bobby.

McCarthy laughs loudly. "I can't tell you how refreshing it is for a woman to have a sense of humor," the senator says.

"I can also see the future," Ethel says, leaning across the table. She waves her fork at McCarthy and Jean as if casting a spell. "Married within the year."

McCarthy grins at Jean, says, "We'd better get to it."

"Laying it on a little thick," Bobby mutters to Ethel sideways.

Kathleen toddles into the room, blanket dragging on the floor behind her. "Say hello to the senator," Ethel says. A bit of early coaching.

Kathleen waves vacantly at the room, covering all of her bases. "Hello there," McCarthy leans forward in encouragement. Kathleen doesn't seem to know what to do with his open palms. She taps one experimentally. McCarthy scoops her up, settles her on his knee.

"Look at those eyes," McCarthy says. "You're going to break hearts someday, young lady."

Kathleen says, "Cheese."

"Would you like children?" Ethel asks Jean.

"Well . . . I quite like working."

"They're wonderful," Ethel says. "At least until they can start driving, and then you'll be getting calls from the police all the time."

"That was just your family," Bobby says.

"You should be very proud, Ethel," McCarthy says, bouncing Kathleen. "Your husband's quite the investigator. Of course he'd have to be. Only the best and the brightest for my committee. Speaking of which, have you heard what Roy Cohn's discovered in London?"

"He's in Bonn," Jean corrects him. "He's uncovered a number of communistically inclined texts in the embassy."

"We've had some of them burned," McCarthy says. "You can never be too safe."

"Burned?" Bobby asks, and he can't quite keep the edge out of his voice. *That's not the kind of thing Americans do*, a small and naïve part of him protests. And what were these so-called Communist texts anyway? He bites down on his tongue to stop this from spilling out.

"It's the same as with a chicken, Bob," McCarthy says by way of explanation. "The quick death is the kinder one. It doesn't do to break a neck slowly."

"They're on to Berlin next," McCarthy continues easily. "And then of course they'll be back and I expect Roy will have some ideas as to where we might turn our investigation next." He turns to Bobby. "Now look Bob, I'd like to ask you something—"

He turns to stone, anticipating McCarthy's next question. *Are you with us or against us?* He must have noticed Bobby's doubts have grown in recent weeks. It's not that Bobby no longer believes there's a Communist threat; it's that he's had a chance to see how McCarthy and Cohn operate now, and they use chainsaws in the place of scalpels. McCarthy barreling through rooms like they're the china shop, he the proverbial bull, Cohn urging him on from the shadows. He's realized now that like the stories of his war injuries, most of what McCarthy tells reporters is overblown, sometimes outright fiction. He gives them new information just specific enough to be printed, just vague enough not to give them anything at all. Bobby braces himself.

But McCarthy only wants to know if Bobby will write the official report on the shipping matter he's been investigating. He lets out a breath.

"I'd be happy to," he says.

At the evening's end, Bobby follows McCarthy to the door.

"A lovely evening," McCarthy says.

"You'll have to come again."

"I know what your wife is up to," McCarthy says. "This talk about weddings. Sometimes you put the idea in a woman's head, that's all it takes. If Ethel's right— you'll be the first to get invitations."

"I wouldn't bet against her."

"I hear your brother may be headed that way soon…it's smart. Make no mistake, it's smart—you don't want anyone thinking you're the wrong way. But Jack—married?" McCarthy shakes his head as if he can't believe it. "Do you know what they used to call him in the House?"

No, but he has a feeling.

"Mattress Jack," McCarthy chuckles. "Old Mattress Jack getting married."

THE CROWDS OUTSIDE St. Patrick's Cathedral wound around the block to catch a glimpse of the bride, as if she was a movie star or minor royalty instead of Bobby's lousy sister. There are close to two thousand people here at the reception, dancing in the Waldorf. Bobby stands at the edge of the room with Jack, watching trays of champagne and canapés float around the room in an orderly figure eight. It's Eunice's day, but McCarthy's their topic.

"Burning books?" Jack asks. Feigning ignorance: "Wasn't someone else doing that a few years back?"

"It's Cohn," Bobby says, "spilling poison in his ear. You should have heard the way McCarthy talked about him at dinner. I don't trust him, not one bit—"

"So you've mentioned."

He wants to tell Jack about his misgivings—but he can't, quite. He doesn't want to admit that Jack was right and he was wrong, running headlong into something just because their father said so. He's still somewhat suspicious to Jack on that front—their father's lackey, far too eager to please. He can feel Jack sizing him up sometimes, deciding where his loyalties lie. He's only recently become worth Jack's attention at all. Admitting he was wrong about the McCarthy job would reverse all that progress instantly.

The band strikes up a new song that sends people hurtling toward the floor. Eunice stands next to the towering cake in a Dior wedding dress, eyeing the people who pass with a nervous smile, dreading the small talk she might have to make. She used to follow Jack, Joe, and Kick around at parties, writing down the jokes they made and the questions they asked in order to rehearse and deploy the same lines in her own conversations.

Their father helicopters around, shaking the hands of the guests, carefully selected invitees from the upper echelons of government, banking, and entertainment.

"Someone needs to get him a drink," Jack says, watching as their father pushes a cameraman aside, looks through the viewfinder, and hauls the camera, tripod and all, to a different position. "Several drinks," Jack corrects himself.

Ted and Pat escape from the dance floor, Pat clutching a bouquet of flowers with one hand and Ted's arm in the other. His sister's coming out of her shoes and she laughs hysterically. Petals weep through the air.

"Why didn't you bring Jackie?" Pat asks. "Didn't she want to see what she was in for?"

Jack's smile is inscrutable. "Do you know something I don't?"

"What were you talking to Dad about for so long?"

"Speak of the devil" is Jack's only response as their father swoops in, raptorlike, looking for something to sink his claws into.

"Go talk to other people," the Ambassador commands. "People who don't share your last name."

"It's a good party, Dad," Bobby says, trying to soothe him.

"Of course it's a good party," their father snaps. "I'm not in the habit of throwing half-assed parties. Now go."

The others scatter, bugs under a light, but Bobby lingers, watching as his father scans the room, his face losing its lines, relaxing into something that would be like serenity in another man. Is he thinking about Eunice, about his daughter getting married, about another daughter and another wedding that he never saw? Kick got married in England during the war; only Joe, stationed over there, could attend. If Kick were here now—his sister would be out there with Ethel and Jean tying cans onto the back of the car. She'd be leading a conga line through the room.

His father puts a hand on his shoulder, he thinks, to impart some paternal wisdom—but no, he's only pushing Bobby toward a table of guests. "Mingle," his father says.

JACK APPEARS IN the subcommittee offices one day after the building has emptied out. It's the first early days of summer, recess approaching, the usual buzz of activity dulled to a quiet hum you can only hear from far-off corridors.

"Walk with me," Jack says, in a tone that can't be refused.

He follows Jack through the echoing halls of the Capitol, empty except for pockets of sunlight trying to hide from the night. He watches their shadows strain away from them, as if they'd like to be attached to other men. He waits for his brother to speak.

"It's time to cut ties with McCarthy," Jack says at last, no preamble. "This fight he's trying to pick with Eisenhower—it's a bridge too far."

A tiny note of aggravation swells behind his eyes, sinks through the roof of his mouth to land on his tongue: bitter. *But you*, he thinks, *you've just been against it this whole time because you think it'll reflect badly on you*. Or maybe he's angry because he's been thinking the same thing himself, but as usual, Jack's beaten him to the punch. Jack, he thinks, and their old man. This has the stamp of his father all over it.

Hasn't he had his own misgivings? Hasn't he found Cohn's book-burning tour of Europe disconcerting? McCarthy's reliance on his chief counsel even more so? Hasn't he stood outside of the hearing room from his very first days on the job and, while others chased McCarthy for a quote, watched the witness emerge, blinking and shaky on their legs like something newly born?

"Is that what they're saying around the Senate chamber?" he asks, listening to the out-of-sync clatter of their footsteps.

"That's what they're saying everywhere," Jack says, "if you look past the praise."

"I guess you would know best," he says, his voice enough to make Jack pause, study him.

"Dad thinks so, too," Jack says, as if this settles the matter. Two against one. What's new? He doesn't answer, giving a hard look to a vein in the marble. "You've had your six months of fun—"

"What does Dad know?" he asks dismissively.

Jack crosses his arms, a line of tension dividing his face. "Dad's gotten a tip. McCarthy's putting his nose where he shouldn't."

"A tip from who?" he asks, crossing his arms as well so they stand there, two brothers, both alike in indignity.

"I don't know," Jack says tersely.

"I don't believe you." His voice is shrill. Jack responds in kind.

"Pull your head out of your ass," Jack says. His voice changes. "McCarthy's poked the bear. The president isn't going to put up with him for much longer."

He sounds like Joe. That's what it is. The bravado he used to win any argument. Their eldest brother ordering him around from beyond the grave.

"They just hate him because he's Catholic," Bobby says. "He's just like us—"

"Like us," Jack scoffs. "Not even close."

"You want me to abandon him," he says, "right when I've started to do good work."

His voice, grown high and sharp, bounces violently off the walls, and he wonders who designed the

Capitol, who got it exactly right, because of course the government should be this hard cocoon of marble, this unflinching catacomb of stone.

"I want you to get out before your association with him blows up in all of our faces," Jack snaps. "We all have to do things we'd rather not—"

"Yeah, right," he scoffs. "When have you?"

He braces himself for Jack's next assault.

His brother says, "I'm getting married."

The shock of this—the sudden sting of happiness for his brother—outweighs his aggravation. Perhaps this is what Jack intended.

"What—she said yes?"

Selfishly, he wants to know if he's the first Jack's told.

Jack drops his head; trying to avoid a shaft of light in his eyes, but to Bobby it looks like he wants to repent. The weary, drooping head of Christ on the cross.

"She's going to."

"How can you be sure?" he asks, thinking if there were one girl who would refuse, it would be her.

"Her father's a gambler," Jack says. "He taught her how to play the odds."

CHAPTER 10

Matrimony

When Jack kneels at the altar, Bobby holds his breath.

To every one of the six hundred guests crammed into the church, his brother looks cut out of a magazine. But the signs are there if you know how to read them. Weight lost from another summer of chewing ice chips because his stomach couldn't handle anything else. The slight puffiness around his eyes from the latest round of steroids.

For all his father's meticulous calculations—the guests, the church, the reception at the Auchincloss estate—they haven't discussed what to do if Jack can't get up from saying his vows. Bobby supposes he and Teddy will have to run over and haul him to his feet.

Pay the photographers for their rolls of film, burn them in secret. But Jack stands without so much as a wince. Bobby relaxes, relieved of an aching back that isn't his own. He wonders, briefly, if his brother's been practicing.

The crowd outside goes wild to see the new couple, surging forward as if Jack and Jackie are royalty who made the mistake of leaving their palace. Jackie spooks, drawing up short. Jack's smile never falters as he urges her forward, toward the photographers.

"It's like a coronation," a voice says beside him.

Jackie's little sister, Lee, her vulpine face unmistakable. If Jackie takes after their father, then it's their mother's face her sister has inherited. Angular, narrow, looking to catch on you like a hook. The kind of face you imagine for Anne Boleyn.

But her voice is Jackie's; the same gravel wrapped in velvet sound. He's not sure if she's talking to him, or just talking, but then she says, "You all know how to put on a show."

"Us?" he says. It's all Jackie. Just listen to the crowd.

"Over here, Senator," the photographers call. But for the onlookers it's only *Jack-ieee!* and they keen her name over and over until at last she escapes into the back of a limousine and only then do they fall silent, as if they choose to say nothing if they can't say her name.

BOBBY QUIT THE McCarthy Committee in July, telling McCarthy that he was considering private practice.

McCarthy was half-drunk and understanding: "If you change your mind, come back and see us."

He wanted to say something like *beware of Cohn*, but it would have looked like sour grapes, so he held his tongue; he wished McCarthy well.

His father, when he gripes to friends about his children, says "Pat always wants something new, Ted draws trouble like a magnet, Bobby can never figure out what he wants to do next." His father has a point. Six months on the job and back to the drawing board.

O'Donnell wanted him to run for Attorney General of Massachusetts.

"The state's too small for two Kennedys," Bobby said.

Ken was quick with a reply: "Establish residency in Connecticut. Be the governor."

Instead, he's joined his father on the Hoover Commission, a group ordained by the president to identify waste in the budget of various federal agencies. Ken made a retching sound when Bobby told him.

This weekend has provided a distraction; it's been something out of nineteenth-century Russia. Making toasts and shattering the glasses in the fireplace. A scavenger hunt where Pat hot-wired a bus and drove it up to the gates of the Auchincloss's Newport estate, Hammersmith Farm. Jackie's mother, Janet—a woman whose chief pleasure in life seems to be finding fault in others and then loudly pointing it out—barred Jackie's father from the rehearsal dinner last night, so he sat up alone in his room and drank himself into a coma, too hungover this morning to walk his daughter down the aisle.

"You should've gone French," he overheard Lee tell her sister earlier in the house, her narrow face displeased, her narrow body buzzing around Jackie like a hornet, fussing with her veil, her train, trying to make things fall a different way.

"I wanted to," Jackie murmured.

It was the Ambassador who decided the bride should wear something traditional, and American-made. Something that would make a splash on camera, none of these simple French designs.

"It makes you look like a boy," Lee said.

"It makes me look like a lampshade," Jackie said, and they both laughed. You could see the resemblance then, the way they laughed.

"I think you look wonderful," Ethel said, creeping up behind him, announcing their presence.

Jackie and Ethel looked at each other for a moment, almost as if they were sizing each other up.

"The best part is this." Jackie held out a wrist, a diamond and pearl bracelet clasped just above her glove. "You all must have helped Jack pick it out. I know his taste isn't this good."

Ethel had smiled, said something bland about jewelry not being his strong suit.

Ethel hadn't exactly jumped for joy when she heard the news of Jack and Jackie's engagement. He thought it was a question of territory; Ethel was used to being the only wife around. All she said when she heard the news was "I'm still betting she makes a run for it." But running is an impossibility in this dress; maybe his father planned for this, too.

Now Bobby follows Lee to the tent on the lawn, through a crush of groomsmen—Jack's Navy buddies, his former roommate and oldest friend, Lem Billings. Jackie's mother had wanted a small, intimate wedding. "Tasteful," that favorite word of the WASP elite, or those who've married into it. But their father wasn't going to be shortchanged, not for Jack. Everywhere you look, you see someone you ought to know. The actress Marion Davies. Arthur Krock, the Washington bureau chief for the *Times*. Chief Justice Warren. And Jack and Jackie in the center, looking like a casting agent's dream for "bride" and "groom."

"They don't make it easy on us, do they?" Lee asks.

At his age, Jack had already published *Why England Slept*. He'd already saved his men from certain death in the Pacific. Bobby is more or less his father's secretary.

And Lee was married earlier in the year. It wasn't a coronation; it wasn't even a particularly interesting man, according to Jackie. If the papers are to be believed, women across the country spontaneously burst into tears, or flames, at the news of Jack's engagement. "The Senate's Gay Young Bachelor Is No More," read the headlines. Jackie beat all of America; she certainly beat her sister.

"One marriage for passion, one for money," Lee

says. "That's my mother's motto. Which do you think your brother is?"

He's aware she's trying to get under his skin. "Both," he says. "Kennedys don't get divorced."

"That's a shame," she says, "because Bouviers are terribly good at it."

"Which is your husband?" he asks.

She only laughs. The dark hole of her throat. "Spin me," she commands.

When she saunters away at the end of the number, part of him thinks he's supposed to follow. He goes to find Ethel instead.

"We all absolutely adore her," he hears Jean say as he passes by.

"That *dress*," one of the gathered women says.

"Doesn't she look top dollar?"

The compliments his sisters rain down on Jackie give them away. If they really liked her, they'd insult her, calling her all the terrible names they reserve for each other.

His father's arm emerges from the crowd, catching him by the collar. "Careful with the bridesmaids," his father says.

"I wasn't—"

"No?" his father asks, releasing him back into the crowd. "You're a man, aren't you?"

"DON'T JUMP," HE SAYS.

Jackie stands alone on the balcony. The shape of her

veil twisting in the breeze momentarily addles him, the way the fabric undulates, the way it seems to breathe. It's one of those perfect late summer days in September, when the sky seems like it might collapse under the weight of its own blueness. He remembers the last time they were on a balcony together, throwing records into the wind. How easily they'd sailed along. He hadn't imagined then that she'd be in a wedding gown soon. Had she?

"You're empty," he says, gesturing at the champagne glass that rests precariously on the balcony railing. "That's not allowed at an Irish wedding."

She twists her ring around her finger. Diamond and emerald and many-carated, he's sure, but another piece she didn't pick. Again: his father. It's a fact that's given Ethel no end of delight; she repeats, every chance she gets, the story of her own engagement ring. Bobby sent her a tray of diamonds and let her pick, but with each re-telling it becomes more grandiose; by the time she's tired of this gag, it won't be a tray he sent, but a truckful.

Jackie leans over the balcony railing, and her veil brushes against the empty glass. It teeters, but doesn't fall.

"It's nice that everyone could be here to celebrate," she says. "Or, almost everyone."

He looks at her with a question mark on his face. The Pope sent his regrets, but apart from His Holiness, people were clamoring for an invitation. He can't think of anyone missing.

"Your sister," Jackie says. "Rosemary."

He looks at her carefully. There's a sense he has sometimes that they're playing parts with each other, acting in a drama, and the audience is just there, on the other side of the footlights, waiting for the next line.

"She's a private person," he says at last. "She doesn't like crowds."

"So I've heard," Jackie says slowly. "It's funny, every time I bring her up, Jack gets that same look on his face. Like he's seen a ghost."

Then stop bringing her up, he almost snaps. He looks away instead, squinting at the small shapes of people moving across the lawn below.

"I was trying to imagine my mother on her wedding day," Jackie says. "I was trying to imagine her in love."

Her veil wafts in front of her face, and when it settles again, she's looking at him.

"How did your parents become your parents?" she asks. It almost sounds like a question she would have posed for her "Camera Girl" column.

Years before, in a century they called Victorian, his father, the son of a stevedore turned whiskey importer, Good Irish (but not the best), set his eye on his mother, the mayor's daughter. Their fathers were dead set against it, which meant it was inevitable.

Their courtship became illicit. They started meeting in churches knowing no one would look for them there. Bobby sees how it must've been: his father bouncing around the corner, full-up with ideas, eager to get to the next place fast. And standing in the church doorway waiting for him is a girl with black hair, an Irish Rose.

Eventually their fathers relent. The two are married. They have a series of children—strong boys, pretty girls. That's how his parents became his parents. Because his grandfathers disliked each other. Because his mother used to wait in a church doorway.

She listens with interest.

He repeats her question back to her: "How did *your* parents become your parents?"

"Let's see…" she says. "Because my mother thought my father had more money than he did, and my father—" She grins wickedly. "My father had nothing better to do."

With one finger, she tips the glass over the edge. It tumbles end over end; it seems to fall for a long time. But it doesn't shatter. It lands in the grass below, unharmed.

THE FATHERS ARE SMOKING cigars as the wedding comes to an end. They're gathered, all, at the bottom of the stairs.

"Why's there always so much waiting around?" Pat grumbles. "I'm running out of cigarettes."

Finally Jack and Jackie descend, showered in rice and flower petals, bound for a Mexican honeymoon. Jackie pauses, kisses both the Ambassador and her stepfather on the cheek. Her real father is nowhere to be seen; apparently, he's swiped a bottle of gin and taken a train back to the city.

"Better than the Astors," the Ambassador says, passing by his children in a sweet flume of smoke. "Tell me what Irish can say that?"

"Do you think they're happy?" Ted asks, and Bobby doesn't know if he means the newlyweds or the fathers, who are, just now, clasping each other's hands as if to certify a deal.

"As long as they look like they are," Bobby says.

CHAPTER 11

Doldrums

HERBERT HOOVER IS SEVENTY-NINE and in perfect health, greets Bobby with a firm handshake and a "Welcome aboard." Bobby's the youngest man in any room by at least three decades.

The official mandate of the Hoover Commission is to examine the budgets of federal agencies and make recommendations to Eisenhower. In reality, it's a lot of sitting around and talking to his father.

"Did you see the *Times* this morning?" his father asks.

He tried not to. The McCarthy Committee is still in the headlines daily. And he's analyzing the spending of the Weather Bureau from an office that looks out onto a dumpster. Now that the summer's over, he doesn't have any distractions—the Cape, his siblings, Jack's wedding—left in his arsenal. It's only this job, the long, slow decline of his days, and the undeniable feeling that he's already peaked in his professional life.

"What did it say?" he asks glumly.

"Why didn't you read it? Are you no longer sub-scribed?" his father asks. "If it's a matter of cost, I'm happy to pay. You all have the idea that the bank of Joe is bottomless anyway—a cook for Ethel, an apartment for Jean—"

"I have a subscription. I was just in a rush."

"McCarthy has taken an interest in the Army," his father says with no small degree of relish.

"Good for McCarthy," he says.

"Au contraire," his father says. A little French. Jack-ie's starting to rub off on him. "Do you think the pres-ident's going to take an attack on his own institution lying down?"

"He's scared of McCarthy," Bobby says. "He's barely said a word about him."

"I assure you that's not out of fear," his father says. "Think with your head, Robert. What's McCarthy's problem?"

"He's got a bastard of a chief counsel."

"Think more critically."

"I don't know, Dad."

"McCarthy's problem is he's invested in one stock—and that stock's taking a hit just now. People are tired of hunting Communists."

"Ah," he says. "I see now."

For the president—as for the Kennedys—McCarthy's only useful until he's not. He's helped the party for the past two election cycles, but you're only as good as your next trick, and McCarthy doesn't seem to have one. Eisenhower's distancing himself from McCarthy for the same reason Joe Kennedy is—not on principle, but because of his waning political usefulness.

At the lunch hour, the Ambassador marches around the city like he's going off to war. He claims it helps his digestion. More likely, he's just glad to be back in Washington and wants to be seen around the capital. Marking the territory, as it were. His eyes, frosty behind his glasses, see through buildings of glass and stone and into the living flesh, the beating hearts of the men inside.

"FBI," his father says. "J. Edgar Hoover. He's been in that office longer than you've been alive. What does that tell you?"

"That the FBI needs term limits."

"He serves at the pleasure of the president," his father says. "That's four presidents and counting who he's convinced to let him keep his job, which means he's either the world's most charming man or he's good at manipulating powerful men.

"How would you like the Bureau?" his father asks. "You're an inquisitive type. Wouldn't you fit in well there?"

"Yes," he says, thinking of investigations, fieldwork,

a job where at least one other person was born in this century.

"Incorrect," his father says, and Bobby's heart falls out of his chest. "Hoover demands total loyalty. He wants allegiance to himself over all else, even the institution." His father shakes his head. "You're no ass-kisser. The character of a place is as important as the job itself. That was the mistake we made sending you to McCarthy."

And the Hoover Commission? The character there is of men who are bored in retirement. When they gather around the table, they complain about the cold, about how the rain of early autumn makes their joints ache. They begin stories, "You should have seen me in my prime…" Those younger men still cocooned inside these old shells, behind glasses and balding heads and liver-spotted hands. He tries not to look at his father in this company; he tries not to see the ways his father fits in.

"What if you were J. Edgar, and one of the president's commissions was investigating your bureau's spending," his father says, "and one man on the commission praised you for the efficiency of your operation, and its unique character compared to other arms of the government. What would you do if you were Hoover?"

He studies his father out of the corner of his eye.

"Would you be willing to do this man a favor down the line?" his father asks. "If you had sensitive information about his sons, would you keep it to yourself?"

What has their father predicted for them?

"You're of an age where you can hear these things," his father says. "I only hope you're listening."

MAYBE KEN'S RIGHT, Ethel tells him. Maybe you should run for something. But that might be worse. That might be the same pain, different symptoms.

Isn't there any future where I don't have to run for office? He wants to ask. But he doesn't dare speak this aloud. He doesn't have the Kennedy gene that makes life charmed and easy for his siblings, natural politicians, ducks to water. He can fake being a Kennedy most of the time. But this ultimate electoral test would expose him to his family as the imposter he is. It would prove once and for all that he's not like them. That he doesn't belong. So for now he's neither politician nor bureaucrat nor lawyer. His life is a series of false starts, of six-month stints in jobs given to him by his father. He dreads November, and another birthday, another year with nothing of his own to show for it.

He can't talk to his siblings—not Pat, who's in love with some actor, Peter Lawford, that Bobby can't bring himself to care about; not Teddy, back at Harvard and busy with school; not Jean, working on a Catholic television program, which has made her suddenly too grand to return his calls. Kennedys don't whine, they'd remind him. So he talks to the Kennedy who isn't a Kennedy.

She and Jack are back from their honeymoon,

living between Hyannisport and Boston, their house in Georgetown not yet ready for occupancy. She thought she might keep writing for the paper, but his father or Jack explained to her that wives don't work, so the Inquiring Camera Girl is someone else now, and she's Mrs. John F. Kennedy. Her boredom overlaps with his often.

"What are you always talking about with her?" Ethel asks, hovering in the doorway with a peculiar expression on her face.

"Same things I talk to you about," he says.

"Then why don't you say them to me?" she asks. But before he can respond, she's gone.

Jackie tells him stories about her father that turn her voice blue; stories about Paris that do the opposite. Don't laugh, she tells him, but when she studied at the Sorbonne, she started pronouncing her name like the French: Jack-*leen*. In the Louvre she'd slip unnoticed into groups of art students. She remembers once hearing a professor lecture about paintings beneath paintings, when an artist changed his mind or made an error in the composition and covered up what was already there with something new. *Pentimento*, it's called. It means "repentance."

Why don't you come down one weekend, he suggests. Stay with us. We can go to the National Gallery. It's not Paris, but it's something to do.

What have you done? his sisters ask when they hear

of the impending visit. Why would you put Jackie and Ethel under a roof together?

No one knows how their feud started, if it's because the Ambassador approves of Ethel, but adores Jackie. If it's because of Jackie's continued unpregnancy, while Ethel, she says, is a baby machine, just put a coin in. Or if it was because of the St. Patrick's Day party early on when Ethel, wanting to make a splash in a green dress, told all of her guests to wear black, but Jackie—even in black—stole the show anyway. Turning heads in a dress the color of midnight embroidered with beads that glittered like a shattered windshield. Intentional sabotage, to Ethel's mind. Showing up late in a chauffeured car and leaving early. Standing by the fireplace the whole time like she was waiting to be painted.

It goes beyond what his sisters feel about Jackie, which is dislike mixed with begrudging acceptance mixed with annoyance. But Ethel and Jackie still hug when Jackie arrives. He marvels at it. Men would never.

Jackie sets a basket of food and wine down grandly on the kitchen table, a thank-you for hosting her. The neat wicker; the care with which a blue ribbon was tied around the handle; the almost architectural arrangement of cans of specialty jelly and tinned saltwater taffy. Nothing could be more out of place on their kitchen table smeared with crayon and peanut butter, the latter of which one of the dogs licks to a high polish.

"I got a red and a white," Jackie says, pointing at the wine, the compositional center of her arrangement. "I didn't know which you prefer."

"Isn't that nice," Ethel says. "The blood of Christ." She lifts a tin. "What's this?" she asks, joking. "Dog food?"

Jackie's face immobilizes. "Pâté," she says stiffly. "You eat it with bread."

"Yes, I know what pâté is," Ethel says, a little offended. There's an awkward pause.

"You can't eat this when you're pregnant," Ethel adds, one hand on her stomach. Is that an actual rule? Or is she just trying to gloat?

"You can save it then," Jackie says. "If ever there comes a day when that womb of yours gets a break."

Ethel studies her like she's deciding something; then her face breaks into a grin.

"I know just the thing," Ethel says brightly. "Some friends of ours are having a get-together—why don't we swing by?"

"She just got in," Bobby says.

"Jackie," Ethel ignores him, laying a hand on Jackie's arm, "you need to start meeting these people. You want to be helpful to Jack, don't you?"

Jackie hesitates, looking down at Ethel's hand—at the diamond she chose herself—like she's inspecting it for fangs. "Of course," she says at last.

Later he'll realize he should have been suspicious of his wife's insistence.

When they arrive, Ethel leads them through the house like she's looking for something, her arm handcuffed to Jackie's.

The chase is over so quickly as to be anticlimactic. Amid the din and clatter and music of many people smoking and drinking, he recognizes the back of his brother's head. He doesn't recognize the woman Jack's talking to.

Jack leans in. He's not just trying to hear her better over the noise. The woman smiles. She touches her neck. Bobby tries to step in front of Jackie, but it's too late; she's already seen. Her cheeks flush. She makes a stiff about-face and leaves the room.

He finds Jackie alone in the basement. "Knock, knock," he says, tapping the door.

Her hand is around her throat, holding her head up like it's a block of concrete. He studies her out of the corner of his eye, examining her for cracks.

"He doesn't mean it," Bobby says. But does he believe this? Does Jack do anything without weighing all the outcomes, tallying every pro and con, or is he only that careful when it comes to politics, and not his marriage?

"If he wants other women, he can have them," Jackie says. "It's humiliating. Watching him chase after women in our social circle. Women who are our friends."

There's no such thing as a friend in Washington, he'd tell her if he was trying to make her laugh. He sits down carefully. Overhead, he can hear the click of a dog's nails against the wooden floor.

Mattress Jack may have gotten married, but it hasn't made him change his ways. Bobby knows his brother sleeps with other women; he knows who some of these women are; mostly, he knows it's better if he doesn't ask any questions. Hear no, see no, speak no evil.

"But I suppose that's just the way things are," Jackie says, not quite achieving the airy tone she's trying for. "The girls pray and the boys play." Her mouth twists into a knot.

He doesn't know what else to do, so he hugs her, not sure if she'll let him. You expect it to be like hugging a rosebush; you expect to come away scratched and bleeding. But she's soft. And smaller than she seems. He can feel her shoulder blades through the back of her dress. She breathes out, and he can feel that, too. The air leaving her.

When they rejoin the group, Ethel looks at him like he's done something criminal. The car ride home is a silent affair.

Jackie goes to the guest room, and he and Ethel go upstairs to fight. You only really know someone if you can tell what they're feeling from the back of their head, is Ethel's theory; hers projects fury down to every last curl.

They check on the children first, moving past each other in silence. Bending over beds. Tucking covers.

Removing Army men and Lincoln Logs from tiny sleeping hands.

Then Ethel stands in the bright light of the bathroom taking her earrings off, and it feels like the whole night has been leading to this.

"Did you know Jack would be there?" he asks. He thinks he already knows the answer.

Ethel glances over at him. "How could I? I'm not his secretary."

Plink goes one pearl into the jewelry dish.

"It's not as if this is a surprise to her," Ethel says. "She knew what she was getting into when she married him."

Plink. The other earring drops. The sound grates. She meets his gaze and then some.

"Don't feel bad for people who've chosen their fate," she says.

"You don't have to be so cruel."

"You don't have to be so kind."

"She's one of us."

"You spend a lot of time on the phone with her these days."

"She's lonely."

"That's part of marriage," Ethel says. "I never remember calling Jack or Ted up at nine at night because you were off studying."

Their eyes only meet in the mirror. Very precisely, Ethel takes a square of tissue and wipes off her lipstick.

"What exactly do you find so interesting about her?" Ethel asks. Now she's not looking at him. "Or have you fallen for this damsel in distress act?"

She's like a jewel, he thinks. Different from every angle. Sometimes I feel like every time I see her, I'm meeting a new Jackie. There are layers and layers of her that I haven't gotten to, and I want to keep hacking away at them, chipping down to the core. But he's not stupid enough to say this aloud. That's only something you would say if you wanted your wife to believe that you don't love her.

"I don't think she's trying to put on any act," he says. Avoiding the first question.

Just then, Joe comes in, looking guilty. He peed. A little. He didn't mean to. It just happened. He hypothesizes that he had too much juice before bed. He also had a large quantity of milk, it seems. And once he started, he couldn't stop. Have they, either of them, tried to stop peeing once they started? Can it even be done?

Ethel cups his chin. "That's all right baby," she says. "Accidents happen."

The routine of changing sheets; changing pajamas; then Kathleen is up and wants to know what's going on and has to be settled again; and by the time Bobby's lying in bed next to Ethel, he doesn't want to fight anymore. He reaches a tentative hand toward her.

"I went to school with girls like her," Ethel says into the darkness. "It's not enough for them to have a beau.

They need every boy they know to be in love with them, too."

That's not what this is, he starts to say. She holds up a finger to shush him.

"I don't speak French," she says. "I haven't lived in Paris. I'm the only other wife in this family. Do you know what it feels like to be a constant point of comparison?"

"I think I have some idea," he says mildly.

"I'm fine with being compared to Jackie by anyone else," she says. "But not you."

She takes his hand, and he thinks she's going to fling it back across the bed; instead, she draws him closer.

THE NEXT MORNING at breakfast, Jackie looks across at him with alert, wary eyes.

"Are we still on for the gallery?" she asks.

He studies the newspaper carefully. Ethel flips the bacon over in the pan and the oil pops.

"I think we'd better save it for another day," he says. "I have to go into the office."

Jackie knows as well as he does that there's nothing about his job that requires working on a Sunday. But she doesn't say anything, only nods carefully. Picks up her mug of coffee and blows on it long after it's cooled.

"I think I might go for a walk," she says at last, and stands abruptly. A moment later, the front door closes.

"Bobby?" Ethel asks. "How many pieces?"

CHAPTER 12

The Other Side of the Aisle

A MONTH LATER, he kills someone's dog with his car. He carries it up to the front door, still warm. I tried to stop, he says, which is true but feels like a lie. That's all right, the owner says sadly. He liked to jump the fence. We knew it would happen sooner or later.

When he gets home, Ethel asks whose blood is on his sleeve, his or someone else's. Someone else's, he says.

Two weeks after that, a group at the park keeps raining baseballs down on their game of touch, too many times for it to be accidental. "Watch it!" he yells, and then another baseball drops near them and he and Ted are crossing the no-man's-land between their groups, Jack behind them on his crutches, all dignity of his office forgotten as he laughs like a hyena and urges them on. Bobby pushes Ted aside even though his brother has the height advantage; he swings first.

When he gets home, Ethel asks whose blood is on his sleeve, his or someone else's. A little of both, he says.

In Palm Beach with his family over the holidays, he alternates between moping and sulking.

"I did try to warn you," Pat says, considering an ornament of a porcelain pig in a Christmas hat. "Put this one up high," she says, handing the pig to him. "Next to the snowflake. I want visual balance."

He does as she says. She steps back, eyeing their work critically. "I told you to be careful of Jack and Dad," she continues. "I told you not to sign your name in their little book. They'll be picking and choosing what jobs you can have for the rest of your life now."

He doesn't answer, staring at the cascade of angels down the tree, one for each of them. Joe's at the top, the oldest and most battered, a Styrofoam cup with paper wings that loses a little more of its gold tinsel hair every year, Teddy's at the bottom, a hasty crayon drawing cut out of construction paper in his brother's typical slapdash fashion.

Outside, Pat's beau—Peter, the actor—takes off his shirt like someone's called "action" and dives into the pool, a perfect, clean arc. He comes up and palms his hair out of his eyes with the ease and style of a leading man. Pat watches all this with a look that has an appetite.

"What do you think of him?" Pat asks.

"I think you can't be serious," Bobby says.

"I knew you'd say that."

"Then why'd you ask?"

"You only dislike him because Dad does."

"You only like him for the same reason."

Pat smiles as Peter floats on his back and spouts a stream of water into the air. Bobby takes some small satisfaction in the fact that his children have probably peed in that water.

Pat's coming up on her thirtieth birthday in May, an occasion that marks some kind of ominous threshold for her. She's started referring to herself more and more as a "crone" and a "spinster," signing her letters *The Beldame of California*. It makes him particularly wary of her decisions concerning men.

"Do you think we ought to…?" Pat steps forward, fingering Rosemary's angel, its wings tiny handprints dipped in gold paint and pressed against the paper, each finger a feather. "I don't want to upset Mother," Pat decides without waiting for his answer, and removes the angel from the tree, wrapping it carefully in a paper towel and packing it away with the other unhung ornaments.

"Maybe Santa will bring you a new job for Christmas," she says. "As long as you've been a good boy this year."

"More like a new family," he says.

THE REST OF HIS SIBLINGS arrive for the holidays, and he no longer has to consider himself as a single entity, but part of a pack—maybe the Soviets are onto something with their collectivism. He lets himself be swept up in their noise and stories and the clatter of their lives for as long as he can.

Then one day, his father calls him into his study. Sitting grandly in his chair, vaguely triumphant even at rest, ready to be painted. Bobby feels like a serf on the other side of the desk, waiting humbly to beseech the king.

In every office his father has ever had, whether in Boston or New York, on Wall Street or a studio lot, there's only one constant. His walls aren't mounted with university degrees, animal heads, or beloved paintings. They're decorated with photographs of his children, the only accomplishment he wants to impress on people. If you didn't know him, you'd think his father was a humble man.

The Ambassador takes his time polishing his glasses before he begins. Bobby doesn't say anything. He prefers to watch the brisk, practiced motion of a task that seems too menial for the man.

At last, his father says, "Your brother seems to think you're less than stimulated on the Hoover Commission."

"Ted said that?"

"No, Jack did."

He's surprised by Jack's attention. Usually it's the other way around, all of them orbiting Jack in a predetermined path, his gravity dictating their motion in the sky.

His father looks him over carefully. "The Democrats on the McCarthy Committee are looking to hire minority counsel. You'd be working under Senator McClellan and the rest, not McCarthy. Your brother suggested that might be of interest to you."

His father laces his hands together in a way that always signals a transaction is occurring. His father's offering him this new job, an exit from the tedium of his current situation—and what does he expect in return?

"As long as it won't hurt Jack politically," Bobby says carefully. He's a stock his father has invested in, the same as oil or utilities, and his ROI is as yet unclear. But if he doesn't earn, he knows his father will have no qualms about weeding him out of his portfolio. You don't accomplish anything by being sentimental, whether it's about stocks or sons. What his father wants from him is security, certainty, assurance—that it's Jack first, always Jack, the first among equals.

He holds his breath and waits. His father nods. This was the correct answer.

The Ambassador says: "We'll see what can be arranged."

HE RETURNS TO the McCarthy Committee in the new year, but this time on the other side of the aisle. Officially, he reports to Senator McClellan now, a stern Arkansan about as different from McCarthy as two men can be. McCarthy used to offer drinks and dinner;

McClellan rarely offers so much as a smile. Unofficially, Bobby still feels slightly torn. Some remaining loyalty to McCarthy refuses to die, twinging anew anytime he sees the senator around the office.

But he keeps his head down; he keeps away from McCarthy, who grows reckless in his pursuit of the Army. It only takes a few weeks back on the committee for him to realize that he prefers working for McClellan who, though somewhat humorless, is methodical about the work in a way Bobby himself is.

Although he suspects McClellan was initially skeptical of him, he must have decided at some point that Bobby was neither a dilettante nor a secret McCarthy lackey, and they work together easily now. With McClellan, there's no performance, no theatrics. No need to guess at how much of what he's telling you is true.

That spring, a new investigation starts. The Army–McCarthy hearings are supposed to look into Communists in the military, but soon McCarthy's on trial as much as the Army. He's managed to piss off plenty of Democrats and most of his own party in the course of his investigations over the past few years. The hearings are an excuse to hit back at McCarthy in the guise of due diligence. Bobby spends long, stifling days at the other end of the table from McCarthy, drafting questions for the Democrats to ask. Only in Washington, he thinks more than once, watching McCarthy cover the microphone with one hand as he confers with Roy

Cohn, do personal grievances play out via official Senate inquiry.

As the hearings drag on, it seems the world finally catches up to the calculation Jack and his father made months ago. Suddenly it's McCarthy with no sense of decency, McCarthy no longer ensconced in a witness-less room with Roy Cohn but out on full display, the hearings televised live for weeks on end. In print, McCarthy's one thing. But on television, he's another entirely. Cruel, reckless, interrupting constantly with a *Point of order!*

Watching McCarthy tear himself apart, Bobby wants to feel relieved, vindicated, anything but what he does—a strange sense of guilt.

By the end of it, the damage is done. It's not just the censure vote being murmured about in the Senate hallways. McCarthy's approval ratings have dropped to the lowest they've been since he entered Congress. He's hung himself with his own rope.

McCarthy has always reminded Bobby of his father—the same certainty, the same refusal to back down from a fight—and now, the same fall from grace. Two Irish boys who made good—and then were unmade just as quickly.

Maybe this is why Bobby still, even after everything, can't find it in himself to abandon McCarthy completely.

One day, as the hearings are winding down, he passes McCarthy in the office. An odd sight, to see him alone, when Bobby's never known him to be without at least one or two journalists trailing remoralike after him, eager for crumbs. The senator so much smaller now, looking no longer like a boxer, but like the man sagging against the rope. It takes effort, Bobby can see, for McCarthy to smile at him. But he does.

They make a little small talk, avoiding the obvious—the hearings and their toll on McCarthy—and Bobby does his best not to flinch when other people pass, seeing the two of them together. On his shoulder is an annoyed angel in the shape of Jack telling him to end the conversation and leave.

"Say, Bob—do you want to swing by my office for a drink? I don't think we ever properly celebrated your return." This, without a trace of bitterness.

He almost says "Yes," unthinking, still the little boy's desire to be included. The angel beats its wings.

"I can't tonight," he says. And then, because he can't resist: "But we'll have you over again for dinner sometime. It's been too long."

McCarthy's answering smile is easy. But something flickers in his eyes. He knows. He knows the shape of the game has changed and the Kennedys are no longer in his corner. Bobby feels seen through, hot with embarrassment. Something must show on his face, because McCarthy pats him on the shoulder kindly.

"Sounds like a plan," he says. "Don't be a stranger."

CHAPTER 13

Surgery

THE PHONE IS RINGING; he doesn't answer, but only dreams he does.

A draft from the hall cuts like ice across his cheek. He's almost asleep again when Ethel says, "It's Jack."

He gets the floor wrong in the hospital elevator and stands, jabbing at the close-door button—"Why do they even put these in if they don't *do what you ask*?"—about to forget the whole thing and take the stairs when the doors shudder closed at last, almost catching his sleeve. Ethel puts a hand on his arm to settle him, but her fingers are trembling. Weren't they just here, seeing Jack off before his surgery—wasn't Jack in a marvelous, teasing mood? "The Hospital for the Ruptured and Crippled," he was saying. "That sounds about right." And his farewell, delivered with characteristic nonchalance: "This is the one that cures you or kills you." And the rest of them were foolish enough to laugh.

Surgery. The watchword of the summer. The start of a hundred arguments. They all, in their free time, became armchair spinal surgeons, leafing through the thick medical briefs the Ambassador had ordered up from experts around the country. They weighed the pros and cons collectively—Pro: A shot at fixing his back. Con: Infection. Paralysis. Death—until Jack got fed up with them and crutched out of the room, saying, "It doesn't require a family quorum call."

The Ambassador had blasted classical music all summer; Rachmaninoff, Tchaikovsky, the terrifying Russians. But Bobby thinks that, for once, it wasn't Joe on his father's mind. Different child, different surgery. Rosemary, and the operation that left her a permanent invalid, left a cone of silence in the middle of their family. Unbidden, un-asked for: the image of Jack and Joe swinging Rosie around the dance floor at the yacht club so fast Bobby thought her arms would come off, his brothers' crazed energy making everyone else evacuate the space.

His mother, Jean, and Ted are a bleak trio in the waiting room. His mother speaks with one of the nurses, her head tilted in its usual way. Do they realize the magazines are two months out of date and might someone consider updating the reading materials?

Jean's hair is still wet, the product of hastily removed curlers. It's the patches of damp on his little sister's shoulders that make all this seem real.

He seizes Ted by the arm. "How bad is it?"

"Dad called a priest."

Ethel pushes him gently in the direction of Jack's room, ungluing his feet from the floor.

He hazards a glance at the hospital bed, and regrets it. Jack waxen and stiff, his face yellow and slack with unconsciousness. The only proof of life is a sheen of sweat haloing Jack's forehead.

Jackie clutches Jack's hand in both of hers. His father doesn't look up; for him, Jack is the only thing in the room, maybe the only thing in the world.

"Infection?" Bobby asks. This is as much as he can manage.

Jackie's voice is strained. "Yes." She tries for something else, but her voice is lost in her throat. She repeats herself. "They said he's in a coma."

Three years ago, during the trip he'd taken with Jack and Pat, Jack had come down with a fever. Just malaria acting up, he said at first. Plenty of soldiers caught it in the Pacific. It's a good disease—a convenient disease, politically speaking. Broad symptoms—symptoms that could explain almost anything. But Bobby knew that this wasn't malaria the same way Rosemary wasn't teaching schoolchildren in Wisconsin, the line his family started using after her surgery. It was his family's version of the truth, which often means its opposite.

There was no time to call his father; his father was asleep on the other side of the world. I need to get my brother to the best hospital you have, he'd said. Pat sat on the bed with a waning Jack, a Jack who looked like he was falling backward in a chair, no longer at home behind his eyes. He remembers the priest's hands making the sign of the cross over his dying brother. The Latin he spoke like the bulb of a tulip, like something waiting to grow. *Per istam sanctam unctionem.*

He and Pat had fallen asleep sitting up, crowded into the corner of Jack's hospital room, like their presence was enough to keep him tethered to the earth. He'd been the first to wake—back sore, legs tingling, Pat's head heavy on his shoulder—to Jack studying him with an amused expression that didn't quite match the bags under his eyes, the IVs shooting out of his arm like highway overpasses.

"You don't look so hot," Jack had said, his voice gravel chucked against a window.

"You're one to talk," Bobby replied.

NOW THEY GATHER at the foot of another hospital bed. Different priest, same words. He seeks out every face except his parents'. His mother and father huddle together in his periphery; it's strange to see them so close together, and then he wonders—why is that strange?

The others go off to find coffee, push chairs together in makeshift cots, sit up half asleep with coats on backward, chins to chests.

Jack's back had been getting steadily worse for a year now; his performance of health grown sloppy—forgetting his lines, walking off set. The edge of his desk is scuffed from where he'd starting propping his foot to tie a shoe; it hurt him to bend. Denied a request for an office closer to the Senate chamber, he'd started sitting in floor sessions all day long, his back pain too great to shuttle back and forth between there and his office.

He'd agreed to this surgery, Bobby thinks, as much because he thought it couldn't make things any worse as because he thought it might help.

For days they hover around the hospital, drinking coffee and interrogating the nurses. Eunice arrives from Chicago with Shriver in tow, and Pat comes from Los Angeles alone. Peter has played soldier, student, and socialite, but he's not quite as willing to play the part of husband.

Bobby's jolted out of a shallow nap by Eunice's voice. "What?" his sister barks into the phone in the other room. They've retreated to his father's apartment under the pretext of stealing a few hours of sleep.

He sits up, and Ethel hands him a cold glass of water. The light coming through the curtains says late afternoon. He has a headache like a fishhook, sharp and glinting behind one eye. He can't remember, but he's almost certain he was dreaming of that dog, the one he killed. He's taken to driving by the house and the yard is always empty, the fence intact, holding nothing in. Is it the worst thing he's ever done?

"I think this might kill my old man," he says.

"He'll outlive us all," Ethel says.

In the other room, Eunice is playing the world's worst press secretary. "There's no change," she barks into the phone at whichever friend or family member had the nerve to express concern about Jack.

"She still on the warpath?" he asks.

Eunice with snakes for hair, telling anyone who'll listen that she knew, she just knew this would happen, surgeons are nothing more than butchers with medical degrees. She was violently opposed to it all summer; he's fairly certain his father was running some kind of shadow PR campaign through her.

"Just be glad the Boy Scout's not around," Ethel says.

"Is he off giving blood?"

"Organizing a canned food drive, I think."

It feels good to make fun of Shriver. Better than plucking petals about Jack. Better than being assaulted by memories of the last surgery in his family.

He leans into Ethel's shoulder. The uncertainty, they always say. That's what gets you when a loved one is sick. But he's not uncertain; he knows exactly what comes next. The bright young senator from Massachusetts dead of complications from a high-risk spinal procedure. No mention of his preexisting adrenal problems. No mention that these should have killed him already. A tasteful waiting period while they regroup.

Ethel seems to guess the shape of his thoughts. "Straighten up soldier," she says. "He still has a pulse."

In the living room, the only signs Eunice was here are a track in the carpet from her pacing and a discarded dark green sweater that she's had so long he thinks of it as hers, even though *JFK* is still stitched in red thread on the tag.

He calls out to her, but gets no answer. "I think she's in the bathroom," Ethel says with meaningful eyes. "Why don't I go down and call a cab?"

He turns Eunice's sweater right side out, folds it carefully, and places it on the back of the couch. Then he goes to the bathroom and kicks the door until his sister tells him to fuck off. Further kicking yields no additional response.

He retrieves a wire hanger from his father's closet. His children are fond of locking themselves inside of rooms, so he has some experience with manipulating locked doors. After a moment of fiddling, the door handle pops. Eunice sits on the floor by the toilet, face shining with perspiration, eyes hollowed out with effort. She wears one of Teddy's button-downs—all of her clothes were her siblings' first—and dark blue crescents of sweat hang under each arm. She flushes, and her lunch disappears down the drain.

He takes a seat at a safe distance, on the bath mat. The stiffness between them since the Senate race has never really gone away. Eunice still angry he got picked over her to manage the campaign, him never having the courage to say, I thought it should have been you, too. Both of them pretending there's nothing wrong.

Although if he's honest with himself, the Senate race didn't cause anything; it only exacerbated what was already there between them. It only ensured that they'd never be close. That Eunice will always see him as a spoiler.

"Jack will be fine," Bobby says in an attempt at comfort. "He always is."

"That's what we thought about Rosie," Eunice snaps, saying the name they've avoided since 1941. Taking their cue from their mother, who stopped including Rosemary in the family letters that fall and has never mentioned her since. It's not cruel, they think; it's how any family survives: in silence. In selective editing. Name a family that got somewhere by telling the truth. But a decade is as long as Eunice can bite her tongue, it would seem.

He remembers backseat games as children, pinching each other's skin and bending fingers back until the other said Uncle, but when it was he and Eunice who played, they never asked for mercy. They'd pinch each other blue; their siblings had to pry them apart to keep them from breaking each other's fingers.

And Bobby doesn't ask for mercy now. He meets his sister's hard gaze. "Did you know?" he asks. "Before she went to the hospital—did you know what was going to happen to her?"

"Of course not," she says. "Only Jack and Joe and Kick knew it was a—a lobotomy." She stumbles over the word and lifts her chin defiantly, as if to cover her discomfort with it. "I found out after, same as you."

He remembers the muted months after Rosemary disappeared, how thin Eunice got. Lost her appetite entirely, and what she did eat, she couldn't keep down.

They're silent for a time, waiting to see if this fragile confidence will hold. With Joe and Kick they were able—allowed—to mourn. But Rosie exists in a purgatory of his family's making. Gone, but not grieved. Sinless, but incapable of salvation.

"I started having these fainting episodes at school," Eunice says. "I hit my head once and had to stay in the infirmary for a few days. Mother and Father didn't know it was because I wasn't eating. They didn't know anything. I told them I got knocked on the head in field hockey."

She runs the sleeve of her shirt over her forehead, wiping away the sweat. "But somehow Jack knew," she says. "He showed up at school and broke me out."

This part, Bobby can imagine easily. It's how Jack was before Joe died: appearing at random in places he didn't belong, half-magician, half-outlaw, roping you into some scheme that was certain to bring down hell on your head—but he made it feel like such a privilege, to be his accomplice, so you always went along with it.

She tells him how Jack drove her to a diner near school and ordered one of everything—chocolate cake with vanilla ice cream, French fries, a tuna melt—and told her they weren't leaving until she took a bite from every plate. She refused at first, she says, and this is easy to imagine too, his skeletal sister sitting cross-armed in a booth, stubborn enough to hold out until the Second Coming.

Jack got the waitresses in on it, she tells him, stringing them along with stories that Eunice was going on a mission trip to Africa and that he, her wonderful older brother, was treating her to all her favorite foods before she left, and they were so charmed they brought out even *more* food on the house. They were probably there for three or four hours, Eunice says. Jack carrying on and playing the gallant brother to the waitresses, making up stories about a family that didn't exist—their father a pastor, their mother a nurse, the small town upstate where they lived. He, Jack, a devout boy destined for a life of the cloth. But then, as the afternoon wore on into early evening, he stopped trying to needle her into eating. The sun had gone long and low, the last light of the day, everything turning golden and holy, the napkin dispenser like a sacred relic, the meatloaf like the body of Christ.

"He cut a deal with me," Eunice says. "If I kept my weight above one-twenty, the two of us would go see Rosie at Christmas. We'd tell Mother and Father we were going skiing with friends and we'd drive out to see her. I didn't know where she was. I didn't think anyone did. Joe, maybe. But Jack said he knew, too.

"The closer it got to Christmas, the more I ate. Second helpings at every meal. I had a bag packed under my bed for weeks, just waiting for him to show up and tell me it was time."

Sweat pricks his palms and under his arms. He's beginning to feel vaguely nauseous himself, and wants to tell her to budge over, to make room by the toilet. But he's frozen in place. He has a hundred questions, and only one worth asking.

"How was she?"

"We never went," she says.

Something small in his chest becomes smaller still. He blinks at the floor.

Eunice pulls her knees into her chest. "Pearl Harbor happened, and then we were at war, and he and Joe enlisted and it just…" She shrugs, trying to pretend she doesn't care. "Maybe he never meant it to begin with. You can never tell how much he's acting and how much he means it."

Yes. It's what makes Jack a good politician, and a difficult person to call your brother.

"But at the time I believed him," Eunice says. "So I ate."

It feels like they've been sitting here in the bathroom for hours, instead of twenty minutes or so. His bones are filled with wet sand; it's harder than it should be to stand up.

"Guess we should get back," he says, avoiding his sister's eyes.

She makes a show of dusting off the front of her shirt. "Guess so."

He knows without having to ask that it'll be a long time before they speak of their sister again.

"You know you'll have to run for something if he dies?" she says, trying to reassert the normal order of things, where they goad and jab and bicker with each other instead of showing their stomachs.

"Do you want to be my campaign manager?" he asks.

For one instant, she's taken aback; the next instant, it's gone. "I'll consider it," she says. "If you can afford my rate."

HE HAS A STORY of his own from after Rosie's surgery. One night in the slow drip of days after Christmas and before the new year, Teddy, who's known to sleep anywhere but his own room, launched himself onto Bobby's bed, landing directly on his shin.

"Christ's sake! Are you trying to break my leg?"

It hadn't really hurt. Teddy was nine years old and child-light, but you have to put little brothers in their place if you want them to take you seriously, so he'd feigned annoyance.

Teddy: immediately remorseful, trying earnestly to overcompensate for his error: Do you need some ice? Do you want me to leave? Did I hit it awfully hard? Oh Robbie, I've really done it now—can you ever forgive me? Lisping his questions in a voice that hadn't dropped yet, still the sweet upper keys of a piano.

"What are you jumping around for anyway?" Bobby asked.

Teddy fondled the ears of the bear he carried everywhere back then. "Can I sleep in here tonight?"

"Don't hog the covers."

Teddy has the same gift of gab that their grandfather did, that pure Irish natter; normally taking him in for the night means a lot of chatter. It doesn't matter if you respond or not. It doesn't even matter if you're awake. Teddy will talk just to hear himself, a one-man radio station. It's lulling, actually. Sometimes he wishes for it still on nights he can't sleep.

But that night, Teddy had burrowed in and been silent. Bobby assumed he'd drifted off. He'd been on the sweet edge of sleep himself when Teddy whispered, "Will I disappear too, if I disappoint Dad?"

Nobody tells you that about brothers; how casually they can ask you to save them. Because a father has that power, the power to make you exist. Or theirs does, anyway.

And how had he responded to Teddy's question?

By lying still in the dark, and pretending not to hear him.

HE GOES TO PRAY in the hospital's small chapel and finds his father already there, slouched forward in what looks like prayer but isn't. His father in profile: the square Kennedy jaw, jowled now with age. Hair that shows just a hint of the red it used to be. A thin line seared into his skin from the arm of his glasses, now tucked away in his suit jacket.

He used to spend years in his father's closet rifling through his suits, the wooden hangers on the rack making skeletal noises against each other. The itch of the wool, or the glossy black sharkskin; this one pin-striped, this one the deep navy of a military uniform. And the treasures you could find in the pockets: Exterior pockets held train stubs, parking tickets, the occasional throat lozenge or peppermint pointing to some meal in some train car on the way from New York to Boston or Boston to Hollywood. Interior pockets: fountain pens; a horn-rimmed hair comb; business cards; curled-up strips of paper with telephone extensions; notes scribbled on hotel napkins. He found a single pearl, once, and a handkerchief with unknown initials spotted with blood.

"He was as good as dead," his father says with an oaken voice, "when he caught scarlet fever. Not even three years old. Too young to fight it off. But I promised God—'If you let my little boy live, I'll give my entire fortune to the Church.'"

And both sides made good on their end of the deal. Jack got better. His father liquidated his assets and donated them to the Guild of Saint Apollonia. He knows this story. But why is his father telling it?

"I came down here to make another deal," his father says. "But I realized..."

His father is not a man who often trails off; his sentences end in hard punctuation: Declarative. Emphatic.

"Realized what, Dad?"

"You can only make a deal like that once," his father says.

CHAPTER 14

Soviets

BUT PERHAPS JACK MAKES A DEAL of his own.

Not long after that day with his father in the hospital chapel, Jack comes back to life, flushed in the face and hoarse. "Well, I know this isn't Heaven," he croaks to the crowd gathered around his bed. They laugh harder than they need to. Relief colors their voices, Bobby's most of all, as they clamor around Jack. All of the terrible eulogies about him—his youth, his wit, how much he had left to give—remain unwritten.

With Jack back from the dead, the world of politics resumes its spinning. Unfortunately for Bobby, his father has decided that after Jack's most recent brush with death, he'd better hedge his bets where his sons are concerned. The Ambassador's attention has refocused from his heir to his spare.

An idea Bobby had hoped would stay dead: a tour of Soviet Central Asia with his father's friend, one of the justices of the Supreme Court. Their visas have been denied every year since he was in law school. He'd hoped the pattern would hold. And then Stalin died. Now Ike and Khrushchev are meeting in Geneva this summer; the Soviets are in a welcoming mood.

Bobby tried to beg off, pleading work—the midterms were kind to the Democrats, who regained both houses, another dividend of the McCarthy hearings. Back in the majority, they regained control of the committees, too; Bobby was made chief counsel in January. He and McClellan, now the subcommittee chair, have managed to turn the subcommittee from a shining example of incompetence under McCarthy into a well-oiled machine, a campaign of its own: organized, meticulous, carefully orchestrated.

Yet his father was unmoved by the argument that he was needed in Washington. After the McCarthy job, he needed to be seen traveling with a liberal, his father said. Justice Douglas fits the bill. It's the kind of trip, Bobby thought uneasily, they made Jack take before he ran for Senate. But his brother is back in Washington now; Bobby's supposed to be safe. Jack returned to work in May, to much applause and banging of drums.

Press courtesy of their father. Fruit basket courtesy of Nixon. The message: "Welcome home."

So why does it still feel like Bobby's being groomed for office? Maybe this was his real objection to the trip: not that it was a distraction from his job, but that it means his father's planning for him to have a new one. The thought is his unwanted companion during the long, sun-struck days he spends traveling through Azerbaijan, Turkmenistan, Tajikistan.

Stalin's picture hanging above urinals. Tablecloths stitched with hammer and sickle. Late afternoon shadows casting harsh judgement on the faces of pedestrians. Prongs of minarets spearing the sky. Stalin's picture hanging in the courtroom. White spittoons outside of every hotel room. The eyes of a fresh dead lamb staring at him for the length of a meal. Camels— groaning, spitting, stinking. Stalin's picture in every hotel room, watching you sleep. Women in red dancing costumes. Dirt runways. Frozen orange ice.

Back home, Emmett Till is lynched in Mississippi. His body chained to a fan and dumped in the river. The photographs of him are distributed for printing in newspapers and magazines. William Faulkner, who's being trotted out in Japan as a goodwill representative of the American South, is quoted instead as saying, "If we in America have reached the point in our desperate culture when we must murder children, no matter for what reason or what color, we don't deserve to survive and probably won't." The State Department isn't pleased with his answer; he was supposed to be putting a *positive* gloss on race in America. The Soviets ask Bobby and Douglas about lynching everywhere they go. About the American Negro. About the bomb, and about *mir*; peace.

They tour collective farms and villages, universities and cities. The sun seems to orbit closer here. The heat is inhuman. When he falls into bed at night, still sweating, he dreams of the cool blue Atlantic fitting over him like a glove.

The dinners held for them are extravagant and endless. They make toasts at every meal, sometimes ten, twelve, fifteen rounds. They're offered sheep's ear. Sheep's brain. Sheep's feet. Many parts of sheep. Camel milk. Lamb kidney. Caviar. He refuses most of it, sticking to white grapes and dark brown bread. But eventually, even this puts him off. He almost gags on a slice of melon. A day later, water starts to turn his stomach. Lukewarm and carrying the tang of metal, he's convinced he's taking small sips of blood. On their way to Omsk, he starts shaking so hard he thinks it's his fault when the plane dips in a current of turbulence. Justice Douglas is speaking to him through a wall of glass, then calling for a doctor.

"No doctor," he says through chattering teeth. He doesn't want some Soviet poking and prodding at him. They've already poisoned him once. What's to stop them from doing it again?

"I told your father I'd get you back in one piece," Douglas says.

He's in bed when Douglas leaves—in bed, though last he knew he was standing on a tarmac, convulsing with chills.

"I don't want to die in Russia," he mumbles.

Joe's laughter fills the room.

"Get a load of that," his brother says. Through half shuttered eyes, he sees the shape of Joe in a high-backed chair, like the ones they have in the dining room back home. *What are our chairs doing in Russia?* he wants to know. Of all his questions, this is the most pressing.

He struggles to get himself upright, but a cool hand pushes him back against the bed.

"Gee whiz Bobby," his sister says. "You'd better hope they've got some ace doctor around here. You don't look so hot."

"Ace," he repeats. "Nobody says that anymore."

Kick just laughs, unconcerned, and adjusts her Red Cross cap. Sitting on the edge of his bed. His sister.

"Am I dying?" he asks, and Kick laughs again, a sound that used to break hearts.

"Not even close," she says.

"Take it from us," Joe agrees.

It feels as if his face is sliding off sideways like the wax of a lit candle, but a quick inspection determines no, still there.

"I need to sleep," he decides.

"All right, Bob. It's been a gas," Kick says.

"Nobody says that anymore, either."

His sister reaches out, her first two fingers in a V for victory. She slides his eyes closed.

FOR DAYS A SOVIET doctor nurses him back to health; his siblings don't return.

When he's finally discharged, a plane is waiting to take him to Moscow. The final leg of their trip in Siberia has come and gone while fever burned through him. Ethel, Pat, Jean, Douglas and his wife all are waiting for him there on arrival. Ethel meets him halfway up the stairs, pulling him to her with such force that she nearly sends them both tumbling.

"What did you do to him?" she asks Douglas, one gloved hand on Bobby's cheek.

"Ah, but ask him what he learned, Ethel," Douglas replies.

They stay in Moscow for a few days, have dinner with the American ambassador, see *Swan Lake* at the ballet. Afterward, his sisters and Ethel try to repeat the steps in the hotel room, spinning around gracelessly in their stockings. Don't quit your day jobs, he says, and they hit him with pillows, and he's glad he didn't die; he would have missed their abuse.

Long after Ethel's gone to sleep, wiped out by jet lag, he and his sisters stay up talking in Pat and Jean's room. It feels good to speak in his own tongue again, not just English, but Kennedy English.

While they've been in Moscow, waiting for him to

arrive, they've seen Gorky Park, the Kremlin, Soviet women in their strange, squeaking shoes. And they've seen Lenin on display in his tomb in Red Square. Jean is convinced there was something wrong with his hands. They were somebody else's hands placed on his body, she speculates. Or maybe it was that his hands looked like the deadest part of him.

They've been idling over their travels, trying to put off, as long as possible, the real discussion they need to have.

"How are things at home?" he asks carefully.

"Didn't you get any of Mother's letters?"

"Yes: 'Your father is golfing. Your sister is swimming. All is well. Forward this to your brother when you're done.'"

"Everything's fine," Pat says in a voice that's too off-hand. *Fine* is a dangerous word. Jean picks at the blanket. There's something they don't want to tell him.

"Jack and Jackie?" he asks.

"Warmer," Pat says.

"Fighting? But I thought—but they'd been getting along."

"Yes, as long as Jackie had him trapped in a bed and unable to walk," Pat says.

Jean shoots her a look that tells him Pat's being particularly uncharitable. Jackie had had to play nurse for months on end, and she did so uncomplainingly, with a steel they didn't think the Queen Deb possessed. The bandages on the suppurating wound on Jack's back she changed daily. The steady flow of visitors she organized to keep his spirits up, even convincing the actress Grace Kelly to stop by once. And most important, he thinks, she carried on as if Jack would return to the Senate, which allowed his brother to believe he would.

Jean runs her thumb along the seam of the blanket. "Jackie had a miscarriage," she says.

Miscarriage. He doesn't know what to do with that word. Apparently Jack and Jackie don't either; Jack's gone off to Sweden to see some old flame. Jackie's gone to Paris to do the same. There's speculation that she's been asking her mother about lawyers.

"They wouldn't get divorced," he says. "It's not allowed."

"Her mother did. Those things are always contagious."

"What does Eunice think?"

"She thinks the same thing we do."

Pat starts, "My psychic says—"

He holds up a hand. "That's not how a mentally sound person starts a sentence."

"My psychic says big changes are coming. The old order of things is in flux. The planetary alignment—"

"They can't," he says again, like saying it will prevent the thing itself. "If he gets divorced, his career's over. The Senate's as high as he goes."

Pat and Jean exchange a look that he doesn't understand. A look between sisters. "I think the electoral component is the least of Jackie's concerns," Jean says at last.

They sit in silence for a moment. He knows it's stupid, but he can't help but feel responsible somehow, like his absence is what caused this latest deterioration of Jack's marriage, like if he'd been paying better attention, he could have prevented it—

"It's not all bad news," Pat yawns. "Tell him."

"Tell him what?" Jean asks.

"Look at her trying to be coy."

His little sister has fallen in love quietly, with a quiet man. His name's Steve and he comes from a family like theirs; the Smiths are wealthy, Irish Catholic, and many. Steve's the youngest of five boys, serious without being self-serious, unflappable, and a capable businessman, working for the tugboat and barge company that his family owns. In other words, he's the son their father always wanted. Like Jean, he seems to prefer remaining in the background, a schoolboy with all the answers who nonetheless doesn't feel the need to raise his hand for every question and show off what he knows. She'll tell you about him, Pat has advised, but you have to go at it *slowly*. Right now, Jean's not in the mood. She swings her legs out of bed and says, "I need something to eat."

They're all hungry then; they split a packet of crackers they find in the bottom of Pat's purse, and this only makes them hungrier. They troop downstairs to look for food; the person at the front desk looks at them dubiously, skeptical of their American appetites.

They find a place still open near their hotel. He and

Jean stand near the door, letting Pat butcher her way through an order in Russian. She returns with three glasses of vodka and a hank of brown bread. "Bottoms up," she says, and doesn't wait for them to lift their glasses. He and Jean exchange a look.

On the walk back to the hotel, they keep Pat firmly in the middle to stop her from running off. She complains that with her arms looped through theirs, she can't smoke, so Bobby is in charge of holding her cigarette, lifting and lowering it to her mouth as she requires.

Back in his sisters' room, he helps Jean wrangle Pat onto her bed. She's snoring lightly as soon as she hits the pillow. Jean sits on the edge of the mattress, watching their sister with an unreadable expression. Bobby pauses his exit and sits next to her.

"Who is he?" Bobby asks.

Jean buries her face in her knees.

"Does Dad like him?"

She pops her face back out. "Have you ever noticed that's the first thing anyone asks?"

Jean: steady, quiet, always watching. She was who he called when Kick's plane crashed while he was in Belgium and who told him that their father hadn't said a word and their mother had said it was God's way of pointing a finger. After Kick died, they were all home for a week that felt like an entire summer and the house broke up into little factions of grief. Jack and Eunice shut up in Jack's room, speaking in low tones.

Teddy wandering around waiting for someone to tell him what to do. He and Jean grew close that week, the closest they've ever been. Siblings go like tides sometimes; you're closer to some than others, then that fades. Moons pass in their orbit, you get close again. They sat in the attic, and he barely remembers what they talked about. Their own mortality and what was playing at the movies. Where they'd go if they could go anywhere and what they wanted most. "To be left alone," he remembers his sister said.

Now she chews her lip. Pat's snoring increases in its intensity, then moves back down to a calmer register.

"The only one who marriage is easy for is you," Jean says quietly. "I think the rest of us would be fine if we'd just gone on the way we always had."

He's never considered that he's better than his siblings at something. Better than Jack at something.

Once, someone told Eunice she looked like Jack, and Jean wanted to know who *she* looked like. The answer she got was: Bobby. It disappointed her greatly. He wonders if it still does. They have the same eyes, no denying that; not just the color, but the doleful shape.

Their mother says that Jean got only the tragedy, none of the good memories. Joe died when she was sixteen, Kick and Rosemary were gone before she turned twenty-one. Maybe it's Jean's eyes that make her own mother believe she was born too late for happiness.

"Do you want to hear about the fight Jack and Jackie

had on the boat?" Jean asks, always quick to turn the discussion away from herself.

"No," he says. He's suddenly a thousand years old. "Why would I want to hear about that?"

"Usually you like to know these things."

Do I? he wonders tiredly. Or am I just told these things and expected to be able to do something with them? Your brother is losing his campaign: Fix it. Your brother is losing his wife: Make her stay.

"Tell me something else," he sighs, tipping his head back until it rests against the wall. Tell me more about Moscow. Tell me more about the hands of Lenin. Tell me more about this man you love.

JACK CORNERS HIM as soon as he's home, commandeering the Ambassador's office to talk Soviets. Their father has taken to evacuating to France for part of the summer now; all the children and grandchildren and in-laws get in the way of his peace. This leaves him and his brother free to treat the office as their own personal war room.

"Farms?" Jack asks. He swivels idly in their father's red leather chair, flipping, occasionally, through Bobby's notes.

Bobby studies his brother; something's changed, but nothing's different. Rumpled white shirt, shorts with a hole in the pocket. Deep tan. He's put on some weight over the summer; you no longer worry about the problems a strong breeze could pose. He wonders if there's a woman.

"Collectivized or state-run," Bobby says. "Douglas said they were impressive compared to the rest of Asia but they don't hold a candle to ours. And they kept asking us about the American peasant—'How does the American peasant live?'"

"What else were they interested in?"

"Negroes. Lynching. War and peace. They have a constant stream of propaganda—everywhere we went they had some public radio on a pole going at full blast."

Jack twists the letter opener and the light off the blade flashes in Bobby's eyes. He's learned when his brother's holding back, so he waits.

"I heard a rumor Adlai Stevenson is considering me for the second spot on his ticket."

Casually, his brother drops this bombshell. Bobby's propelled to his feet in an instant. So that's what it is, he thinks, looking his brother over again. He wasn't so far off the mark; this is a kind of courtship.

"You're joking," he says, and in the same breath, "What does Dad think?"

Jack smiles ironically. "He thinks it's one of the 'ten most moronic fucking things' he's ever heard."

"And how does Eunice feel about you sniffing around her old boyfriend?"

"She says as long as I don't make it a habit..."

Since his brother returned to the Senate, he's been going full throttle: speaking engagements, commencement addresses, his fifteenth-year reunion at Harvard, all to dispel any rumors about his health. He shows up in a sweatshirt and sneakers at community picnics so he can toss balls around. The first rule of politics: A tight spiral will convince the majority of Americans that you're in perfect health.

Bobby supposes this Stevenson idea is the next step in all that. But something about it bothers him.

"Why would he want you?" Bobby asks. What does the figurehead of the party gain from allying himself with a relative unknown?

"And you call yourself my brother."

His mind is racing, weighing the worth of being second spot on your party's ticket if that ticket is almost guaranteed to lose—but he stops: his brother has made no indication of what he actually thinks.

"Do you want it?" Bobby asks.

Jack says, "We'll see."

HE'S NOT EVEN HOME a month when the president has a heart attack.

A fog covers the event, like a ship approaching an ill-fated harbor. Just how bad is it? Will he be able to return to office? Will he run again next year? These are the questions the Republicans ask with dread, the Democrats with delight. One man's heart attack is another's opportunity to retake the Executive Branch, as the saying goes.

"He's under an oxygen tent," Bobby reads.

"Don't bother with the papers. We'll know he's finished if they keep him out of sight," his father says. His father, who's about Eisenhower's age.

Suddenly, the second spot on a Democratic ticket doesn't sound so bad to the Ambassador, now returned from France, but it's not Stevenson he wants to ally Jack with. If he's serious about this, his father believes, Lyndon Johnson's his horse. And Bobby can't fault his father's logic; the Southern majority leader with the articulate young Northerner? It would be a strong ticket. A way of pulling together alienated wings of the party and giving them at least a hope of a chance in November.

His father gets a table in a restaurant where the steaks come bloody and the napkins come in shapes: a swan, a sail, a bishop's hat. The man to get a message to Johnson is Tommy Corcoran, a longtime intimate. Bobby's here to see how things are done, to see, as his father says, what it feels like to be the man in the back booth. His father has given up on the idea that any of his sons will have a head for money, but perhaps he can still teach them a different kind of business.

"He'll be late," his father says as they settle into their seats. He's ordered a cola, but hasn't touched it, so Bobby doesn't drink his, either.

"How do you know?" he asks.

"You're always late if you have something to offer instead of to ask."

He wonders if his father learned this lesson from Roosevelt. A year's worth of waiting in some room kept too hot. And when he was finally let in to see Roosevelt, a nettle of anger had worked its way into him, slowly, surely. The anger of generations: unreasonable, outsized. That he'd always be the Irishman asking the WASPs for a leg up.

But Roosevelt had remembered with a mind as cold and faceted as a diamond, or else his clever wife had remembered for him—that his eldest son was abroad recently and how did his trip turn out? And the anger fizzled out of his father like fingers pinching a flame and he accepted commissioner of the SEC when what he'd wanted was a cabinet post. It was better to take something instead of nothing.

Corcoran hustles over to them in a wool suit jacket. He'd planned for the day to be colder, but the autumn has surprised them, offering up one last warm afternoon. His forehead has a light sheen of sweat.

"Apologies," he says, extending them both a hand. "Traffic."

"Not at all," his father says with a gesture that only certain men can perfect, bringing a waiter scurrying from across the room. "What are you drinking?"

First comes the ordering of food. Asking after families. Talking football.

"Your youngest plays for Harvard now, doesn't he?" Corcoran asks. He scrapes at an oyster with a toy fork, loosening it from its shell. Squeezes a lemon. Tips his head back to swallow it whole.

"He earned his varsity letter against Yale," his father says with no small degree of pride. Never mind that Yale trounced them this year.

"And you're still with Senator McClellan?" Corcoran turns to Bobby. "How do you like him?"

"He's tough but he's fair," Bobby says.

Corcoran chuckles. "He could chew up nails if you ask me—but from what I hear you're a tough SOB yourself."

Bobby starts to say, *My reputation is undeserved*, but his father cuts in.

"That he is," the Ambassador says. "You don't want to cross Bobby. He can hold a grudge better than any man I've ever met." He says this like it's a good thing.

"Does Senator Johnson have thoughts on next year?" the Ambassador continues.

Corcoran sucks his teeth. His glass rattles lightly as he stirs the ice with a straw. "He's waiting to see how the president fares."

"Heart attacks come in pairs," the Ambassador says. "He could have another one in two months. You'll lose your chance if you wait too long."

"What do you think?" Corcoran asks. He leans back expansively in his chair. "Do you think he should go for the big prize?"

"I wouldn't be here if I didn't," his father says.

Corcoran chooses his next words carefully. "It wouldn't be a fundamentally incompatible match," he says, "but I'd be lying if I said there weren't . . . *concerns* about Jack's health."

The Ambassador remembers his cola; he pours it into a glass, and the ice crackles and sizzles and seethes. "He's healthy as a horse," he says. Not even a flicker of emotion.

"You can't blame me for asking," Corcoran says. "He's as big around as a napkin ring. We've heard he's got rickets—"

"Malaria from the war," the Ambassador repeats the standard line. "And I've built up enough goodwill with the press"—by goodwill he means dollars—"that they'll never print anything more than that."

Bobby knows he isn't here to speak, but he can't help himself. "How's Senator Johnson's health?" he asks testily. "He had a heart attack himself in July."

He expects a reprimand from his father; what he gets is approval, a silent signal of the sort he's seen pass between the Ambassador and his older brothers a hundred times. A hard-driving son of a bitch, he remembers. Well, who says that's a bad thing?

Corcoran's eyes narrow slightly. "That little thing? That was nothing."

"Excellent," his father says. "Now that we've all coughed and bent over, do you have any other objections?"

"Well," Corcoran says slowly, and Bobby knows what's coming next as surely as if he's reading Corcoran's mind because it's always next.

"There's the matter of religion," Corcoran says. And then, after a calculated pause, "It doesn't matter a whit to us, of course, but we can't say the same of other Southerners."

You fucking hypocrites, he thinks, not for the last time. His father only nods, expecting this.

"You don't have support outside of the South," the Ambassador says. "You need the votes from Northern cities. We can deliver that. It's a balanced ticket. Southern insider. Fresh-faced Northerner."

" 'Fresh-faced' can read as 'inexperienced.' "

"Voters need something to get excited about," the Ambassador says. "And it's not going to be Humphrey or Symington."

"Where does Jack stand on nuclear armaments? Tariffs on goods from Soviet allies? And what about race?" Corcoran asks. "It's a sensitive subject down South."

"He knows you have to go along to get along."

Corcoran looks unconvinced.

"You may have heard he's rather good at getting people into bed," the Ambassador says. "Even Dixiecrat governors."

Corcoran chuckles. "Takes after his old man?"

"You're damn right he does."

Bobby can tell it's a no even as his father and Corcoran continue to parse Jack's record. What he sees is a Johnson camp unwilling to gamble. A Johnson camp who only agreed to this meeting so as not to burn a bridge with one of the richest men in the country. Evidently, the Ambassador reads it, too; when Corcoran places his hands on the table to push himself to his feet, the Ambassador says, "What's his number?"

Corcoran's eyes flicker. He wasn't expecting this final offer, though he should have been. Bobby's surprised his father waited this long.

"You put him on the ticket, you'll have my full financial support," the Ambassador says.

You can see Corcoran counting this out in his head. All the millions the Ambassador's made. But even this last overture isn't enough.

"It's certainly an interesting offer," Corcoran says at last. "I'll make sure to pass it on. You give Jack my regards."

Corcoran leaves. His father signs the bill without looking at it.

"Never get the oysters," his father says, studying the empty plates in front of them with mild distaste. "Oysters are for commoners or amateurs."

"He made up his mind before he came," Bobby says.

"Yes," his father agrees. "What makes you sure?"

"He never unbuttoned his jacket," Bobby says. "He called him 'Jack' the whole time. They think he's just a boy."

His father fixes him with an approving gaze, a gaze that says, *We'll make a man out of you yet*. His arm around Bobby's shoulder as they spill out onto the street: it's the same way he used to hold Jack and Joe.

THEY WAIT TO SEE how the political winds blow.

Bobby isn't left idle. The Ambassador has decided that apart from his continuing committee work, he needs to raise his public profile and round out his résumé on foreign affairs, the way Jack did. Bobby still suspects some run for office is in play; he's aware of the pendulum above him, descending lower with each swing. Still, he does as his father says, writing every article, speaking at every engagement his father sets up, discussing his firsthand observations of Soviet life during his trip with Douglas, and more broadly, how the West might win the Cold War.

At best, he has a kind of frenetic energy when he speaks, the words pouring out of him in a half-intelligible slur. At worst, he's wooden. Some mix of a real boy and a puppet.

Others put it more bluntly still: "Eunice says you're the worst speaker she's ever heard," Jack says.

"Eunice would find fault with Churchill."

His brother's laughter rattles the line. Jack's in a good mood these days; he's got a new doctor. His faith in her comes from the simplest of things: her discovery that the left half of his body is smaller than the right, something overlooked all these years by experts the world over. She prescribes him shoe lifts to make up the difference, Novocain for the still frequent muscle spasms. A regimen of steroids that has Jack stabbing himself in the thigh with a needle twice a day. "The healing power of a woman's touch," Jack jokes.

As if to prove he's here to stay, Jack and Jackie have bought a new house across the river, once General McClellan's during the Civil War. It's big for two people.

"Well it has to be," Jackie says. "We need room for Jack's ego."

The ego that continues to entertain ideas of a spot on Stevenson's ticket.

"Early endorsement with a press conference," Jack says. "That's the best way to keep Stevenson interested."

Bobby looks at Jack's hands, watches them twitch and jitter against the knees of his pants. His brother is no longer merely intrigued or interested by the idea. He's prepared to run headlong after it. Get a hand, a foot, a finger in the door. Anything to keep it cracked open. Anything to get onstage in Chicago at next year's convention.

Bobby wonders about the wisdom of this. The Stevenson of four years ago excited him, but now he's more concerned with the political future of his brother than his country. His calculus is a careful one; the answer must always be, *Good for Jack.*

"Do you really think he can beat Eisenhower?" Bobby asks.

"Even if he doesn't, it's national exposure. And if he does…"

If he does, it's two terms as vice president and Kennedy in '64. Bobby is warming to the idea. But an endorsement for Stevenson isn't going to seal the deal.

"They'll want the state delegation," Bobby says. The state delegation that's currently controlled by a chairman who hates his brother and isn't going to just hand it over. "You really want to get involved with local politics?"

Jack says, "Who's going to listen to me about Berlin if I can't bring Boston to heel?"

Bobby *tap, tap, tap*s one finger against the crook of his elbow, slogging through the coming months of internecine Massachusetts political battles in his mind. They'll have to get a new chairman, a Kennedy ally, on the ballot and convince the state committee members to vote their man in, all this while pretending to be uninvolved.

Messy and unpleasant, yes, but the payoff—his brother nominated to the party's ticket as a first-term senator. His brother who last year was as good as dead.

His brother is waiting, he realizes, for his answer. As if he has a choice. As if he'll ever have a choice.

"I hear Chicago's lovely in the summer," Bobby says.

CHAPTER 15

The Ticket

RAIN LASHES THE WINDOWPANE.

"It's a doomed ticket," his father says, voice crackling over the connection. Away in the South of France, his warnings are limited to phone calls. Jack has stopped picking up. "The Democrats don't have a chance in hell this year. *Don't let your brother do this.*"

It's not Adlai Stevenson's fate as presumptive Democratic nominee the Ambassador's worried about in the coming presidential election. It's the rumor swirling that Stevenson's considering naming Jack as his running mate at next week's convention.

"When Stevenson loses," his father says, "your brother will take the blame. I can see the headlines now."

Bobby can see them, too. *Too young, too inexperienced, too Catholic.* All the error laid at Jack's doorstep, handicapping him for future runs. We can't give it to a Catholic, they'll say. Last time we did, we lost. It's what they still say about Al Smith, the only Catholic ever nominated to the top of the party's ticket. Losing by a landslide in 1928, he's been a curse to Catholic candidates ever since. His brother's name will join Smith's as party wisdom and warning.

"Eisenhower's weak," Bobby says. "Stevenson may pull it off."

"Eisenhower will clobber him in November," his father says. "Our party has a tradition of choosing idealists over candidates who can actually win."

"Jack said he's not going to actively pursue it," Bobby says.

Never mind all the effort they put into controlling the state committee in order to deliver Stevenson the Massachusetts delegation. Never mind that even though the critical vote was the day of Jean and Steve's wedding in New York, Jack was in Boston to shake the hands of the committee members as they filed in to render their decision. Bobby remembers the lead in his gut that afternoon, waiting by the phone as the wedding went on like a summer storm in the other room. If they'd lost the committee vote, his brother would have been exposed as impotent in his own state because of an election for which he wasn't even on the ballot. It was this that galled Bobby more than anything; the idea of his brother sticking his neck out that far for Stevenson. And when they'd won, serving the Massachusetts delegation on a silver platter to Stevenson, he'd responded with warm thanks, but no commitment. Still unsure if he wanted to gamble on a sick young Catholic.

"Not going to pursue it?" his father snaps now. "Jack got you a floor pass for the convention. He wants you there with him, and it's not out of brotherly affection."

A floor pass giving Bobby the same convention access as any of the other delegates. Jack finagled one for his little brother out of a friend who owed him a favor. It felt like being knighted when his brother chucked it at him and told him to pack his bags.

"You're not his friend," his father says, and the words lose none of their sting on their way over the ocean. "His pals can tell him how wonderful Stevenson is. *You're* his brother. Are you up to the job?"

Was it a job for Jack and Joe? He thinks *brother* meant something different then. It meant Jack and Joe pushing one of their father's cars down the driveway at midnight, not starting the engine until they got to the street in the hopes their sleeping father wouldn't hear the noise. It meant Jack and Joe throwing a party for which they charged admission while their parents were out of town and then, when they were discovered by the painting they'd failed to put back into place, being forced to deposit their bounty in the church donation box.

"He's past the point of listening to me," his father says. "You're the last one who has his ear."

Bobby doesn't think that's true, although he wants to believe it. He thinks of his brother sometimes as a cabinet of curiosities, the wood so smooth it's like velvet, a million little drawers, and Bobby can open more of them now than he once could, but he stills finds so many of them locked no matter how he rattles and yanks on them.

"Don't let him do anything stupid," his father says. A clap of thunder punctuates his words.

"Wouldn't dream of it, Dad."

CHICAGO. FIVE DAYS in August. There's an energy in the air; it bites at you. The national ticket on the line. If you're Stevenson, you feel "cautiously optimistic" or perhaps "quietly confident" in the press. In private, you're up to two packs a day. Frontrunner or not, these things can never be guaranteed.

The brothers enter the hotel suite as one person. But the differences emerge quickly. One is tall and narrow, almost Lincolnesque; the other shorter, just as lean, but healthier, more substantial. The one is *classically handsome*; the other has a profile they compare to a raptor. The one is the Candidate, the other, the Campaign Manager. They've taken dismal little rooms next to the stockyards where cattle used to be led en masse, the slaughtering site for Northern appetites. Fitting for a political convention.

The troops are gathered: O'Donnell and O'Brien a scheming pair in the corner. Ted Sorensen, the aide

Jack's increasingly come to rely on for everything from speechwriting to policy positions, with his ever-present legal pad. Eunice, blending in with all the men even in a three-hundred-dollar dress. And Jackie. A candidate needs a wife, and that wife needs to be her: young, beautiful, and heavily pregnant. She sits at a slight remove, watching the rest of them with almost an anthropological interest, politicians in their natural habitat. Bobby imagines her unforgiving field notes. Social organization: Centers around one "chief," and all members of tribe are eager to satisfy his desires, believing his success will be their own. Customs: Unnecessary amount of backslapping; tendency to refer to members of other tribes as "bastards" or "sons of bitches"; frequent reference to "the Ambassador" who may be a great elder or feared deity. Methods of communication: To speak over each other without listening to a thing anyone else is saying. Shared beliefs: Delusion.

He gives them their marching orders while they wait for Stevenson to be nominated: test defenses, probe support. What does California think about Kennedy? What about Indiana? Who's afraid of a Catholic? Who's not? Talk to as many people as you can. The key is to get people thinking about you; if they're thinking about you, you've won half the battle already.

The heat grabs at them as they make their way from the hotel to the coliseum, trying to sap them of their strength. When they enter the cool concrete of the arena, Jack pauses, taking it in.

The red, the white, the blue. The bunting. The giant stars ringing the perimeter of the arena, emblazoned with the name of each state. The men in their suits and the women in their sashes. The signs that say AMERICA NEEDS STEVENSON and MADLY FOR ADLAI. The smaller, less numerous signs that say BACK JACK. The scaffold in the middle of the floor erected for the cameras. The spotlights that beam twin cones of light down on the stage as if to emphasize, *There's the prize.* The delegates. The journalists. The candidates. The hopefuls.

The convention.

"What do you think?" Jack asks, his gaze sweeping over the room.

Bobby wants to be awed—a national convention, his brother in the hunt—but awe is strangely missing. Feel for it, try to force it. Nothing.

He doesn't tell Jack this. He says instead, "We're a long way from East Boston."

FANFARE, MOSTLY, IS THE SCHEDULE for the first day. Opening speeches. Appearances by party grandees like Truman and Eleanor Roosevelt.

He and Jack and the others find party leaders, Eunice and Jean find their wives. The men talk to the men, the women to the women. And Jackie? She leans over the railing of the box, bent awkwardly over her stomach, and asks Bobby, "How do you do this all day? I've had to tell three people my water broke just to end a conversation."

Tennessee's Senator Kefauver and his camp, still hoping to rob Stevenson of his prize, are everywhere that first day. To the public, Kefauver's known for his hearings into organized crime, so popular at the time that newsreels of them were shown for free in movie theaters. Around Washington, he's known as the Claw for when he's alone with women in the Senate elevator. He wears a coonskin cap on the campaign trail, his trademark; that kind of thing plays well in Tennessee. It used to be he'd carry a live raccoon, but apparently it didn't behave for the photographs.

To cap off the first night, there's a short film introducing the keynote speaker. The narration provided by the one, the only, John F. Kennedy.

The lights go down, and his brother's voice comes alive in the darkness.

Measured, even, unmistakable. Rendered slightly hollow by the loudspeakers. It belongs to Jack and it doesn't, the same way the man on screen is his brother and isn't. In the light of the projector, the room turns blue and spectral. Jack looks down the barrel of the camera, explaining what the Democratic Party means to people. A philosophy. A point of view. A way of life. Whatever it means to you, his brother intones, it will be found in the course of this video, which will cover the notable moments in the party's founding. City streets, laughing children, people filing into a white clapboard church. Jack talks them through the party's history, from Thomas Jefferson through Truman.

On the face of it, it's nothing remarkable, mawkish even. But the strange alchemy of his brother makes it more than the sum of its parts. Bobby can feel the energy of the crowd rising, and he thinks he understands why; they've gotten used to being the party that lost Korea, or gave away Berlin. The party that's weak on Communism. All of the slurs the Republicans have branded them with under Eisenhower. But the man on screen reminds them that they were something nobler once. And they like it.

At the very end, the applause tells him that the vice presidency no longer feels like a long shot; it feels like something they could reach out and pluck off a branch, forbidden fruit, theirs for the taking.

The Candidate smiles and bobs his head in humble acknowledgement. The Campaign Manager senses an opening, propelling the Candidate toward the stage. This isn't part of the programming, but the Campaign Manager doesn't care. *Let them see him,* he thinks, as his brother ascends to the stage to accept his applause.

His father cautioned him about conventions: ruled by emotion, a notoriously difficult thing to calculate. But the emotion in this room is palpable; the emotion in this room is pride. Pride in being a Democrat. Pride in being the party that produces men like him. Men like the youthful senator from Massachusetts who has so eloquently captured the way they want to see themselves.

Perhaps we can win this thing, the audience is thinking.

And the Campaign Manager is thinking, too.

"TOMORROW," JACK'S SAYING, "let's test some of the wheat states."

In the darkness of the cab, Jackie's cigarette blooms orange.

"Do you have to do that in here?" Jack asks.

Jackie, with a voice like a dull knife: "I guess I do."

"Let's start circulating your agricultural record," Bobby says.

Jack ignores him. "How many of those have you had today?"

Jackie shrugs. Three years into their marriage, and they pick at each other like children. Gone is the one-time intimacy of a brush with death, the days of Jackie reading to Jack in his hospital bed as she sponged sweat from his forehead. Now they carry themselves stinger-first, like scorpions.

"They're terrible for you," Jack says, rolling down the window to let a little air in.

Jackie rests her hands on the crest of her stomach. "It's late, darling, let's not fight."

It sounds like the opposite of what she wants.

At the hotel, Jackie's the first out. Her cigarette sizzles a slow death against the pavement. Jack stalks after her.

It's past one in the morning and the others filter in and out of the suite of rooms that make up the Kennedy command center, lit up and giddy, rehashing the film, speculating on its impact. Even Ken O'Donnell, who normally has the brooding aspect of a Brontë character, is smiling.

Jack flips a switch, suddenly in good humor again. He floats around the room like helium, making everyone lighter, a joke for Sorensen, a clap on the back for O'Brien. Jackie sits in the corner.

Late, but they're not tired. Late but they could go for years. Someone wants to go parlay with the Stevenson camp; Bobby axes the idea. Let the word spread that his brother is the convention's breakout star. Let the BACK JACK signs multiply. Then they'll see what Stevenson's thinking.

"Not bad for a first day," Ken says.

"Need to get Jack in bed." His brother needs to be fresh. How you handle the candidate is as crucial as how you handle the voters.

"You want me to send these yahoos packing?" Ken asks.

"That's all right," Bobby says. This may be the high point. Let them enjoy it.

Eunice pulls him aside, her displeasure palpable. The cords in her neck stand out like a fighting dog's. She was with Jackie for most of the day, trying to teach her how to chat up delegates and insinuate herself with their wives; how to be informed on her husband's positions without being overbearing; how to gracefully exit an unproductive conversation. It seems Jackie was a less than eager student.

"She's terrible," Eunice hisses. "A liability."

The Washington wives expect someone who speaks their language. Jackie knows French, Spanish, a little German, but not this.

When the governor's wife had hugged Jackie and asked about the baby, Jackie snapped, "Who are you?" Now all the women think she's aloof. A wife in politics may be shy, reserved, even circumspect, but never "aloof."

So maybe that explains her mood in the car; she's used to being good at things. She thought she had a handle on the primitive culture of politicians, but living among them has complicated her theories and proved how far in the outgroup she still is.

"She's still new to this," Bobby says. "What do you expect?"

"Can't we bench her? Say it's the baby or something…"

In the corner, Jackie smokes irritable cigarette after irritable cigarette. After a while, she leaves the room. Jack, deep in conversation, doesn't notice, or pretends not to.

Bobby finds her in the room across the hall, sitting alone in the dark.

"Jackie?" he asks, as if, in the dark, she's disappeared.

"He's going to put himself in the hospital again,"

she says, but her voice is slack. This isn't what's really bothering her.

He fumbles for the edge of the bed opposite hers, buying himself time.

"Eunice says you're doing wonderfully."

"You're a worse liar than Jack," she says.

"You know, Jack's hands used to shake," he says. "Even if there were only four people in the crowd. He'd grip the edge of the podium so people couldn't see. We used to give him hell about it."

Her silence says suspicion.

"The only one worse than him was me," he says. "Sometimes if I was introducing him, he'd let me go on and on just to make himself look better in contrast. And Eunice would—this made him cross—she'd stand at the front of the crowd and mouth his speeches because she thought he'd forget."

Two *thunks*. She's kicked off her shoes. "But do you hear," she says, "how even when you're falling flat on your face, you have each other?" His eyes have adjusted to the dark now. He can see her looking at him. "Who do I have?" she asks, then sketches a laugh. "Because it's certainly not Jack."

He can feel them in the room then, sighing and shifting and swishing their dresses: the other women in Jack's marriage. A memory comes to him, Jackie's father at her wedding, grilling him about his new son-in-law. *Your brother a good man? Yes. Going to treat her like a queen? Yes. Ha. You can't fool me—I know how men like him work. I am one. But it doesn't matter a whit, you know why?*

And then he told Bobby something that's stuck with him these years, an arm collared around Bobby's neck, the reek of booze. He said, "Men do these things. And women forgive us. It's the fatal flaw of each sex."

Bobby says to her now, "You *do* have Jack. And the rest of us. You're a Kennedy, too."

"I'm not," she says. "I thought I could be. I tried in the beginning. I thought if I bent a little, it would make you all—it would make Jack—bend a little, too. But that's not what happened. I contorted myself— and you all have stayed exactly the same shape."

He thinks about these funny arrangements we call family.

"Why don't you lie low at Eunice's apartment," he suggests. "There's no reason for you to deal with the convention madness until you have to. Not with the baby. We'll only need you if there's a real chance he gets it. Just to show up in support of Jack."

"It's not just tomorrow," she says. "Or the next day. If he keeps going, which he will, I'll have to do more and more—I see Pat Nixon, I see her on television all the time."

The words run out of her, low and urgent. He can hear what she's trying to say beneath them: She's scared of being exposed, laughed at, alone. And what comfort can he give her, when he's felt these same fears a thousand times? When they don't go away with experience, but instead intensify with every passing year?

He's speaking before he realizes what he's saying. "You just have to find something to deflect it," he says. "Something that keeps people from ever really being able to see you."

"You mean something to disappear behind," she says, a critical note in her voice. "You mean erasing yourself—"

"No, I mean—Jack uses his charm, right? It's how he makes sure people only see the surface. Or Pat—she has California, being married to an actor—it gives people an idea of her without her having to explain herself to them."

He leans over his knees and addresses the floor. "That's all we have to be. Just an idea. They don't want the real thing anyway. They wouldn't know what to do with it."

She's quiet for a long time. So quiet he can hear them across the hall, laughing and carrying on, drunk on the day's success as much as the beer. Then she says one word:

"*Pentimento*."

"Exactly," he says. "Think of it like that. One painting people see, and another beneath the surface."

BOBBY CATCHES ONLY a glimpse of Mrs. Roosevelt as Jack exits her suite, pearls and a long floral dress. The proof of his brother's new status as the convention's star isn't in the girls who run up to them with convention programs asking for signatures, or the reporters who follow them with a renewed interest, asking if they've been given any sign from the Stevenson camp—"You tell me," Jack says, tossing a smile over his shoulder. It's here, in the fact that Eleanor Roosevelt agreed to sit down with Jack for half an hour. Don't let her matronly facade fool you. She still has sway in the party by virtue of her husband. Stevenson listens to her. If Jack wins her over, he might just win over Adlai, too.

But Jack emerges from her room with a tight face.

In the stairwell, Bobby periodically peeking down the shaft to ensure no eavesdroppers, Jack says, "She grilled me about McCarthy, why I didn't vote to censure him."

"What else?"

"That's practically all we talked about. None of my voting, none of my politics—"

"What did you say?"

"That I was recovering from a difficult surgery and didn't feel we could convict a man of censure for violations committed before the current term, that the proper time to take action would have been when they occurred—"

He can see his brother reworking the conversation in his head, trying to unpick the thread where it all got tangled. She was never going to give him a chance, Bobby realizes. She just wanted to dangle it there and then yank it away as soon as he jumped. It's the same thing her husband used to do with their father.

"Damn it," Jack spits, his mouth bracketed with tension.

"Forget her," Bobby says. "Fuck her."

"She's going to tank me."

"Johnny. Do you want to work for Stevenson if he keeps his balls in Mrs. Roosevelt's purse?"

This garners a weak smile.

"Let's go," Bobby says. "On to the next."

"The next" being a meeting with Stevenson himself. Bobby stands outside in the hallway and tries not to look like a student loitering between classes.

Lyndon Johnson lumbers around the corner, intent on the cigarette machine. With a flock of men following him like crows, the senator is giving what sounds like a well-rehearsed monologue about the history of the Johnson family—the Johnsons of yore used to be cattle kings; they trailed beef from Texas to sell at these very same stockyards.

"Back in those days, you could sell a steak for a tidy little profit," Johnson says. "Even bad meat, tough meat. You know why?"

The men around him hang on his words. Johnson feeds change into the machine, building suspense for the group with each *clunk* of the coin. It's the first time Bobby's seen, up close, the particular gravity of the majority leader.

Johnson frowns at the cigarette machine. "Anyone got a nickel?"

As he looks up, he sees Bobby. A giant paw swipes through the air, landing like a thunderclap on Bobby's shoulder.

"How are you sonny?" Johnson asks. "Can you spare a nickel?"

Sonny, Johnson says like he doesn't know exactly who Bobby is. It's not that he flatters himself, just that he expects a man like Lyndon Johnson to keep close tabs. Instead, Johnson acts like Bobby's a Senate page, waiting for him to come up with the coin while his hand sits heavy on Bobby's shoulder.

Bobby can smell his sweat, and the coffee on his breath, and the aftershave he used this morning leaking out through his open pores. This is the core of a convention, he thinks; it breaks men down into their component parts, skin, hair, flesh, blood.

"I don't have any change," Bobby says.

"Nothing?"

Bobby shrugs.

Johnson's eyes cool. Bobby remembers what Jack told him once about "Le Roi Lyndon," how the quickest way to get into his good graces isn't to vote for his issues or solicit his advice, but merely to call him "Leader." Deference is his toll. Pay it, and you'll be rich beyond measure. Don't, and you'll be branded the worst thing you can be in Johnson's book: Not a team player. He's aware that what he's just done is akin to an act of war.

Another man offers the change. Johnson holds up the coin.

"The reason they could make a pretty penny off of even a sick cow was that they knew what they were selling," Johnson says conspiratorially, slotting it into the machine, "but the Yanks only knew that they wanted their steak, and they wanted it now."

His audience caws with laughter.

"Supply and demand boys," Johnson says, taking his cigarettes and leading them away. "Simple as that."

Jack emerges from the Stevenson suite a moment later.

"They've offered me the nominating speech tomorrow," he says as they cruise the hallways. They've perfected a way of speaking out of the corners of their mouths.

"So you're out of contention," he says.

"I'm not out," Jack says.

"They don't give the nominating speech to someone who's being considered for the ticket."

"I may not even give the speech."

"Well which is it?"

"If they push through a strong civil rights plank for the platform, they need a Southerner to nominate him. If it's the weaker version, they need a Northerner, and I get it."

"Did you ask whether you were still being considered, speech or not?"

"They said I was."

It sounds an awful lot like waffling, but Bobby doesn't say this to Jack. He wishes he could have been in the room, listening to what Stevenson said, listening to what he didn't. The annoyance that washes over him is becoming familiar.

It's hours before the party platform is finalized. Hours before they know where they stand—to speak, or not to speak.

And then they get the word: it's the weaker civil rights plank. So Jack gets the nominating speech. Fine by him. Stevenson's people send over a draft, but it's the kind of thing you'd expect from a first-term state senator, not the party's two-time standard bearer.

"We'll have to do the whole thing over," Jack decides, looking it over in dismay.

It's one o'clock in the morning. The nominating speech is to be delivered at twelve noon. Jack dictates a new outline, then leaves Sorensen to the writing. Bobby goes to his own room, but sleep eludes him.

When he ducks back into the suite, Sorensen's marking up a draft. He knifes through sentences, filets an entire paragraph, killing the speech over and over, executing this word, anointing a new one to take its place. The intensity of his concentration has heated the room; plates of discarded food sit on the side table, sweating with grease. Sorensen nods at him in acknowledgment, still slightly wary of him even after three years working for Jack, wary of this younger brother who he sees as a copy of the father, with the father's whims and prejudices and hardline cold warrior views. Wary, but he understands they're all on the same team: Jack's team. He gestures for Bobby to sit.

"Do you think he's still in the running?" Bobby asks.

"Yes," Sorensen says, hunched forward over the page, "but only because Stevenson can't make a decision to save his life."

Should we be hitching our star to this wagon? Perhaps Bobby is his father, for his father's doubts plague him now, every reason they shouldn't ally themselves with Stevenson: Losing ticket. Taking the blame. Hurting Jack's chances down the road.

His shirt sticks to him; he pulls it away from his body and has only a moment's reprieve before it glues itself heavily back to his skin. The air conditioning unit blows tepid air into his face. He sets the stage in his mind: his brother sits across from Senator Kefauver, who'll surely be the top contender for the second spot when he loses the nomination to Stevenson. And what does Bobby want? For his brother to win?

No. For his brother to have the stage to himself.

"All this effort," he says, "just for second place."

Sorensen says, " 'The struggle itself towards the heights is enough to fill a man's heart.' "

Bobby considers this. "Whoever said that was a wuss."

"Camus," Sorensen says. "Not a wuss, just French."

In the adjoining room, Eunice is churning out BACK JACK signs on a carpet that contains at least half a century of cigarette ash. Posterboard is spread in front of her, a black marker in one hand.

"Thought you'd gone home," he says.

She grunts a response. He watches her for a moment, her hand gliding over the poster, the letters emerging in thick black capitals.

"You know we've ordered more of these from the printer," he says. "You don't have to make them."

She looks up impatiently. "When Stevenson or the press see a hundred new professionally printed signs for Jack, what do you think they're going to assume?" she asks, her voice thick with condescension. "They're going to assume—correctly—'the Kennedys have had some signs made up.' Whereas if they see people holding hand-lettered signs, they'll think it's a sign of actual support for Jack, that these people took the time out of their day to draw up a sign for him."

She's right, of course. Her brain is built for the tactical problems of politics. For a moment, he feels sad for his sister, that her talents should be relegated to this: making signs on a floor in the middle of the night. Everyone knows who Jack had to become when Joe died; less remarked upon is who Eunice became when Kick died, then Rosie went away, and she found herself the eldest girl. If she's bossy and condescending and a know-it-all, maybe it's because she thinks this is what an older sister is supposed to be. What she wishes someone were to her, still.

"We lost Eleanor Roosevelt," he says as Eunice dips a brush in a pot of glue and pastes the sign to a wooden stick. She sets it aside to dry, and pulls the next blank poster in front of her.

"I heard," she says. "I followed her into the ladies' room, actually. Thought I might convince her to give Jack another chance."

"And?" he asks with the forward lean of his body.

B A C K, she writes out, focusing intently on the letters. "I was standing there pretending to wash my hands, trying to find an opening, and she just turns to me at the other sink and goes, 'You're one of Joe Kennedy's girls, aren't you? You have that same swindler's set of the mouth. I always thought your father should sell cars.'"

They exchange a glance and then a laugh. It's only funny in the retelling; he's sure at the time Eunice had gotten that look about her that you could pull out of a freezer: eyes frozen solid, jaw clenched like a block of ice.

She sits back on her heels, capping and uncapping the marker in her hand with a little *pop*. "So then I introduced myself and she said she'd known one other Eunice and that one had been a terrible dullard. Was I a terrible dullard? And I said I didn't think so. And she told me in that case I should quit pretending to wash my hands and spit out what I'd followed her in there to say."

In the other room, Sorensen's typewriter clatters and then stops; you can hear him muttering quietly to himself, trying out a line. Then he bangs on the keys some more. *You liked her*, he thinks, looking at Eunice's face.

"I told her I wanted her to support Jack as vice president and it was ridiculous to hold the McCarthy thing against him. It was years ago. Why couldn't she let it go?"

"What did she say?"

Eunice flutters her fingers, and the tendons in the back of her hand play like piano keys.

"She said it wasn't personal, just politics. Jack made a political choice then to keep quiet on McCarthy and she was making a political choice now to remind people of it."

"Did you tell her he has a strong—"

"Liberal voting record, yes, those were the next words out of my mouth, but she sort of—" Eunice slashes the air. "Cut me off cold. She said it wasn't that she thought Jack was really for McCarthy or really for the liberals or anything else. That didn't matter to her. It's that she was afraid he didn't stand for anything."

Bobby scoffs. "I'd have punched her."

Eunice rolls her eyes. "I said if Jack could just have ten more minutes with her, I was sure he could convince her—"

She stops short. Her eyes fall back to the signs spread out in front of them.

"What?" he asks. "What did she say?"

"She said Jack had had his turn to convince her, and now it was my turn to try."

"What did you say?" he demands.

"I don't really remember—I was too angry. So I just started, I don't know, rattling off about delegates and polling and how the party was a house divided that couldn't stand unless you could find someone to walk the line between liberals and Southerners, and that all this nonsense about being too far to the left and too far to the right was bullshit because most people live in the middle, and maybe she'd prefer some liberal on the ticket but that wasn't doing the party any favors, and as much as I liked Adlai, idealism only gets you so far. And then I got to the end and she…"

"She applauded," Eunice finally says, her eyes gone lunar with the remembered praise. "She asked me if I'd ever considered running for office. She said women do now. And surely my father had the money for it."

Bobby's silent; he wants to hear his sister go on.

"I asked her how she did it—got people to take her seriously in politics—and she said her husband used to tell her that politics was just the systematic organization of different hatreds, and all I had to do was find something people hate more than women. I think she was joking of course, but…"

Eunice trails off. It's definitely there now: a glimmer of admiration has crept into his sister's voice.

"Her husband," Bobby says testily, "the man who ended our father's career."

Eunice is silent, bent over the poster, spelling out their brother's name.

"What?" he demands. "You don't actually think you could run?"

"And why couldn't I?" she bursts out. Her anger sends the marker off the page in a jagged line, ruining the poster. "What would be so crazy about that?"

Now isn't the time to start fights within their own ranks. He should make peace, he knows, but how do you make peace with a hornet's nest? Blow in a little soothing smoke?

"You know what Dad says," he offers, hands shoved deep in his pockets. "If you'd been born with a pair of balls, you'd be president."

"*If*," she snaps. "That's the defining word of my life."

She gets up and storms out, trampling over all the signs. Sorensen's typewriter goes quiet. A door slams.

So, he thinks. Now we've lost Eleanor Roosevelt and our own sister.

HE CAN'T THINK about their argument right now. It's noon; they barely make it over to the convention hall in time to get a copy to the TelePrompTer.

He remembers Jack just back from the war, in a

perpetually untucked shirt and sneakers, remembers wondering if his brother wanted a seat in Congress because he wanted it, or because it was there. And now in his Brooks Brothers suits and ties carefully selected by Jackie, it's the same question, but is it the same Jack?

Jack is given ten minutes for the speech; he uses perhaps six. Hunched over the rostrum, wreathed in smoke, he speaks on colonialism, the cracking of the grand alliance of the West, failures of Republican leadership, the dangers of the hydrogen age.

"These are critical times," Jack says. "Times that demand the best we have—times that demand the best America has."

This line demands applause, and the crowd complies willingly. But Bobby, even as he smacks his hands together with the rest of them, wonders: Is the best America has Adlai Stevenson? Is this what leadership for the atomic age looks like? A former governor who's already lost once?

"The time is ripe," Jack says. "The hour has struck. The man is here, and he is ready."

And for a moment—that line—Bobby imagines his brother's accepting something rather than giving it away.

AFTER THAT, STEVENSON'S nominated with a minimum of drama. Bobby watches him accept the nomination with a twisting feeling in his gut. When's he naming the rest of his ticket? Could be tonight. Could be tomorrow. They hear only vague, crystal-ball answers.

The hours have the drag of a heavy suitcase. Jack's cagey. He lies flat on the bed and then springs back up and paces. "It's Kefauver," he says, trying to convince himself.

Then an hour shy of midnight comes the announcement: Stevenson's throwing the selection of his vice president to the convention.

It's over, is Bobby's first thought. It has to be over because they're not prepared for this. A part of him is relieved. Then he looks at Jack, sitting on the edge of the bed with an expression Bobby remembers from childhood. Jack used to make a game of guessing which way his father would pass the meat at dinnertime, deciding every night whether to sit on the old man's left or right in order to get the first bloody slice instead of whatever stringy bits were left at the end, after it had made its way around an entire table of ravenous siblings. And it's that same hunger on his face now.

He looks at his brother, and his brother doesn't look beat.

"He didn't want to choose," Bobby says. "It amounts to support for Kefauver."

"Or he wants me but doesn't want to offend Kefauver," Jack counters. He sits forward, and through his shirt, Bobby can see the outline of his back brace.

"Kefauver already has hundreds of delegates in his pocket."

"He's too liberal on civil rights. The Southerners hate him. We can win their support."

"In twelve hours?"

Jack stands and shrugs back on his suit jacket. " 'If we live, we live to tread on kings.' " His shirt collar sticks out, but he doesn't seem to notice.

Bobby pushes a hand through his hair. They were prepared to woo Stevenson, not delegates. No one can deny Jack's had an outsize role at the convention, but does this a vice president make? All his instincts warn him against it.

And yet if anyone can do it, it's his brother, who's something like a myth to him, and something like a man. Just once, he'd like to push a car down the driveway with his brother. He shrugs off his jacket and rolls up his shirtsleeves.

"You'd better call Dad," Jack says.

"*I'd* better?" he asks, but he's already dialing.

Ted answers. "Shit," his brother breathes, understanding in an instant. "You're going for it?"

"Can you get Dad?"

"Your funeral."

Bobby holds the receiver a foot away from his ear and his father's voice is still clearly audible. He expects the phone to start smoking. When the connection's lost, he doesn't try to call back.

Jack peeks his head in the door.

"I don't think he's pleased," Bobby says, dialing another number for another Kennedy.

Eunice picks up on the fourth ring. "We're going for it," he says. "We need you."

A long, deciding, deliberate pause. "I'll be there in ten minutes," she says, their feud temporarily shelved. "Who do you want me to talk to first?"

Some brothers scheme to throw house parties, to borrow an expensive car without asking, to take a trip to that part of town their parents don't like. These brothers scheme how to win the second highest office in the land.

Bobby instructs the others: Find whoever you can. Get them on our side. These are the only orders he can give.

THEY SPLIT UP to cover more ground, trawling for delegates in the wee hours of the morning. The streets are rotten with Kefauver people, Humphrey people— Humphrey making a play for it, give him a break.

He imagines his father running through the same Chicago night twenty years ago. Not running—that's not his father's style. He slows the Ambassador down to a dignified lope. That year, the convention had been split three ways: Roosevelt, Garner, Smith. Enough people were skeptical of Roosevelt's internationalist tendencies—nobody wanted to be pulled back into Europe's problems—to cause gridlock. The Roosevelt people were turning frantic, unable to get through to

William Randolph Hearst, the newspaper mogul powerful enough to block Roosevelt's nomination. Hearst wouldn't answer any of the Roosevelt people's calls, refused to meet with them.

But Joe Kennedy was an old friend. Joe Kennedy brought Hearst around, and Roosevelt got his nomination.

Bobby bursts into a bar, the most likely place for delegates at this hour. Here's his Hearst: a man picking idly through a bowl of bar nuts, a beer half-gone in his other hand.

"I'm Robert Kennedy," Bobby says. "Will you support my brother for vice president?"

"Hate the cashews," the man says, plucking out the offending nuts. Bobby supposes this is the closest to a rapt audience he's going to get.

He starts on his spiel: Jack's accomplishments in the space of thirty seconds. But the man holds up a hand.

"Already committed to Kefauver," he says. The hard sound of a peanut between his back teeth.

Bobby starts to turn away, but then he spins back.

"Why Kefauver?" he asks.

"He sent me a Christmas card," the man says.

Bobby almost collides with Ken on his way out of the bar.

"No luck," Bobby says.

"Where should we try next?" Ken asks.

"The urinals," he says, only half-joking. That's American politics at its core: a mad scramble in the dark. An impromptu conversation with another man as he tries to take a piss.

He picks up his pace.

IMPOSSIBLE TO SAY how much progress they've made by morning. He hears a version of his story from all but Eunice, who brags that Delaware is in the bag.

"A woman asking to see them in the dead of night," he says. "I wonder what your secret was."

When the balloting begins, he leaves his brother in the hotel room, looking slightly the worse for wear. It's been a long night. A night full of mistakes. They left Carmine De Sapio, the New York political boss with almost a hundred delegates, waiting for half an hour. Jack nearly tripped over television wires into a Kefauver press conference. They're all exhausted. Jack's hands flutter, moving from his hair to the television remote to his socks.

"Don't come down until it's certain," Bobby says, and Jack nods distantly, more a motion of the eyes than the head. Nothing more embarrassing than drinking the wine of victory prematurely or more foolish than conceding before you have to.

The convention floor is a bovine mass, a cattle call of men. Sweating, smoking, yelling. The Kefauver people are many. The Kennedy people are young.

The balloting begins with Alabama.

First ballots aren't where you win—they're for narrowing the field. The goal now is only to keep in contest with Kefauver, hope he doesn't make it to 687. It irks him again, Jack running for second place.

He and O'Donnell bull-rush McClellan, begging him for the Arkansas delegation.

Bobby's boss raises a brow. "How long have you been awake, boys?"

"Which way are your delegates leaning?"

"My delegates aren't leaning any which way," McClellan says.

"Can we talk to them?"

"No," McClellan says, and he feels temporarily stung. "But only because they're not my delegates, as a senator. They're Governor Faubus's."

This is something they should have known. Something Kefauver certainly does. McClellan places a hand on Bobby's shoulder.

"You've got to do the work beforehand. You can't let a little good press convince you you're a viable candidate and then go running around like chickens with your heads cut off."

McClellan's right. All they can hope for now is momentum; that elusive convention magic that can topple a clear winner, the fever and frenzy undoing months of someone else's work in one fell swoop.

As the balloting continues, Bobby moves from delegation to delegation, telling whoever will listen what they want to hear. Strong on civil rights, he promises New York. Good with labor, he assures Pennsylvania. Moderate on civil rights, he tells South Carolina.

His voice creaks out of his throat. Next time, he's thinking—but he cuts himself off.

Suddenly Georgia of all places is pledging her delegates to Kennedy.

They've stolen one of Kefauver's Southern neighbors. O'Brien wallops him on the shoulder as he runs by. Upstairs, Jack runs a finger over and over the scorched mark in the arm of the chair from a cigarette put out long ago. A blip, or a pattern?

Not long after, Louisiana goes to Kennedy, too.

A two-man race. If Humphrey and Gore withdraw, delegations will start to switch. More votes—how many more?—will be released for the Kennedy camp to wolf down.

The words of someone in the Oklahoma delegation— he doesn't know who, but he'll make it a point to find out—float to him over the noise of the floor. "Never Kennedy," the voice says, loud and wanting to be heard. "He's not our kind of folks."

Heat floods his head. *To them we'll always be Irish.*

Bobby runs on.

GIVE US THE SOUTH, he's praying as the second ballot begins. *Give us the South and I'll be good for a year.*

Kefauver has strength in the West and Midwest. If they can piece together the South, the Northeast—

"They want him, Bob!" O'Donnell hauls onto the floor, two bright spots of red flaring in his cheeks. He was at a nearby bar, grabbing a beer as the first ballot wound down. "Every guy in there was cheering for Kennedy," he says. "Every truck driver, every cop— you'd have thought we were in East Boston."

"Good," Bobby says. "So he's picked up support with drunks."

As the second ballot begins, though, Kefauver takes an early lead. Pulling so far ahead, it seems over already. Whatever steam they gathered on the first ballot is just that: hot air, dissolving. Upstairs, Jack ties his shoes for the third time.

Seeing it slip away, Bobby stops trying to sweet-talk delegates and snaps at them instead, "What did Kefauver ever do for you?" The dull trickle of minds moving toward the safe choice. Indignant, he almost trades fists with a California delegate who looks at him the wrong way; Ken points him to the exit: *Get some air.*

It's ten degrees cooler off the floor. For the first time, he allows his exhaustion to hit him.

Eunice comes storming around the corner barefoot, holding her shoes in one hand, the better to run.

"What are you doing?" she snaps. "Get your ass back in there."

"It's over," he says, slumped against the wall.

He understands now—the scales falling from his eyes—precisely how amateur their operation is. They who run around passing messages via human telephone while the Kefauver people stroll by with shiny black walkie-talkies. They who are known for their sleek political machine and precise campaigning exposed as boys playing at being men. They who don't know where the levers of power lie at this level, much less how to push them. And for this, he can't blame Stevenson.

She pushes him hard on the shoulder. "The Southerners hate Kefauver. Everyone I've talked to this week has said as much. Stop wasting your time on New York and New Jersey and focus on the South."

She fixes him with a gaze. The distant thunder of the men on the floor; closer, the ticking second hand of her wristwatch. He sees it in her eyes: Don't you dare waste what I'd kill for.

Back on the floor, the energy has changed. Like a hive starting to swarm. No, like a herd starting to stampede. Panicked animals running in the same direction.

Eunice was right; Kefauver's enemies have caught up to him. The South is switching or sticking with Kennedy, and Bobby's there to urge them on. Then New York and New Jersey abandon Mayor Wagner one after the other for Kennedy. For the first time all day, they're ahead, 402.5 for Kennedy to Kefauver's 245.5.

He sees Eunice back in the stands now, looking like she might at any moment hurdle the railing and drop to the convention floor. Even Jackie cheers, waving a STEVENSON FOR PRESIDENT sign.

Lyndon Johnson steps to the podium.

He leans over the rostrum with hands as broad as

Bibles. Texas, he announces, will give her delegates to "The fighting senator who wears the scars of battle… John Kennedy of Massachusetts!"

Now the switching begins. Suddenly everyone wants to be with Kennedy. Kentucky asks to be recognized—they switch their votes to Kennedy. North Carolina follows suit, recasting half of their votes for Kennedy, too.

They're forty votes shy of the whole thing. Bobby's throat goes dry; his heart is making an escape from his chest. He tries to yell for Kennedy, but no sound comes out. His voice is gone.

Upstairs, Sorensen offers Jack a hand in congratulation. Jack waves him off. Not yet. He knits his fingers together and leans toward the television.

Call for a recess, Bobby silently begs. Call for a recess, then on the third ballot we can win. A frenzy is setting in, a force beyond their control. The sudden support for Kennedy is generating a backlash—some Kefauver delegate elbows him hard in the ribs as he passes. The Kennedy fever is morphing, being matched, the crowd churning. For every action, an equal and opposite reaction.

Tennessee asks to be recognized. They switch their delegates to Kefauver. A recess! A recess!, Bobby thinks. My kingdom for a recess! They're hemorrhaging votes. Oklahoma eagerly switches to Kefauver, followed in rapid succession by Minnesota and Missouri.

And it slips away just like that.

Jack's fingers dig into the arm of the chair.

Bobby finds a phone. Says, "I think you'd better get down here."

SAY THAT, TO EVERYONE ELSE, Jack looks like an excellent loser. Say that he looks glamorous and gracious as he stands up there on the podium, blue banners draped over the stand, delivering an off-the-cuff concession speech and throwing his support to Senator Kefauver with humor, with charm. Say that even before he dismounts the stand, there's a rumor moving through the crowd, a rumor that sounds like *Kennedy in '60*, except Bobby isn't really listening.

He's watching the spring loaded behind each of his brother's gestures, the way Jack has to spit out his smile, the anger in his stride as he descends to the floor again.

At the inn, Jack climbs onto the bed trying to find a spot where he'll be seen above all the Kennedy people clogging the room as he thanks them for their hard work. Jackie—is it possible the Kennedy competitiveness has gotten to her?—sheds a single, angry tear.

When the others have finally cleared out and they're alone again in the hotel room, anger makes them switch places. Jack grows hot; Bobby, cold. Jack whips his tie off and flings it to the ground, pacing the room with dark utterances that could strip the paint off the walls.

Bobby sits, selects a pen. Scribbles, from memory, each state, their delegation count, the number for

Kefauver, the number for Kennedy. Jack pours himself a drink but doesn't drink it, only presses the curved edge of the glass to the hollow of his closed eye.

"I fucking hate losing," Jack says at last, the words puckered with venom.

Losing. That word that's almost forbidden in their house.

"Stevenson will lose to Eisenhower," Bobby says. "Kefauver will lose with him. You walk away with national recognition and no harm done." He's surprised at the cool logic to his words. You tell the Candidate what he needs to hear, you convince him this was all for the best, and then you, the Campaign Manager, find a way to make it so.

Jack, still entombed in anger, seems hardly to hear him. His only spotlight now is the pale light through the window.

"Joe would have won," Jack says quietly.

Bobby doesn't know what to say, so he says nothing. He thinks of cattle as far as the eye can see. That feeling he had during the nominating speech comes back to him, picturing, for a moment, a different candidate, a different campaign. *Sooner or later* and *Someday* are for other men. *Now,* he's thinking. *Now we'll have to.* He rolls a piece of paper slowly into a tube, tapping it against one knee as he thinks. He wants to remember this feeling, because to remember it is to learn from it. He holds it close enough to feel its pulse.

"I wanted it," Jack says, his voice tight, "but this

whole week…I wanted it and at the same time I felt…" He shakes his head, searching for the word.

"Impatient," Bobby supplies. It's what he felt walking onto the floor that first day. Impatient all this wasn't theirs yet.

Jack looks at him, and nods slowly. Bobby hears the *click* of another drawer unlocking.

Some brothers would pat themselves on the back for coming so close. For some brothers, to try is enough. But these brothers look at each other, and they think the same thought:

"Never again," Jack says.

"Never again," Bobby agrees.

PART II

1956–1959

CHAPTER 16

The Next Campaign

HOT AND CLOSE, the August night clings to him as he drives, pushing eighty. The windows are down to wake him up, and then kept down because the wind against his skin proves, somehow, that he's real, that he's here. The trees on the side of the road are Wizard of Oz trees; they run up to the edge of the pavement and then freeze when he looks at them. He keeps thinking he sees something up ahead about to dart into the road; someone's dog who jumped the fence. Someone's dog he's about to kill.

It's been a week since the DNC, and he thought they were done losing. He thought he and Jack said "Never again" the way you prick your fingers and promise in blood.

When the phone rang, he figured it would be someone in need of help on the campaign trail looking for a boost from the newest star of the Democratic Party. Some journalist wanting to know what the senator's planning next. When the phone rang, his mind went to politics.

But it wasn't about Jack. It was Jackie. In labor; being rushed to the hospital; hemorrhaging. Can't be, he thought. Women like her don't bleed.

Muscle memory kicked in from his small black pile of tragedies. He got the name of the hospital. He got his keys.

"Where is she?" he demands of the nurse in the ER. "What happened?"

"Perhaps you'd like to speak to the doctor, Senator Kennedy?" He doesn't bother to correct her mistake.

"Is she all right? Is the baby—?"

Her eyes say enough. She doesn't want to be the one to tell him. He repeats himself; he shows no mercy.

"Mrs. Kennedy is resting," the nurse says. And as for the child: "Stillborn."

He remembers his lessons on the limbo of infants. The purgatory for the innocents. He always pictured the beach on a gray day, the sand dull, the water dark and fitful, no houses in sight, just the wind through the reeds and so many small souls scattered like shells.

"Are you sure?" he asks, and the nurse nods helplessly.

Jackie's mother waylays him outside of the room.

Her lips are bright red; the color of a skinned knee. "Oh Bobby," she says, gripping his shoulder. "It's just awful, isn't it? Have they told you?"

He tries to brush past her, but she refuses to be ignored. His brain turns to static and he looks at Janet and he wonders: Who hears that their daughter's in the hospital and takes the time to put on lipstick?

"It's just awful," she repeats. She wants him to ask her how she is. He obliges, if only to end the conversation sooner.

"We were all so excited! Now—" She shakes her head as if it's too terrible to say. Says it anyway: "Now I'll have to go all the way into the city to return what I bought the baby."

He pats her on the back clumsily. Reaches deep within himself for a well of sympathy.

"Why don't you get some rest?" he suggests.

Janet nods; she was hoping he would say this. She clutches at him with cold hands. "She hasn't come out of the anesthesia yet," she says. "Someone will have to tell her."

WHEN HIS FIRST CHILD was born, Ethel's hospital room was filled with balloons and flowers and his siblings all playing with the rubbery end of his daughter's nose, joking that she was about the size of a football if anyone wanted to get a little exercise.

This room is only an imitation of a real space. Something poorly drawn from memory. Where there should be a pink, glowing mother there's only a woman. Flat, gray, unconscious. Her hair still damp with sweat at her temples. He sits here with the body of his brother's wife.

Every time his mother gave birth, his father gave her a piece of jewelry. When Joe was born, before the Ambassador had made all his money, it was a single silver hairpin. For Teddy, she picked out a diamond and ruby bracelet that cost as much as a car. His mother showed him once what she chose for his birth: a golden brooch inlaid with mother-of-pearl and turquoise. "The jeweler told me this was his most exclusive design," she explained, proud of her own good taste, although he's never seen her wear it.

An emergency caesarean section, the doctor told him in the hall, also mistaking him for Jack. We did everything we could, he kept saying, probably trying to fend off a malpractice suit. Don't worry, Bobby could have told him. We're not going to sue. My old man won't want to draw any more attention to this.

He sits and waits for Jackie to wake up, listening to the lisp of the clock's second hand as it sweeps around, piling minutes on top of each other. It feels like a violation to look at her unguarded face, so he looks only at her hands resting on top of the bedcovers. There's something he forgot, he realizes.

He calls the nurse back in. "Was it a girl or a boy?" he asks, expecting the answer to clarify things for him one way or the other.

"A girl," the nurse says. It doesn't clarify anything.

Jackie comes out of sleep slowly, confused.

"Bobby?" she asks.

He doesn't want to be the one you call to deliver terrible news. But he's here, so he must be; he's here, so he is.

He takes her hand. He tells her quietly. He waits at any moment to taste red in the back of his throat, but it never comes.

She blinks twice. It's like this: if you were looking at a marble statue and suddenly saw a flicker of life behind the stone, just a twitch of a cheek, just a glance of the eyes.

"Does Jack know?" Her voice scrapes against him.

His brother is on a yacht somewhere in the long blue neck of the Mediterranean, slinking out of the public eye for a spell before the strategizing begins anew. He left right after the DNC, left his heavily pregnant wife who asked him not to go. Worse, he took Teddy with him. They both know what that means: Ted, young, unmarried, and a known playboy, provides perfect cover for when Jack wants other women around.

"He's at the airport," Bobby lies.

"There was so much blood," she says. It's how these stories always start, or end. Her eyes are all pupil. "It was like the beaches at Normandy." She's trying to make him laugh.

"Try not to think about it," he says.

Maybe this is terrible advice. Maybe he should be

telling her to pour it all out now because his brother has no room for the bleak and bitter emotions: Grief. Sorrow. Despair. Instead, Jack pretends they don't exist. Bobby learned this long ago; he learned this when Joe died and Jack carried on like nothing had happened, regaling friends on the front porch long into the night, their laughter bouncing across the yard until the Ambassador hauled open his window and yelled down to Jack, "Have some respect for your brother!"

After that: the sound of car engines pulling away.

"What did he say on the phone?" she asks.

"Not much. He was in a rush."

"Your father told me—before we got married— your father said, 'Jack's the kind of boy who can love the whole world without ever loving another person.' And I thought, well that can't be true. I see how he is with you all. But he turns into someone else some- times, doesn't he?"

"Can I do anything?" he asks.

"You're always doing something," she says. She wets her lips with effort. "You can distract me from this hor- rible room."

He tells her a story he would tell his children: when he and his siblings were young, they would fill the salt- water pool at Palm Beach with creatures from the sea. Star fish. Pompano flashing in the sun. Once even a small nurse shark the size of Teddy with a hide that looked like the bottom of a fountain, dappled with sil- ver, a tail like a feather. They kept it in there for a week, feeding it with other fish, watching it swim in circles, reaching out a hand to try and touch that peculiar skin, rough when you were expecting something cold and smooth.

"What happened to it?" she asks. Her eyes are closed. The track of a tear runs from each corner, down her cheeks, wetting the hollow of her throat.

"We let it go," he says.

But he can't remember what actually happened. Which image is more believable, a group of children hustling a flopping shark down the beach to set it loose in the ocean, or a groundskeeper scooping its body out of the pool and into a black garbage bag to leave at the curb with the rest of the trash?

He feeds change into the phone in the lobby. He calls his father; the old man listens as Bobby explains in terse, telegram sentences.

"Should we tell him?" Bobby asks.

Eventually they'll have to, his father says. But now—right now? To have him come back when Jackie is a woman, burning? He's only just won the national limelight; rumors of marital problems would—he stops himself.

"What do you think?" his father asks.

He thinks if Jack's in the room with her, he's liable to be turned to stone by a single glance. But he also thinks:

"If he doesn't come back, he's going to lose the vote of every wife and mother in the country."

"Holyhood," his father says at last. The cemetery where they have the family plot. "Make the arrangements."

He understands then that he's picked up another part of his brother to be responsible for.

When he returns, Janet's taken his seat. Her daughter is asleep again.

"It's nice that one Kennedy could be bothered to get out of bed," she says. After a moment, she stands and leaves—he thinks she only came in here to say this to him.

He flicks off the lamp, plunging the room into a twilight of hospital room instrumentation. Jackie's voice comes out of the darkness: not asleep after all.

"Ruthless Bobby," she says. "But they don't know you like we do."

JACKIE'S LITTLE SISTER, Lee, arrives not long after, laying claim to Jackie's room, guarding her sister jealously, like a dragon guards its clutch of treasure. The steps and halves come next: Jackie's favorite, Yusha. Nina. Little Janet and James. Eventually Ethel, Jean, and Steve arrive. Four Kennedys in total now, but none of the ones who count.

"Jack?" Ethel asks.

"On his way," Bobby says, and this time it's the truth.

"Press outside," Steve says quietly. "Mostly Boston papers."

Bobby's impressed that his brother-in-law is here,

that he's identified the reporters, that he understands this is something Bobby might like to know. Can't help the comparison in his mind: if Shriver were here, he'd be out angling to make a statement. Lawford would be off flirting with the nurses.

He goes to the bathroom to splash cold water on his face. Lee follows him in.

"This is the men's," he says, hunched over the sink, testing the water with his fingers. Lukewarm. The faucets are gear-shaped and silver. They throw back his reflection, maimed.

"She won't say it, so I will," Lee says, and he thinks, *Oh good*.

"We're going to the press. And we're going to tell them all about your brother—every rotten detail."

He can't blame her for the attempt. He'd be doing the same if it were his sister.

"Who will you go to?" he asks.

"*Time. Life*. Whoever wants to print it."

"My father is old friends with Henry Luce—who you may know happens to run *Time* and *Life*. So no luck there—who else?"

He tests the water again, feigning boredom, knowing this will get under her skin. Maybe it's cruel of him, but right now he wants to be cruel.

"*The New York Times*," she says. "I know plenty of journalists over there."

"My father's golfing buddies with their New York bureau chief, so you go right ahead."

Jackie's face has a softness that Lee's is missing; the little sister bloodless, bone and wire. It's like someone gave an artist the same description of a woman but told him to draw one like a rose, the other like a thorn.

"She thinks you're the sweet one," Lee says. "Boy have you got her fooled. I told her there isn't a human one in the bunch. They walk and talk but there's nothing behind their eyes, no pulse. Tin men, all of them."

The water at last runs cold.

He splashes it against his skin, runs a hand through his hair.

"Are you done?" he asks, yanking a paper towel from the dispenser.

"I just hope your precious papa can afford to keep her around," Lee says. "I can tell you this: it's going to take more than an apology from your brother."

The bathroom door clangs shut behind her. He crushes the paper towel in one fist and sends the pulp into the wastebin.

JACK'S ALWAYS BEEN the late one. Not that the rest of them are punctual. But Jack—he puts his own spin on it. As kids, he was the one coming in halfway through meals, the last into the car every time they tried to go somewhere, the one still trying to find a jacket while the rest of them were dressed for Mass. Because he was late meeting them back at the front gates of the club pool and their mother would leave without him, Jack would be the one who caught rides home with the mailman. Punctuality is next to godliness, that was always her rationale for leaving him behind, or something like it.

It was like his mother and Jack were playing some game of chess with each other, both of them the black pieces, both of them the rooks. Hard to say who won—his mother, pulling triumphantly out of the parking lot at exactly three o'clock, or Jack, sloping off the mail truck with a stack of letters under one arm and a wet towel around his neck an hour later. His mother with the power to set the rules, Jack with the power to break them, one by one.

Entering the hospital, his brother telegraphs discontent down to his stride, which bites against the linoleum, resounding with the report of a rifle. His eyes today are gray and humorless—they make you think of sharp things in unexpected places: thumbtacks hidden in the carpet. He runs a hand through his hair, the only sign that someone is in there. He disappears into Jackie's room without so much as a glance at the rest of them. Lee exits a moment later, shooting a withering glare at Bobby.

Teddy stumbles in with his hair half sticking up—"Does anyone have any cash? The taxi driver—" He gestures helplessly.

Steve is on his feet before Bobby can move. "I'll handle it," he says, and motions for Teddy to take his chair. The door to Jackie's room snicks shut.

"He told the driver to run every light," Ted says. "If

it started to turn, 'Go through it, go through it. I'll pay for the fines.'"

Bobby thinks it's too late for this to count for much. "Any press at the airport?" he asks.

"He bit their head off," Ted says. "They tried to ask him about the convention and he just lit into them."

Jack emerges from the room sometime later with a jaw like iron and a gaze to match. With a flick of his head, he commands Bobby to follow.

"She thinks it was the convention," Jack tells him, palming a Styrofoam cup of lukewarm coffee, giving a hard look to the liquid inside. "She thinks it was politics. 'All of your insanity,' she's calling it. Did she say anything to you?"

He weighs whether or not to tell his brother how the little sister tried to blackmail him in the bathroom. He decides not to; his brother isn't seeking honesty. Jack's haggard beneath his tan, as if wearing the suit of a healthy person over someone pale and tired. His brother is seeking absolution.

"I talked to the doctors," Bobby says. "They don't know why it happened. Some women just have a harder time with it."

"Maybe it's me," Jack says wryly. "Maybe I'm not meant to be a father." He slumps against the wall, pressing a hand to his forehead. "We would have called her Arabella," he says, and Bobby thinks of a tiny pink music-box ballerina. Then Jack straightens up. "I want to see her," he says.

This time Bobby leads.

The morgue attendant greets them quietly, pulls Bobby to the side.

"There's a chapel through there," he gestures. "We could have the baby brought in. Sometimes it's easier—"

Bobby shakes his head. No use for his brother. No sugarcoating. Give him the facts as they are.

Afterward, Jack's quiet on the elevator back up. "Will you pray for her?" he asks Bobby eventually, studying the dial as it ticks past floors. "It won't mean anything coming from me."

"Of course."

"I'm sorry Johnny," Bobby adds—quietly—because these things aren't usually said out loud, not in their family.

The iron returns to his brother's jaw, to his words.

"We just—" Jack starts. Falters. Tries again. "We just have to keep going."

MAKE THE ARRANGEMENTS, his father said; the arrangements are made. Ethel goes with him to pick out the casket.

She surveils the pint-sized boxes on display. Turns to the funeral home attendant. "How do you do this for a living?" she asks.

The burial is this: the priest in his white vestments. White for innocence. Innocence for children. The rest of them stand there with their grubby souls, impure, faces drawn. Everyone is here except Pat, still recovering from her own delivery a few days before. It's good she didn't come; her baby is a healthy little girl. Seeing her would only rub salt in a fresh wound.

There are no tears. No harsh words. None of the emotion from the hospital has carried over. These things aren't for other people to see. But the rifts are still there, if you look closely—the Kennedys on one side of the grave, Jackie huddled between her mother and sister on the other.

It's August—too hot for mourning. They shift, graveside, trying to edge into the shade as the first of their number makes use of the family plot. Kick buried in England. Joe's remains never recovered. The first Kennedy they bury is a baby girl they never knew. For once, he's not trying to catch Jackie's eye. Jack is somewhere above them all. Bobby thinks to take his pulse.

Right now, at Bobby's instruction, there are movers dismantling the nursery in his brother's house. Disappearing the crib. Ridding the house of what was expected.

Summer is ending; over.

The priest says his words and the Kennedys say, "Amen."

SAINT BOBBY, JACKIE STARTS calling him, but the Stevenson people have other names. They correctly assume that he's here to further the Kennedy cause, not theirs.

A stint with Stevenson was decided upon for Bobby

even before they left Chicago. They need to understand from the inside how a national campaign works, so Jack's sent him here, into the heart of the beast. He makes no attempt to hide his endless note-taking, no effort to win the friendship of the others on the campaign. He's an interloper at the back of the bus, a blue eye, watching.

They swing through the Midwest, the towns that become critical only near an election. Bobby writes down the groups Stevenson speaks before, possible contacts, privately rating the former governor's effectiveness.

Today he sits on the train tracks, his arms around his knees, studying the gathered crowd, trying to gauge their interest. Stevenson speaks from the rear of a train, a stack of flat white notecards in one hand. Get him on TV, Bobby thinks. Less of this golden age of the Republic whistlestop nonsense, more commercials.

Stevenson's doing a refrain on nuclear armaments, warning about the danger of war in this age, and living forever in the shadow of a radioactive mushroom cloud. The crowd shifts from one collective leg to the other. They use campaign pamphlets as fans. It's another instance of wrong place, wrong time: Stevenson speaks about tax hikes to the mothers of veterans, segregation to coal miners. Knowing your audience is more important than knowing your speech. It's why Jack highlights his war record in blue-collar districts and his travels abroad when speaking on foreign affairs.

Adlai pounds one fist against the railing of the train car, and the gesture rings hollow. It's hard to pass off a phrase like "As nuclear fission broke the pattern of science, so atomic explosion may break the pattern of history" with real conviction.

Arthur Schlesinger, one of Stevenson's speechwriters, is unmistakable in an electric green bowtie, watching the delivery carefully. He's written this speech, or part of it. Schlesinger—famous historian father, himself the author of numerous books—is the mold of a Stevenson man: undoubtedly liberal, Ivy League educated, unashamedly pretentious.

"Not bad," Schlesinger says afterward in a moment of self-congratulation. To Bobby's surprise, they turn to him. Sometimes, he's the Voice of Catholic America, and they'll quiz him on different saints, but today they want to know what he thought of the speech.

"He should speak off the cuff," Bobby says. "It'll make him seem more sincere."

This was the wrong thing to say. The mood shifts instantly.

"Is that right?" Schlesinger asks.

He's hit a nerve. Maybe they suspected as much themselves. He's heard them complain about the hours on end Stevenson spends moving sentences around in a speech, time that could be better spent elsewhere. As he leaves, he hears Schlesinger mutter something about McCarthy. His other role: Bobby the Antichrist, because he worked for McCarthy once for a whole six months.

In spite of the loyalty of Adlai's men, Bobby can feel it: Stevenson's campaign won't work. He's capable of real eloquence—but his scheduled appearances are often delayed, the result of constant deliberation on his remarks. That photograph of Stevenson from his last campaign—a hole in the bottom of his shoe. Such a humble man. Such simple tastes. This is who he wants to be to the electorate: a new Abraham Lincoln, orator of the Plains.

But what happens when you stack this against Eisenhower, pretty words versus military might? Stevenson should be on the offensive—against a popular incumbent, you have no choice but to attack. He should be doing everything he can to strike a contrast that cuts in his favor: remind people of Eisenhower's subterfuge in Indochina. Remind them of the economy. Instead, Stevenson polishes his rhetoric until he can see his reflection in it.

Bobby calls Jack periodically, always from whatever hotel is across the street. Jack is campaigning, too—nominally for Stevenson, though his speeches would suggest otherwise. The references to Adlai are loose footnotes, a vague gesture at the end. The speeches are about Jack's issues, Jack's interests—colonialism, the Soviets, America's global position.

And through it all, Jackie remains in Washington.

CHAPTER 17

The Shape of Power

IT'S LATE BY THE TIME THEY LEAVE Libertyville the next day, and the bus is nearly full. He drops into his usual seat at the back.

A presence to his left; Arthur Schlesinger stands in the aisle. Bobby gestures for him to sit.

They hit every pothole on their way out of town. Forget surgery, Jack needed one ride through middle America to realign his back. Bobby thinks of the Jeeps of Tajikistan with open tops and no seatbelts, getting thrown to the floor every so often when they hit a rut, providing comic relief for his Soviet chaperones.

He uses the scant light from the window to read dispatches from the subcommittee.

Before the convention, Clark Mollenhoff, a journalist, had come to see him with a lead he swore would make Bobby's head spin. A Detroit labor boss, high up in the Teamsters union, but operating like a mobster.

"Intimidation or money," Mollenhoff told him. "Those are the only two languages Jimmy Hoffa speaks. His local union—they get new members to enroll by telling them they'll blow up their trucks if they don't."

As chief counsel, Bobby's gotten used to it, the flow of journalists in and out of his office with investigations they swear will be *headlines for years*. He'd brushed Mollenhoff off, didn't think their committee was the proper avenue for investigating labor, had never heard of Hoffa. But he's decided to turn his attention to the Teamsters after all, the truckers and warehouse workers with a finger on every aspect of American life, from the delivery of milk to the hauling of freight. After the convention, Mollenhoff had caught him on his way out. "Kefauver did his crime investigations years ago and it got him enough clout to kick your ass."

Past the haze of fury, a cold logic had kicked in. "Come see me in Washington," he'd told Mollenhoff.

Since then, Bobby's sent his investigators to retrieve Jimmy Hoffa's tax records and they've come back with a reported income that far exceeds the salary he's paid by the union. Perhaps more suspect than what they've found is what they haven't; for his various business dealings, Hoffa only ever uses cash. There are no records of anything.

After a while, he gives up on trying to read in the flashes of streetlight. Schlesinger holds his own papers only an inch from his nose as he squints to make out the print.

"Do you want to switch?" Bobby asks. "There might be a bit more light over here."

"That's all right," Schlesinger says. "I think it's hopeless either way."

To speak or to fall away into being strangers again. They weigh their options.

"I liked Stevenson's acceptance speech at the convention," Bobby lies. He thought it was, like most of Stevenson's speeches, too lofty, condescending, full of words but not conviction. "Did you write that?"

"Parts of it." Schlesinger tilts toward him by a degree. "Your brother was fantastic," he says.

Bobby nods his head in thanks.

"I was sorry to hear about his—and Mrs. Kennedy's—loss."

"Yes," Bobby says, searching Schlesinger's voice for any malice, any trace of a rumor about the senator yachting while his wife was in the hospital.

Nothing. Nothing but honest sympathy. Is he already so jaded that he finds this hard to believe?

He turns the conversation back to politics. He and Schlesinger agree on the important matters, namely their party's most convincing argument for the White

House: If Eisenhower has another heart attack, do you really want *Nixon* as your president?

"What makes a good president, in your opinion?" Bobby asks him. Surely a man who makes a living as a historian has an answer he can use.

Schlesinger tilts his head to the side. "If you take Roosevelt for example—he had a way of using the best in the people around him. A personal magnetism; he could be sadistically charming with the press. Every man in the room believed they knew him best."

Yes, Bobby thinks. His father was one of them.

"But above all," Schlesinger says, "he understood the shape of power."

"The shape?"

"Yes, yes. That's all politics is. A shape. A system. Take the presidency, for example: a web."

"I'd think it was a cone," he says. "Power radiating out from a point."

"No, no," Schlesinger says. "No move can be made by the president without shaking and stirring the remotest fibers and tendrils of the whole thing."

He pictures Eisenhower's head atop an arachnid body. There's something to help you sleep at night.

"But then any movement of the web will also shake him," Bobby says.

"Precisely," Schlesinger says. "This interconnectedness is at once the greatest strength and consummate weakness of the presidency. In order to exist in such a system, to keep the web intact, the people around him must subordinate their needs, their lives, to his, which breeds either fanaticism or envy."

"Which is better?"

"Both are fatal. After six months, every Cabinet officer becomes a natural enemy of the president for exactly this reason. They've either become devoted to him, in which case they're too blinded by his wants and his agenda to help him see the country objectively anymore, or they want to replace him."

"So Stalin may have had a point with his purges?" he asks, and Schlesinger laughs.

"From what you know of Roosevelt," Bobby asks, "does he seem to have been destined for it all along?" Maybe what he's really asking is: Do we have any say in it?

"The Greeks believed that character is destiny," Schlesinger says. "Whatever happens to you happens because of who you are."

He doesn't know whether to be reassured; you shouldn't ask these questions on an American highway at night. You end up thinking about your whole life.

After this, the silent animosity stops. Occasionally he and Schlesinger sit together again on days the bus is full. They're not friends; there's no such thing in politics. But nor are they enemies. This is perhaps the best Bobby can hope for.

CHAPTER 18

The Loneliest Place

FUNNY TRICK OF THE AMERICAN election system, that you enter the hardest stretch of campaigning as the world turns cold, as it tilts away from the sun. You race against daylight hours. You hope the electorate can be enticed out of their homes in the evenings with the promise of average coffee and a chance to see you speak.

They call politics nothing but a popularity contest, but it's not so simple as that. Politics isn't who voters like the most, but who makes them feel the most. To inspire a feeling—how do you do such a thing? He suspects you're either born with it, or not.

He watches the candidate—this candidate.

He'll give Stevenson this, at least: he's good in

small groups. When a woman, impressed with Stevenson's speech, tells him that every thinking American will vote for him now, Stevenson says, "That isn't enough—I need a majority." When Bobby explains to the others that Saint Anthony is for finding things, Stevenson, passing by, says, "Let's hope he can find me some votes." Not a skill to be underestimated—not when campaign stops are just as often a dozen people in a town hall as they are a packed auditorium.

He watches the men around Stevenson. Who's the person that tells him "no?" For Jack, it's Bobby, the perpetual contrarian by design, the only one who can refuse Jack without fear of repercussion. Who's the man they send to build bridges, who you know instantly is here and means business? For Jack, it's Ken O'Donnell, who's stern but efficient and knows without being told what Jack wants. Who's the one who can bullshit with the old guard and the new? For Jack, it's O'Brien, the complete opposite of O'Donnell in temperament but no less effective. He can talk a blue streak with the power brokers who matter and still come back with results. Who keeps things friendly with the press? For Jack, it's Sorensen, who gives the journalists advance copies of Jack's speeches to save them time on their stories and let them focus on the intangibles—crowd reaction, Jack's delivery. But Stevenson doesn't seem to have these people.

Bobby's inside the campaign and outside of it, but good for summoning the Catholic vote. He introduces

Stevenson to the bishop of Denver. He offers suggestions for Catholic crowds.

They'll return east soon. Stevenson will try to capture voters in New York, Pennsylvania—the states where Jack being on the ticket could have helped him. Bobby will return to the committee.

He's returning from another hotel, another surreptitious call to his brother, when he spies Stevenson, his coat collar turned up against the chill. The candidate waves him over.

The pavement is littered with light, the reflections of storefronts and streetlamps scattered like coins in the puddles left over from an earlier shower. Smoke from the governor's cigarette twists away on the breeze, breath turned gossamer turned nothing. Bobby doesn't know how this conversation starts, so he remains silent. He shoves his hands in his pockets. Studies the nearest stoplight as if, in its silent flicker from yellow to red, there is some devastating truth.

"What town are we in?" Stevenson asks. "I've been sitting here scratching my head..."

"Sunbury," Bobby says.

Stevenson shakes his head. "The campaign fog," he says.

He can't help the frisson of resentment he still feels for Stevenson. About the convention. About the way he strung Jack along. It sizzles in his chest, makes his mouth taste black. He tries not to let it show on his face.

Stevenson's letter to Jack after the convention: *I had hoped to see you before you left Chicago, and left, may I say, a much bigger man than you arrived!*

Bobby's looking at a man who's gotten smaller. Stevenson is stooped under the weight of another day. On the trail, his baldness is a joke: a funny comparison between him and Eisenhower. There are placards that sometimes read: *We Want Stevenson—That's the Bald Truth!* or *Men with Hair for Stevenson!* Here, it's a resignation. A concession of defeat to the long slog of years in the middle of a life.

Stevenson has toyed with his brother, spurned his father. Accepted the Ambassador's campaign donations and asked his father to keep it quiet after the check cleared, not wanting to piss off his liberal friends by accepting money from Joe Kennedy.

Stevenson rubs at his neck wearily. The streetlight changes back to green: *Go.*

"We're grateful for your help," Stevenson says. "You and Jack."

Bobby wants to ask who "we" is. Wants to ask, *Was it the Irishness? The Catholicism? The youth? What did it finally come down to that made you kill the movement for my brother?* Because he doesn't believe in coincidence; he still thinks of the sudden shift in support on the floor from his brother to Kefauver. There are only a few people who would have been in a position to push that button, and Stevenson is one of them.

"We're glad to help in any way we can," Bobby says finally.

"Jack's got a bright future ahead of him," Stevenson says. A compliment. A consolation prize. "It's wonderful for the party that the next generation…I'll be excited to see, ten, fifteen years…"

Bobby masks his expression. Inwardly seethes at the idea that Stevenson would dare dictate a timeline for his brother's rise through the ranks.

"It's a long game," Stevenson continues with a short laugh. "Most men don't hit their political stride until they're fifty, sixty. Older than that, even."

Bobby senses, in Stevenson's musings, a warning. *Be bold, be bold, but not too bold.*

"For what it's worth," Stevenson says, turning to him conspiratorially, "I think Jack would make an excellent vice president."

At last, Bobby's patience runs out. He fixes Stevenson with a stare that's like the final flash of talon over the throat of something soft. Moonlight glancing off of bone, and then a spurt of red.

"I think he'd make an excellent president."

Stevenson laughs good-naturedly and agrees—of course he does. He's the face of the Democratic Party. Two-time standard bearer. What does he have to fear from Jack or from any of the Kennedys? They're a flash in the pan. One good performance on the national stage does not a president make.

Bobby may not have the ability to charm men the way his brother can—but he can dissect them. He can pick apart a laugh, a smile, the twitch of a brow, to see what motive, what menace, lies beneath. What he sees in Stevenson, as clearly as if it were carved into granite, is a man who suspects that this is the furthest he'll go.

Stevenson's campaign manager emerges from the hotel behind them with a bead on Stevenson. Stevenson sighs, grinds his cigarette out of existence beneath his sole.

"Thank you for the company," Stevenson says, and seems to mean it. His mouth twitches with humor. "It gets lonely on the long and dusty trail."

"Lonely?" Bobby asks as the candidate turns to leave. Stevenson is surrounded by people all day. Voters, press, advisors.

Stevenson pauses. "Hasn't your brother ever told you? The campaign trail is the loneliest place for a man."

He's never asked Jack about this.

"Has this campaign made you lonelier than in 'fifty-two?"

"I suppose it has," Stevenson smiles. "But no campaign makes you as lonely as the next one."

IT'S A CLEAR DAY at the end of October, the sky open, blue, endless. Miles of Midwestern wheat burn gold in every direction. A group of children is yelling near the platform where Stevenson tries to speak, playing a game that involves pounding each other into the dirt. They come away with dead grass stuck to their hair, patches of earth clinging to their small shoulders.

Schlesinger's bowtie today is a ripple of silver, a fish caught in a net.

"Are you staying with him through the general?" Bobby asks. His own departure from the campaign is imminent, and he already feels a queer nostalgia for it. These are his last days of watching someone else run for president. When he returns to Washington, it'll be Jack running.

"I've come this far," Schlesinger says with a glimmer of weariness. "Might as well see it through to the end."

One of the children has found a stick and brandishes it like Excalibur, battering the others with a *Take that! And that!* The adults who might claim them make no move to. Campaign aides shift nervously, no one eager for the indignity of taking a stick to the shins.

"That's a glowing endorsement," Bobby says.

"No one looks forward to losing."

He's surprised to hear Schlesinger admit this. Surprised that a liberal is capable of a rational, clearheaded thought. One poll has it that Stevenson may only win seven states.

"He's tired of it all," Schlesinger says. "He's never enjoyed campaigning. But he's doing it for the party."

Bobby looks at Stevenson with his notecards: perhaps not a man as obsessed with getting the lines right as he is with getting them over with.

"You think he's sick of politics?" he asks.

"It wears on a man."

Some men, he doesn't correct Schlesinger.

"Enthusiastic crowd," Stevenson remarks as the children howl. The adults are restless, muttering. Stevenson tries to start again, but can't be heard. "Louder!" someone calls. A few aides have moved in now but are beaten back by the stick boy.

Bobby steps forward. "Hey," he says, clapping his hands to get the children's attention. They turn to him as one. The stick boy brandishes his weapon, preparing for a new foe.

"I'll beat anyone from here to that lamppost," Bobby says, and takes off running, a score of children tumbling after him.

This is his first and final gift to the Stevenson campaign: he buys Adlai time to finish his speech. It's the least he can do; he's decided he's voting for Eisenhower.

CHAPTER 19

The Christmas Fight

THEY'LL ALL AGREE AFTERWARD that it was the worst fight his family's ever had.

And like those other, notably bad fights, it'll be given a name.

"The Golf Cart Debacle" they call the time Jack and Joe wrecked one of the carts so badly the roof was sheared clean off, and the Ambassador yelled at them about entitlement for what felt like a week straight.

"The Sangria Sister Fight" they call the time Pat and Eunice drank too much and started strangling each other because first Eunice used all of the hot water back at the apartment, then Pat, in retaliation, stole her necklace and dropped it down the garbage chute.

This one they'll simply call "The Christmas Fight."

But when he arrives home for the holidays in winter 1956, he still has hope that it'll just be a bad fight, not the worst.

He hovers around Ethel as she gets dressed for dinner, watching her assemble herself. Most women put their hose on by bunching up each leg one at a time; Ethel's method is to stick both feet in, hold the waistband, and jump up and down until it's sorted itself out.

"Are our wills up to date?" she asks, her pearls banging hard against her collarbone as she jumps.

His father is going to kill him, they've agreed. He hasn't even told Jack what he's up to yet. They're each other's only allies; his other siblings are sure to turn to his father's side because, in his family, it tends to be the winning side.

"The Excommunication," he remembers. That's another one. When Kick decided to marry a Protestant she met in England. Their parents were livid; he's certain they'd have gone over and bodily removed her if it had been safe to travel. He's ashamed now of how quickly he and his sisters turned on her, writing her damning letters about how she would be forfeiting her faith and her family. He imagines his sister opening them, hoping for congratulations, and finding instead rebuke after rebuke. Jack and Joe were the only ones on her side. "The power of silence is LOUD," he remembers Joe writing to their parents after they'd shut Kick out, a rare disagreement with their eldest son.

After that, his sister was persona non grata with her

own family. And it all ended up being for nothing anyway. Her husband, killed by a sniper, never came back from the war. She was a widow longer than she was married and then she was dead.

He remembers how she used to cut the funnies she thought he'd like out of the newspaper and mail them to him at school, sometimes crossing out what was printed and writing in her own captions. He wishes badly that he could apologize to her. Maybe he deserves to be cast out in the cold now for how he treated his sister then.

Ethel looks at his face and starts her wartime Churchill, which is better than her Orphan Annie and not nearly as good as her Humphrey Bogart.

"We shall fight on the beaches," she growls. "We shall fight in the air. We shall never surrender!"

She resumes her demented hopping. The glass vials of perfume and hand cream rattle against each other on the bureau.

From downstairs, Pat shouts, "Put them on like a normal person!"

"Never surrender, never surrender, never surrender," Ethel chants and jumps in a circle on the rug. Unclear if she's still talking about his predicament, or addressing her hose. Slowly, inch by inch, the stockings crawl up her legs.

BOBBY'S BEEN DIGGING this hole for himself in the weeks since he left the Stevenson campaign. He's been traveling the country, following up on his investigators' leads, speaking to union members and journalists about threats, blackmail, membership dues paid at strange intervals, pension funds that disappear. The oddly lavish lifestyle of the higher-ups in the Teamsters union. Shakedowns, extortion, harassment for the journalists investigating and the union members who ask too many questions. Calls to their house at midnight with no one on the other end. Black cars driving by at night.

There's enough there to launch an investigation, and McClellan agrees. But he also knows that the first rule of politics is: Don't fuck with labor. Unions are a nation unto themselves; they don't want Washington bureaucrats poking around telling them how to govern their members, and the smart bureaucrats listen, because the union vote can decide elections. In order to win the presidency, they have to lock up the New Deal constituencies: white Southerners, Black Northerners, and blue-collar workers. If they fail to capture even one of these three, they don't get over the finish line. In other words, Bobby's investigation could make the Kennedys an enemy to labor, and kill Jack's candidacy in one swift stroke.

HIS FATHER IS GOING to have his head.

As he follows Ethel down the stairs to dinner, he wonders uneasily if he's making the same mistake McCarthy did: Biting off more than he can chew.

Nosing into an institution that wants none of his interference.

The others are already seated, carrying on four, five conversations at once. Pat, alone—Peter rarely comes east—explaining how she talked herself out of her latest speeding ticket. Eunice giving Jean what's probably an unsolicited lecture. And Teddy talking about a tort law class to Steve and Jackie, hamming up his own stupidity, even though he's been working hard to keep up with his classes, calling Bobby from the library late at night to fret about an upcoming exam.

Bobby sits heavily, leaden with dread. Across the table, Jack studies him carefully.

When they bow their heads to say grace, Jack kicks him under the table. He looks up over his crossed hands.

"Heavenly Father, we thank you for this meal..." the Ambassador intones.

You look like shit, Jack mouths to him.

Thanks, he mouths back.

"...and for allowing us all to be here together..."

What are you hiding? Jack asks.

Nothing.

Liars go to Hell.

Bobby shrugs and widens his eyes in his best imitation of innocence. Jack shakes his head, unconvinced. He's not winning any awards with that performance.

"...and for our many blessings..."

Work? Jack asks.

Bobby feigns a sudden inability to lip-read. *What?*

"Amen," their father finishes, and the others lift their heads. "Amen," he and Jack say, a beat later than the rest.

Don't force the issue, he and Ethel have strategized. Let it come up naturally. Bobby saws his food into ever smaller pieces and waits for his father to ask him about work, ignoring Jack, who's still staring at him, and Eunice, who's staring at Jack trying to figure out why he's staring at Bobby, and Pat, who has now alerted to Eunice's alertness, the rising drone of energy among his siblings like a hive waking up, their collective realization that *something* is off, even as they continue their conversations.

The Ambassador's voice cuts through the noise of the table, silencing his siblings in an instant.

"Well, Robert?" his father asks. "Anything come of it?"

He's loosely aware of what Bobby's been up to, but Bobby has intentionally obscured and downplayed the finer points.

Bobby sets down his silverware. The room is so quiet he can hear the candle flame burning its wick in the centerpiece. "Yes," he says carefully. "We've found quite a lot actually."

His father's eyes narrow with displeasure. "Go on," he says.

Bobby runs through the highlights: *Labor unions. Racketeering. Corruption.* And most importantly: that he, Bobby, is going to be the one to investigate.

The words pulse out of him even as his father's fist knuckles white around his glass.

When he finishes at last, his father takes a long drink of water.

"The Bear," they call his father sometimes, because this is how he approaches the market—cynically, in expectation of the worst. But it's also because of this, Bobby thinks, watching his father's head drop: because, in his anger, he looks like he could maul you with one swipe of the claws.

Eunice, unsurprisingly, is the first to come to their father's side. "You must be joking," she says. "It would be an electoral disaster."

Jean's eyes flicker to Bobby, uncertain. Pat is quiet, her fork suspended midair. Jack's expression calcifies into something unreadable. He can sense all of them weighing the risks; to ally themselves with their father, or with Bobby.

"We're not screwing with labor," his father says in a low, dangerous voice. His hand is still in a death vise around his glass, but it's the ticking muscle in his jaw that tells Bobby how angry he actually is.

"Their own leaders are robbing their members blind," Bobby says, his hands tightening into fists in his lap. Ethel's ankle bumps against his in silent support.

"Leave the union to sort it out for themselves," his father says. "You're punching above your weight."

"They have no incentive to clean themselves up," Bobby says. "And no incentive to stop."

Now he's making his case not just to his father, but to his entire family as well. Even Jean has decided she's against him. "It's too close to the election," she says, her eyes filled with a kind of apology as she sticks the knife in him nonetheless. Next to him, Ethel's arguing with his other sisters, launching volleys across the baked ham. Only Jack is curiously silent.

Ted stands—Ted is on his side. It's the worst ally he could have; no one takes Ted seriously. "I think he's doing the right thing," he says, drawing breath as he prepares to launch into a speech. "When men of principle—"

"Sit down, Teddy," Eunice says. "The big kids are speaking."

"If you're bored, we can find you something else to do until 1960," his father says at last, when he's satisfied that his lieutenants have kicked the appropriate amount of shit out of Bobby.

As if his whole life is just one clock ticking down to 1960. As if he has nothing else to live for but his brother's campaign.

For a moment he remembers that odd nostalgia at the end of his stint with the Stevenson campaign, as if he was saying goodbye to something bigger than the campaign, and he wonders if there wasn't something else mixed in with that emotion, if he didn't also resent that the path had been decided for him.

"I won't hear any more of this," the Ambassador says.

For a moment, Bobby sees his father as the world must: Tyrannically certain of himself. Ruling his children's lives with an iron fist. But the Ambassador has forgotten what everyone says: that Bobby Kennedy is every inch his father's son. A pain in the ass. A headache waiting to happen. A hard-driving son of a bitch.

"I'm not asking your permission," he says to his father, words that come out, for once, exactly as he intends: flat and black and taking no quarter.

The room goes still. He feels suddenly, perversely thrilled. He's said something he can't take back; and more startling, he doesn't want to.

"My office," his father says.

Only Jack has the nerve to follow. Teddy moves like he wants to, but Jean stops him, shaking her head.

The sound of the Ambassador's displeasure is wood cracking against wood as he slams the door behind them. Bobby tries not to flinch.

"What the fuck are you thinking?" the Ambassador spits.

But Bobby's angry now, too; his face hot, his pulse in his ears. "I think that I'm doing my job," Bobby says. "In case you'd forgotten, I'm counsel for the Subcommittee on Investigations. That occasionally requires *investigating*."

He's surprised to find that he can manage sarcasm. Jack is, too; his face says: *Little Bobby finally grew a pair.*

"Think!" his father roars, flinging a finger at Jack. "If they hear a Kennedy's sniffing around, trying to meddle with unions, they'll brand him an enemy to labor and he'll be dead in the water before he even begins. *Use your goddamn head!*"

"It's not *him*," Bobby hisses. "It's *me*."

"One Kennedy's the same as another to the rest of the world," his father says. "Is your one-man crusade worth your brother's political future?"

What about my future? He wants to ask. *What about me, my life, the things I want to do, the things I could do if I were born into any other family?* But these will always be the wrong questions.

"I'm not going to drop it," he says. "It wouldn't be right."

"I hope your principles are worth it," his father says disgustedly, "when they write about how Jack Kennedy's aspirations were dashed by his brother's selfishness."

Guilt is what he's supposed to feel. But he lets not a single trace of emotion pass across his face. You taught us too well, Dad, he thinks. Win at any cost.

"If that's all it takes," Bobby says, "it must not have been a very strong candidacy to begin with."

It's a new thing, realizing he can walk away from his father. He always thought these small blasphemies were reserved only for Jack and Joe. He stands suddenly, the movement jerky, like a colt see-sawing its way to its feet. And he leaves. He swears there's something like respect in Jack's eyes, but he doesn't wait around to find out.

Only Teddy, ever loyal, follows him out into the spitting rain. Ethel remains at the dinner table, putting up a passionate defense of him. For a brief moment, he wonders what other families fight about at the holidays.

"Go back inside," he says as Teddy jogs up to his side. "You don't want to be seen with me."

The raindrops cling like small diamonds to Ted's eyelashes, giving him a girlish delicacy.

"You're my brother," Ted says simply.

Oh, Teddy, he thinks. That's a stupid thing to risk your neck for. Unconsciously, they've both turned toward the water, and they hunch into themselves as they walk into the wind.

"I'm serious," Bobby says, trying again to shake his brother. "I'll be lucky if I stay in the will after this one."

"That's the benefit of being the youngest," Teddy says, grinning. "No one cares what I do."

Around the time Teddy got expelled from Harvard, Bobby remembers wondering aloud to Jean how he could have been so foolish. His sister had gone quiet, and then said, "You don't pay him enough attention."

In the years since, it hasn't gotten better. He pays Teddy all the attention he can—but there's less of it to go around every day, with a presidential campaign to plan. Jean was right then; she's still right now. Little brothers need feeding. He ought to know.

He looks at Teddy, who's taller than him by a good three inches, and heavier by thirty pounds, but who nonetheless hasn't outgrown the pudgy eight-year-old

Bobby holds in his mind, and he thinks: families make these little holes in each other and then plug them so quickly without ever patching them completely.

"I guess we can always stay in the garage," Bobby says, and Teddy's laugh makes him feel like he's won something.

When they were in boarding school, they'd escape to Hyannisport on the weekends, just the two of them. The house shut up, the town emptied out after summer's end—and he and Teddy would break into the garage and hide out without their parents' knowledge, surviving off of whatever provisions they'd managed to bring with them. Sitting on cots in the garage with musty sleeping bags tied around their shoulders for warmth, eating beans right out of the can, commiserating over the tribulations of school.

He and Teddy weren't like Jack and Joe, didn't charm their teachers, didn't slip in easily to the groups of boys their age and become their leaders. They struggled, they fought, and just when they started to make some headway, they usually changed schools. All told, by the time they got to college, they'd gone to ten different schools apiece.

He is a quiet boy who does not show much promise, but he seems happy nonetheless, he remembers one of his teachers writing about him on a report card he was supposed to deliver—sealed— to his parents, but ripped open on the train home.

Those weekends with his brother still have a

dreamlike quality, almost like he's remembering them from a life before this one. The bare trees. His breath visible in the cold garage. He and Teddy wheeling around the island on a bike with half-flat tires, Teddy standing on the back, his hands on Bobby's shoulders for balance.

"Dad won't stay mad forever," Teddy says now, thoughtfully.

"Why? Because it's Christmas? He's not the sentimental type, in case you hadn't noticed."

Ted turns and gives him a toothy grin. "He knows that he needs you now more than you need him."

CHAPTER 20

Convictions

AT FIRST, HIS FATHER rages at him.

When the stick doesn't work, he tries the carrot. He dangles other, less politically damaging jobs in front of Bobby. What about the State Department? he coaxes. Or if you're so interested in investigation, why not one of the alphabet agencies—NSA, CIA? When neither carrot nor stick work, the Ambassador turns to surrogates. Jean tries to reason with him; Pat reminds him how much money he stands to lose if their father disinherits him; and Eunice simply lists, in all its permutations, his failures of intelligence. But Bobby remains unmoved; he'd like to say it comes from the clarity of his moral conviction, but he suspects the reality is something meaner: like the child denied a toy, being told he can't have it only makes him want it more.

He develops a simple yet effective escape strategy; when his sisters start a counteroffensive, he retreats to Jackie's corner of the house. Though it's never been spoken aloud, the others know that they're allowed in Jackie's domain by invitation only. Saint Bobby's the exception to the rule. The two of them have a routine for when he jogs up the stairs and raps on her door. She answers solemnly, like a priest in a church doorway. "What do you seek, my child?"

"An hour of sanctuary."

She kicks open the door and ushers him in. "Enter, and be at peace."

Time has looped, and deposited them back to her early days in the family, when they'd talk on the phone. Except back then, they were still essentially strangers, still finding their footing with each other. Now he's sat at her bedside and delivered the worst news of her life, and instead of it making her hate him, it lets them speak without the artifice they once had.

Once, her stubborn self-isolation from the rest of the family was a sign of her outsider status. Now it's a sign of her power. She no longer cares about proving herself to the Kennedys; it's they who're desperate to keep her happy. Because despite his bluster to Lee in the hospital, even a miserly judge would grant Jackie a divorce now, after what she's been through.

Why does she stay with Jack? It's the question on all of their lips. Is she biding her time, waiting to ruin him closer to the election? Is there a journalist somewhere finalizing a story?

Ethel and his sisters whisper about some deal struck between Jackie and the Ambassador, a payoff for her to stay with Jack. In their version, the events of the summer were the final straw for Jackie, the culmination of four years of absence, four years of looking the other way, four years of being married to Mattress Jack. She's demanded a million dollars up front, plus a million dollars put into a trust for any future children she and Jack have together. Ethel pesters him to find out if it's true. It's the first thing he's refused her in all their years of marriage.

He doesn't care if his father did pay her; it's probably the least she deserves. But he also doesn't think this is why she stays. A woman as smart as Jackie can always find more money, which means a woman as smart as Jackie would never stay with someone for money alone.

There's a different reason; a better reason. What it is, he hasn't yet found the courage to ask. They have an unspoken agreement during these hours he hides out with her: they don't talk about his brother.

He sits by the window and watches her. Even at rest she looks like she could be selling something—eye cream, shampoo, the book in her hand.

"We went through your things," he surprises himself by saying. "The first weekend you came to Palm Beach."

"Oh?" she asks, arching a brow. "Find anything good?"

"Just clothes," he says.

"Just clothes," she repeats. "Well that's all I am. Just clothes. Just *things*. Just ghosts knocking around an empty house."

"I'm sorry we did it."

"Don't be," she says with a droll smile. "I went through your things, too."

She reaches for her cigarettes, turning away slightly as she lights one. A self-conscious gesture, one he remembers from the first time he met her.

"Did you hate us in the beginning?" he asks. *Do you now?*

"I wonder if I did," she says in a thoughtful voice. As if they're not the same person, the woman from back then and the one sitting in front of him now.

He knows he's not supposed to speak of his brother, but he can't help himself from saying, "I wish you'd met Jack before my father made him go into politics."

Jackie doesn't reprimand him. She cocks her head to one side and looks at him funnily. "Do you think Jack lets anyone tell him what to do?" She laughs shortly. "Not even your father could have *made* him go into politics. He chose to."

Can that be true? Could he have gotten the first chapter wrong all this time? He tries to play it back from the beginning, not Jack the reluctant heir, but Jack free to reach for the full extent of his ambition with Joe gone. Jack not running because he was forced to, but because he wanted to. That can't be right. Can it? That's not the Jack he knows. But then, he realizes, looking at Jackie, maybe it's the one she does. Maybe it's possible they're both true; her version of Jack and his.

"We all choose," she says. "He chose to run for office. And you chose to run his campaign."

She shakes her head ruefully at whatever expression is on his face. "You Kennedys," she says gently. "You stage-manage fate. You direct destiny. And then you pretend you had nothing to do with it."

She pauses and looks him over. "Maybe that's what I thought the first time I met you," she says. "That you were very good at convincing yourselves of your own inevitability."

THE HOLIDAYS ARE less enjoyable as the family pariah, and he's relieved to return to Washington. When he says goodbye to his father, standing defiantly in front of the old man's desk—his father has refused to leave his study, even though he must have heard them packing up the car—his father won't look at him. His rage has dimmed and cooled into something more permanent. Bobby sighs and leaves.

By January, the Teamsters have gotten wind of his investigation and try to kill it in the cradle. A subcommittee on investigations, they argue, has no business looking into labor. They instruct their members, if called to Washington, to plead the Fifth, to be as uncooperative as possible. Having risked his position in his own family, Bobby can't afford to have the hearings fail. A compromise emerges: a select committee made up of four senators from the Investigations committee, four from Labor. In theory it'll be bipartisan. Fair. In reality, no senator from Labor wants to touch the investigation, except for the usual anti-union nuts. The investigation is going to look like a hatchet job unless Bobby can do the impossible: convince a single senator, someone he knows for a fact wants to make inroads with the unions, to join the select committee.

Unfortunately, the man he needs is also the one most likely to refuse.

"Don't you think one Kennedy on this thing is enough?" Jack asks. "Dad's blood pressure only just came back down."

He's come to his brother's house to abase himself, and he follows Jack as he makes his way, limpingly, down the hall.

"I'll do your homework for a week," Bobby offers.

Jack turns and squints at him: "Or maybe that's your game. Send Dad to an early grave so you can have whatever political pet projects you want."

Resentment arrows through him. It's not a *pet project*, he feels like saying.

But he bites his tongue and follows his brother into the living room. The last time Bobby was here, everything was blue and gold like a French tearoom. Now the color is gone and a heavy teak sideboard dominates the room. Jack's house is inconstant; the walls are painted over, the furniture swapped out, new carpets are laid—then the next time it's all changed again. He keeps this observation to himself; his brother wearies of Jackie's constant remodeling.

Jack eases himself carefully into a chair, his hands clenched on the arms. "Lyndon Johnson says I can't survive as a serious contender in 'sixty if I start going after labor now."

Johnson? Since when does his brother care what Johnson thinks?

"He's only saying that to scare you off," Bobby says. "He'll come back in three years and tell everyone you're not strong enough on labor reform."

"I'd considered that."

"Don't think of it as attacking labor," Bobby says. "Think of it as cleaning up corruption across American life."

Jack toys with the strap of his watch, unconvinced.

"Wait until we pick up steam," Bobby says. "I'm already up to my ears in reporters. And it's only going to snowball. Once people see the hearings on television—it'll be free publicity."

Partly, he's trying to sell his brother. Partly, it's true. He has journalists calling every day, stopping by the office to try to get a quote, a look at a document, a tip on where the investigation is heading. They'll have headlines for months to come, nothing to scoff at when you're planning a campaign three years down the road.

It's hard enough to sustain relevance in your state for years at a time, try nationally.

"Labor's a serious investigation for serious politicians," he says. "It'll show the press you're more than just a pretty face."

He thinks he spies a faint look of interest on said pretty face.

"Fight for the little man," Bobby says. "Take a stand against the crooks who would rob their own—"

"Don't get on your soap box," Jack says. "You do it for the morals, I'll do it for the headlines."

He senses his brother isn't done, and he waits—has learned to wait. Jack knits his hands together, chews his cheek.

"What do you think of this house?" Jack asks, studying the crown molding like there's something very interesting written there.

"It's a good house," Bobby says.

"Take it," Jack says.

Bobby laughs. "Yeah, sure."

"I'm serious," Jack says. "I know you and Ethel are looking. There's enough room here for your circus."

"You might want to run it past Jackie first."

"It was her idea." Jack doesn't meet his eyes. "She says it feels like a mausoleum."

The word drops like a stone between them. He's come to ask his brother for something; his brother has something to ask of him in return.

"I'll talk to Ethel," he says.

CHAPTER 21

Hoffa

THE INVITATION COMES through Jimmy Hoffa's lawyer: Hoffa wants to have dinner to discuss Bobby's investigation and the union in person. Man to man. See if they can't come to a better understanding.

His father and Jack shadowbox in his head: His father saying do it, meet the man, never turn down an opportunity to look your opponent in the eyes. Jack saying what does it accomplish, waste of time, you know you're going after him regardless of how much you like the steak.

But he's become intrigued by Hoffa, the more he reads about him.

Born poor; fatherless at the age of seven. Grew up in

Detroit, auto-town, geography as destiny. Dropped out of school in the ninth grade to start working.

One reporter writes: "His stubby build, a wife named Josephine, and a passion for power made it inevitable that he would become known as the Napoleon of the Teamsters."

Not a boy who played nice, who got along well with others. A boy who, with his older brother Bill, used to throw sucker punches in the schoolyard. Who learned early the language of violence. Who learned early to make the first one count. He's had his head cracked open like an egg by a police nightstick; he's got a rap sheet the length of his arm; someone shot his brother once believing it was Jimmy they were filling with lead.

He got his start in the labor movement at a Kroger grocery warehouse. When the company refused to start talks with his union, he told his men to open up the trucks carrying the strawberries. This was the Depression; he knew exactly what a strawberry cost: hours growing in the Florida sun, laborers to pick them, refrigerated trucks needed to ship them. And under his supervision, all that sweet fruit went to rot in the hot air, flies pulsing over the produce like a corpse. Not the most subtle of tactics, but he's not the most subtle of men. They say strawberries were ruined for him forever after that, but he won his contract.

When asked once to sum up his career in the labor

movement, Hoffa offered four sentences: "I got a job in a department store—stock boy. Then I got a job at Kroger's. And that's my whole life. Pretty simple life."

Pretty simple life, Bobby repeats to himself, calling Hoffa's lawyer to accept the invitation. Pretty simple life, he repeats as he jogs up to the lawyer's house on the night of the dinner.

They both answer the door, the lawyer and Hoffa. He wonders briefly what kind of man he's dealing with who needs counsel with him just to let someone in.

Bobby's first time meeting the man and he's looking down at him. But what Hoffa lacks in height, he makes up for in build. "Sturdy as a prizefighter," the papers have written about him. "Built like one of the trucks he drives." He's barrel-chested, constructed like a piece of furniture. Each joint and beam slotted carefully into place, made to articulate with the next. Function, not aesthetic. That's Hoffa.

"The famous Mr. Kennedy," Hoffa says, eyes glinting. "Pleasure to meet you." He thrusts out a hand like he's pulling a weapon.

"Likewise," Bobby says. They shake.

"Who wants a drink?" Hoffa's lawyer asks, leading them inside. Bobby declines. Not in this company. Imagines his ruddy-faced Irish ancestors looking on and shaking their heads, murmuring amongst themselves, Good God, boy, you don't turn down a whiskey free of charge.

Hoffa, too, shakes his head. "Not me. I don't touch the stuff."

He looks at Bobby to see how this lands. Bobby becomes aware, at once, that the game has begun.

At dinner, Hoffa is both elbows on the table, a napkin tucked into his collar like he's at a diner. He's playing the working-class man, but a fat gold ring sits on one pinky, the ruby stone like a bubble of blood.

"How did you come to be involved in the union?" Bobby asks.

Hoffa grins, like this is funny. Looks at his lawyer as if to say, Get a load of this guy.

"I'm a working man," Hoffa says. "Nobody handed me anything."

The implication is clear: to Hoffa, Bobby's nothing more than an Ivy League millionaire's son. He may as well be sitting there with a silver spoon in his mouth. Bobby decides this can suit him for the evening.

"How much does someone in your position make?" he asks.

"Look, I don't got no trust fund," Hoffa says, jabbing right back.

"How much schooling did you have?"

"They can't teach you what I know in any school."

"You've been arrested a number of times, haven't you?" Bobby asks.

Hoffa smiles. A point of pride. "You see this?" He rolls up a sleeve, offers a battered forearm. "I've been beaten on picket lines more times than I can count. Met my wife on a picket line. We were both bleeding."

So romance isn't dead, Bobby thinks. "You must be lucky, never to have served time," Bobby says.

Hoffa shakes his head. "No such thing as luck for working men. Nothing ever sticks to Jimmy Hoffa. I'm like a cat—nine lives. You might want to keep that in mind."

The tough guy routine would almost be funny, if not for the beatings; the acid thrown at journalists; the murders; the letters arriving at Bobby's office every week with tips from people too afraid to sign their real names. *Anonymous. A Working Man. Seeking Help.*

"There are disturbing reports coming out of your union."

"A few bad apples don't mean you gotta upset the whole apple cart."

"What would you do," Bobby asks carefully, "if you were president of the union? How would you clean things up?"

Hoffa's smile shows teeth. He only says, "What? Am I on trial already?"

After dinner, they decamp to the parlor. Going through the motions of polite company. Hoffa sits. Bobby stands by the fire.

"They say you've got more of a temper than your brother," Hoffa says, eyes bright, gauging his response.

Bobby says nothing. Hoffa takes his silence as an invitation. Hoffa's lawyer looks nervously between them.

"Yeah," Hoffa nods to himself. "They say Jack's a regular prince but you're just like your bootlegger old man."

The lawyer shoots a warning glance at Hoffa. Hoffa holds up his hands. "Their words, not mine."

"Whose words?" Bobby asks.

Hoffa shrugs. "You hear things." He flexes his fingers, the stone on his ring catching the flame of the fireplace, erupting with light. "Everybody's got a story about the Kennedys."

"I've heard stories about you as well," Bobby says.

Hoffa is nonplussed. He picks at a bit of food in the back of his teeth. "What do they pay you on a Senate salary?" he asks. "Can't be much."

Bobby's been waiting for the bribe all evening. He has his answer prepared. "As you pointed out, I don't need the money."

Hoffa snorts. "You're the only one." He grips the front of his jacket by its lapels. "So what do you do it for then? Morals?" He laughs at the thought. "Or are you trying to make a name for yourself?"

I do it because my brother died during the war, he could say. *I do it because my father ran out of runway before he could campaign for president himself. I do it because once, when I was very small, I jumped off a boat before I knew how to swim.* But none of this would make sense to Hoffa. Sometimes it doesn't make sense to him.

"I suppose I do it because it's there," he says. "It needs doing."

Hoffa grunts and twists his ring around his finger. "You know," he says, "I can be persuaded into supporting your brother in 1960."

"I thought the Teamsters only backed Republicans," Bobby says.

"The ends justify the means, Bob, you ever heard that?" Hoffa asks. "Better the devil you know than the devil you don't. We got a million members. Think about that."

He can imagine it: Him going easy on Hoffa in the hearings, Hoffa answering the questions vaguely but politely. Nothing comes of the investigation. The union gets a slap on the wrist and carries on as they were. Perhaps, in 1960, Hoffa welcomes Jack to speak to the union in Detroit. Hoffa throws the considerable political support of the Teamsters to his brother. His brother is president. Hoffa is pulling the strings.

He sees no reason to stay. He's formed his opinion of Hoffa. Hoffa has formed his opinion of him.

Hoffa doesn't move as Bobby makes his farewells to their host. It's only with his hand on the door that he hears Hoffa, his voice so low it's almost not meant to be heard.

"We weren't ever gonna be friends, were we?" Hoffa asks, looking over one shoulder at Bobby. Strange to meet a man before you go to war with him. He can't imagine what it ever accomplished.

"Just remember I'm not as bad as everyone thinks I am," Hoffa says.

CHAPTER 22

The California Kennedy

QUESTIONS: MANY. SLEEP: LITTLE.

As the hearings begin, there are almost daily public sessions. He's no longer in the back, hidden by other people's shoulders, the way he was at the Army–McCarthy hearings. He's front and center, leading the questioning.

The papers aren't shy about his youth, his inexperience, his poor cross-examination abilities. He accepts that he doesn't have a brilliant legal mind; he wasn't like his friends in law school who could argue novel theories of the case, who had strong opinions about originalist versus textualist interpretations of the Constitution, who could slice a case apart and assemble clear yet elegant summations. To Bobby, the law isn't beautiful, or even particularly interesting. To him, the law is utilitarian. Its beauty doesn't matter if it's doing the job it's supposed to, which is correcting wrongs, protecting people, leveling the playing field. Law should reflect a degree of morality if it's the one thing that separates us from the beasts of the field. It's like religion in that way, something you have to put faith in for it to work. Something that's less about miracles and more about the daily, grinding work of belief. Something that's practiced, but never finished.

When he's not in hearings, there are leads to follow up on; investigators to send out into the field; staff to instruct; documents to examine; cases to construct; money trails to follow.

He's good at this work for the same reason that he's good at managing campaigns: because it requires no particular brilliance, only the ability—the desire, even—to work hard, to give yourself over to the task completely. Because more important than any innate talent is simply the ability to organize, marshal troops, and divide up tasks. It is, like a campaign, a closed system, a machine whose parts Bobby understands, as well as how those parts interact.

The hearings start in February, and they're as newsworthy as he predicted. It's the first event since the Army–McCarthy hearings that's caught Washington and the public's attention at the same time, and as the months go on, they only increase in popularity. These are good days, good press. Even the Ambassador's come around, due partly to the positive headlines and partly to Jack's joining the committee. He might be fine casting Bobby into the cold, but not Jack. Now his father says that investigating labor was the smartest thing Bobby ever did. He's enjoying the bargain: two-for-one coverage of his sons on television and in magazines. Articles with titles like, "The Rise of the Brothers Kennedy." *Rise,* his father says, reading it over and over, savoring the word.

But his siblings still treat him with suspicion, wary of this independent venture, and maybe a little jealous that he defied their father and got away with it. They wish they'd thought of it first. Publicly, they're supportive, showing up to sit with Ethel at the hearings. But privately, they grow distant. It's little things at first. A joke they tell that he doesn't understand, and when he asks them to explain, they wave their hands and say, *You had to be there*, which he wasn't, because he was working. Then it's Eunice, showing up unexpectedly at his office to discuss Kennedy Foundation business, which she actually runs although he's the chairman, and she says, I *told* you I was coming, and he knows, he knows—but he must have forgotten. Then it's dinners, a ski trip, weekends at the Cape that they don't even bother to invite him to, knowing he'll say he has to work.

Something impossible is happening, something he never imagined. It's a fundamental law of the universe, as certain as gravity, that's governed his existence thus far: his certainty that regardless of whatever else may happen, he's a Kennedy first. But now his siblings are becoming strangers to him. His own family is recounted to him secondhand where once he would have lived it. He reads his mother's round-robin letters about the family goings-on like he's reading about strangers. Since when did Pat get a new car? Ted is doing what? Jean has a trip planned to where? A distance is widening, and he's both afraid that it'll never be repaired and afraid of what happens if it is.

What worries him most, though, is the day Eunice and Jean come to his office after one of the hearings and tell him that Pat's out of sorts again.

They each have their unspoken responsibilities: Jean and Ted are each other's keeper, Eunice used to look out for Rosemary, and Jack for Kick. Pat has always been his. He doesn't believe that she could have sunk so low without him noticing. He can always sense her blue moods coming on—a certain tone in her letters, more frequent calls than usual—and head them off. He's sure Eunice and Jean are mistaken, and says as much.

Eunice stares at him baldly, with a threadbare patience. "It's not like you've been around," she says curtly. He looks to Jean. She shifts uneasily in her chair, which amounts to agreement.

"How bad is it?" he asks, studying the mountain of documents on his desk, the boxes of evidence stacked around the room. There's some restless spirit inhabiting his office, he's convinced, that moves and rearranges the towers of testimony when he's not looking. What it's trying to communicate to him, he can't be sure.

"Go see for yourself," Eunice says, standing and pulling her gloves on. "That is, if you have time in your busy schedule."

AT HER FRONT DOOR in Santa Monica, Pat launches herself at him, hugs him tight, tight, tighter. Hugs him like a woman who's angry with her husband—when suddenly any other man, even a little brother, looks like a saint by comparison.

"You're squeezing the life out of me," he says.

"Stay a week," she says. What did he do now, Bobby wants to ask, seeing the red blood vessels swimming in her eyes.

"Just the night," he says. "I have to get back."

He only has a day—this day—to be Bobby.

"Boo," she says.

He shrugs. "I'm a hot commodity these days."

She keeps her arm around his neck as she leads him forward. "I got us dinner reservations tonight at a place in Hollywood. You're going to hate it."

His gaze slides to hers and they cackle, laughing still as they enter the house. He's thinking smugly that he was right after all, it's not nearly as bad as his sisters made it seem, and he looks forward to rubbing Eunice and Jean's noses in it.

The house is empty—empty of her children, empty

of Peter. Empty of the actors and actresses she calls friends. It occurs to him that his sister's life out here is something of a mystery. When he sees her, it's in Washington, or Hyannisport, where she's the same Pat he's always known. But California Pat—what does this woman actually do all day?

"Do you want any?" Pat asks, pulling a bottle of white wine from the refrigerator. There's one answer to his question. Her wrists tense as she cranks the corkscrew.

"It's a little early for me," he says.

She shoots him a glance over her shoulder that says *Get over yourself,* and pours him a glass anyway.

They stack cushions from her deck chairs at the edge of the pool and lie there with just their feet in the water, growing lazy in the sun, the sound of the ocean like a deck of cards being shuffled ad infinitum. He uses a forearm to blindfold his eyes.

The two of them used to crawl into the dark belly of the sailboat with a cup of ice cubes on the hottest days in July, when they'd exhausted their mother's patience and couldn't beg any money off of her or their siblings for ice cream. So they'd chew ice, grind it between their molars, taste that nothing taste while the sea slurped against the side of the boat. Sometimes they could talk about things down there that they couldn't anywhere else, with anyone else.

Above them now, a sliver of the moon, misplaced in the daytime sky, snags against the blue.

"You know, it'll drift away someday?" Pat asks. "It recedes from Earth an inch and a half every year."

"Where did you hear that?" he asks, skeptically.

"I read an article. Someday it'll be far enough that Earth's gravity can't hold it anymore, and it'll spin off in its own orbit."

"And what then?"

She pauses. Kicks her feet idly. "We'll have to find something else to look at."

His sister today is playing the part of a woman scorned. Her glass rests over her heart, leaves a circle of condensation like a bullseye on the center of her chest.

"Tell me we've got some campaigning to do soon," Pat says. "Anything to get me out of this state."

"Sick of your Hollywood pals?"

"They're lovely, of course," she says quickly. "But you try to talk about...I don't know, the test ban treaty, and they look at you like you've grown three heads."

"You're always welcome at the hearings."

"Euny and Jean said it's just a bunch of people taking the Fifth. Sounds about as interesting as dentistry," she says. As an afterthought: "No offense."

None taken. It wears on all of them on the subcommittee.

"My friends say I'm going to be dancing on the White House lawn soon."

"We can dance in November."

His sister splashes her feet idly. "Do you remember

how close the count was in 'fifty-two?" she asks. "Seventy thousand—"

"—Seven hundred thirty-seven," they finish together. He remembers.

"Jack said it was because of me," Pat says softly. She sits up a little to take a drink. Speaking around the wine in her mouth, her words are watery. "Me and the girls—the teas—it all came down to the women's vote, he said."

She swirls her wine, and it dances a spiral around the glass. "But I heard him tell O'Donnell once that the seventy thousand was because of him—because of Kenny, Worcester, the blue-collar vote." Her gaze takes a bite out of him. "Which was it?" she asks. "Who got him the seventy thousand?"

His sister is a mother now; a wife; most startling of all, a *Californian*. When he looks at her sometimes, he gets the same feeling he does with his mother, like she's a woman who was hired to play the woman he actually knows.

"Everyone doing their part," he says in a measured voice. "That's what wins elections."

She looks at him like he's a stranger. She says, "I remember when you hated politics."

THE NANNY RETURNS with the children. He stands in the pool, catching his nephew over and over again, watching his face crack open with delight every time he takes the leap. Pat crosses one tanned foot over the other, amber colored in the late afternoon light, humming along to the record player as she refills her glass. Loose limbed, she knocks her glass off the table and into the deep end of the pool. Bobby retrieves it, gives it to his nephew to return to his mother. Running across the pool deck, it looks like he's holding a cupful of sunlight. Pat throws it right back in.

There is no dinner. They don't make it that far. Pat slumps over the kitchen island, batting away every bit of food he tries to coax into her, an olive, a wedge of cheddar cheese, a pretzel stick.

"Trying to lose weight," she mumbles.

She looks as thin as anything to him, but he doesn't bother to share this. His sisters will only be happy with their bodies when you can slide them under a door like an envelope.

A bouquet of roses sits in a crystal vase on the counter—an apology? A romantic gesture? Pat rips the brown petals off the flowers and leaves them scattered over the counter.

"Animal cracker?" he asks, proffering the jar.

She eyes a zebra listlessly and bites its head off, chewing for longer than necessary.

"When Jack comes, he just wants to cad around with Peter," Pat says. Her eyes are glassy. "But you'll spend time with your dear old sister."

She practically falls off her stool trying to hug him.

Before he can get her on her feet, she's suddenly furious, sweeping the vase off the counter with the back of her hand.

The vase doesn't shatter; it turns out it's cheap plastic, not glass. It bounces harmlessly against the tiles, brackish water spilling over the floor.

"Leave it," Pat says, seeing him move to clean it up. "I swear to God, Bobby. Just stop trying to help for once in your life."

Then she turns and walks out of the room with the intense focus and careful foot placement of the insensate drunk.

She flops onto the bed like the victim of a hit-and-run, limbs askew, neck cranked to one side.

"What am I doing in California?" she asks him.

He thinks they're down in the boat again, talking about secret things.

"Come home," he says. "You belong with the rest of us."

"I can't," she whispers. "I won't be like Mother—living back East, turning a blind eye while my husband's in Hollywood—"

He touches her cheek and the tips of his fingers come away wet.

"I know," she says. He didn't say anything: she's responding to a lifetime of "Kennedys don't cry."

She has the same face now that she did at sixteen. And she let men treat her badly then, too.

But maybe he'd treat her badly, too, if she weren't his sister.

It's an awful thing to think, but he thinks it. We can't always think only the things we'd like to. Can't always be only the men we'd like to be. Sometimes we're like other men—men we dislike, brother-in-laws we scorn—and they're like us.

He fights through the tangle of her hair to unclasp her necklace—he's read about women being strangled to death in their sleep by their jewelry. Or maybe he saw this in a movie once. Cause of death: a diamond choker. A strand of pearls. A golden chain flecked with emeralds.

"Where do you want this?" he asks, palming the necklace.

Pat plucks it from his hand and chucks it into the corner of the room. It hits the wall with a sound like marbles being poured over a wooden floor. A gift from Peter, then.

"It wouldn't be so bad," she says, "if the papers weren't always writing about how happy we are."

IN THE MORNING, Peter still hasn't returned. The children have been spirited away again by the nanny. Pat's house is quiet, a film set after the shooting has wrapped, as if her family are hired day players who disappear as soon as the episode's finished.

Bobby goes to the kitchen, where the upset roses still lie on the floor, and mops up the green water with a paper towel. He throws the wilted roses in the trash, beneath more paper towels, so Pat won't see them. He sweeps the petals off the counter and into his hand and lets them blow away in the sea breeze off the back porch.

Pat slouches downstairs earlier than he expected, her mascara giving her raccoon eyes. She pours herself a large glass of water, then glares at it moodily without drinking it. Her shirt is on inside out.

"Are you leaving soon?" she asks glumly.

"In a little."

He pushes the water toward her with the tips of his fingers. Irritation flashes across her face.

"You'll feel better if you drink me," he says in the voice he uses with his children.

Pat eyes him, then takes a small, begrudging sip.

"You're leaving us behind," she says. "Jack, I understand. But I never thought *you* would."

"I'm not allowed to have a life?" he asks impatiently. He feels irked for a moment at how much his family needs him, at the shape they want him to bend into for their sake, even if it means deforming himself.

"I'm happy for you, Bobby," she says, smiling sadly. "You don't need us anymore."

He remembers what Ted said after the fight with his father: *He needs you more than you need him.* Need, need, need. He thinks it until the sound falls away from the meaning. What is need? What is need except a hole you expect someone else to fill?

He pulls a jar of pickles out of the fridge, and carefully pours the juice into a mug.

Pat knows his game. "Don't start with the Irish mammy folk remedies."

"It works."

He pushes the pickle juice over to her. She stares into the mug, then downs it in one gulp, shuddering as she swallows.

"It was nice before politics," he says, to keep this inconvenient snarl of emotions in his chest at bay as he watches his sister.

Pat squints at him. "It's never been nice," she says. "What family are you talking about?"

She walks to the fridge. He knows she's about to pull out another bottle, tell him she has a terrible headache and needs the hair of the dog, and then by the time he has to go, she'll start crying and begging him not to and telling him how alone she is.

"Wait," he says. "I have an idea."

OUTSIDE IT'S STILL too early to have warmed up. The sand is damp and chilly beneath their bare feet.

Pat hesitates at the edge of the water. "It's freezing," she says, dipping a toe in.

"Chicken."

He yanks his shirt over his head and charges into the water before he can change his mind. The cold clears out every thought in his head. It reminds him of the freezing pools of boarding school, a mountain lake one summer, morning laps in the Navy.

When he surfaces, Pat's gone. He squints at the windows of the house, looking for her silhouette, until she pops up next to him and spits a column of water into his face.

They swim out further and further, jumping as the waves roll into them. A woman walking her dog on shore stops to watch for a moment, perhaps considering if they need help, perhaps wondering if they're someone famous, before turning away and urging her dog on.

Bobby jumps on Pat and holds her under. He lets her go after a ten count, and she comes up spluttering, wiping the seawater from her eyes. She lunges at him and he lets her force him underwater in retaliation.

I'll try harder, he vows to himself. I'll be a better brother. It's the kind of promise that, even in making, you don't intend to keep.

She lets him up, and they stand, panting. After a moment, she lets the waves sweep her feet out from under her until she's floating on her back. Pockets of air balloon in the shoulders of her shirt. Her hair is a Medusa's head of snakes around her face. He thinks she means to let the tide take her; then she thrusts out a pale hand.

"Don't let me float away," she says.

And he doesn't.

CHAPTER 23

His Place in History

IN MAY, NEWS Bobby can hardly believe.

"McCarthy's dead," he says, sinking into his office chair. He claps a hand to his head like some silent-movie character, emotion telegraphed in overexaggerated pantomime. Hepatitis, they're saying. Not even fifty years old.

O'Donnell scarcely looks up, but at least has the decency to cross himself.

"What do I do?" he asks. There's a ringing in his ears.

"Send flowers," O'Donnell suggests.

He sends the office home instead. He calls Jack.

"You're not going to the funeral," Jack says. This is not up for discussion. Jack's been cozying up to the liberals since the convention and is in no hurry to jeopardize his new standing with the intellectual wing of the party. "I don't need the papers saying 'Kennedys Mourn a Monster'—and I certainly don't need Eleanor Roosevelt in my shorts again."

"He wasn't a monster," Bobby says. His voice sounds strange to him.

Jack says, "Say a prayer. Light a candle. Be done with it."

Pat is equally unsympathetic.

"Can you believe it?" Bobby asks, feeling something like despair in the center of his chest. He knew McCarthy was sick—knew that he drank too much—but this?

"He was an alcoholic, Bobby, of course I can believe it."

"You dated him—am I the only one who's upset by this?"

"I went on *a* date with him," Pat says. "It's not like he was one of us."

"He was a friend of the family—you wouldn't be sad if Lem Billings died? Or Kenny?"

"Billings stood me up last time I was in New York."

"Patricia," he says. "A man is dead."

"I'm clear on that point," Pat says with the voice of someone who's waiting for her nails to dry.

"It's so *permanent*," he says, trying to make her understand.

"My," Pat says, "what a brain you have."

THIS IS HOW they write about him:

A turbulent chapter in American history has closed with the death of Senator Joseph McCarthy of Wisconsin—admired by some as an anti-communist patriot, but denounced by others as a witch-hunter....

The strain of the two long series of hearings had sapped McCarthy's physical strength and the censure vote was a severe psychological blow. He became more subdued in public and private and began to have repeated attacks of illness. When his name got into the newspapers, it was usually because he had entered a hospital for treatment....

His place in history will be based almost entirely on a four-year span of his life which began in 1950 with his sensational attack on the State department, and ended in 1954, when the Senate voted to condemn his actions....

The Wisconsin Republican's death at 6:02 p.m. ended one of the most controversial careers in modern United States politics....

By the time of his death, he had become just another senator. . . .

They write: "He is gone and we will not miss him."

THE JOURNALISTS COME to Bobby, trying to sniff out a new lead, asking him to denounce the senator he formerly worked for.

It makes him sick—the same sycophants who once praised McCarthy's every move want to smear him now that he's gone.

"I'm not going to do it," Bobby snaps at them, perhaps unwisely. "The man is dead."

Soiled. Unpopular. Tarnished. But still a US senator.

McCarthy's given a funeral service in the Senate chamber at the request of his widow.

"She's got balls," Jack says. "I'll give her that."

"It's like giving Chamberlain a ceremony at Munich," Ethel says.

It's a strange place for a send-off. The institution that so publicly rejected him.

"It's her way of winning," Jackie says firmly. "All she can do now is make them look."

Most of the senators—both parties—turn out. Sam Rayburn, the Speaker of the House. The vice president. Roy Cohn.

And then there's the burial itself. Bobby slinks into Appleton, riding there on a military jet with the other government officials who want to pay their respects. He sits up high in the choir loft, a bird in the rafters. He asks one of the journalists who's friendly with Jack not to write about his presence. The senator would approve of the pomp and circumstance, he thinks—an honor guard of Marines bearing the casket to the grave. A crowd of mourners outside a thousand deep. The stars and stripes draped over the casket, folded into perfect triangles, and handed to McCarthy's widow, her face washed clean with grief.

"Don't feel sympathy for the dead," his father told him once, after Roosevelt died. "Feel sympathy for the man who has to take the job next." But the strange rules of Wisconsin politics mean that McCarthy's seat will remain vacant for some time.

"I feel so strange," he tells Jackie a few weeks later, the two of them sitting in the yard of the house that's his now. "Everyone's saying how terrible he was. Maybe it's true, I don't know—can't I be sad?"

"Permission granted," she says.

She grasps one pearl on her necklace like she means to pop it. It's a gesture he's seen her make before, signaling unease, a certain distance. He tries to intuit the cause: Jack...or her father, recently diagnosed with liver cancer. He opts for the safer of the two.

"How's your father?" he asks.

"Still terminal," she says, and nothing more.

His children reach for fireflies, trying to capture them in their open, ungentle palms.

Jackie's pregnant again, though he doesn't know how. She and Jack hardly look at each other when they're in the same room. Most women trying for a baby would be happy to learn that they're pregnant, but Jackie's started planning her own funeral.

"Women still die," she says. "Even now." She considers her hands. "I have this horrible vision," she says, and describes it to him: her body pale with loss of blood, the sheets red. She can see it so clearly it's like it's not even a vision so much as her death foretold. That's a strange word, he thinks. *Foretold*.

She gives herself a shake; her earrings swing.

"You'll be fine," he says. Something he has no way of knowing.

"In some ways it's the best thing I could do," she says. "He'd have another woman in our bed before the grave had even been filled and I'd be there in the corner saying 'Boo.'" She grins at the idea of being Jack's ghost, hiding his keys, tapping inside the walls, writing her name in the fog of a mirror.

It may not be love that makes you want to haunt someone, but it's something.

She's fuzzy-edged in the dusk. Her profile is classic, her eyes sad.

For a moment, he feels guilty for having all these children. The small pack of them roils en masse toward some invisible boundary and then falls back, skittish. There's almost enough light to see them, almost enough light that he can't see them at all. Five of them now. It feels greedy, sitting next to her.

A phantom detaches itself from the others, screeching in pain, solidifying into a boy as it nears.

His boy. His son.

David thrusts out a hand, bleeding. Alive.

CHAPTER 24

Chief Counsel

THE SUMMER WEARS ON. The work continues.

When the president of the Teamsters is forced to resign as a result of Bobby's investigations, Hoffa is the presumptive heir. Bobby feels as if he cleared the way; it makes him that much more determined to get Hoffa.

In August, when they have Hoffa on the stand, Bobby rips into him like a snarling dog; Hoffa hits back. Each day, they jab and weave and do their best to exhaust each other. Hearing about the fireworks between the chief counsel and the union leader, the audience soon doubles, triples, until it's standing room only, then people are fighting for seats, then they're standing out in the hall, hoping to hear if not see, to brag to their friends that they were there.

The chief counsel, moving constantly through the documents in front of him without interrupting his questioning, against Jimmy Hoffa, squat, crew-cut, and with a face like a balled fist. Almost uncivil, how they talk to each other. Like they wish this were taking place in a bar instead of the caucus room. The press in the back take bets on the hypothetical matchup: It'd be Hoffa easy, look at him. I wouldn't count Kennedy out, it's always the quiet ones who hit the hardest.

His own siblings seem surprised by the person he becomes when the hearings are gaveled in for the day. His sisters come by his office afterward and look him over with slightly puzzled expressions.

"I see now why they're always calling you a son of a bitch," Pat says.

At the hearings, Jack sits to his immediate left. His sisters, one, two, three, and Jackie and Ethel sit in the audience. You'd almost think it wasn't the Senate Select Committee on Improper Activities in the Labor or Management Field against the International Brotherhood of Teamsters, but the Kennedys versus Hoffa.

The papers call him the same old thing: Ruthless. Vicious. Aggressive. Somebody writes, oh so cleverly, that after Jack's book *Profiles in Courage*, perhaps another Kennedy will pen *Profiles in Bullying*. They say he badgers witnesses. They compare him to McCarthy. "Mr. Kennedy knows," they write, "and when he knows, he is very sure that he knows." His name is printed less often as *Robert F. Kennedy, younger brother of the senator from Massachusetts* and more as *Robert F. Kennedy, committee counsel.* For the first time in his life, people are mistaking Jack for him instead of the other way around.

Out at lunch one day, a woman vigorously pumps Jack's hand, thanks him for the great service his hearings are doing for the country, and asks if he would be so kind as to sign her napkin.

"My friends will be just delighted that I met *the* Robert Kennedy," she says.

Jack forges a signature without bothering to correct her. When she's gone, he looks at Bobby, slightly miffed—and, Bobby thinks, slightly irritated. *Do you hate me?* he almost asks.

Something's changed since that fight with his father; he feels, for the first time, like a person in his own right. Not the seventh of nine. Not one of many. For once he's Bobby first, a Kennedy second.

He finds that something's taken root in this version of himself; something black, something red. He keeps the staff until nine, ten—and even when he lets them go, he himself stays and works. He walks past the Teamsters' building and sees the lights still on. He turns back. As long as Hoffa's working, he will, too.

By ten, he promises Ethel. By Eleven. Twelve.

He's rarely home at a normal hour anymore. Tonight, it's two in the morning, and he and Ethel are sitting at the kitchen table, Ethel eating a second dinner with him. You don't have to get up, he's told her, not really meaning it, because say he did come home one night, and the lamp didn't flick on when his tires touched the driveway, and the front door didn't swing open with her greeting of "Howdy partner," and she didn't sit with him to hash out the developments of the day—what would he do then? He'd have to wake her up.

Tonight, it's raining; one of those late-night storms that makes the whole house humid and Ethel's hair curl wildly off her head. A car swings by outside, headlights strafing the room, and he and Ethel both look, waiting to see if it'll stop and idle outside the house the way cars have started to do now. The gawkers have picked up recently; he blames his and Ethel's appearance on television earlier in the month.

A few weeks ago, the house had been filled with producers and camera operators setting up for the filming, brisk and efficient as they checked shots and marked spots with tape on the floor. The klieg lights scorching him with the light of an atomic explosion. They'd gone over the camera angles and the lines beforehand. He knew what Ed Murrow would ask, and he knew what his answers were supposed to be. But he was still nervous, sweating, a makeup artist with sympathetic eyes dabbing powder on his nose. Jack wasn't there to capture the spotlight; Jack wasn't there to hide behind. Bobby the moon, passing temporarily in front of the sun.

Ethel's a natural on camera; her face bright and

open, welcoming you in, and so it had been during the filming. Whereas when he's on camera, he appears to be peering out of himself from a threshold down the hall. Ethel made the prewritten jokes sound unrehearsed and fresh. He stumbled haltingly through his own lines, relieved when he got through it without a major slip of the tongue.

After the program was over, he did the usual telephone tree with his siblings. Ethel was much better than him, they unanimously agreed. Did he mean to look like a shy child alone in the recess yard, or was that part improvised?

He called Jack last. "Did I do okay?" he asked.

Jack's voice was cool. "You did well."

He wandered through the house, picking missed spots of gaffer's tape off the floor. Satisfied, at least, that he proved his father wrong about the hearings; dissatisfied by something else he couldn't name.

The car outside keeps going, not a gawker after all, and he relaxes.

"Have we gotten any more fan mail?" Ethel asks, after a time.

He nods heavily. There's some publicity he hasn't told his father about; some publicity Jack wouldn't be jealous of.

He gets letters at the office that say, *I'm going to cut off your wife's head and mail it to you in a hat box.*

He gets letters that say, *I'm gonna throw acid in your babies' eyes on their way home from school.*

He gets letters that say, *I've got a gun and I'm coming to your office to blow you away.*

He's thought about asking Jack if he gets letters of his own—but what's the point? Nothing can be done. Kennedys can take care of themselves.

ONE NIGHT IN OCTOBER, Jack drags them out into his yard, seemingly unconcerned that the Soviets are on their way to launching missiles from space. He wants to see this thing called *Sputnik.* It's the time of year when night comes on early and doesn't let go. The stars are yellow and distant. A breeze rattles through the leaves that are left, and in the silence after, it feels like the whole world is holding its breath.

"What's it mean 'sputnik?'" Jackie asks, standing next to him with a jacket pulled tight around her shoulders, far enough along now that the bump of her stomach shows, her face tilted to the sky. Lovely in the moonlight.

" 'Death to capitalism,' something like that…"

"Satellite," Jack calls, trying to find the best vantage point in the yard. "It means 'satellite.'"

"It's too late, Johnny," Bobby says. "It has to be dawn or dusk. The sun's reflection on the metal…"

But Jack ignores him, swiveling to the right with binoculars clapped over his eyes, binoculars he bought specifically for this purpose, to get a glimpse of the future. His brother's cool reserve cracked by a metal ball in the sky.

"How will it come down?" Jackie asks. "Or will it stay up there forever?"

"I think they said it'll fall into the atmosphere and burn up."

"Hm. They should've called it 'Icarus.'"

A step into the future, they're saying. A step toward sending men up there. The thin fingers of the bare treetops snatch at the moon.

"I'm freezing my ass off," he calls.

"Quit bitching," Jack replies.

"You looking for the *Sputnik*?" Jack's neighbor asks from the next yard over.

They chorus their reply.

"I've got it on the radio," the neighbor says, and Jack bolts over, quick and thin as a greyhound.

Bobby offers Jackie his arm. "I'm pregnant, not an invalid," she says. She takes it anyway, after a moment, and they pick their way across the dead grass.

He looks up; the stars pulsate. He wonders: if our fates are written up there, might we not send a satellite to change them?

Jackie's fingers close over Bobby's wrist, pulling him back to earth. "We want you to be the godfather, by the way," she says.

And suddenly he isn't concerned about the Russians, the bomb, what might come from outer space.

"Me?" His chest prickles with heat.

"Who else?" she asks.

"Jack agreed?"

"Jack suggested it."

They crowd around the radio, listening to the sound being transmitted back to earth from high above them, the peal of Soviet victory bells: a steady beeping somewhere between a kettle boiling and a vital sign.

"Do you hear that?" Jack asks, breathless, and Bobby sees the little boy his brother must have been in those eight years before he was born.

Jackie looks at him, too. There's something like love in her face, but Jack doesn't see it: his gaze returns skyward, searching.

"We hear it," Bobby says, and shoves his cold, blue fingers into his pockets.

CHAPTER 25

Reelection

THAT WINTER, THE PAPERS WRITE: "Senator Kennedy couldn't lose if he came out against the Pope."

If Jack were any other man, he could pencil in a few appearances in Massachusetts after Labor Day, march in a parade, make one television spot reminding people to vote, and let the ballots roll in. But he's not another man; he's this one, and he doesn't have the luxury of sitting around. Not because of a challenger—but because they need a landslide to prove his electoral strength ahead of 1960.

The campaign schedule is brutal. They have to give people a reason to turn out in an off-year election, which means more appearances, more speeches, more charm. Not just in Massachusetts, but around the country. This election is a dress rehearsal for the big one.

Ted's been put in charge of the state campaign, flying up every weekend from law school. He calls Bobby, asking his advice, reminding him of himself six years ago: *Tell me how not to screw this up.* He could tell Ted: it doesn't matter who's on the opposing ticket, sometimes Jack's still running against Joe. When his back hurts at the end of a day he'll be annoyed with the press and treat them like journalists instead of comrades, which is what they're used to, so after the last event, be sure to hustle him to the hotel. Keep crutches on hand even though he'll say he doesn't need them. When he wants to stop and talk to people after events, let him, even if it means you're late to the next one—he has an instinct for crowds, and he can find the one girl in a textile mill who's a generation off the boat, whose family lives a county over from ours and it doesn't matter that we already have the Irish vote in the bag, you just have to let him. He won't hold babies, but he'll seem to hold a stranger. He hates the PT-109 story, but make sure it's in the campaign literature, make sure he talks about it with the veterans and the Gold Star mothers, Sorensen will know what to do. When he seems like he's running out of steam, send him to a high school, or a college. He likes the way young people ask questions, doesn't matter that they can't vote, they'll go home and tell their parents about meeting the senator. Mrs. Lincoln, God love her, is a wonderful woman and a terrible secretary—don't leave her in charge of anything important, O'Brien and O'Donnell will know to bypass her but others might not. You have to understand that sometimes he's the Candidate, sometimes he's your brother. You have to understand it's not personal, it's politics. Remember that he's not a liberal, a hawk, a cold warrior, a dove; he's a winner. That's the only position that matters.

Could tell Ted, but doesn't. This is information that's only useful to him, because this is the Jack he knows; for Ted, it'll be someone different.

He comes to Boston one weekend and lets Teddy prove he's in charge by asking his little brother to show him around and introduce him to staff. A ceremonial transfer of power, he thinks, asking Ted a question about the campaign that he already knows the answer to, quietly kept in the loop by O'Donnell, O'Brien, and Jean's husband, Steve, so that he can course correct as needed. Ted walks around headquarters with his chest puffed out, the big man to see. He proudly displays a map of Massachusetts with a pin stuck in each town he's visited. It's a replica of the one Jack keeps, except Jack's is a map of the entire country.

Steve is with them, trailing discreetly at their heels like a sleek-coated hound, only speaking when Ted addresses him. He doesn't need any of the spotlight; he lets Teddy take all the credit as his own.

Teddy might be in charge of the campaign, but Steve's in charge of Teddy. The truth that Bobby discreetly conceals from his little brother is that Teddy wears a hollow crown; there's nothing he could do that would actually hurt the campaign, because there's no decision he makes that hasn't already been reviewed by Bobby, their father, or one of the others. They come through and turn straw to gold, and when Teddy wakes up in the morning, he's none the wiser.

He doesn't tell Ted this, of course. He lets him worry in the hopes it might do him some good. At some point when he wasn't looking, his brother became this idle princeling who racks up speeding tickets and catches flights just to follow women abroad, and if he appears in print, their father says, it's in the gossip column. He's no longer a little boy looking for a place to sleep; he's one of those men sitting in the back of a club with an oily smile. He's acting like a Rockefeller or a Roosevelt, old families who can afford to have one or two sons every generation turn out silly. But the Kennedys are still new to the ruling class, and not even on firm footing yet. For them, every son has to count. Our great-great-great grandchildren—they can be fools. We have to be made of sterner stuff.

Ted has been explaining his idea for a multi-town speaking tour that Bobby wrote off as too time-consuming to be realistic five minutes ago. Teddy pauses to look back at him, and Bobby realizes he's waiting for a response. He chews his lip as he looks at Bobby, and for just a moment, Bobby can see him, the little boy Ted, rise to the surface.

"It's an interesting thought," Bobby says. "Why don't you talk to O'Donnell about it?"

Relief washes over Ted. "Good," he says. "I'm glad you think so. I wasn't sure…"

Behind Teddy's back, Bobby meets Steve's eye and shakes his head. Steve nods: *Message received.*

Sometimes Bobby misses the way things used to be in his family, before politics. Even if it was never nice, as Pat claims, it was simpler. Their subterfuges and betrayals were only the normal kind—borrowed clothing, tattling on each other to their parents, refusing to let one or the other of them in on a secret. Those days are gone, he reminds himself. They're in the attic, gathering dust.

Teddy's latest girlfriend meets them at the union hall where Teddy's set to give a speech and shake hands. Another mostly useless exercise, both the girl and the speech; Teddy will have a new one next week, and the union vote is already sewn up. But it's good practice, he supposes.

The girl, Joan, hovers nervously outside, clutching a handbag in front of her with both hands. She's a quatrefoil of blonde hair and an ice-blue dress a full hand shorter than most women's. Bobby registers her more as the things she's wearing than as an actual person so that he has the strange feeling they're approaching a mannequin. Cursed with beauty, he thinks, watching her blanch under the gaze of three new sets of eyes. Some women, like Jackie's sister, know how to flaunt it, and others, like this one, don't know what to do with it, overwhelmed by the attention it brings them, allowing their clothes and their bodies to deflect so much notice away from them you forget they're a human, and not a rack to display things on.

She and Ted seem unsure of how to greet each other. She takes a few nervous steps toward him—maybe a hug? He goes in for a kiss right as she turns her head, and lands on her cheek instead. She tries to correct, and turn it into French kisses on either side of the cheek, but Ted thinks she's trying to kiss him on the mouth and leans forward, and they crack heads. Joan pulls back, rubbing a hand on her nose. Ted shoves his hands in his pockets, embarrassed but pretending not to be.

"I think it's locked," Joan says, motioning at the building. "I've been standing out here for ages." She pulls on the door handle as proof.

Bobby hesitates, then moves past her. "It's a push," he says gently, holding the door open for her. She flushes bright red as they all file inside.

It's not his first time meeting Joan. Teddy brought her home for Christmas after a previous stint with a model had flamed out. His brother does this with his girlfriends; dates someone extremely inappropriate—a woman fifteen years older or a Russian ballerina—then when they break up, he finds himself the opposite, a nice Catholic girl to see for a little while. The Penance of St. Edward, the rest of them call it.

The first night at dinner with the family, Joan caught herself on fire. She was reaching across the table to hand Pat the salt, and her sleeve dipped into the flame of one of the candles. Joan had pulled back, her arm held aloft like she was trying to signal a passing ship.

It was all over in a matter of seconds; Eunice calmly tossed her water onto Joan's sleeve, putting out the flame, then, with a disapproving look, as if Joan were a naughty toddler, she'd blown out the candles. Joan sat there with her smoldering, charred sleeve, maneuvering peas onto the tines of her fork and trying to carry on as if nothing had happened until their mother said, "Why don't you go change, dear?" and then she'd gotten up and run from the room, and the rest of them had opened the windows to air out the smell of burnt fabric.

Only Jackie's eyes had held any sympathy, watching Joan dash from the room like a hunted rabbit. She'd followed her out, and when Joan had returned to the table, it had been in one of Jackie's sweaters. This pink angora: a sign of her patronage.

By the time they finished dinner and moved into the living room, he and his siblings had more or less written the girl off.

They were arguing about whether to play Monopoly or Scrabble or just put something on TV, but then Joan sat down at the piano, and started to play. Something sweet, a light trill of notes, a slow melody like rocking a baby to sleep. Then it became something so familiar it took Bobby a moment to place it. He was surprised when it was Jack who started singing, not Teddy. He hadn't heard Jack sing in ages, had forgotten the clear, rich sound of his voice lifted in song, has gotten so used to it in speech instead. Like hearing a stranger. Like hearing a memory talk back to you.

And he remembered, suddenly, the years when they were all still together, a whole unit, the years before the war, when their mother would play like this before dinner, with Jack accompanying her, sometimes changing the lyrics at whim to lines he thought would make them laugh. *Amazing Grace, how sweet the sound, that saved a wretch like Eun-yyy.*

Joan, finding Jack's range, effortlessly shifted the tune on the piano, matching it to the natural tenor of Jack's voice.

If she can just keep playing a little longer, he remembers thinking, Kick will round the corner, sliding on the wood in her stockings, tweaking Jack on the ribs as she skates past. Joe will slope through on his way to the dining room, his cheeks still pink from a fresh shave. And Rosie will make her slow, determined way down the stairs, a flower Eunice picked for her tucked behind one ear, stopping by the back of the piano to watch, quietly mesmerized by the motion of the strings. They'll go into the other room and have dinner again, and it'll be twenty years ago instead of now. He could tell from the glazed eyes of his siblings that they were thinking the same thing. Just a little longer. Just a little longer to summon the whole family. They didn't want it to end.

But it did. Jack sang the last line and Joan closed with a cluster of notes, a repetition of the first bar of music, trailing off quietly. Only then did she look up, realizing their gaze, and flush bright red. They burst into applause, possibly the first standing ovation they've ever given a guest, and Joan hooked her hair behind her ears, abashed and pleased, swatting down their praise.

"I see you've taken a shine to the little match girl," he said to Jackie the next day.

"She's very young," Jackie said. "Girls need looking out for at that age."

"Motherhood is making you soft," he said, and she looked up at him where he was perched on the arm of the loveseat, in a way he took to mean *Don't push your luck, pal.*

Still recovering from her pregnancy, she'd taken to sitting barefoot with a stack of books piled beside her, reading through them one by one, moving only to take care of her body's still human needs. This time around, things had followed the script. A healthy little girl in the cradle at the end of November, named Caroline, for Jackie's sister. A room full of chattering family members. A press release that at last said "Child to the John Kennedys." At the christening, Lee had played the godmother to his godfather. She'd worn a mink coat and a smile like a splinter, a little chip of wood working its way under your skin.

"Proof that they've gotten along at least once," Lee had stage-whispered to Bobby.

"Don't worry about Joan," Bobby said as Jackie turned a page in her book. "She'll get out before we do any permanent damage. That's how it goes with Teddy."

"Wham, bam, thank you ma'am," Eunice agreed. She'd sunk so far down in the middle of the couch he could only see her knees, her hand scribbling something furiously. A grant proposal if he had to guess. Or a request for research. A demand for something she wanted yesterday, not understanding that the rest of the world didn't move at her furious clip. She's steered the Kennedy Foundation away from throwing cash at a haphazard assortment of charities and toward an actual mission: funding research into mental retardation. It keeps her as busy as him these days.

"Is that what you said about me?" Jackie asked. " 'She won't last long?' "

"No, we said other things about you," Bobby said, and she gave a rueful laugh and shook her head.

Since the birth of her daughter, something had changed about Jackie; there had been a newfound ease. She had taken his sisters' ribbing and had given it back to them. She had demanded things from Jack instead of asking, had required that they eat dinner alone in their house at least three times a week when they were all in Hyannisport. She had taken to sitting on the loveseat like it was a throne, and she, the queen. Something a little regal that he had remembered from when he first met her, but that had gotten lost somewhere along the way. Now she'd recovered it. Now she'd even agreed to go out on the campaign trail with Jack.

His sisters and Ethel had thought the change had had something to do with Caroline, the security she'd provided—a child makes it infinitely harder to leave your wife, was their logic. But Bobby had thought differently; Caroline hadn't been something to tie Jackie to Jack, but something that had at last been her own.

One of the dogs trotted in to lap up water from the Christmas tree stand, the bobbing motion of its head making the lower-level ornaments jingle.

"She's not the sharpest shed in the tool, is she?" Eunice asked. "All rumors about blondes confirmed."

"Keep your voice down, she's in the other room."

"By the time she figures out I'm talking about her, we'll have our next president."

"I don't think she's stupid," Jackie interjected. "I think she's shy. And intimidated."

Eunice made a noise that suggested it was all the same to her, pen still moving at a relentless pace.

"You're a fool if you marry any one of us," Eunice said darkly. "No offense, Jackie."

"None taken," Jackie said lightly. "You married Shriver, after all."

Eunice's pen stopped. She sat up, her face appearing above her knees. A smile spread slowly across her face.

"Who knew the Deb had a sense of humor?" she asked.

UP ON STAGE NOW, Ted is being introduced. Joan claps enthusiastically with the crowd as Teddy steps forward and takes the microphone. Bobby looks at her, and it's not without sympathy. If it were even a few years ago, he would have tried harder with her. But as it is, he's short on time; on the long list of things he has to do, getting to know Ted's flavor of the week doesn't make the cut.

As Teddy starts his speech, Bobby leans over to confer with Steve, though he already knows what his brother-in-law is going to say.

"How's he doing?" Bobby asks.

"He's a nice kid," Steve says quietly. Only in politics is this a liability.

"He works hard," Steve continues. He's not trying to smear Ted for his own gain, only delivering the honest report. "And he learns quickly. His heart's in the right place. But…" He pauses, sucks his teeth. "They don't take him seriously."

It's not a matter of age. Bobby was about Ted's age when he ran the first Senate campaign, and men cowered and hated him. It's something else.

It should be Steve, comes the traitorous thought. The

third Kennedy brother. He's more like them in some ways than Teddy is. Hungry for it. Determined. Whereas Teddy's the baby, used to things being handed to him. Not his fault that he's always been coddled. They've neglected Teddy; the training wheels should have been off by now. You're only as strong as your weakest link. Jack took Bobby into his confidence, made him grow up and get serious. Bobby should have been doing the same to Ted. But the committee work has occupied his time, and if not the committee, Jack's campaign.

"What can we do?" Bobby asks.

"He just needs time," Steve says.

It's the one thing they don't have.

Up on stage, Ted goes on obliviously, his smile gleaming as he pauses for laughter.

Joan looks up at the stage with an uncertain expression. "Isn't he wonderful?" she asks, as if trying to convince herself.

"THE PARTY'S SPLINTERING," Sorensen says. "You saw it at the last convention. We ought to be focusing our attention on capturing the Black vote instead of wooing Southern governors. *That's* the direction we're headed—"

"The Southerners aren't going to bolt the party," O'Donnell counters. "At least not this election, which, if you'll recall, is the one we're trying to win. If we start going after the Black vote, the Southerners will throw their support to Johnson, just watch—"

"The Black vote in Northern cities more than out-weighs losing the South—"

Hard not to picture Sorensen and O'Donnell as knights errant as they argue against each other in Jack's office, jousting with their conflicting strategies. O'Donnell the old veteran with a battered shield, and Sorensen the young challenger with a flashy new suit of armor.

Sorensen has been traveling around the country with Jack since the convention, writing his speeches, making contact with the people in each state it'll be important to know come 1960. He's less a man and more a copy of Jack's brain walking around, offsite storage for the things his brother doesn't have time to think about. But O'Donnell and O'Brien have been around since before Sorenson was a twinkle in Jack's eye, and happy to remind him of it.

Jack watches them argue with mute interest. He can intuit his brother's line of thinking: *I don't care if they fight as long as they're fighting for me.*

They've learned from the mistakes of Chicago; they need to start currying support years ahead of time, not for the Senate reelection but for the big one. Getting friendly with the powers that be on a state-by-state basis. Tracking delegates, predicting who'll be selected for the next convention. Sending Jack to speak in strategic locations. Mailing Christmas cards. Their biggest advantage right now is time: the fact that they're moving while others haven't even started. The usual

Kennedy tactic of starting early, but pretending they're not. Starting early but pretending it's only reelection they're seeking. Starting early, but telling the press Jack merely travels where he's asked to speak, that there's no broader plan. Lie, lie, lie. Run, run, run.

Bobby can sense O'Donnell stewing. "Another self-important liberal," O'Donnell seethes as their meeting winds down, shooting a dark glare at Sorensen who's across the room getting one last word in with Jack.

"You know he drinks daiquiris off the clock?" O'Donnell asks. "Just like Jack. I swear he picks up a Boston accent—"

"He helps my brother." This is the only argument that matters.

"Yeah," O'Donnell begrudgingly concedes. "Yeah, he does. But if I ever start getting that moony-eyed over Jack, hit me or something."

"What, you don't believe in the Kennedy magic?"

"Magic," O'Donnell scoffs. "If you call straight teeth and a trust fund magic."

When they've gone, Bobby closes the office door, loosens his tie, and lies down on the floor. After a moment, Jack joins him, lowering himself to the ground in increments, testing each movement for the pain it'll cause. They do this sometimes, on the nights they're tired, although lately this is every night. He's become familiar with Jack's office ceiling: the hairline crack in one corner of the molding, the one bulb in the light fixture that burns a slightly different shade of yellow.

"It's what we expected," Bobby says. Beside him, Jack sighs, needing no further context. They speak in a kind of shorthand now. Sometimes, even their own siblings complain they can't understand them.

"Poor Teddy," Jack says. He shifts, trying to find a more comfortable position for his back. "The only thing worse than being the eldest is being the baby."

Bobby hazards a glance at his brother. Jack's eyes are closed tight. Bobby recognizes that he's in some pain from the thinness of his lips, the clenched fist resting over his heart.

Only last week their father ripped O'Donnell and O'Brien a new one over the reelection schedule. "You'll schedule him into an early grave!" the Ambassador roared. "He'll be in the hospital within a month! Cut it back," his father demanded with the ruthlessness of a Hollywood studio head.

But after he'd hung up, it was Jack who said, "Leave it how it is. Just tell my father you've made the changes he wants."

Stubborn—stubborn enough that he'd quite literally break his back. He sees in Jack something swooping close to the sun.

"The campaign's fine," Bobby says now. "Teddy will learn." He doesn't know if he believes it, or only wants to. "How's Jackie handling it all?" he continues.

It's not just Teddy who's been getting a dress rehearsal. Jackie's never campaigned before—the DNC doesn't count. Of late, she's been out on the trail with Jack, learning what's expected of a politician's wife. Bobby expected her to be a net neutral at best, at least while she got the hang of things. All reports indicate otherwise. A typical scene reported by O'Donnell:

Jack jogging down the stairs of the plane in a show of health. No other senator in America gets the kind of airport welcome his brother does: crowds of constituents pressing in against police barriers, television cameras on hand to capture what would be, for any other politician, a routine arrival.

His oxfords clicking against the tarmac, Jack steps forward to greet the waiting crowd. By now he's perfected a way of shaking hands where he barely touches the voter, preventing anyone from latching on.

Parents hold up their children for a better look. Girls jump up and down in the back. People strain forward to hear what he's saying, bending toward him like they're sunflowers, he the light-giving sun. Others try to get a touch on his sleeve, this holy idol they've journeyed a long way to obtain salvation from—

And then Jackie appears.

The Wife—*thin, attractive, with wideset eyes that are apt to give her a slightly inquiring look, wearing one of the pastel-colored dresses she favors and white gloves to the wrist*—emerges from the plane.

Her ankle appears first—*shapely, narrow, fitted inside of hose and a black kitten heel*—lands on the first step, and then the rest of her body follows. She descends carefully, her hand sliding down the railing. Each step is precise. She has a way of making ordinary movement look choreographed. She moves so lightly that even in the dead silence that's fallen over the crowd, they can't hear the click of her shoes. At the bottom of the stairs, she stops and brushes her hair out of her eyes with one hand. Shyly, she looks up. Almost like a young girl, with her thin calves and her coat buttoned all the way to the top. But also like something else—something that's still taking shape and can't yet be named. It starts from the back of the crowd and moves forward, until they're all yelling the incantation of her name in different pitches and with a different urgency than what they showed his brother. There's almost a violence to it.

They've forgotten about Jack in an instant; he was the warm-up act. It's her they're really here for.

She walks toward the police barriers, accepting bundles of flowers as they're handed to her. She sniffs a rose coquettishly and then stoops down to hand it to a little girl. She shakes hands. She steals the show completely. She sniffs another rose in the bouquet and then, like a benediction, tosses it into the crowd. A hundred hands reach up.

"Do you think she likes it?" Bobby asks. "Campaigning?"

"I think she likes winning," Jack says. "I think she might be a Kennedy after all." He lets out a long sigh that he seems to have been holding in for some time.

"She's going to have a price," he adds. "I guarantee her cooperation is conditional."

How does he know? What augury has told him this?

"Because she's her mother's daughter," Jack says. "If Janet taught her one thing, it's how to make her husband pay."

CHAPTER 26

Engagement

HIS FATHER DOESN'T INVITE his children to visit; he summons them. He and Jack meet him at the Palm Beach house.

Their father is waiting for them out back, practicing his putt on the veranda. He lines up his shot and sinks another golf ball into the open mouth of the drinking glass set on its side to serve as a target.

"We're going to have Ted get married," the Ambassador says. "Robert—my ball."

Bobby looks at Jack and sees his confusion mirrored. "To who?" he asks.

"The ball, Robert," his father says, motioning with his club. Bobby fishes the ball out of the glass and rolls it back to his father, who stops it with the long edge of his putter.

His father adjusts his grip, shifts his weight between his feet until he finds a position he likes. "That girl he's been seeing. She's a good Catholic," his father says, eyeing the cup. "It's unlikely he's going to find another. And she's young enough—"

The club connects with the ball. The ball connects with the back of the cup. Ironic, that his father excels at the short game in golf, when he plays the long game everywhere else.

"Young enough that she'll be easy to handle. Easy to train," his father finishes his thought.

And young enough that she won't understand what she's getting into until it's too late, Bobby thinks. To Joan, they're the glamorous family she's seen in magazines. She won't look past the cover story.

The Ambassador taps his club impatiently against the ground, and Bobby understands that he's to stay here, squatting next to the cup, so as to be his father's ballboy.

"He's not ready," Jack says. His eyes are hidden behind black sunglasses, but Bobby thinks he can read unhappiness in the set of his mouth. "Let him have a few more years of being a bachelor."

"We don't have a few more years," their father says. He leans on his club. "The press already think you're a playboy. We can't have your brother running around making a fool of himself as well. Not while you're campaigning. Imagine you're running a primary while trying to deal with another headline about him yachting with loose women."

Jack takes his sunglasses off. "'Loose women?'" he asks. "It's nineteen fifty-eight, Dad. We call them 'party girls' now."

"Ask him," their father gestures at Bobby. "Ted's own campaign staff doesn't take him seriously. Why should a voter in Indiana?"

He does a few practice swings, a gentle swivel of his body. The sun knifes off the head of the club, slicing a purple line in Bobby's vision. Jack steps forward. Now it'll happen, Bobby thinks with relief. Jack will make him see reason. Jack will make him listen.

His brother plucks a club from their father's bag, gives it an experimental twirl. "You use a five-wood?" he asks.

"It's good on the rough," their father says. "Better than an iron."

"I don't know about that," Jack says. "The iron has better—"

Bobby stands up abruptly. "A marriage is for *life*," he says. "Teddy hardly thinks past tomorrow's breakfast. It'll end badly."

It's not that Teddy has malice in his heart, just that he's careless. What makes their father think he's going to be able to handle a wife?

Jack slots the club back into the bag. "We'll find a way to keep him busy during the campaign," he says, looking to Bobby for confirmation.

Bobby nods. "We'll send him out West. Keep Steve with him."

Their father is unmoved. "A wife is good cover," he says with a pointed look at Jack. "Wouldn't you agree?"

The Ambassador lines up his next shot. The ball rolls smoothly toward the cup. At the last second, Jack nudges the cup with the toe of his shoe. The ball misses and rolls off, into the grass. Their father gives Jack an annoyed look. Then he turns to Bobby. "The ball's not going to fetch itself."

They go on like this for another half hour, he and Jack arguing against the marriage, their father insisting on its necessity, until eventually he and Jack are beaten into submission. There are still some fights they're incapable of winning against their old man. If Bobby's thinking like a strategist instead of a brother, he can admit it's a smart move. The best tool you can have if you're prone to slipping up in the spotlight isn't an attorney or an apology, but a woman standing faithfully at your side.

They slouch back out to the car. Neither of them is staying the night; Bobby's back to Washington, Jack is off to his next speaking engagement.

Heading back to the airport, his brother hurtles along the interstate like he doesn't care if they reach their destination, stitching the car in and out of lanes without a signal.

"We can try again," Bobby says. "Find him when he's in a good mood—"

Jack flips down the sun visor, then flips it back up with an impatient hand. "It's done, Bob. I'm not happy about it either, but we have to accept it."

Bobby worries the air vents. "Try and picture Teddy sitting down to dinner at five o'clock to eat ham and potatoes. He's not built for marriage."

"He'll get used to it. We all do."

It takes him longer than it should to recognize something in his brother's tone is off. He turns to Jack. The realization dawns on Bobby slowly.

"I don't believe this," he says. "You've been conspiring with Dad. You wanted this to happen."

Everything they just went through was a three-man play, only one of the actors didn't have the script beforehand.

" 'Conspiring' is a strong word," Jack says.

Not in our family, Bobby thinks. Not by a mile. He likes to think he's left behind the days when he and his brothers would get into fistfights with men in the park. But right now, he'd like nothing more than to hit his brother, to whale on him like a stranger, to get his anger out with his hands.

"You rotten son of a bitch," he spits at Jack instead.

Jack puts a mocking hand to his heart. "You wound me," he says.

"Why did you do it?" Bobby asks. "Don't you care about Teddy at all—"

"It's for the best," Jack cuts in flatly. "He has to grow up, Bob. You did."

His throat is tight. A second heartbeat pulses in his temple. He tries to parse his anger, to rank it by how much it stings. First, what it means for Ted. Second, that he didn't see this coming. Third, the one that stings most, the fact that Jack took their father's side instead of his, when it's the two of them that are supposed to be partners now. He thinks for a moment. Fourth—he adds a fourth—the fact that his brother knows all of his thoughts, but he still doesn't know all of his brother's. A small part of him admits that he's angrier on his own behalf than on Ted's.

"You're a lousy brother," he says, and though he speaks to Jack, the words are actually directed at himself.

"Tell me something I don't know," Jack says, cutting a three-lane change from the left lane, just barely making their exit.

Behind them, horns blare. Other drivers lift their middle fingers in outrage. But Jack's unconcerned, lifts a breezy hand in apology. He knows that everyone forgives him in the end.

A FEW MONTHS LATER the announcement is made. The final Kennedy to be wed. He and Jack take Teddy out for something like a bachelor party. Although Bobby's anger lingers, Teddy doesn't seem to notice anything amiss. He's at his most Irish tonight, spinning through every bar they enter, shaking hands with the bartender, chatting up the women, buying a round for the men, ensuring he's on a first-name basis with the whole place by the time they leave.

He chats excitedly with Jack and Bobby about what he'll do when he finishes law school next year, his plans for the three of them once they all live in DC. Bobby can tell what he's thinking: It'll be like this all the time. Nights whirling through the city, a three-man social club. Touch football during the day. Lunch together in the Senate cafeteria. It's what Bobby thought early on, too. He doesn't have the heart to tell Teddy that nights like tonight are the exception, not the rule. Most of what he and Jack do is work. Grinding work. Slogging together through the problems of electoral politics. They don't have fun together—"fun" is something they've learned is best kept to other people.

His father was right, what he told him before the DNC: He's not Jack's friend. He's not his drinking buddy. Not his pal. He's his coconspirator, his campaign manager, his brother.

But he lets Teddy believe what he wants, for tonight. Watches him drink and laugh and flirt at the bar. He wonders if his brother's been given the pre-wedding skirt-chasing talk yet. *Be discreet. Keep things ship-shape on the home front. Have a child within the first year to keep her occupied.*

"Lighten up," Jack says, reading his mood, and Bobby feels Jack slip a few degrees further away. He used to think it was all at once, how his brother became this Jack, then another. But now he knows it's a more delicate calibration.

"Easy for you to say," Bobby says. "Don't you feel any guilt at all?"

"Oh, I do, Bob, but I save it for confession."

"You know, I walked in on him and Joan the other weekend," Bobby says. "You'd expect them to be necking. Do you know what they were doing? A puzzle."

"Maybe if you'd given them another minute," Jack says.

Teddy leans against the bar, grinning. His little brother in the body of a man. The woman he's talking to tilts her head to the side, exposing a long column of neck. Teddy says something to make her laugh. *Be discreet*, his father said, but once, long ago, the actress Gloria Swanson came to visit them in Hyannisport. Roaring into the driveway in a red Rolls Royce with a whole troupe of valets to carry her bags, her small daughter, also named Gloria, immediately swallowed by the horde of his sisters. Bobby was on the roof, where he used to nest like a bird in the summer because he liked to watch his family from above, to track their comings and goings from the eaves. The car door opened and the starlet emerged, pale leg, the buckle of her shoe sparkling in the sun, a cream-colored dress billowing around her, one hand to her head, holding a hat in place over dark curls. She looked up immediately, as if she knew he was there, and lifted her hand. Not a wave. Nothing so friendly as that. More of an acknowledgment that he was looking at her, and she was someone to be seen. Bobby knew from his sisters—not because of anything said aloud—that there was something wrong with her, something to dislike.

His father emerged from the house then, the gravel crunching under his shoes, his stride insistent, urgent. His mother followed slightly behind and Bobby wondered if she could see it, how when his father grabbed the starlet's hand, he was doing more than saying hello. Whatever greetings the three of them exchanged were lost on the wind. His mother, after a moment, started directing the valets, leading them inside in a train of suitcases and hat boxes. His father and the actress were left alone—or so they thought—and this was when his father kissed her and the actress let him for just a moment before her hands came up to his chest, pushing him away, pointing to the roof. Bobby had already disappeared behind one of the eaves. She was pointing at nothing, and he remembers feeling his father's laughter deep in his gut.

Pat told him he couldn't have remembered it, that there's no chance he was on the roof at three years old; then whose memory is it? he wanted to know. You probably made it up, she said, because you know now what was happening then. Then who scraped my hands trying to hide on the roof? he wanted to ask, who got dizzy up there from the smell of seaweed mixed with perfume? No use arguing, though; when his sisters know something, they're very sure that they know.

"It's out of our control then," Jack says, remembering this with him. His brother slides out of the booth, his eyes on the women at the bar. "It's something in our blood."

BUT NOW HIS BROTHERS change: they're meeting their wives for dinner, and they're dutiful husbands again. It's the same night, but they're different men. The girls have been having their own party for Joan, and they all convene, laughing, outside of the agreed-upon restaurant.

They enter the restaurant in twos and threes. It's the kind of place their father would like, the interior unchanged from the thirties: thick curtains, tables big as boulders, light fixtures that defy gravity. Ted doesn't seem to know quite what to do with Joan; he moves her first to one arm, then the other, like she's an unwieldy parcel. Not heavy, just awkward.

Pat breaks free from their group to talk to the maître d'. "It's under Kennedy," she says with drunken jauntiness. Her earrings are tiny diamond chandeliers; when she turns her head, they spit light.

A cry behind them. Ted and Joan have gotten stuck in the revolving door, the tail of her skirt trapped. Ted tries to push on the door and it only pulls the dress tighter, to the point of tearing. An usher rushes over to help, and after a bit of maneuvering, manages to free her. Ted beams, feeling mildly heroic as he reaches for Joan's arm, but she brushes past him with her head down, her cheeks red.

"In the worst case we could have cut her out of it," Ted catches up, squeezing Joan's arm. She doesn't seem to find this funny. She bites her lip and stands stiffly, not saying a word.

"If we make it to the table without someone tripping on a banana peel, it'll be a miracle," Eunice says, and then the others pick up the thread, pointing to table corners and chairs and saying "Watch out Joan!" She's trying to smile and play along, but she's biting her lip the way a child does when she's taken a spill; it's not the pain, but the embarrassment.

"What's the occasion?" the waiter asks. People are always asking this when his family's together; usually there is no occasion, just a lot of them.

"He's going to win an election," Eunice says, motioning to Jack. She seems to have honestly forgotten why they're here.

"And they're getting married," Jean fills in hastily, always eager for everything to be all right, for everyone to get along. Joan starts to blush again, red creeping up from her neckline.

"Right, that too," Eunice says, plucking at her bundle of silverware. She'd normally be in bed by now, and has about reached her limit of social graces for the evening.

Pat crooks a lacquered nail at the waiter. "I'll have a martini," she says. "Two olives, or I'll send it back."

Bobby motions the waiter over. "Strike the martini," he says quietly. "She'll have a coffee."

Pat doesn't notice his sabotage. "Have we been here before?" she asks. Eunice yawns.

As the food comes out, the conversation turns to how the rest of them got engaged. Pat was in Tokyo visiting one of several men when Peter decided he was willing to take the leap. When she got engaged, the Ambassador told Jean that she could have a big wedding and a small present or a small wedding and a big present. Ethel holds out her hand to Joan; not asking her to kiss the ring, merely to look at it.

"When Bobby and I got engaged—"

"Yes Ethel, we know," Jackie says dryly. "You were sent a whole tray of diamonds because Bobby loves you best."

"And don't you forget it."

Time hasn't dulled their dislike.

They sit together sometimes at the hearings—not by choice, but to avoid rumors of a rift. Ethel chatting with the camera operators and Jackie as stiff and still as if she'd been carved there in marble. They always seem to be in colors that clash. Occasionally he sees them making small, sideways conversation and wonders what on earth they talk about.

Tonight, they don't take their animosity any further; tonight's about Ted and Joan's uneasy union, not theirs.

"Give us the story," Pat prompts Ted.

Ted and Joan look at each other; there's a beat that goes on slightly too long. Neither of them wants to tell it.

"You have asked her, haven't you?" Eunice asks. Joan turns a deeper shade of red.

"There's nothing to tell, really," Ted says, shrugging. Joan looks at her plate.

"You have the soul of a poet," Eunice says. Pat giggles and reaches for her drink; she ignores the coffee in front of her and pulls Jean's martini to her instead.

Joan picks at the tablecloth, then looks up at Jackie for a life preserver. "What about you?" she asks. "I don't know if I've ever heard how you and Jack met."

Jack and Jackie look at each other, as if trying to remember themselves. Usually they tell it like this, they make it a bit of a joke: Jack will say, "We were at a dinner party with friends and I leaned in over the asparagus and asked her out," and Jackie will say, ironically, "And how could I resist?"

Jack does his part, the first part, but when it comes to Jackie's half of the story, she picks moodily at her food, then sets down her fork in such a deliberate way, Bobby can't help but read it as a warning sign.

"I'm not even sure they were serving asparagus that night," she says, folding her hands together on the table. Jack seems caught off guard, but only for a moment.

"The broccoli, then."

Jackie purses her lips. She seems to decide something. "I was engaged to another man first," she says to Joan. "But I broke it off."

"Why?" Joan asks.

"Because I could," she says meaningfully, looking

only at the girl. Bobby's aware of his sisters exchanging glances.

There's something urgent in Jackie's voice now. "I broke it off even though I'd said 'yes.' Even though the announcement had gone out. Because as long as you haven't walked down the aisle, it's not too late to change your mind——"

Pat upends her plate into Teddy's lap. "Oh dear," she says, moving hastily to mop it up with a napkin. Oil glides down the front of his shirt. Pat's suddenly making a big show of her drunkenness, and Bobby sees something calculated in it. He tries to catch her eye, but her eye evades capture.

"They make a very strong martini here," she says to the table at large, shaking her head like it's the restaurant to blame. She plucks the speared olive out of Jean's glass, and slides it off the stick with her teeth. The stick rattles as she tosses it back into the empty glass. "And I think I asked for *two* olives," she says.

BOBBY TAKES TEDDY into the bathroom to clean him up. Teddy stumbles into him at the sink and says, with whiskey-loosened lips, "I'm sorry I'm not Steve."

"What?" Bobby laughs. It sounds false even to his own ears. It's as if his brother has pulled his own traitorous thoughts out of his head and read them back to him.

"That's what you want, isn't it? You and Jack?

Someone who's like you. Someone who's actually *good* at politics—"

"You're doing fine," he says, running the tap to warm. "Don't beat yourself up." He pumps a bit of soap onto a damp paper towel and starts scrubbing at Ted's shirt, avoiding his brother's eyes. The stain doesn't lift out, only spreads into an abstract shape.

Ted says, "You're being kind. Didn't you say that once? That kindness in our family's fatal?"

Bobby ignores him and wets a new paper towel.

"I don't want to marry her," Teddy says, apparently ready to get every last thing off his chest.

Bobby scrubs stubbornly at his brother's shirt. "She's a lovely girl," he says.

"I hardly know her," Ted says, approaching a wail. "She doesn't want to either."

"Talk to Dad," Teddy continues. "Tell him—tell him something! He'll listen to you." His brother's eyes are wide with desperation, his breath hot with drink. Bobby feels like he's on the verge of being swallowed by his family's need. He can feel it looming over him, coming down like a hood. He remembers his little brother asking him in the dark: Will I disappear, too, if I disappoint Dad? Ted, here, grown up but still asking him the same question, asking Bobby to save him.

"Teddy," he says in a voice calmer than he feels, "we all have to do things we don't want to do."

His brother takes a few gulping breaths, like a child getting worked up.

"Take this off so I can dry it," Bobby says quickly, motioning to Teddy's shirt. His brother fumblingly undoes the buttons, then slumps down the wall in his undershirt, finally coming to rest on the tile floor.

Bobby stands at the hand dryer, punching the button over and over, listening to the blast of air, feeling the warmth on his hands, ignoring the tears rolling steadily down his brother's face.

HE GOES ALONE, this time.

Jack can't be counted on as an ally, so he opts to plead Teddy's case again on his own. His father is neither expecting him nor surprised to see him, used to the peripatetic nature of his children, their constant comings and goings a trait inherited from him. The first trees are spangled yellow and red, the geese arrow south through clear skies, and the day is still just warm enough in the sun that you can convince yourself summer isn't so far gone.

"See that?" his father asks, pointing out at the water.

A handful of boats, their sails so white and pristine they look like restaurant napkins folded and laid out on the tablecloth of the Atlantic.

"Been here all morning," the Ambassador says with a note in his voice Bobby can't quite read.

"Do you know them?" Bobby asks.

"No, but they know us." Before he can puzzle this out, his father says, "They have cameras."

Satisfaction, he realizes. That's what he hears in his father's voice. And Bobby can see them now, their lenses pointed at him and his father, pointed at the house. His mind goes to the cars idling outside of his house, the gawkers, and he feels suddenly exposed, and also embarrassed to feel this way, because what does it matter, a few photos of him and his father in the yard? It's good to be paid attention, good for people to take an interest in them. Or, good for the campaign, anyway.

And this is where his father's mind is, not on Teddy, which is a done deal as far as he's concerned. He's oblivious to Bobby's reason for coming here.

"I know it would certainly be a weight off Jack's shoulders the sooner you're able to focus on the campaign full time..." the Ambassador says.

Bobby hears the suggestion in his father's voice. And once he would've quit his job right away; once, in fact, he did this. But he holds on, stubbornly, to his committee work, this renegade existence unsanctioned by his father.

"Your sisters say all you talk about anymore is Jimmy Hoffa," his father says.

"They exaggerate."

"Hoffa isn't the priority—your brother, that's where your attention ought to lie."

He knows this. And yet—he tries to think of how to explain without sounding disloyal—it's something of his own. Something that makes him more than an ambassador's son or a senator's brother in the eyes of the world.

I want to talk to you about Teddy. He has the words. But then he swears he can hear the click of camera shutters echoing over the water, and he realizes that he came here more out of guilt than conviction; he doesn't actually believe he can change his father's mind. He came here for something else. He came here to say he tried without actually trying.

He used to think his father could read their minds, peer straight into their heads with his laser-blue eyes. He used to think there was nothing his father didn't know about them. But this age has passed, he's sad to find. He realizes now that his father has no idea what any of his children are thinking. The Ambassador recognizes only the thoughts and desires that are in accord with his own, and anything else is extraneous. Anything else simply doesn't exist. And that's been the key to his father's success. Not money or political connections or whatever else they usually chalk it up to. Only blinding faith in the rightness of his own vision. Only belief that obliterates all else.

"I remember what it was like to be young and to want to work," his father says. "Why—there were weeks I stayed up seven days in a row, working all day, entertaining all night."

This has the gloss of one of his father's trademark exaggerations.

"Mother says you were an old man from the day she married you. Always in bed by eight at the latest—"

"You wouldn't believe some of the nights I've had, Robert."

If he goads the old man just a little, he may just get a story out of him instead of a lecture. And Bobby wants this, suddenly; he wants to go back to that younger age when his father knew everything, when in the beginning was the word, and the word was with his father, and the word was his father. He shuts his eyes against the sun.

"Everyone drank during Prohibition, Dad. That's hardly the epitome of a grand old time."

He can hear in his father's voice how the Ambassador's eyes flare with the challenge. "I'll tell you what we did—we'd have the president around to Marwood— you remember that house?"

He does, but vaguely. He never lived there; none of them did, although that was his father's excuse for buying a mansion when he first went to Washington. Room for the kids. It had the feeling of Versailles. It had the feeling of another man. Bobby suspects that women who weren't his mother slept in the bedroom more than she did.

As his father speaks, the scene blooms to life behind Bobby's closed eyes: The president and his men pulling up in their black limousines, already a little drunk from the drive over. The president wheeling up to the house in strong strokes, his chair flashing in the moonlight. And then, inside: the dining room table set out like a state dinner, fine china and candelabras, and the president rolling to a stop at the center of the table, where a chair had already been removed to make space—

"Why the center?" Bobby asks. "Why not the head?"

"I'll tell you why," his father says, pleased to be asked. "He said you always missed the punchline at the head of the table, and as president, you hear precious few jokes as it is."

Resume the scene: the party seated around the table, the waitstaff bringing in glasses of Scotch. His father has spared no expense; the Roosevelts of the world drink Haig & Haig, so that's what he serves. If you can buy the same whiskey, maybe you can be the same man. The main course isn't veal, isn't steak, but bright red lobster on a bed of lettuce, flown in from Maine that morning. Lobster for the president. And some of the others, if they hail from inland states, don't know how to eat it, poking at it uncertainly with a fork.

"That's how you know you've arrived—are you listening?—when you can serve a food that other men don't know how to eat."

The dinner party guests grow lethargic on the food and drink and summer air, the night so hot that not even open windows and ice cream can cool them down, so his father has mint juleps brought out, an old Southern trick for dealing with the humidity, or at least getting you drunk enough that you don't mind. And they start singing, eventually, all of them. Old songs, songs they learned as boys. Songs you can't sing around women. The room yellow and the night black, and the crickets and cicadas singing back—

"Did the president have a good voice?" Bobby asks.

"Of course. What kind of story would it be if the president couldn't sing? He could sing and he could spin a yarn as well as any Irishman. He was a marvelous time when he wanted to be."

His father sounds—does his father sound?—wistful.

He opens his eyes, and the vision disappears. Those men are gone now. It's just his father, alone in the yard. Alone with his memories.

Not alone—with his son. He tests the moment, seeing how much it'll give beneath his touch. "Are you glad you knew a piece of history?"

"History," his father scoffs. "He was only a man— like us, like anyone. Flesh and blood. A pile of bones. No more alive than anyone who ever lived."

He thinks that that's not really an answer, but perhaps—perhaps it's a matter of rephrasing it for the witness to make it clear what he's asking: *Are you glad that you knew* him? *Was it the man or the history that mattered in the end?*

But this will keep until another time.

ON ELECTION NIGHT, Bobby watches from across the room as Jack, Teddy, and Jackie pose for the UPI reel, smiles slashing across their faces. He's only flown in for the night, for the victory. They've gotten their landslide.

After the first Senate election, Bobby threw up in a wastepaper basket. Emptied his guts after the press had gone, the metal rim of the trash can digging into his forearms. The relief of victory tasted like stomach acid. This one tastes like the lit end of his brother's cigar, the dry, spiced smoke that trails him in a sweet train.

"*Looking down the bumpy road toward 1960,*" the papers write, "*Jack Kennedy has moments of discouragement. He takes from his wallet a cartoon showing a harassed office worker, standing on his chair, thumbing his nose at his desk, and crying 'I quit!' Says Kennedy: 'That's the way I feel sometimes.'*"

But this is only a bit they've decided on for the reporters; something to soften the bite of "ambition" they so often accuse him of. Tomorrow, his brother will be back on the road, back on 1960, back on the edge of his seat arguing with Bobby over their strategy.

Election to the Senate. This was all they wanted, once. This was everything, once. The campaign of six years ago a pentimento, those men painted over, still there but hidden. Still there but repented for, the composition improved, the dreams enlarged.

He remembers them singing in 1952; for this one, he'll remember most the steady clack of the television cameras, turning them to image.

CHAPTER 27

Repentance

THOSE DAMN TEA PARTIES, Lodge said of their victory over him in '52. That's what gave them the edge. But Bobby knows it wasn't the tea parties alone. A campaign doesn't stand or fall on one act. It's the overall effect, the sum of its parts. What beat Lodge was Eunice knocking on every door in an apartment building, even the ones of confirmed Republicans. What beat Lodge was Jack shaking an extra hand. What beat Lodge was Jean visiting a ward not on her itinerary. What wins is unending work.

Christmas 1958 hardly registers for him: Mass, the children unwrapping presents, a brief patter of rain against the glass. New Year's: sparklers sizzling to death in a bucket of water, the multicolored artillery of fireworks over the treetops, his sisters saying "Only one year to go," like it's a good thing. The whole world, not just the Kennedys, is looking ahead. They're saying that in the sixties, the Soviets will put a man on the moon. Women's skirts will rise high above the knee. People will keep moving out of the cities, and telephones will have keypads instead of rotary dials. What wonders the coming decade will bring.

Next year, 1960, is going to be the longest year of their lives. A year measured in miles of road, in vote counts and polls. A year measured in hands shaken and babies held and paper cups of whiskey passed around frigid campaign buses late at night. A year of hotel rooms and small towns and motorcades. A year where exactly three things matter: the primaries, the nomination, the general.

But first it's early 1959 and he has an awareness of each hour, and how it should best be spent. He arranges minutes on an abacus in his head. Every moment now could be the moment that tips the balance.

Jack's become the most popular Democrat in the party, a landslide victor in his latest race, and a total politician, with the wife and smiling baby to prove it. He's by far the frontrunner, and this is what Bobby's afraid of, that they'll peak too early. Because they're not running alone anymore; by the spring, other undeclared candidates have started to make their bids known the way presidential campaigns are always announced in this country: by vehemently denying any such campaign exists.

All across the country now, there are meetings going on like the ones he and Jack and the others are having. In law offices and conference rooms and restaurants. Feelers put out. Plans laid. He can almost hear it sometimes; the low murmur of other men's aspirations. Lyndon Johnson, Richard Nixon, Hubert Humphrey, even Adlai Stevenson, who perhaps thinks "third time lucky." Some of them aren't serious enough to worry about as real challengers. But others are; Lyndon Johnson, for instance, gives Bobby a particular unease, and he comes to associate the sight of his gangling form around the Capitol with a stomachache. Pavlovian, how it comes on.

"I'd have the nomination if the convention was tomorrow," Jack says, watching the field of contenders grow day by day with increasing annoyance.

"Another year is nothing," Bobby says, because the first rule of politics is you can't let the candidate see you're as worried as he is.

"It's time," Jack says. "We act like it's these other things that matter—policies, experience, money—but all it really comes down to is time. If you get the timing right. If you understand your times." Standing behind his desk, he idly knuckles a muscle in his back, his teeth set against the pain. "Think about Chamberlain," Jack says. "You look back at him and think 'How didn't the poor bastard see it coming?'"

"Nobody's going to call us poor," Bobby says. "Dad made sure of that."

"Dad got it exactly right, didn't he? Investing early in the movie studios?" Jack asks, a note of hope in his voice, like maybe it runs in the blood.

"Investing early in the movies, the stock market, Governor Franklin Roosevelt of New York…"

Jack cocks his head to the side. His hair falls in his eyes. "But he was never around." Bobby thinks of his own children then, of scooping them up three, four at a time, trying to figure out—are you bigger than you were last weekend, when I last held you? Pressing his face into their baby soft scalps. A postcard from his daughter saying, "Dear Daddy, Where have you been it is time to come home all your children miss you."

"Can't you be both?" Bobby asks. "A father and a man committed to a cause?"

"Can you ever be both?" Jack asks, and this is one of those moments where he slides into his brother's head: They're fathers when they have the time. Family men when *Life* magazine needs new color stills.

Jack turns to study the map on the wall that bristles with pins: his progress like a palimpsest over a map of the nation.

"Catholicism," he says.

"Youth," Bobby says. "Inexperience."

They trade weaknesses. It's not masochism; it's what everyone else will be saying soon enough, if they aren't already.

"Dad."

"Money."

"Massachusetts."

Wrong state, wrong age, wrong religion, they write of his brother. His handicaps, in their eyes, are manifold. His strengths limited mainly to his popular appeal, and his hair.

"We'll need a disproportionate number of Catholics," Bobby says. "To outweigh bias from other wings."

"Saints and martyrs," Jack says, still considering the map. Bobby knows he's not looking at all the ground he's covered, but at the white space between each pinhead. "That's all the difference between us and them."

"Transubstantiation, too."

"Saints, martyrs, and God in our bread and wine," Jack says wearily. "If Martin Luther had only kept his mouth shut…"

The Catholic candidate for president, or a Catholic who happens to be candidate for president? This is how they talk about Jack, the political commentators. He'd offer a third category, sometimes: a Catholic who just happens to be Catholic.

Would the religious furor settle down if he told them how Jack used to sneak paperbacks into church in the waistband of his pants? How he held dime novels inside of the Bible during Mass so that he always appeared to be in deep contemplation of scripture? He thinks of a conversation he had with Arthur Schlesinger recently. Bobby was trying to pick his brain about why

Al Smith, the first and last Catholic candidate their party put on the ticket, lost so badly.

"You mean, do I think he lost because he was Catholic?" Schlesinger asked. "It certainly doesn't help a candidacy when Americans can be convinced by the Klan that you're the Antichrist."

There was an old joke about Al Smith, how people believed that if he was elected, the Pope would move stateside and rule the country from Washington. After the election, the punchline goes, Smith sent a one-word telegram to the Vatican: "Unpack."

"But if we ask the inverse," Schlesinger had said, "would Smith have won had he been a Protestant, I don't know that it comes out in his favor, either. The Republicans had a boom economy, which is the number one consideration for voters. Not to mention that Smith was a Tammany Hall product, which likely turned off a fair number of people. And you must consider—women had only been able to vote for two election cycles at this point and Smith—this was not a world-class campaign. He certainly wasn't sending his brother out four years ahead of time."

"It sounds like 'Catholic' is still the cause of death," Bobby said.

"It wasn't his faith," Schlesinger said. "It was his failure to find a good way to address it."

And is that the only way to win in this country? To deny what you are? To distance yourself from it? To *address* it?

He picks up a pin and fiddles with it. These questions don't bother Jack, he knows. He's long been aware his brother's faith is different from his own. "Flimsier" isn't quite the right way of putting it, though it does bend. Religion irks Jack for the same reason it comforts Bobby; because it's always there; because it has an answer for everything.

Jack's a Catholic because he was born a Catholic. He still goes to church out of habit, and because the only thing more suspect than being a Catholic lawmaker in this country is being a godless one. He knows all the rules and rituals because he was taught them. As for Christ dying on the cross for him, Jack's suffered more pain in his life than Jesus on the cross for three days, and probably thinks the old boy should have gotten a little more out of it for his troubles. Though the crucifixion and the tomb were a good bit of political theater, even he can admit.

Bobby presses the pin against the pad of his finger until blood wells to the surface. *Drink of my blood and eat of my flesh.*

His brother, the hope of Catholic America, of immigrants, of their father, of their family. He looks over at his brother, who's both a boy and ancient in the lamplight, and he wants to ask Jack: *Is it heavy?*, but of course it is; any dream is, whether it's yours or someone else's.

The time is coming, he knows, to bear a little of his brother's burden. To shift his attention to the campaign full time, to be the Campaign Manager instead of Bobby. A moment lost now can't be made up on the other side.

An official campaign apparatus is starting to take shape. His father has—ever so discreetly—rented out a suite of offices near Bobby's own for campaign headquarters, putting Steve in charge to provide cover. The proximity of the office isn't just for convenience; it's also a reminder to his son of where his responsibilities lie.

But something in him still resists. He catches himself daydreaming about other versions of his life, free of politics, free to do what he wants. He imagines staying on the committee, finding his way to the next job, something at the DOJ, maybe, where he could prosecute the criminals he's only been able to question, Hoffa included.

The only problem with his private imaginings, he thinks, looking across at his brother, is that Jack's nowhere in the frame.

Questionable loyalty of campaign manager. Another weakness to add to their list.

CHAPTER 28

The Round Table

IN APRIL THEY GATHER in Palm Beach. The first official meeting of the Kennedy brain trust. They sit in a loose circle of lounge chairs on the hard-packed sand, intimates only, "The Round Table," as Jackie has taken to calling it in a voice rich with irony. Sorensen has taken the seat next to Jack, and he polishes his glasses on the tail of his shirt and tries not to gloat as O'Donnell and O'Brien stare at him murderously. Steve sits nearby in that quiet, watchful way that reminds Bobby so much of Jean, self-contained but at once aware of everything going on around the circle.

And his father. The Ambassador an outlier among their group, in age and role. Unlike the rest of them, he won't be publicly campaigning for Jack. It would draw the wrong attention, open them up to attacks of Jack being nothing more than his father's puppet.

Bobby—the Campaign Manager—listens to their progress reports one at a time. As they travel around the circle, a dread builds low in his gut and works its way steadily up through his chest to his throat, then his head, as if being drilled from deep in his core. It's the same feeling he had when he took over Jack's Senate race: months ahead of everyone else, yet somehow still late to the dance. How have things been going on like this? He asked Jack back then. But this time he knows the answer to his own question.

It's because of him. Because he's been distracted, playing the Chief Counsel instead of the Campaign Manager.

A silence. The sound of the waves.

Bobby says, at last, "Frankly I'm appalled that more work hasn't been done."

"Thank you for your frankness," Jack says levelly.

"An hour lost now can't be made up on the other side," he insists, aware of how cold his voice sounds.

"We would have brought you on earlier, Bob, but we didn't want that voice in our ears for the whole year," Jack says. The unspoken accusation in his brother's eyes: we would have brought you on earlier, but you refused.

They move on. He ignores Jack's look and whatever it's trying to tell him.

They turn to the primaries; sixteen states hold them. Other candidates have the luxury of sitting them out—Stevenson, who can hope to be drafted at the convention, Symington, who plans to ride Truman's endorsement all the way to July—but Jack will have to enter them to prove his popularity extends beyond the Northeast and the pages of *Time* and *Life*.

They debate now which to enter.

"Wisconsin," Sorensen suggests. "It would bait Humphrey into entering—he's their third senator, after all. A win there takes care of him."

"Indiana or Illinois," O'Brien says. "Prove that he can appeal to farmers."

"West Virginia?" O'Donnell asks. "If you win there, they might just have to hand you the whole thing."

"Too risky," Bobby says. It's win or go home for each primary they enter. "Whatever we decide, it has to come up Kennedy every time."

They turn to Steve with his abacus brain: "How many primaries can we reasonably afford to enter?"

Hotels, radio and television ads, printing pamphlets and posters to paint each town Kennedy, greasing the right palms—it adds up.

His father has said very little. His father, who's used to dominating rooms, struck silent. Moving out of the spotlight so his son can have a chance at what he couldn't. But he speaks up now.

"Whatever the cost," the Ambassador says, "we'll pay it."

Bobby flicks a glance at his brother. "There goes our inheritance, Johnny."

"I don't think he left you much anyway."

He remembers his father's bargain with God once: every penny I have if you heal him. Now he makes a similar bargain with the American people: every penny I have if you make him your president.

"I expect progress and lots of it by next time," Bobby says by way of bringing things to a close for the day.

The others linger, clustering around Jack, but Bobby strikes off down the beach. His head is a riot of states, delegates, poll numbers—he tries to organize them, to line them up in black and white, smooth marble pieces on a chess board.

By the time he returns to the house, it's getting dark. Jack has gone. Only his father is left, a hard caramel clicking against his teeth as he mutters to himself and sorts correspondence in his office.

Bobby lies down on the couch in this room that was once off-limits to him. He shuts his eyes.

"Given any more thought to when you'll leave the committee?" his father says finally. Nearly everything is going to plan for the Ambassador—Jack reelected, Ted married at the end of November, these items listed in order of importance. All except his third son, who refuses to get in line.

Bobby says nothing. He can feel his heart beating beneath his hand, on and on it goes, with no reward.

"Soon, Dad," he says. A promise just vague enough to keep.

His father shifts forward in his seat, and Bobby braces himself for another onslaught. But his father surprises him.

"He should have lost his first Senate race," the Ambassador says thoughtfully. "Would have, if not for you."

"It wasn't me," Bobby says. Quick to distance himself from the crime. "It was everyone. Jack almost hospitalized himself—"

His father nods. "Jack works as hard as any mortal man. You take it a little further."

He studies Bobby with that gaze that's always had a physical weight.

"It's just like with the boat. You weren't any higher than this desk, didn't know how to swim. But you dove straight into the water. Not afraid. Tough as anything. 'He's a Kennedy all right,' I said."

Bobby lets the words settle over him. His father used to tell that story a different way.

And yet the Ambassador gives no sign he's aware of this revision. Perhaps this is a sign itself, the carefully neutral expression from a man whose emotions normally move across his face like weather systems.

Their father, their first author. He rewrites Bobby just like that.

It's what he's been wanting to hear for years. That

he's like the rest of them, like a Kennedy, like his brothers, after all. And now that he's got it, he finds he no longer wants it.

It isn't relief he feels, sitting across from his father, but a sick kind of knowledge, of being in on the game at last, only to realize you haven't won anything; the game was rigged. This was how it was going to end all along.

Sitting there, looking back at his father, that day in the hospital chapel comes back to him. His father promising a fortune to save his little boy. But it wasn't your boy you were trying to save, Bobby thinks. It was a dream. And then he thinks of Rosie, and her own hospital stay—and what was promised for her? he wonders, heat flashing through him. Or didn't you bother?

And does he imagine it then, or does his old man look cowed? Looking at his son, seeing himself reflected back.

"The two of you have something he and Joe never did," his father continues, looking away from Bobby now, as if unable to meet his eye. "A kind of… intuition."

And is this the truth, or another convenient fiction of the sort that his family, his father, excel at crafting, the kind that make you fall in line with the narrative? You ignore the things going on offstage, the people relegated to smaller parts. You ignore the story itself as long as you're a part of it. You're so grateful for a speaking part that you don't realize you didn't get to choose your role in the first place.

"Soon, Dad," he repeats. Beneath his hand, his heart drums on.

IN THE SUMMER, they gather in Hyannisport. They play their oldest game: *What would you do if you were president?* But now they're not asking each other. Now everyone is asking Jack.

Can Win, Will Lose, Don't Know. These are the answer choices in newspaper polls. Potential presidential contests stacked on top of each other: Kennedy vs. Nixon, Rockefeller vs. Stevenson, Nixon vs. Johnson. Bobby frets; he thinks only in threes: *Can Win, Will Lose, Don't Know. Primaries, nomination, general. Father, Son, Holy Ghost.* Some days, he thinks it's already been won or lost. They say that no campaign is really decided until after Labor Day, but on bad days, Bobby thinks that every campaign is already decided before you even announce your candidacy. It's decided by the state of the economy, how afraid people are about national security, whether or not there are enough houses to live in, all of which are determined by factors out of their control: global inflation, what Russian physicists are doing with missiles, zoning laws. It's decided years ahead of time, by forces set into motion so long ago and so distantly from them that it would be impossible to map their origin. All campaigns are essentially a formula of these factors, and the solution to the equation is one of two outcomes, victory or defeat, solved by adding the candidate. The most he can do is place his candidate into an already written equation.

But then other days he feels less algebraic about it.

Outside, the unzipping sound of bodies ripping through the surface of the pool. The children—his, Pat's, Jean's—explode against the water.

"Have you come to join us on lifeguard duty?" Pat asks, her hair beneath a red silk kerchief that gleams in the sunlight when she turns her head. In the water, the children shriek like birds. It's a fine line between laughter and screaming.

"Rockie doesn't have a Jackie," Ted says, continuing whatever conversation he and Pat were having before. "Or a Bobby—"

"He has the richest father in America," Pat says. "He makes us look like paupers."

Never too early to start speculating on who they might be up against. The Republican nominee could be Nelson Rockefeller, not content with the governorship of New York. That's a problem, another millionaire's son. Some retired general will run, too, trying to offer himself as a continuation of Eisenhower. Taft is dead, or he'd surely be in contention. And then there's the obvious. Jack studies *Time* magazine with an implacable intensity. He demands every article about Nixon in Moscow; Nixon showing off the American kitchen; Nixon going toe to toe with the leader of the Soviet world, granted access the likes of which no Western diplomat has been given before.

Khrushchev—impromptu—invited Nixon out to his private dacha for a night where they dined and discussed their respective systems of governance.

Jack can make as many speeches as he likes—Indochina, Algeria, Poland: it's not the same as real diplomacy. But Bobby wants Nixon anyway.

"Nixon would kill the age issue," he argues. He and Jack are close enough in years, came into the House in the same class. That's one black mark removed.

"He plays dirty," Pat says.

"The only way he's ever won a race is by calling his opponent a Communist," Bobby says. "That won't work on Jack." He turns to Teddy. "What do you think?" he asks. "Does he have support out West?"

His brother has been in the far reaches of the frontier, riding bucking broncos and doing ski jumps to prove to Western delegates that the Kennedys are invested in the country as a whole, not just the Eastern Seaboard.

"Yes, Ted, tell us about the West," Pat says, and he can tell from her voice that he's missing something.

Teddy shrugs. "Mostly they like Johnson."

"Joan wants to move out there," Pat says. Ted glares at her.

"Move away?" Bobby asks. No chance, he's thinking. If Jack wins, his father will want all of his sons in Washington. But also: Ted would have confided this in him, once.

"It was just a thought," Ted says quickly, without meeting his eyes. "We hadn't really discussed it."

Pat takes a drink. "Kennedys don't do well out West," she says. "Take it from me." There's something flat and displeased in her voice, and Bobby thinks that whatever she was discussing privately with their father earlier didn't go her way.

Bobby studies his little brother, who's become absorbed in retying his swimming trunks.

There's something new in his brother's face now; he saw it for the first time the morning after Ted's bachelor party, when he still wanted to believe that Ted was too drunk to remember their conversation in the restaurant bathroom.

Ted had slung his legs out of bed and run a hand down his crumpled face, and Bobby had asked, "How's your head?"

And that's when he'd seen it, a quick flash of hurt that this brotherhood was unequal. What wouldn't Bobby do for Jack? And what would he do for Ted? It clouds the air between them.

"Even if we did move, it wouldn't be until after the election," Teddy says, and Bobby feels a flash of envy for his brother, that this is an option he has.

ONE NIGHT, HE FINDS PAT curled like a cat on the couch, so small and flat he almost doesn't see her until her eyes wink open with light. He's on his way to the kitchen, hungry again, always hungry because of too many nights working late.

"You know you have a bed," he says to her.

"Make me one, too," Pat says.

He returns, expecting her to have drifted into sleep again. But she props herself up, expectant. He hands her a sandwich and moves to leave, but she says, "Sit with me a minute," and starts carefully dismantling the crust from the bread.

The house is quiet around them; not only quiet but inert, as if they've stepped out of time.

"What were you talking to Dad about earlier?" he asks. "Jean said you were in there for ages."

She takes a bite of her sandwich and chews. "A divorce," she says at last. Seeing the look on his face, she laughs meanly.

"What are you going to do, write me a letter telling me I'm going to hell?"

His cheeks burn. Pat knows he regrets writing nasty letters to Kick. Pat knows because she knows all his private humiliations and flaws and mistakes, and he knows hers, and they know their siblings'. He used to think it was a good thing, the unusual closeness of his family. A point of pride. Now he wonders if what he thought was intimacy isn't something else, something closer to parasitism. What makes us think we'd be good for the country, he wonders. We're not even good for each other.

"You were looking out for me," he says to her now, "when I took over the first Senate campaign. You were the only one who was. You told me not to do it."

She smiles sadly. "Didn't exactly work. Dad and Jack got to you anyway. Molded you in their image."

She did it, he thinks. She got out. Got away. He's so close to telling her about the seed of doubt that's grown inside him, not only about their family, but also his role in it. So close to confessing his fantasies of defection, of asking her to explain to him how she cut and run.

"Patty…" he starts, but she leans over and rests her head on his shoulder, and something about her proximity makes him fall silent. The opportunity vanishes.

"Do you know you used to beg to sleep in my room?" she asks. "You hated your own bed. And you were an awful sleeper, a kicker. But I always let you."

And he wants to correct her, no, that was Teddy, but it seems important to her that he remembers, important that it was him, so he allows this revision, he says, "Yes. Of course."

He looks at the plate balanced on her knees, at the pattern of blue fishes painted around the rim, at the crusts of bread.

"So are you leaving Peter?"

"No. It's too close to the election. But I'm not staying with him either."

"What does that mean?"

She sits up. A sly look crosses her face. She takes a moment, deciding whether or not to take him into her confidence.

"I met someone," she says. The words seem to hang in the air, defying their own gravity.

He's aware that she's chosen to trust him, aware that what he says next could determine what she tells him for years to come. *Who?* is the wrong question. *Why?*, ditto. It occurs to him that his sister wakes up hungry, too, but for different reasons.

"Humphrey Bogart?" he asks.

"Swear you won't tell anyone?"

He says, "I'll take it to the grave."

CHAPTER 29

Eight Years

JACK'S ALREADY ON THE FLOOR when Bobby enters his office. He lowers himself onto the rug next to his brother and gives him the rundown.

They still like Jack down South, where Bobby's been with Eunice, who's better versed in civil rights than he is, provided that he favors gradualism on the question of race. When he goes up North next, it'll be a different story to the liberals, it'll be firm executive action on the question of race, but that's a headache for another time.

He's got Pat and Jean looking into hotels and secretarial pools in Los Angeles, where next summer's convention will be, getting ahead of other campaigns on nailing down the logistics. And Teddy—he lasted three seconds on a mechanical bull in his latest swing through the West, but they'll work on getting his time up.

Jack is quiet, his eyes closed. Bobby studies the thin lines etched at the corner of his eye, the bracket at the side of his mouth. Unlike in his early campaigns, he looks old enough now to run for office. *I'll have to be different*, Jack said long ago, during his first Senate race. And he is different from that early Jack. A seat on the Foreign Relations Committee. Major labor legislation up again this term. The most popular Democrat in the party.

He wonders how many Jacks are contained within his brother, if he's a nesting doll of political faces, what the very last piece is, the one that doesn't open up to reveal another.

Jack wets his lips. "Have you nailed down a campaign manager?" he asks. "Or am I to expect Teddy to run this one, too?"

Bobby looks over again, expecting the ironic twist of Jack's mouth, the shape of a joke on his brother's face. But it's missing; Jack means it.

"It was different in 'fifty-two," Jack says. "You were hardly out of law school. Didn't have a career of your own." He winces at some spasm of pain invisible to Bobby. "Now you're chief counsel of a Senate committee. All the papers say it could be a five-year investigation."

Is this what his brother's been thinking, watching

the success of the hearings? That he's going to be down a campaign manager?

Or maybe, he realizes, Jack's been looking for an excuse to get rid of him, and this is it. All his old insecurities rise to the surface in an instant; none of the intervening years matter. He's backstage again at the Lodge debate, uncertain if his brother wants him to stay or go, trying to read the desires of a stranger, certain whichever one he chooses, he'll choose wrong.

"If you want someone else—a professional—to run your campaign, I understand," Bobby says. How strangely formal he sounds.

Jack opens his eyes, distant and clouded with pain. He doesn't answer Bobby's unspoken question, the same one he asked his sisters years ago: *Does Jack want me there?*

"You're making a name for yourself. You keep going with the committee, get the right political winds, doors will open. Running for office, if you want. Or higher-level bureaucracy. The DOJ. You could run a whole division."

"All that will still be there after your campaign," he says cautiously.

"Maybe. Maybe not. You know how fickle Washington is. You'd be stupid to walk away from it now," Jack says. Taunting him? It's hard to read Jack's expression beneath the tautness of his face. Is this supposed to be a guilt-trip, or advice, or a third, unconsidered option?

"I told you," Bobby says, "and I told Dad. I'll quit the committee soon and I'll run the damn campaign."

A flash of irritation on Jack's face. "But do you *want* to?" he asks.

"Since when does what I want have anything to do with it?" he snaps. "Since when does what *you* want, for that matter?"

He feels hot around the collar and pushes himself up into a sitting position. Here it is again, his family's oppressive want, the thing he's never allowed to refuse. Take my blood, take my bones, take everything I have. That's the expected response. But now he looks down at Jack and finds himself thinking about the younger version of his brother, just back from the war—if he'd had a little more courage, if he'd stood up to their father and said "No, Dad, I'm not going to run for office," couldn't everything be different now? Was this not the original sin?

He resents that Jack suddenly, the gaunt soldier with the newly nervous hands, the boy, really, who wasted all his fight against the Japanese and had nothing left in the tank for their father. If he'd only put his foot down—maybe Eunice wouldn't have this anger that sits in a hard shell on top of her skin; maybe Pat wouldn't be so sad; maybe Jean would be loud instead of holding everything inside; maybe Teddy wouldn't self-sabotage because it's impossible to live up to his other siblings. And Bobby; maybe he . . . maybe he— maybe he?

"Would you have done it for me?" Bobby asks. "If our situations had been reversed—would you have dropped everything to come run my campaign?"

Jack's eyes answer before his voice does, but they say the same thing: "No. Probably not."

Bobby looks away sharply. He's surprised to feel pain. So that's it, he thinks. He and his brother aren't confidantes or accomplices or friends; they're just two people who happened to be thrust together by circumstance. A part of him has suspected it all along.

"That's always been your problem, Bob," Jack says pityingly. "You always choose the rest of us. And the rest of us always choose ourselves."

He's suddenly tired of it all, tired of being a Kennedy.

"Is that what you want me to do?" Bobby demands. "You want me to choose myself? Fine." He propels himself to his feet. Blood pounds an irritated beat in his head. "Do it without me then," he says. "I'm done. I don't want to be a part of this anymore."

He stalks out of the room, leaving his brother on the ground.

IN HIS CAR, Bobby rolls the window down and the wind whips inside, scattering the loose papers on his passenger seat, scattering his thoughts. He drives without a destination, taking his cues from the stoplights. He goes whichever way is green, anything to keep from stopping. He circles Washington in an expanding loop, hardly recognizing streets he's been driving for years now. Then he gets a green arrow. And he gets on the highway.

The miles glide by beneath him. He's the only one on the road, save for the occasional trucker. He's a man of method and plans, but sailing down the dark asphalt, he has no plan, no destination, no idea how far he'll go. He's suddenly stateless, a nation of one.

For a while, he's able to remain thoughtless, suspended in orbit by his own forward motion. He focuses only as far as the beam of his headlights. The country slides by outside his window, dark and discreet and never changing. But then he sees something up ahead, an interruption in the pattern of pine trees and grass darkening the side of the road. The object is indistinct at first, then unmistakable as it comes into view. A white cross on the side of the highway. For some reason, it feels like it was placed there for him. For some reason, it makes him stop.

The guilt comes on fast after that. What is he, some wannabe Judas? Deny his family thrice by morning? He opens his door, and retches out the side of the car. The night air is feverish; the humidity chokes him, even after sundown.

He looks at his own bile on the gravel of the shoulder, shining in the moonlight. He starts the car again.

OUTSIDE HIS BROTHER'S office, something makes him hesitate. "Johnny?" he calls.

But there's no answer except for a faint sound

beyond the office door that he can't hear clearly enough to place. He thinks maybe his brother's gone home, except that the light's still on, spilling underneath the door.

A part of him knows already what he's going to find. Then he pushes open the door, and enters.

A record spins on the turntable. That's the sound— the empty needle sound, the slight pop as it slides over a groove, spinning on and on, the music played out.

Jack's become so good at acting around his pain, sometimes even Bobby has trouble determining just how bad it is. But there's no mistaking this. He's in the same spot where Bobby left him hours ago.

Jack's eyes roll sideways toward him, the whites prominent.

"I can't get up," Jack says, and suddenly the harsh words of earlier cease to matter.

He's never thought of his brother as helpless, until now. He'd always assumed there was no pain Jack couldn't overcome through sheer determination. Even after his surgery, when things looked bad—he came out of that fine. Yet Bobby's aware of the need to conceal this revelation, not to let it show on his face. He pulls off his jacket and tosses it on the chair.

"All right," he says in a level voice. "I'll help you. No problem." As if he's a man who's come to inspect underneath the sink.

He kneels at his brother's head.

"Have you been down here the whole time I was gone?" he asks.

"I was just waiting for it to pass," Jack says in a shaky voice that Bobby recognizes is the voice of him in extreme pain trying to maintain a normal human affect. Bobby knows about his treatments, and where he can go for emergency care in each of the major metropolitan areas around the United States, where discreet doctors have been in touch with his father and know that if a call ever comes, they're to drop everything to treat Jack. But even all this is only a sliver of what Jack actually goes through. Masks worn, pain concealed. Stupid, to think he understood it before.

"I'm going to sit you up," Bobby says. It's not the first time he's dealt with a medical crisis of his brother's. Not the last, he thinks grimly. He wrangles Jack into a sitting position, his arms under Jack's shoulders, Jack's teeth gritted with pain, a soft hiss of air escaping between them as Bobby lifts him upright. Just that small adjustment has made a cold sweat break out on Jack's forehead.

"Do you think you can stand?" Bobby asks.

His brother is silent for a long time. But at last, "No," he says.

Bobby looks around the room. Knows better than to suggest an ambulance, medics with stretchers, another stay in the hospital.

"I'll get you onto the couch, first," he decides.

Working his brother back up to verticality in stages. Hearing no objection, he takes this as approval, and starts to drag his body across the rug. His tall frame makes him an awkward package, his legs dragging and tangling behind him. The dead weight of his body sags in Bobby's arms.

He remembers the Senate campaign—Jack stripping off his shirt at the end of the day, the raw, red burn marks his crutches left under each arm, his own stigmata. Is there grace in suffering? Or is it just something we tell ourselves to undergird with reason what's otherwise senseless, unbearable pain?

"Stop, stop," Jack says, panting. Drag marks on the carpet show the trail of each of his legs. Bobby reminds himself to swipe the weave of the fibers the opposite way before he goes, erase any evidence. He doesn't set him down, only loosens his grip beneath Jack's arms, lets them both catch their breath. His brother's shirt is damp, his cheeks flushed red with exertion. He leans against Bobby's shins, panting, and Bobby looks down at the clean white skin of his scalp, the soft monochrome weave of his hair. It makes him feel for some reason tender to see the unprotected top of his brother's head.

All this effort and all this pain, and they've moved approximately two feet from where Jack originally started. What's his plan? Drag his brother thumping down the steps of the Capitol and out to the parking lot? They're not going to make it to the car, he realizes. Not like this.

"New plan," he says. He leans Jack against the coffee table—Jack looking up at him dolefully, with basset-hound eyes—and rolls Jack's chair out from behind his desk. Jack shakes his head.

"Do you have a better idea?" Bobby asks. Jack doesn't.

He places the chair close by. Just a few inches up, he tells himself.

"On three," Bobby says, getting into position. But he lifts on two, the same trick the doctor uses when his children have to get their shots. Needle going into the soft baby flesh of an arm or a thigh. Wail of pain. Pain, just not when you expected it.

He realizes too late the fatal error in his calculation. He's so focused on the motion of getting Jack up and off the floor as painlessly as possible that he fails to account for the chair.

As he tries to lift Jack into the seat, the chair skitters backward and away from them. Bobby stumbles forward, losing his grip on Jack, falling down hard on one knee. Jack slips out of his grasp, making a high, animal noise as he hits the ground.

He thinks for a moment he's killed his brother. Jack lies very still on the carpet, his head turned away from Bobby. One hand is splayed out, palm down. He's afraid to move, afraid to touch his brother.

"Just leave me," Jack says at last, in a hoarse voice. "I'll be better by morning."

His brother's eyes are closed, and tears of exertion run down his face.

Bobby turns out the lights and locks his brother's office door. He calls Ethel and tells her he'll be home in the morning. His brother lies silently on the floor through all this. Then he bunches up his suit jacket into a pillow and lies down on the floor next to Jack.

"You don't have to stay," Jack murmurs.

And since they're saying pointless, futile things, Bobby says, "Do you need to start using a wheelchair?"

Jack opens his eyes. Turns his head. Looks at Bobby with something close to hatred. "They're not going to elect a Catholic in a chair," he says.

So this is how it'll go then, Bobby thinks tiredly: more football, more sailing, and when the cameras are off, lying on the floor, unable to get up. A long con, his brother's political career is. An impressive sleight of hand.

He turns on his side, away from Jack.

"What are you going to do if something like this happens next year?" Bobby asks.

"What do you care?" Jack asks sulkily. "Thought you'd tendered your resignation."

"Changed my mind. Decided I didn't need it on my conscience if you lost."

Jack makes a sound that's not quite a laugh. "That might be the first good thing Catholic guilt's done for me this campaign."

Bobby looks down at them as if from above, as if they're two small figures in a shoebox diorama, Jack sprawled out flat, Bobby curled into himself, a comma in a black suit. How would you explain this, he wonders. How would you explain why the diorama is labeled *Brothers*, and all the terrible, wonderful things that means.

Jack says, "Do you ever hate me?"

Bobby turns on his other side, back toward his brother, and finds Jack looking at him steadily, his eyes murky with what Bobby takes at first to be pain.

"For what?"

Jack shrugs. "Stealing your life?" Jack lifts a hand to his hair, brushing it back idly, waiting for an answer.

"Do you ever hate Joe?" Bobby asks.

"I used to," Jack says. "The whole Senate race I could hear him laughing at me. Every speech I screwed up. Every voter I didn't convince. I used to talk to him in my head..."

Jack's eyes wander to the middle distance. Maybe he's picturing Joe, or maybe he's thinking of that race, the man who ran it.

"Do you still talk to him?" Bobby asks.

"No," Jack says.

He can guess why. Can peer into his brother's head and see out his brother's eyes: Whatever wisdom the dead can give us is the wisdom we decide for them. We can only chase them so far; we can only get so close. The best we can do is take their fate and make it our own; take these men, and make them something like us.

"One of the first things Dad told me," Jack says,

"my first race—he said they'll come and they'll do their pieces and profiles and even the ones who try awfully hard will never get it quite right. But at the same time, even the dumbest son of a bitch will never get it entirely wrong."

"That sounds like our father."

"Do you ever wonder why we do it?" Jack asks. "Politics, I mean."

This from a man who's running for president. But he thinks about it longer, and realizes the answer isn't quite as simple as it would seem.

"Because it can make a difference in people's lives," Bobby says at last.

"Yes," Jack says, "but that's not why we do it."

"Enlighten me, then, oh font of wisdom."

"So that people will remember us. What we said. What we stood for."

"I don't want that," Bobby says.

"What do you want?"

What does he want? He thinks of Stevenson mid-campaign, standing exhausted and alone on a street corner, saying, "It's a long game." Remembers McCarthy before that, in his office, telling Bobby he'd always thought politics would be temporary. Remembers Jack after the Lodge debate, saying "I've spent too much time in politics to do anything else."

He doesn't want to be like Stevenson, McCarthy, any of the rest of them. And perhaps, he realizes for the first time, that means he doesn't want to be like his brother either.

"You want an out," Jack says softly, reading it in his face a moment before he comes to it himself.

"Not now," he says. "Not next year. But someday, yes. I want to do something besides this." He wants his children to remember him, not to remember his absence.

Jack seems to study Bobby from a great height.

"Can you give me eight years?" Jack asks.

Eight years. The age gap between them. The length of two presidential terms. Nineteen sixty-eight, and he's free.

"Eight years," Bobby nods.

Jack nods; he gives his blessing.

"We're agreed?" Bobby asks. "Just like that?" Nothing in his family is ever this easy.

"Sure we're agreed," Jack says. "Because I don't think you'll actually be able to walk away. You think you can, but you can't. You'll be back in a week."

"You wanted to lose the first Senate race," he reminds his brother. "You never wanted to be in it to begin with. You told me once if you lost you could do anything."

"Yeah, well. We're a long way from East Boston," Jack says, and what he means is: *We're a long way from those men*. The ones who sat in that hotel bathroom. The ones who didn't know what they'd do if they won, or if they could win at all.

IN THE MORNING, momentary disorientation. He wakes up believing himself in his childhood bedroom, dresser on the left, door on the opposite wall.

Then his brain corrects itself. Jack's office. The brother in question sitting calmly at his desk, looking through some papers. Has the gall to look at Bobby over the top of his readers and say, "Good morning, Sleeping Beauty."

Bobby picks himself up off the floor and pulls on his rumpled jacket. He starts several times to say something to his brother, then cuts himself off, can't form the words. Eventually, he just moves to leave, and Jack stands.

"I'll walk you out to your car," Jack says. Trying, Bobby thinks, to show he's recovered, prove a point, win the argument perpetually being raised by his health.

But as they make their way out of the office, down the hall, outside, he catches sight of Jack's face in profile as he limps, and finds his brother's face chastened. He's embarrassed, Bobby realizes, and stops, not wanting Jack to walk further than he has to. The cross his brother carries not made of wood, but simply his own blood and bones. They have the same stubbornness, he and his brother. Bobby broke his leg once in the Yale game and kept playing, so why should he be annoyed at his brother for doing the same thing? Same stubbornness all Irish have, stubbornness that makes you cross an ocean, gamble on a new life: the stubbornness to survive when the world wants to grind you beneath its cold heel.

"I think I can find my own way to the car," Bobby says.

Jack's face: relieved, grateful.

"Call me if you need me," Bobby says. Sadly, knowing his brother won't, even if he does. Jack nods, ready for this episode to be over. He reaches as if he means to pat Bobby on the shoulder, but then runs a hand through his own hair instead.

We all choose, Jackie told him. And he supposes, right or wrong, this is what Jack chooses for himself.

They part ways. At the bottom of the steps, Bobby looks back just once. Watches his brother make his slow, struggling way up the steps, leaning heavily on the handrail with the stooped posture of an old man.

He thinks then of the younger Jack home from the war, but not with anger this time.

The first time Jack ran for Congress, he missed the filing deadline for declaring his candidacy.

By the next morning though, Jack's ballot containing the necessary signatures had miraculously appeared in the courthouse.

Jack, a few of his Navy buddies—Bobby remembers them persuading a window open after hours as he stood watch on the street. Jack climbing out of the window that night, skimming a hand over Bobby's hair, and saying, "Don't look so sour, Bob. We got it done in the end, didn't we?"

He remembers the candidacy that almost wasn't. The Jack that almost was. He remembers it because he knows his brother doesn't. Not that Jack forgets; only that the past, to him, is a relative in another state that he never visits, out of sight and out of mind, whereas Bobby—sometimes he feels like he's drowning in the past. Sometimes he feels like it's all he is; the deaths of brothers, and sisters, and surgeries gone wrong, and stillborn children, but also—he realizes, watching his brother limp up the steps—also good things: the brothers and sisters who live, the surgeries that are survived, the children born alive.

Jack reaches the top of the steps, and for just one moment before he disappears, the light forks across his back so brightly Bobby can see them all; the Jack on the surface, and every Jack beneath, painted over, but still there.

FOR WHAT FEELS like the first time in his life, he knows exactly what to do next.

He takes his daughter with him, and he drives back by that house, the one where he killed a dog once. It's a guilt trip he hasn't made in a long time.

"What's here?" Kathleen asks, peering out the car window. Her hands leave fingerprints on the glass that join an army of other fingerprints and initials and smiley faces drawn by small hands.

There's a puppy behind the fence; it trips over its paws running up to greet them. It seems to want to force itself through the fence and into their arms, but it's too big to fit through the gap, and too small to jump, he notes with relief. The owner comes out onto the porch and for a moment Bobby's terrified he'll be recognized. He puts an arm around his daughter, ready to lift her and run back to the car—but the owner only offers them a bag of dog treats.

Kathleen feeds the puppy through the fence, laughing when it nips her with its sharp little teeth, laughing because it should hurt, but it doesn't, not at all.

CHAPTER 30

Kennedy for President

"HOW LONG DOES IT TAKE to get to the hotel and back?"

It's Jack saying this, a reflection speaking to him out of a mirror. Jack who's been up to this point almost preternaturally calm but has finally found the thing that will break him: not the expectations of the watching public, not being selected as his party's torchbearer, but the fact that his shirt didn't look quite right on camera during the screen test.

So you are nervous, Bobby thinks. Thinks again.

It's September 1960, almost a year since that night in Jack's office: Here's the senator from Massachusetts, sitting in the makeup chair with his eyes closed as a woman dusts him with powder, pieces of tissue tucked into his collar to protect his shirt—the hated shirt, Bobby amends, the first thing that's upset him this entire campaign. This single button-down has gotten into his head better than anything opposing campaigns have said or done all year. The Nixon campaign ought to consider hiring it on.

They've been here for an hour already, sitting for the screen test, arguing about lighting and camera angles with the producers, being reminded of the rules for the evening's debate.

Also rebuffing the repeated advances of the studio's makeup artist, who's come by at ten-minute intervals the entire time they've been sequestered here, in the green room, to ask if the senator's sure he doesn't want just a little powder before he goes on?

Don't let the studio artists touch him, their father warned him beforehand. They may as well be undertakers. Don't use any of that pancake makeup shit. That's what we used when we wanted someone to look like a villain.

So, true to form, they've snuck in their own makeup artist to give Jack a touch-up behind closed doors with just a few minutes to go until his brother will walk out onto set and debate the vice president on live television.

"I'll go check on the shirt," Bobby says. On his way out the door, he pauses to study his brother's face for a moment unobserved.

The next president, Bobby repeats to himself, as he's been repeating to himself for nine months now. But he hasn't yet been able to convince his brain that he's looking at anyone other than his brother. He moves at a deliberate, unhurried pace as he makes his way from the green room to the studio floor. No need to let anyone watching from the Nixon camp know that anything's amiss.

There's no audience this time, no crowd to count as he passes the studio stage. Only the television cameras. The panel of reporters who'll be moderating. Each candidate. The one guest from each campaign allowed on the studio floor. They're expected to lose, he knows. Nixon is apparently so unworried by their impending face-off he hasn't prepared at all. He was a champion debater in high school; he's gone toe to toe with Khrushchev in the Kitchen Debates. He doesn't have anything to worry about with Jack Kennedy.

Jack's own preparation was typical of his brother. Earlier, at the hotel, Jack laid out flat on the bed in shorts and an undershirt, a stack of notecards on his stomach. But it was he who quizzed them—Bobby, Sorensen, O'Donnell and O'Brien—instead of the other way around. When he decided he was ready to be asked some questions, his own answers were jokes, had them in stitches. As they practiced, Bobby sat on the corner of the desk, trying to imagine the atmosphere in the Nixon suite. Nixon in a suit jacket even at leisure, practicing hand gestures in the mirror. When to glower, and when to shake his head. Which answers to deliver forcefully, and which to land softly. Nixon's advisors all Executive Branch, advertising agency and Manhattan lawyer types. Jack's inner circle: a Nebraskan, a bar owner, a family friend, his little brother. Bobby wonders now, briefly—the way he has every thought these days, as quick as he can, in a flash of intuition, he doesn't have time for anything more—if he should have managed Jack a little more carefully.

Rounding the corner, he runs into Nixon's campaign manager, Robert Finch, a man with the clean-cut look of the Mercury Seven astronauts. They greet each other as cordially as can be expected.

"Our guy's running a fever of a hundred and four," Finch confesses.

Trying to level set, Bobby thinks. He smiles pleasantly and murmurs his wishes for Nixon's good health, crossing a finger, childishly, behind his back.

"They've sent a makeup artist around," Finch hedges. "I'm not so sure about how it looks. Did they come to you too?"

"Oh yes," Bobby says. "They've already been in to see the senator. Don't worry, it'll look great on camera."

Finch's shoulders sag with relief. "See you in there," he says.

Bobby bids him farewell and does his best not to skip down the hallway. He arrives back at the green room and the makeup artist is gone. Jack's eyes jump to the door as he enters.

"Where's the shirt?" Jack asks, his eyes animate and probing, like the eyes of a mad Russian czar who thinks his advisors are keeping something from him. Nobody has come by with a shirt for Kennedy.

This is it, Bobby thinks. The moment every campaign manager dreads—the event, the speech, the instant his candidate finally cracks, the pressure becomes too much, he falls on his face.

Bobby starts unbuttoning his own shirt. "Switch with me," he says.

"It'll be too small," Jack says uncertainly, but he's reaching up to unknot his tie even as he says it.

Now I've given him the shirt off my back, Bobby thinks, handing it over, and I'd give more if he asked. He pulls on his brother's shirt, and it smells like Jack: the sharp cedar of his aftershave, the faint, earthy tinge of his sweat hiding beneath it.

Satisfied with Bobby's shirt, Jack sits back and is still. Bobby inwardly breathes a sigh of relief.

But no sooner has his brother relaxed than a studio hand knocks at the door. It's time. Two minutes out. Can the senator make his way to the stage, please?

Jack stands, but Bobby blocks his path. The instinct clarifies for him. "We'll be along shortly," Bobby says, closing the door again on the studio hand. Jack looks at him strangely.

"It's time to go, Bob."

"No," Bobby says, nodding at the clock on the wall counting down to showtime. He remembers Lodge breezing in at the last minute some eight years ago, and he silently thanks their former opponent for this lesson.

"Let him wait," he says. "At twenty seconds we'll go."

Playing chicken with the vice president of the United States. Out on the studio floor, Nixon is already taking his seat, his feet positioned slightly apart on the floor, as if he's bracing for turbulence. He looks across the stage, at Jack Kennedy's empty chair, wondering where his opponent is. Let him wait. Let him wonder.

The clock hits twenty and he opens the door, leading Jack to set. His brother walks onstage bloodlessly, cool as anything. Nixon tries to say something to Jack, some word of greeting, but Jack ignores him and takes his seat.

Bobby stands behind the monitor. Nixon's campaign manager wasn't lying; he looks like a clown in grease paint. There's a brief argument about cutaway shots; the camera operator agrees not to cut to Nixon while he's mopping sweat off his forehead, but otherwise it's fair game. Does the Kennedy campaign have any objections? No, no objections. The good thing about being a Kennedy is you assume someone's always watching; you assume you're always on camera.

All right, someone calls. Quiet in the house.

There's a brief, beautiful silence. Bobby can hear every thought in every man on set's head with perfect clarity.

Bobby looks at the square of the television monitor, at his brother's face captured within it. *The next president, the next president, the next president*, he chants to himself.

A producer holds five seconds on his fingers, and he counts them down—four, three, two, one—until there's nothing left.

And then it begins.

ACKNOWLEDGMENTS

THANK YOU TO MY INCREDIBLE AGENT, Chad Luibl, for taking a chance on me to begin with and for caring about this story as much as I do. A first novel is a hell of a ride, but it was made less daunting with you in my corner.

Thank you to my amazing editor, Kathy Pories, for her support and collaboration and for helping me hone this story to its strongest possible version. Thank you to Roma Panganiban for her early read and insightful notes. Thanks also to my copy editor, Chris Stamey, for his diligence, and to everyone at Algonquin Books and at Little, Brown who had a hand in bringing this book to life.

Thank you to all the teachers and professors I've had over the years, with special thanks to Dr. Joanna Ruocco, who read this project in its earliest form and encouraged me to develop it into a novel.

Thank you to the other artists, writers, and friends who've influenced this book directly or indirectly, too many to list here. Thank you to the Kennedy scholars past and present whose work I relied on while researching, and to archivists everywhere for the work you do, with a nod to the exceptional custodians at the John F. Kennedy Presidential Library in Boston.

Thank you to my sisters, Hadley and Reese, and thank you to my brothers, Griffin, Brett, Whitaker, and Murphy, though I doubt some of you (Murph) will have read this far. Thank you for teaching me how to exist.

Lastly, thank you to my parents, Kelly and Kevin. Thank you to my dad for reading me the Kennedys' speeches. Thank you to my mom for reading me everything else. And thank you for giving me what other daughters are denied: the same treatment as your sons.

RAISING READERS
Books Build Bright Futures

Thank you for reading this book and for being a reader of books in general. We are so grateful to share being part of a community of readers with you, and we hope you will join us in passing our love of books on to the next generation of readers.

Did you know that reading for enjoyment is the single biggest predictor of a child's future happiness and success?

More than family circumstances, parents' educational background, or income, reading impacts a child's future academic performance, emotional well-being, communication skills, economic security, ambition, and happiness.

Studies show that kids reading for enjoyment in the US is in rapid decline:

- In 2012, 53% of 9-year-olds read almost every day. Just 10 years later, in 2022, the number had fallen to 39%.
- In 2012, 27% of 13-year-olds read for fun daily. By 2023, that number was just 14%.

Together, we can commit to **Raising Readers** and change this trend. How?

- Read to children in your life daily.
- Model reading as a fun activity.
- Reduce screen time.
- Start a family, school, or community book club.
- Visit bookstores and libraries regularly.
- Listen to audiobooks.
- Read the book before you see the movie.
- Encourage your child to read aloud to a pet or stuffed animal.
- Give books as gifts.
- Donate books to families and communities in need.

BOB1217

Books build bright futures, and **Raising Readers** is our shared responsibility.

For more information, visit **JoinRaisingReaders.com**

Sources: National Endowment for the Arts, National Assessment of Educational Progress, WorldBookDay.com, Nielsen BookData's 2023 "Understanding the Children's Book Consumer"

9 781643 757995